WARCRY
CATACOMBS
BLOOD OF THE EVERCHOSEN

WARCRY
CATACOMBS
BLOOD OF THE EVERCHOSEN

RICHARD STRACHAN

BLACK LIBRARY

A BLACK LIBRARY PUBLICATION

First published in 2020.
This edition published in Great Britain in 2021 by
Black Library, Games Workshop Ltd., Willow Road,
Nottingham, NG7 2WS, UK.

Represented by: Games Workshop Limited – Irish branch,
Unit 3, Lower Liffey Street, Dublin 1,
D01 K199, Ireland.

10 9 8 7 6 5 4 3 2 1

Produced by Games Workshop in Nottingham.
Cover illustration by Alexander Mokhov.

A CIP record for this book is available from the British Library.

ISBN 13: 978 1 78999 828 3

See Black Library on the internet at

blacklibrary.com

Find out more about Games Workshop
and the worlds of Warhammer at

games-workshop.com

Printed and bound by CPI Group (UK) Ltd, Croydon, CR0 4YY

From the maelstrom of a sundered world, the
Eight Realms were born. The formless and the divine
exploded into life.

Strange new worlds appeared in the firmament, each one
gilded with spirits, gods and men. Noblest of the gods was
Sigmar. For years beyond reckoning he illuminated the realms,
wreathed in light and majesty as he carved out his reign. His
strength was the power of thunder. His wisdom was infinite.
Mortal and immortal alike kneeled before his lofty throne.
Great empires rose and, for a while, treachery was banished.
Sigmar claimed the land and sky as his own and ruled over a
glorious age of myth.

But cruelty is tenacious. As had been foreseen, the great
alliance of gods and men tore itself apart. Myth and legend
crumbled into Chaos. Darkness flooded the realms. Torture,
slavery and fear replaced the glory that came before. Sigmar
turned his back on the mortal kingdoms, disgusted by their
fate. He fixed his gaze instead on the remains of the world he
had lost long ago, brooding over its charred core, searching
endlessly for a sign of hope. And then, in the dark heat of
his rage, he caught a glimpse of something magnificent. He
pictured a weapon born of the heavens. A beacon powerful
enough to pierce the endless night. An army hewn from
everything he had lost.

Sigmar set his artisans to work and for long ages they toiled,
striving to harness the power of the stars. As Sigmar's great
work neared completion, he turned back to the realms and saw
that the dominion of Chaos was almost complete. The hour
for vengeance had come. Finally, with lightning blazing across
his brow, he stepped forth to unleash his creations.

The Age of Sigmar had begun.

PROLOGUE

It was a land that rang with bitter wailing, night and day. In shallow valleys and amongst the wind-scoured rocks, scavengers were knifed by rivals and cut-throats indulged their dark desires on hapless victims. Those left bleeding in the wake of a warband's ruinous pursuit would howl their agony to the unfeeling air, and the tendrils of the breeze as they coiled over the blackened earth brought always the sound of pain and misery and death.

It was a land where men and women fought and died, killed and were killed in turn, spilling blood for pleasure or for what passed as coin, or killing only to stay alive for another miserable day. In ramshackle huts and lean-tos, in hovels made of scraps and animal skins, they slept with knives in their hands, and every turn of the sulphurous breeze drew another shriek across the air. The wind blew on, a choking fume, and the screams rose and fell and rose again.

It was a land that lay deep in the damned nexus of the Eight-points, the realm that sat both between and beyond realms, a land devoid of peace or sanctuary or hope.

It was the Bloodwind Spoil.

PART ONE

CHAPTER ONE

THE STORM BREAKS

On the edge of the blasted wasteland that was the Desolate March, the settlement of Spite prepared for the Feast of the Black Spire.

Spite was a mean collection of squalid huts and tumbledown shacks, and as the evening crept through its meagre streets the wind began to blow from off the plains. The mountains of the Fangs, like a ragged jaw, loomed dark in the distance. The horizon flashed and muttered with thunder, and great banks of cloud roiled like silt in brackish water across those distant peaks. The storm was moving closer.

Ankhad huddled into his cloak as he moved through the streets, a bucket of water sloshing at his side. Uneasily he passed the towering model of the Black Spire, the seat of the Everchosen, which had been cobbled together from bone and rusting scrap in the middle of the town square – the centrepiece of the ceremonies that would take place later that night. He turned his gaze from it. Archaon Everchosen, the lord of this benighted land... Ankhad had never thought it advisable to pay too much attention to the

Three-Eyed King; there was always the chance that the Three-Eyed King would start paying attention to you.

The wind picked up, stripping the plain of its ferrous topsoil and scouring it across the night. Lightning stabbed towards the earth, probing its way from the mountains to the edge of the March. The air in Spite was febrile and tense, and the gathering storm had only made it worse. Ankhad had already passed a scuffle or two, mutants and scavengers squabbling over a crust of bread or a scrap of salvage, rolling in the dust in bitter argument. No doubt blades had been drawn and buried, although it was death to shed blood on the Feast of the Black Spire. He cut through the derelict market and watched the other looters gather round to watch as another fight broke out.

Like corpse-hawks, he thought. *Waiting for the scraps...*

He hurried on, toting the bucket he had filled with muddy water at the well. The clouds seemed to drift closer above the settlement, thick and menacing. Spite's rickety walls shivered in the wind, rattling with blown dust and sand. Ankhad grimaced at the smell in the air, the rank scent of fear and festering meat.

Above him, the clouds flickered and pulsed with light. Thunder rumbled across the land, shaking the very air, as coarse and violent as if the mountains themselves were being ground together. Ankhad flinched as the air cracked and trembled around him, and then, as he reached his hut on the edge of the settlement, a spear of red lightning crashed down with a deafening bark against the scrubland outside the gates. He heard her scream.

'Ilthis!' he said. He pulled back the heavy hide that served as the hut's door, and the smell assailed him at once – a coppery tang, the harsh, metallic scent of her lifeblood pouring out onto the earth.

She was dying. Ankhad knew that. He knelt at the side of the bed and squeezed her hand. Sweat ran greasily down her face and her skin was grey. She twitched and mumbled, her green eyes staring into the hut's dim light, seeing nothing. Below her waist the sheets were drenched in blood.

'Ilthis,' he said softly. He dipped a rag into the bucket of water and wiped her brow. Her stomach heaved and twisted. He could see the child toiling under the skin, stretching it as if trying to break through. 'Ilthis, can you hear me?'

She shook her head, her breath harsh and stuttering.

'I don't know what to do. Please... tell me what to do? Don't leave me here, not on my own.'

He pressed his forehead to the back of her hand. Her skin was cold.

How could this bright thing be so cold? he thought. *This pillar of flame, this incandescent life so fierce and free.*

The storm ravaged the settlement outside. He heard the rain begin its deafening percussion against the roof, but when he looked to the window he saw that the glass was sheeted in red. *Blood rain*, he thought, and fear twisted uneasily in his gut. *On this day, of all days.*

Ilthis writhed on the bed and wailed again, but her voice was strained and weak now. It trailed off into silence. She shuddered, and then the walls were rattling around him, the wind threatening to tear them down. Ankhad wiped the cloth across her face. When he passed it over her eyes, he knew that she would see nothing at all now, ever again.

The green had faded to black. She was gone.

Now, at the moment she left it, he thought of the moment she had first come into his life. There had been a whipping storm then, too. Savage winds on the outskirts of Carngrad, the rubbish and detritus of another skirmish in the scrubland, the smell of dead meat and spilled blood on the air. A sandstorm had been blowing in from the Corpseworm Marches, and then stumbling through the whirlwind in the aftermath of the fight came Ilthis, trailing a scavengers' caravan of looted silks. She had wandered, as if led by fate, into a warzone. He had taken her and everything she owned as a prize, one of the easiest he had ever won.

Fool, he thought. *To think you could ever own such a woman! She tamed me, as no one ever could. She owned me, and I was hers entire.*

'I'm so sorry,' Ankhad whispered.

The skin of her stomach buckled, undulating in the candlelight like some fevered tide. He let go of her hand and drew his knife.

They came for him not long after the last scream had died.

Ankhad heard the tramp of their feet across the muddy ground. Lothin, as close as Spite came to a town chief, was the first to the hut. When he threw back the flap Ankhad saw that his face was streaked with blood from the rain, his hair matted to his scalp. The settlement outside was a morass. The lightning, as it stabbed across the sky, fused and cooked the raindrops into weeping scabs, and they fell on Spite like bloody snowflakes.

Lothin was small, hunched, his head swollen with festering lumps. As he entered the hut, he was flanked by his enforcer, Grulsham Mof, a quick and deadly fighter with a great, spiked club in his hand. Others milled about the entrance, apprehensive and uncertain, some slinking off to lose themselves in Spite's ramshackle streets, others bearing weapons and girding themselves for a fight.

Fine, Ankhad thought. *A fight is what you shall have…*

'Ankhad,' Lothin cried, his voice almost drowned out by the thunder. 'What have you done?' He shifted his weight from one foot to the other. One of his eyes was cloudy with cataracts; the other two were sharp and black, and they looked almost sad.

'What needed to be done,' Ankhad said. He still sat there by the bedside, next to the peeled and opened body of his dead wife.

When the baby cried, everyone stepped back. Lothin raised his knife.

'You said it wouldn't be for another month!' he said. 'Not on Feast Day, Ankhad! Don't you know what this means?'

'Life comes when it must,' Ankhad muttered. He turned and stood, and the baby he had cut from his wife's belly mewled in his arms. He had wrapped the child in a cloth, red and filthy from its birth. Born in a bath of blood, lifted from its mother's corpse, the child opened its mouth and cried again.

Others pushed past Lothin to crowd the hut's entrance, a stinking mob of scavengers and mutants cursing and muttering to themselves, scratching with fused claws or peering into the gloom with bulbous eyes. Ankhad stood there, warily watching them. The bag he had hastily packed was at his feet, and his knife, its blade cleaned of Ilthis' blood, was tucked into his belt. He was a big man, rangy and tough, seasoned where others would have been whittled down by all his years in the Desolate March. Although he was far older than most of the scavengers who crowded his door, the years hadn't diminished his sense of danger. Ankhad had heard the rumours others told about him. Some said he had been a warrior once, a pilgrim from the outside realms come to lay his sword on the steps of the Black Spire. Others claimed he was no more than any other native of the Bloodwind Spoil, a cowering scrap merchant, a ragpicker just like the rest of them – only luckier, because he had found in Spite a cursed little settlement full of ragpickers smaller than he was. Let them say what they wanted; he did not care.

'A child born on Feast Day is for the gods,' Lothin said in his rasping voice. 'It's always been thus. And this storm, the blood rain… The omens cannot be denied. It must die.'

'You would spill blood on the Feast of the Black Spire?' Ankhad said. His voice was low, his bearing outwardly calm. 'Let me tell you then – so would I.'

Grulsham Mof stepped forward, his club in his hands, but Lothin held him back. He looked uneasy. Where others dominated through violence, Lothin's strength had always been in his cunning, even in his sense of diplomacy.

'Tarnot's already broken that rule,' Lothin said. 'He killed Mad Rhukar in the marketplace. He dies tonight, as he must, but there's no need for you to join him.'

Beyond Lothin, out in the street, Ankhad could see Tarnot cast down into the mud on his knees, his arms bent behind his back. He was a young man, his eyes wide-spaced on either side of his head like a fish's, his lank hair plastered to his face from the bloody rain. He grinned wildly.

'He started it!' Tarnot protested. 'Shanked me in the back, he did.'

'And you tore out his throat with your teeth,' Lothin called wearily over his shoulder.

'You never said,' Tarnot shot back. 'What's it to be in the end then? Stoning? I think I'd like a good stoning, if I've got a choice.'

'You, we'll drown in the water trough,' Lothin said. 'The baby... I'm sorry, Ankhad, for what it's worth. But the child must be burned. The True Gods demand it. It's their right.'

As if it understood their words, the child cried again, and from the crashing skies came an answering rumble of thunder, the flash-crack of red lightning. Ankhad flinched. The spire at the centre of the Eightpoints hung heavy on his mind then, stabbing its weight deep into his marrow. He looked down into his son's face, and for the briefest moment, as if illuminated in the lightning flash, he saw a mask of shadow pass quickly across it – a mask in the shape of an eight-pointed star.

'I will kill every man, woman and child here before I let you harm this baby,' Ankhad said, and he knew they all believed him. Cudgels were hefted, and the press of bodies in the street grew nearer. Ankhad dropped his hand to the hilt of his knife. Over Lothin's shoulder he could just see Tarnot, struggling against his captors and straining to stand up.

'Ankhad,' Tarnot shouted. 'It's over for me, but it doesn't have to be for you.' Through the press of bodies, their eyes met. 'Run!' he shouted.

The fight, such as it was, lasted mere moments, but it was long enough.

He owed Tarnot nothing. They had passed no more than a handful of words in all the months he had lived in Spite, but something had made the other man help him. Whatever it was, Ankhad silently thanked him for it.

He saw Tarnot break free and snap an elbow into his captor's face, sliding then through the mud to launch himself at Lothin's back. Grulsham Mof, with no room to swing his spiked club, dropped his weapon and punched Tarnot in the side until his ribs cracked, but by that point Tarnot was lost under a scrum of bodies and Ankhad was kicking his way through the mouldering planks of the hut's wall. He had the baby clutched tightly in his arms and he paused to swing his pack up onto his shoulder – and then the wasteland of the Desolate March was there before him, strobed with red lightning, black and forbidding and no less dangerous than the streets of Spite.

'Run, Ankhad!' he could hear Tarnot shout, before his voice was muffled into silence. 'Run!'

Ankhad ran, and the miserable little town of Spite was smothered in the blood rain behind him.

CHAPTER TWO

SPIRITS OF THE DEAD

On the shores of the Blood Lake Basin, the weeds had blistered in the heat. The red water lapped in lazy corrugations at the shale, crinkling into a rank crust at the line of the shore. Around it, almost encircling the wide expanse of water, was a vast ring of mountains, and the shadows they cast were beginning to lengthen. Night was creeping near. Kurguth, First Fang of the Untamed Beasts, second in command of the Split-Tongue Tribe, flexed the pain from his arm and shivered as the darkness came closer.

Like something hunts my spirit in the shadow-lands, he thought. *Or some doom reaches for me, across all the rancid acres of the Bloodwind Spoil...*

He stood on the shore and stared out across the crimson water. A pale steam was rising from it, a haze that made the further bank indistinct. As wide as an inland sea, the distance from one shoreline of the Blood Lake Basin to the next was too great for anyone to see, even on a clear day. But then Kurguth's eyes had always been good. Far-hunter, wide-ranger over limitless plains, he bowed to no one in the sharpness of his senses. Not even Burak, their Heart-eater, the leader of their tribe, could run faster or throw a bone spear further, or fight longer and harder and drink deeper. He was Kurguth Eight-Lives, who had crossed the Skull-pike Mountains in one night to outrun his enemies, who had fought Khask the dominar in single combat and won.

He touched the dried scrap of Khask's skin that hung from his belt, the trophy he had taken from the field after his victory. *A year now, since that day*, he thought. He remembered the feel of his bone blade slicing into the Iron Golem's chest as the dominar lay dying, the wheezing cry as Kurguth slipped the knife tip around his pectoral muscle and *pulled*... It had been a worthy fight. When the hard lands around the basin plummeted into night, Kurguth still sometimes walked with the limp that Khask had given him, but the memory of that fight kept him warm. He remembered Burak too, after the Golem had been pushed back from the tribe's territory, his frenzy and exaltation, standing on the edge of a broken archway and ululating his fiendish war cry across the veldt.

'Get back to Carngrad!' Burak had shouted. 'Back to your forges and your stone prisons, you mewling dogs!'

That had been the peak, Kurguth knew. *We clasped the mountain's tip in our talons that night, and we looked down on the ants below us. But something has gone wrong since then, so wrong. None of us are the same. Burak most of all...*

He could see Mayra standing on a lip of stone that stretched across the foreshore, staring off towards the declining sun. The Beastspeaker's bone whip was coiled in her hand and she had her arms crossed against her chest, her skull helmet at her feet. He could feel her sadness from here, the grief that lay like a curse against her. Kurguth sighed. His muscles ached, and the welt on his arm was still burning. He felt the pain deep in him like a rebuke, the mocking evidence of their failure. He stretched his arm out again and headed over towards her.

'Do you know why the water is so red?' Kurguth asked, pointing at the lake. 'They say so many beasts have been slain on its shores that their blood has stained it for eternity.'

'We have had good hunting here,' Mayra admitted. 'The Bloodwind Spoil has been… *stranger* than I thought it would be, but the prey has not been lacking.'

Her eyes flashed then, dark and pained.

'I feel your sorrow,' Kurguth said. 'Words mean nothing, but the feeling is the same. My heart beats for your loss, and my blood shares it.'

'Words are masks for truth,' Mayra said. She didn't look at him, still staring out across the water towards the falling light. The sunset stained the bloody tide, and the basin was lit with shards of scarlet. 'But truth is always welcome.'

He laid his hand against her shoulder and she reached up to take it. She was a head shorter than him, lithe and supple where Kurguth was all brawn and sinew, but he knew the power in her. He respected it. He knew her whip could slash the jaw from any warrior she faced, and with her bone blade she was faster than almost anyone he had ever seen. But the true power came from inside, as it did with all Beastspeakers. The creatures of the Spoil sensed it too. They could taste the mastery in her, perceive in ways Kurguth couldn't imagine that she was an apex predator, someone who dominated not through force but through sympathy. She shared with those creatures a fellow feeling, Kurguth knew. She revelled in the hunt, savouring the taste of blood from a savaged prey. The beasts knew her, and she knew them. And now her beast was dead.

The memory of the hunt was still vivid. Neesa, their rocktusk prowler, had leapt at the last minute to bring the lasherbrute down, springing up from a hunkered run to launch herself at the creature's flank. Mayra had seen what was going to happen. Kurguth could still hear the echo of her scream as she called Neesa back, but it was too late. Burak had been ahead, sprinting along the cusp of the shallow ravine, Kurguth on the other side readying his harpoon. The plains-runners who had lured the beast down into this killing spot looked terrified as it reared and turned, its tusks clawing a spray of dust from the ravine wall, the leathery tentacles whipping out to catch one of them across the face. The plains-runner had fallen, shrieking, his eyes torn away, and the other had been trampled under the lasherbrute's hooves. And then Neesa had struck, her claws buried deep in the creature's hide, her fangs savaging at the bulge of muscle on its shoulder. The lasherbrute spun around faster than any of them would have believed possible. Neesa's grip had failed and she flew across the ravine to strike the wall, and then the lasherbrute's tusk was buried to the hilt in her chest. Kurguth had tried to throw his harpoon, but a tentacle snaked out of the ravine and slashed against his arm. Burak had jumped down to head it off, but the lasherbrute flung Neesa's corpse aside and barrelled him out of the way. In the mouth of the ravine, the rest of the warband sprinted to catch up, the lasherbrute scattering a cloud of dust in its wake as it disappeared across the plains. Mayra had buried her face in Neesa's mane and howled. The hunt had failed.

Kurguth turned now to look back at Burak on the shore, kneeling into his prayers. Neesa's body was laid out before him, and some of the plains-runners were gathering wood for the campfire. Burak leaned forward and pressed his forehead against Neesa's side, then leant back with his hands raised and his lips mumbling. His eyes were open, staring into who knew which world of signs and omens.

Burak the Bloodseer...

Kurguth shivered, although the day was still warm. He still gripped Mayra's shoulder, and she turned to follow his gaze.

'He still wears it,' she said. 'I see the sunlight glint against it like the glint in a madman's eye. Do you believe me now? Our Heart-eater has fallen prey to the lust for iron and steel.'

'I believe nothing,' Kurguth muttered. 'I see or I don't see. I cannot choose what is true.'

'And what does your heart see? He wears that thing around his neck and our hunts have been sour since. We've been turned from our path. The Devourer mocks us for it, and now Neesa is dead.'

Kurguth grunted. He would have given anything to change the subject, but he couldn't deny that Mayra spoke something like the truth. Around Burak's neck was a shard of metal taken from the field when the Iron Golems were defeated, a broken circle of tempered brass from a drillmaster's skirt. It was worthless to anyone but the most despised scavengers who littered the Bloodwind Spoil, and certainly not worth a moment of an Untamed Beast's attention. Their totems were bone and skin, teeth and skulls. Their banners were bloody rags of hide, and they slept not in the stone houses of the weak but under the maddening open sky of the Bloodwind Spoil, the caustic wind cleansing their bare skin. And yet still the flicker of brass had caught Burak's eye, and he had stooped to pick it up, his fingertips playing into the hole where the disc had been affixed. He had stared, and smiled, and drifted into reverie...

'Come,' Kurguth said. He drew her close, smelling the scent of her, feeling the coiled tension in her body. 'The light slackens, and night is near. We will say our farewells.'

Mayra nodded and kissed him. Before they left the spur of rock, she reached down for the bone helm and threw it far out into the bloody water, where it broke the surface and sank. Kurguth looked at her, saying nothing.

'I will make another,' Mayra said. 'Neesa will be with me, always.'

Darkness is when the spirits speak.
Let slip your shackles.
Step from thy meat and drift, a trail of dust.
Move now, Neesa, in the Devourer's mind.
Let your spirit soar along the hunting paths.
The Devourer of Existence is hungry.
Be His feast.

Burak the Bloodseer toiled at his prayer, the scent of death in his nose from the prowler's dusty hide. The itch of prophecy was in the Heart-eater's mind, clawing at his thoughts. He took some knucklebones from a bag at his hip and cast them in the dust. The bones fell in the shape of fangs. He cast them again, rocking back on his heels, and in the failing light they were like two figures on the plain, running for sanctuary. He cast again, gathering the bones from the dirt, and they became four paths leading to a hidden hollow.

A cry fell across his second sight. He saw it lance up from the earth and buckle in the air, bending then like the flight of a falling arrow to spear him in the heart. Burak gasped. His hand, fingertips bloody with Neesa's life essence, strayed up to brush against the brass disc around his neck. He saw Kurguth, his First Fang, when they were both still young, no more than eager boys – two plains-runners on the Jagged Savannah in Ghur, the Realm of Beasts, years before the bellowed call of the Devourer of Existence had drawn them into the Long Hunt. In those days they could cross fifty miles of the savannah and be barely out of breath at the end of it. He saw Kurguth's proud face, his dusky skin, his lean body not yet filled out to manhood. *Rivals in everything back then, Kurguth, my brother...* He saw Kurguth's fist striking his face, Burak sprawled out in the fighting circle. He saw Kurguth, the first to run down a razordon in their initiation rite, furthest to throw his spear, fastest to sprint from the grassland to the peak of the Bloody Claw. And yet now Burak was Heart-eater, not Kurguth. Burak was the leader of the tribe and had taken them from the Jagged Savannah to the monstrous half-place of the Eightpoints. Burak had led them to the Bloodwind Spoil, this crazed landscape of fiendish mountains and baking plains, of wrecked civilisations and ravening warbands. It had been Burak, not Kurguth...

Because Burak *saw*.

The cry fell across his sight again, trailing thunder, dragging a ribbon of fire behind it. A black spearpoint in a savage plain, higher than any mountain, trembled and fell. He squeezed his eyes shut and felt the campfire's flames against his skin. He was aware of the cool air beyond the fire's embrace. Night was falling and the tribe drew near. He felt Neesa's spirit shift, prowling the shadows, her low growl crackling below the sound of the fire. He touched the disc again, secured around his neck by a length of cord. Even with his eyes closed he could sense Kurguth's shame, Mayra's anger.

Fools, he thought. *They are blind. Nought is won by sacrifice that isn't precious to give up.*

They worried that he was being seduced by the trappings of stone and armour, of high walls and metal. They couldn't see that he wore the disc not from lust but from revulsion, from pain. What could be the greater sacrifice than to deny your own nature, to trap a wild beast under lock and key? The Devourer of Existence saw. The Three-Eyed King saw, and he nodded his praise.

Ekrah the Preytaker whispered something to the plains-runners who sat beyond the fire's reach. They had dressed their young comrades for death already, those killed in the hunt that morning. Reverently they had stripped the bodies of their totems and left them sky-buried for the raptoryx, the scavenger birds who would shred them bare. Neesa was different. She had been with them since she was a cub, had been a part of them in ways the plains-runners had not. She was as much Mayra as Neesa, and to bid farewell to the prowler's spirit was in some way to bid farewell to a shard of the Beastspeaker's soul.

'Great Devourer,' Burak intoned, his eyes still closed. 'Hear now the purring of your daughter, her growl for meat and blood. Heed her call and swallow her down so she may partake of your every hunt.'

He buried his hands in Neesa's mane, felt how the muscles of her neck had grown stiff. He lifted his jawbone axe, the blade a line of serrated teeth still embedded in the bone, and he severed Neesa's head with one ferocious blow. Her blood had thickened with death and it trickled from the wound. Mayra raised her face to the blackening sky. In the undercast light of the campfire, her face looked like a mask. Burak passed the immense head to her. She cradled it in her lap, the prowler's yellow teeth grimacing, as fierce in death as she had ever been in life. Mayra stroked its bloody muzzle, and tears flowed freely from her eyes. Later, she would flense the flesh from the bones of Neesa's skull and fashion a new helm to protect her in battle. Such was the way of the tribe. Those who died gifted their totems to the rest, to shield them against future harm.

Burak slit the beast from neck to navel and reverently pulled out its guts. He laid them to one side, intoning prayers, smearing handfuls of blood against his face. Others too dipped their hands into the smoking cavity of the prowler's chest, and when they had anointed themselves in turn Burak cut choice pieces of her meat and passed them round. Eaten raw, the meat would impart a shard of Neesa's spirit into them all.

He sensed her out there beyond the fire's light, growling, her red eyes gleaming. He grinned and ate, swallowing down the bloody flesh and feeling her essence grow strong in him.

He found Neesa's heart amongst the offal – his by right, as Heart-eater of the tribe. It was huge, powerful, bigger than his fist. That such a thing should fall still… He raised the organ above his head so all could see, and with the tribe's eyes on him he put it to his mouth and bit deep, the dark heart's-blood running down his chin and spattering onto his chest.

'Brothers, sons,' he said through a mouthful of meat. 'Sisters, daughters. Hunters on the holy veldt, sworn to slaughter. Eat with me of our sister, Neesa, and take–'

He looked down into the crescent of flesh, glistening and moist. The edges of his vision faded to a troubled mist. In his own chest his heart stuttered and fell still, and from the back of his neck he could feel the icy tendrils of prophecy begin to creep. The world drifted into silence, neither warm nor cold, neither hard under his feet nor as insubstantial as a dream-song. He looked again into the meat of Neesa's heart, the shape of his teeth where he had gnawed the flesh, and from those shapes came breaking now the suggestion of new teeth, yellow and blunt, gnashing silently together, and between them flickered the lids of golden eyes that peered sadly up at him from the weeping tissue.

Burak, Bloodseer…

He saw as if imprinted on his mind the shape of the Black Spire, the spike rammed down into the very centre of the Eightpoints – seat of the Everchosen, leaching life and sanity from the earth, caparisoned in a mad geometry of buttresses and battlements, black as jet, black as night, black as a murderer's desire. The Spire rattled and groaned in a web of thunder, and deep in its evil heart, the Three-Eyed King called for help that only Burak and the Split-Tongue Tribe could give him.

Hunt, Bloodseer, the gnashing mouth whispered from Neesa's heart, the stench of its breath buffeting across Burak's face. The embedded eyes stared with frantic lust. *Hunt, before it is too late...*

He saw a man sprinting over a quagmire of blood and earth, a child in his arms.

A moon's turn to the Mountain's Throat, Bloodseer...

He saw a warrior grown fierce and strong, gathering the might of the Spoil to his banner.

The path will open when the sacrifice is made...

He saw war come to the Varanspire, the clash of arms, the falling of the citadel. All was ruin. All was fractured and lost, and the Great Hunt was led astray.

Bury the child, Bloodseer, skin its hide... In the temple you must skin its hide...

The mouth screamed silently in his fist, the eyes ruptured and leaking.

Seek it in the Fangs! Take its hide! Seek the temple!

'I will,' he whispered, hoarse, his voice trembling. He looked down at his hand. The meat was blank, no more than the chewed rag of Neesa's heart once more. 'I will do as you command,' he said, and then his vision was black and he was falling, plummeting down into a lonely abyss.

Kurguth caught him before he struck the ground. Burak's teeth were gritted and he was spitting foam, his eyes rolling back in his head. His hands were clenched so hard Kurguth feared the fingers would break, and he had crushed Neesa's heart into a bloody paste.

'The vision is on him,' Mayra said at Kurguth's side. She made a warding sign and spat on the ground. The flames of the campfire stuttered and leapt, snapping like a banner in a breeze.

'Help me!' Kurguth cried, straining against Burak's frenzied strength. 'Jaws of the Devourer, help me before he chokes!' Mayra took his legs and together they managed to lay him on his side. His body jerked and thrashed, and beyond the fire the rest of the tribe were praying. Ekrah slashed his arm with his knife and sprinkled drops of blood against Burak's feet, so his spirit would have firm ground on which to hunt and an easy trail to find its way back home.

Kurguth held his palm against Burak's sweating brow, trying to draw the pain of the vision from him, but he was no seer. He could fight, and run, and take any pain the mortal world could throw at him, but the dark paths of the vision quest were a trail even he couldn't follow. 'Burak,' he whispered, 'brother, hear my voice. In the darkness hear the light of my words calling you back. Kill the prey with your second sight and bring the spoils home.'

Slowly, the Heart-eater fell still. The trembling stopped. His eyes fluttered and closed. His fists unclenched, and the purple stain that had spread across his face began to fade.

'Kurguth,' he croaked. 'I saw your spirit like a column of flame, like a hookbeak cresting the dawn. I followed it, I...'

'Rest now. The tribe needs your strength more than it needs your visions.'

Burak pulled himself up by Kurguth's shoulder, sitting there on the shores of the Blood Lake Basin with Neesa's butchered corpse before him.

'This was no vision,' he said. 'This was a command. The Everchosen needs us, Kurguth. We will at last find entrance to the Great Hunt.'

'What did you see?'

'A child. And the Mountain's Throat. And a temple where the child must die.'

Kurguth frowned. He helped Burak up and glanced warily at Mayra, her whip coiled in her hand and Neesa's severed head at her feet.

'I don't understand. What has a child to do with us? Or the

mountains? We have no need of temples. The plains are our temples.'

'The child will cast down the Everchosen,' Burak groaned. 'It will destroy the Black Spire and shatter all the power of the Eight-points. Unless we can stop it. And when we do stop it,' he said, smiling with all the certainty of the god-touched, 'we will be at the Devourer's right hand as he leads his holy hunt. I swear it.'

'And what of the lasherbrute?' Mayra demanded. 'The hunt starts anew when light falls. We have revenge to make, for Neesa.'

'No,' Burak said sadly. 'Others run as we falter. Others wake as we sleep and rise to kill first. We're not the only ones to seek the child – we must move now. Will you trust me on this, my brothers and sisters? Trust the truth I am telling you.'

Kurguth nodded, although he couldn't meet Mayra's eyes. The Beastspeaker bared her teeth and crouched next to Neesa's head, but when she looked up there was no more defiance in her face. Ekrah drew his serrated blade and hefted it to his shoulder, nodding slowly.

Burak sat by Mayra and joined his hand with hers, their fingers intertwined in Neesa's mane. He grinned, his gums black, his teeth filed to points and the dried blood flaking from his face.

'She still has a part to play,' he said softly. He looked off into the shadows. There, a black shape limned with a dusky light, he thought he saw Neesa's spirit form prowling on the borders of death. 'The child hungers and will starve before we reach it, and the sacrifice will be lost. Go, run, Neesa!' he shouted. He laughed. 'Go, find it, give it sustenance so we can kill it while it lives!'

He watched her spirit pace the foreshore with a wary tread, and then she was leaping up into the air, the gleaming redness of her eyes shooting away like twin comets searing across the darkness of the Blood Lake Basin towards the distant Fangs – and the sound of Burak's laughter chased them all the way.

CHAPTER THREE

SERPENT'S SIGHT

Far over on the other side of the Bloodwind Spoil, the Hag's Claw Forest trembled in the breeze. It lay like a stain against the edge of the Tormented Lands, a jungled morass of emerald glades and shadowed pathways, brooding and sinister. Strange beasts prowled the deeper habitat, hunting for prey. Deadly fungi thrived in the damp confines of its heart, and deep in its verdant chambers the harrowmask flowers bloomed. Their pale green petals were marked with the tapered black blot that gave them their name – a mark like a mask, disguising their hidden motives. As he lay there in the dirt, Ashrath Silenthis, Trueblood of the Splintered Fang, thought that their scent was sharp and at the same time somehow indistinct. It cut like a knife, he thought, but it didn't linger. It was like the smoothest poison...

He had no time for further reflection, because at that moment Su'atha, his second in command, stabbed at him with a blow that would have skewered him in the dirt if he hadn't rolled aside at the last minute. He parried the follow-up strike with the broken shaft of his trident and kicked out at Su'atha's greaves to force the Pureblood back a step. Ashrath flipped up onto his feet and threw his ragged net aside, swinging the trident shaft at Su'atha's face to keep him occupied while he tore his broken helmet from his head. Ashrath was cut in several places, but at least they weren't using poisoned blades. He was fighting for his life, but there were rules to a challenge, after all.

'Yield, while you still can,' Su'atha said, circling around. The clearing was trampled and bare; they had been fighting for only a few minutes, but it felt like the best part of a day to Ashrath. He knew the Pureblood was good – his best fighter – but he had thought himself wise to all his moves. His second mistake. The first being, of course, to have accepted the challenge in the first place.

But what Trueblood could have backed down and still retained the leadership of his band? Ashrath had been placed in an impossible position, and as the two fighters circled each other he cursed himself again for pushing things to this point. Everything had gone wrong since Carngrad, since the fire-worshippers had smoked them from their temple and chased them out of the city. And now this – murder in the dirt, death in the Hag's Claw Forest on the far side of the Bloodwind Spoil, amongst a field of bitter flowers. *Damn them all.*

'I will never yield,' Ashrath said. His breath came heavily, but the longer Su'atha talked, the more time he had to regain his strength. He could feel Ma'sulthis' venoms fading in his veins, but just a moment's rest was all he needed. The Pureblood, strutting for the rest of the warband, was enjoying the chance to grandstand. It was not enough to win, Ashrath knew. The victory had to be accompanied by the abject humiliation of the vanquished.

Su'atha clashed his sword against his scale-mailed chest, his eyes glinting from the narrow vision slit of his helmet. His right arm was armoured wrist to shoulder, and he held it out before him like a shield.

'I promise you, though,' Ashrath said, 'surrender now and I will see your body buried in the snake pits, as is only right. I would do you that honour, though you spit in the face of your leader like the sewer worm you are, most cursed of serpents.'

'The Coiling Ones curse *you*, coward,' Su'atha said. 'No Splintered Fang should have run from the Scions of the Flame as you did, and you ran only to lose us in this miserable swamp. You follow portents and rumours like a child following a trail of sweetmeats. Your path is done. You are a legless lizard, no true serpent.'

'My path has barely begun, fool. I am a Son of Nagendra. You were at the ceremony – you know the Great Snake's venom runs in my veins.'

'*Blasphemy!* Blasphemy and delusion, there is no end to your failure. I will give you one choice, Ashrath. Death by a thousand cuts, or death by the killing blow. Choose now, for I will not make the offer a second time.'

The rest of the Horned Krait were gathered in a rough circle around the edge of the clearing. Some of them sat in the dirt, their weapons laid across their knees, eagerly watching the fight. Others stood as if poised for combat, unsure which way the band would fall when the victor emerged – whether those still loyal to Ashrath would defend his legacy, or whether those who had sided with Su'atha would fight to stake his claim. Old vengeances would be fulfilled, Ashrath was quite sure. Ancient slights would be paid in full, with a dagger in the back or a whip across the eyes, or the slow drip of poison for those who liked their revenge as cold as possible, as cold as the snake. His eyes met Essiltha's, and the aelven warrior almost imperceptibly inclined her head, a gesture as cryptic as Ashrath had ever seen her make. He looked away.

Did she mean for him to accept his fate, to die? Or to encourage him to fight? They were inscrutable, that race.

Of them all, only Ma'sulthis seemed to pay no attention to the challenge. Off to one side, sitting cross-legged against the trunk of a black-barked woe tree, the Serpent Caller mumbled in prayer, his hood covering his eyes, and the coils of his great serpent, Kathenga, wrapped around his body. The snake's massive head moved lazily from Ma'sulthis' shoulder, the forked purple tongue flickering to brush his skin, its eyes like shards of agate or chalcedony, crystalline, unseeing. Ashrath risked a glance in his direction, but the Serpent Caller gave no indication of how he desired the fight to end. His whole expression, what could be seen below the snake-skull mask, was blank and disinterested. It would end as it must; after all, the Coiling Ones moved as the serpent moves, with cryptic certainty.

Fight like the serpent then, Ashrath told himself as he warily circled Su'atha. *Strike true, and let speed be your most dangerous weapon.*

The Pureblood's helm, with its plume of emerald hair, glowed with a dull green lustre. This deep in the forest, thick in the twisting passageways and stagnant bowers, what light fell from the maudlin sky was blocked by the blackened woe trees, their branches clasped together like beseeching hands. But as Ashrath angled round, he could see a coin of light catch briefly against the peak of Su'atha's helmet, a dapple in the shade. He gestured with the broken shaft, swinging it wide and then jabbing in at the Pureblood's sternum. The wood was still heavy enough to break an arm, or cave in a skull if need be. Su'atha parried with his sword, but Ashrath had gained another foot of distance between them, and he had subtly pushed the other man half a turn around the clearing.

The serpent, lidless, sees all...

He stopped suddenly, holding the shaft low at his side. He could see the broken tines of his trident far over on the other side of the clearing, too far for him to reach. Unblinking, letting a thin half-smile creep casually onto his lips, he fixed Su'atha with his viridescent eyes. He was amused to see the first quiver of uncertainty on his opponent's face.

Let the victim try to strike or run; the result is the same. The snake always strikes first.

As Su'atha danced forward and cut low with a great cleaving swing of his sword, Ashrath moved like the pit viper and rolled under the blade. Coiled and precise, he struck like the banded mamba, jabbing the splintered end of the broken shaft deep into the back of Su'atha's unarmoured thigh. The Pureblood roared with pain and whipped round with a blow that would have taken Ashrath's head clean from his shoulders if he had still been standing there to take it. Instead, spinning the broken length of trident like a staff, he turned and took a half-step back, and as Su'atha lunged forward the Pureblood was paid with that coin of light precisely in his eyes. He fumbled, squinted – and then Ashrath snapped the staff's heavy stock into a crunching blow to his throat.

Su'atha collapsed, retching blood. He dropped his blade and staggered to the edge of the circle, where he was roughly pushed back into the centre by the jeering crowd. The Horned Krait had made its choice, and any who followed Su'atha's claim had by now smoothly insinuated themselves back onto Ashrath's side.

The serpent is, after all, true to its nature...

Su'atha fell to his knees, his face darkening as he drew off his helmet. He gulped air, tried to reach for his sheathed knife. Ashrath kicked his arm away. He took the knife from him and considered the blade, the greasy steel gleaming with a faint purple tinge.

'Serpent's Sight?' he said. He held out the knife, watched the way the dim forest light caught and smouldered in the steel. 'This is a dangerous poison, Su'atha. Many are the years of exposure before an initiate can gain immunity. Have you, I wonder, had the time to match your strength to the strength of this?'

Su'atha reeled in the clearing, still clawing at his throat. There was a time for mercy, Ashrath thought, and a time when mercy made nothing but a fool of the weak. Ashrath Silenthis could be called many things, but weak was not one of them.

The warband drew closer, anticipating death. Essiltha crossed her arms, a mocking smile on her face. Her eyes, black almonds, glimmered. They all deserved this display, Ashrath knew. The challenge should never have come in the first place, and he despised himself for allowing Su'atha to reach a point where he felt emboldened enough to make it. He should have stamped on this rebellion earlier, much earlier. All these weeks of strife, dragging themselves from Carngrad to the borders of the forest, trying to escape defeat through atonement... It had been a trial with no end, no purpose.

He remembered Lord Rakaros standing in the maelstrom of fire and smoke, the Scions of the Flame laughing as the temple of the Splintered Fang burned, their warriors butchered on the ground and the snake pits aflame. Then the long journey to the Hag's Claw Forest, the atoning promise to find the lost Shrine of Nagendra that legends said was hidden deep in the jungled heart of this foul quagmire. They had followed all the signs and omens, but no sight of it had they found. Instead, they had discovered only starvation and fatigue and death: acid vines that burned the skin from a man's bones; the staring cyclops eye of the swamp-polyp before its barbed tongue lashed out to disembowel the unwary; the drifting spores from the hag's claw plant that, once breathed, metastasised in moments to choke the lungs with virulent fungal clusters. It was death, this place, nothing but death.

He looked down at Su'atha. *A leader must be swift in decision, my friend, as the snake is swift. If only you had learned that, perhaps our positions would now be reversed?*

'Let us see, then,' he said, 'how well you endure the Serpent's Sight.'

The cut on its own was nothing, a mere scratch with the poisoned blade against his cheek. But the moment steel met skin, Su'atha began to screech through his constricted throat; his arms went rigid at his side, his shoulders hunched, and a purple foam began to bubble from his lips. It was in the eyes that the most dramatic effect took place, though. The pupils seemed to swell and elongate, stretching from the top of his eyes to the bottom like a serpent's, each one swimming in a pool of blood. Corrosive purple tears poured down his face, and as the Pureblood's screams became ever more frenzied, he fell back and writhed across the floor of the clearing like a snake trying to shed its skin. The eyes bulged from his head – and then suddenly, with a wet, sucking pop, each split along the line of its pupil and fell away from the socket, and from the boiling cavity of Su'atha's skull came a narrow plume of purple smoke.

'The Serpent's Sight,' Ashrath said softly, into the silence that met the Pureblood's end. He held up the envenomed blade so all could see. Then, with great care and deliberation, he slowly licked the poison from the steel.

'You took a great risk, Son of Nagendra,' Ma'sulthis said in his hissing, croaking voice. He adjusted his snake-skull mask and placed a dried snakeskin against Ashrath's bare shoulder, touching his forehead lightly with a venom sac from a spine-rattler. 'Serpent's Sight is a most holy poison, and only the initiates of the Scaled Temple have full immunity.'

Ashrath shuddered under the priest's attention, his fists clenched, the sweat breaking out in thick beads across his face. His teeth were grinding together, and his eyes felt like they were going to burst from his skull. It was as if a thousand burning needles were scraping and jabbing their way through his intestines.

'It's just as well,' he gasped, 'that the temple knows no greater initiate than you...'

'Ah, but we are a long way from Invidia, are we not? Deep into the Eightpoints we find ourselves, young Trueblood, no longer to see the jungles of our distant realm. How can you be so sure I have the antidote on my person?'

'Damn you, Serpent Caller, must you let me suffer so!'

The shadow of his hood covered most of what his mask did not, but Ashrath was sure that a ghost of a smile played briefly across the Serpent Caller's lips. From his belt he took a vial no bigger than his thumbnail, luminous with a sickly purple liquid.

With rigid hands Ashrath took and uncorked the vial, tipping the contents onto his burning tongue. The effect was immediate; his eyes cooled and his vision cleared, his muscles relaxing so that he slumped back onto the oily grass. He dragged air into his lungs, smelling the sharp and fleeting scent of the harrow-mask flowers that lit the glade with their subtle green. Kathenga, coiled around the Serpent Caller's shoulders, swept its blunt head from side to side and fluttered its bifurcated tongue as if tasting the flowers' perfume. Light shattered in the blind amber eyes, like clustered crystal.

'Was the display necessary?' Ma'sulthis asked. He sat and bent over his collection of ampules and bottles, holding one of them up to the serpent's head. Kathenga, hissing softly and as if knowing what was expected of it, stretched its maw and presented its ivory fangs to the bottle's mouth. Ma'sulthis milked the smoky venom from the creature's poison sacs, adding a few drops from various of his other stores. 'Su'atha was defeated in single combat – the poisoning was... an additional measure, perhaps?'

Ashrath sat up and took the bottle Ma'sulthis offered him. 'An essential measure,' he said. 'It was not enough for him to be defeated, but for the manner of his defeat to show my mastery, both of combat and of the holy poisons with which we pray.'

'And what would you have done if my stores of the antidote had been dry?'

'I would have died as Su'atha died,' he said with a smile. 'In agony.'

He tipped the jar to his mouth and drank deep, and he felt the venoms coiling in his gut. They swam and shifted through his veins, insinuating their way into his nerves and muscles, lighting his eyes with green fire. All the pain and exhaustion of the fight drifted off, like smoke on the breeze. He handed the jar back to Ma'sulthis.

'More often do you seek the venom's strength, Trueblood. Take care, as I have said before, that the venom does not master you.'

'It won't,' Ashrath said. 'Have no fear, priest. Nothing can master me.'

'Take heed, Ashrath – even the greatest leaders can be defeated by their over-confidence.'

Behind them, further off across the clearing, the warriors of the Horned Krait sat around their campfires. Ashrath could hear their muttered conversation, their chanted songs. Dissatisfaction had been neutered for the moment, but without doubt it would rise again, as the snake rises after sleep to hunt.

'You fought well, my master,' a voice said, silken and foreboding. Ashrath looked to see Essiltha cross the clearing towards the campfires. She raised a harrowmask flower to her nose and inhaled deeply. He couldn't tell if he was being mocked, but he nodded all the same as she passed on her way.

'I am never sure if that one means to provoke me or not,' he muttered. 'Always picking those damned flowers... All of the warband need purpose, though. The search for Nagendra's Shrine was a fool's errand, a quest with no more substance to it than rumour and legend.'

'Rumours and legends are the essence of the Bloodwind Spoil, Ashrath Silenthis. The whole of the Eightpoints is a land built upon ancient myth. Some say that Nagendra's teeth fell to make the mountains of the Fangs, when the solar drake Ignax tore him down. His flesh fell to make the serpents of the realms, is it not so? He bred the Coiling Ones, who guide our path, do they not?'

'They do,' Ashrath grudgingly admitted. 'But it was a mistake, the first I've really made, and it nearly destroyed us. I need something more than myth. I've led us to the Bloodwind Spoil on the promise that we would find glory in the Everchosen's legions, that we would become the true heirs of the Coiling Ones, true children of Nagendra. You ministered at the ceremony back in Invidia, Ma'sulthis – you know what I promised when I took the leadership. And what have I given them but dust and ashes in our plundered temple, and death in the turbid silence of this miserable forest!'

'Do not despair, Ashrath, do not give up your hopes. While you fought,' Ma'sulthis hissed, 'the Coiling Ones came to me. Drawn by death, drawn by blood and poison, they spoke to me through Kathenga's mouth. His tongue flickered with the fire of their holy words!'

Ashrath narrowed his eyes, his heart beating faster in his chest. Rarely did the Coiling Ones, the children of Nagendra, speak. When they did, the wise man listened.

'They showed me a child of the Spoil, and a man running to Nagendra's Fangs. They showed me the Spire of the Serpent's Tooth, which gnaws upon the earth and bleeds its poison into the ruptured lands.'

'The Varanspire,' Ashrath whispered. 'Archaon's seat.'

'They showed me this child, and he is more precious than all the jewels of the realms combined, more powerful than a thousand kingdoms.'

'Who is he?'

Ashrath gripped the Serpent Caller's arm. Ma'sulthis grinned, and behind the snake-skull mask his sallow skin seemed to glow.

'He is Archaon's heir,' he whispered. 'He is the Blood of the Everchosen, the Heart of the Spoil. And only you, Ashrath Silenthis, can save him.'

In some distant day of the forgotten past, he must have had a name. There must have been a mother to bear him, a home of sorts, a sense of life lived as one moment accruing to the next. Even here in the depths of the Bloodwind Spoil, cowering from the febrile tides of its brutal skies, peering into air that was always murky with fume and the bitter exhalation of the burning earth, he must have had a sense of his life as something that progressed from day to day, month to month, year to year. He must have lived, once.

Now, he did not live; he merely survived, and he had no name. He was the Beggar, to himself if not to the other citizens of Carngrad. To the denizens of that unhappy city, a shanty settlement of rusting iron and worm-eaten wood, of stone notched with a thousand sword swings, he was nothing at all. He meant as little as the scrawny rats he chased along the stinking alleyways, gnawing them to the bones as he crouched in puddles of filth, his patchy beard matted with their entrails. He was the Beggar, although in truth he begged nothing, for not one of the warriors, slaves and cheating merchants who called that city home would have even stooped to spit in his eye, let alone pass a coin into his proffered cup. To ask for help in Carngrad was to invite only misery. If you needed something, you took it, and all the Beggar needed was the rats.

He saw one now, skittering through a heap of mouldering cloth at the roadside. An oily rain had fallen earlier that night, and the muddy street was slick underfoot, but the Beggar was a practised hunter. He lay in the muck and slithered carefully towards it, his fingers twitching with anticipation.

A splash of sound further down the street made him pause. Turning his head with infinitesimal care towards the sound, he saw a ragged shadow in a cape of black feathers slashing madly at a prostrate figure.

A Crow... the Beggar thought. He tried to shrink into the dirt.

The shadow cackled horribly, and then it seemed to merge with the shadows around it and disappear. The Beggar stared into the darkness, dimly aware of the ravaged figure on the ground. There were pockets there, he thought, that could be rifled, and who knew what they might contain...?

The choice was agonising – rat now, or the prospect of plunder. Which was it to be? Rat, or dead body? He stared at the rat and licked his lips, but his fingers itched to search the body's pockets. But then the body might be of someone just as inconsequential as the Beggar, with nothing in his pockets but pebbles and fingernails... But then why would one of the Crows cut him down so savagely? A Crow wouldn't bother its business with a beggar – they always had more dangerous prey in mind. Oh, it was too much!

He looked to the rat, hunkered on its hind legs, washing its cankered face with its paws. The red eyes twitched. It skittered around to look at him. It was now or never. Rat tonight, or pebbles? Or maybe gold, precious gold... or market scrip? Or fingernails? Or... rat! Yes, rat... but here was a rat before him, just waiting to be eaten.

The Beggar's stomach growled in sympathy. He wriggled in the mud, and then his choice was made.

It must be rat.

Honed by the long years of necessity that were to the Beggar no more than a glinting madness in his mind, he lunged from the dirt and propelled himself forward on all fours. The rat turned to leap, but as it jumped out of the Beggar's grasping reach his fingers curled around its tail.

'Ha!' he screeched. 'Victory is mine! A feast, a veritable feast of rat! Oh, for rat and a cup of zephyrwine!'

But in his glee the Beggar had forgotten that the rat must never be underestimated, and that in the battle of wills between rat and man, it is rarely the man who wins. The rat whipped round, preternaturally fast, and sank its festering teeth into the back of his hand. He barked with pain, reflexively opening his clenched fist, and the rodent scurried off to freedom in the grimy alleyways of Carngrad.

He didn't know how long he lay there in the mud, weeping to himself. For the Beggar, time moved in fits and starts. Eventually, though, he became aware of a shadow that had fallen across him, blocking out the stuttering ruby light of the aether-lamp further up the road. He raised his head from the ground, his face plastered with muck. A figure stood before him, staring down with what the Beggar took a long moment to understand was concern.

'My poor friend,' the figure said, in a rich, mellifluous voice. His robes trailed in the mud, rattling with chains, and at the head of his staff there glowed a burning ember. His face was hidden behind an elaborate latticework mask. 'So tired and hungry. This is a vicious place for those in need, truly it is. Please, take my hand. Come with me. You look so cold. Come with me, and I promise we'll get you warmed up.'

It was a city where cannibal meat markets abutted temples to forgotten aspects of the Ruinous Gods, where fighting pits rang with the clash of steel, where rickety streets hosted the tread of a hundred flagellating cultists, each scouring their flesh with blessed mortification. It was a city where the alleyways were the scenes of a thousand hurried stabbings, and where secretive chambers in backstreet reliquaries were the site of unnumbered bloody rituals. It was a city where debts were paid with murder, where the gangmasters of the Talons held court and toasted each assassination with a goblet of tears, and where the warbands of a dozen fractious cults clashed nightly in an endless play of bloodshed and mutilation.

It was Carngrad, and a more cursed and vicious place in the Bloodwind Spoil would be hard to find.

But it was also a place, as the Beggar knew, of strange sanctuary. Many were the tattered caravans that wandered in from the plains of the Kardeb Ashwastes, or that staggered across from the dry misery of the Tormented Lands. For if Carngrad was anarchic and unruly, then the lands around it were worse. If Carngrad was a patchwork zone of mayhem and death, then it was a haven compared to the lawless wilds of the Spoil. Or so the Beggar had always assumed, anyway.

Within Carngrad, certain sanctuary could be found too. Some sections of the city were official truce zones, the peace kept by the bodyguards the Talons recruited from the gladiatorial ranks of the Spire Tyrants. Some temples, dedicated as they were to the Three-Eyed King, were places where vendettas must be laid aside. It was to a place such as this that the Beggar saw he was being taken, a simple and unadorned stone temple in a courtyard off Cadavers' Avenue. Two torches burned on either side of the black door, the lintel stone roughly scarred above them. The robed priest who had helped him off the ground held the Beggar's elbow in a firm and reassuring grip and gently guided him onwards.

'Food you shall have,' he promised, 'and rest such as your weary bones need.'

'Food would be lovely,' the Beggar muttered, for a moment unsure if he had actually spoken the words aloud. 'Would you have any... *rat*, do you know?'

The robed figure laughed softly. He held his staff ahead of him, and the twin doors of the temple slowly swung open.

'Rat will be the very least of it, my friend. But first, you are dirty from your misfortune. Come, soon you will be cleansed.'

They passed through a low atrium bare of decoration, the flagstones wide and dusty underfoot. The man led the Beggar through another set of doors, into a long, cool chamber which was similarly austere. There were hollow niches along the walls, empty of icons or statuary, and in the middle of the floor was a circular depression. Above it, admitting the night air's fitful breeze, was an opening in the ceiling that showed the red, mist-wreathed skies above Carngrad.

'Is this all you bring me, Votremos?'

The voice boomed from the shadows at the other end of the chamber. The Beggar flinched. Instinctively he turned to go, but the chamber behind him had silently filled with half a dozen others, young men and women dressed in simple half-cloaks and leggings who surged forward to take hold of him. Whimpering, he was dragged towards the depression in the centre of the stone floor.

The shadows at the further end seemed to flicker then, as if a flame were kindling into life. The Beggar stared, and the shadows swam before his eyes.

'He doesn't look like a worthy offering,' the voice said. 'Is there such a paucity of choice on the streets of Carngrad that this beggared halfwit is all you could find?'

'Forgive me, Blazing Lord,' the robed figure said. The brazier embedded in his staff began to glow, as if responding to the form the Beggar could see emerging from the darkness. Torches burst into flame along the walls as the figure passed – and then he stepped into the guttering light, revealed.

In heavy black boots and bronze greaves, he stood upon the stone floor, his eyes blazing behind the sockets of his flared mask. At his hip was sheathed a massive two-handed blade, and his shoulders and upper arms were guarded by linked spaulders of scorched metal. Chains rattled around the tabard at his waist, setting a clinking accompaniment to the scene.

'For our purposes,' the robed man continued, 'he will do well, however. Look more closely, Lord Rakaros. Do you not see that here is one so soiled by decadence that his soul calls out for cleansing?'

'Indeed,' the lord said. He took off the bronze mask, and a smile more terrible than his fuming eyes lit up his face. 'Initiates – prepare him.'

The Beggar tried to break free, but the initiates' grip was too strong. He cried out as they bound his hands, his bare feet scrabbling on the stone floor as they dragged him towards the centre of the room. Two more initiates brought to the circular depression a wooden stake that reached its pointed tip to the skylight in the ceiling. They tied the Beggar to the stake and arranged bundles of kindling around his feet, scattering a swatch of crystal stones amongst them. The stones glowed with an inner fire, reeking amidst the bare wood.

'Let me go!' the Beggar shrieked. 'I... I've changed my mind! I don't want any food, or rest, or anything! I swear, I just want to go back!' He twisted his wrists against the cords that fastened him to the stake, but the bonds had been cruelly tied.

'You have been brought to the Crucible,' the lord said, the one the robed figure had called Rakaros. He stood before the Beggar, radiating heat and power. 'Do you know what that means?'

'No... no, I don't, I...' he stuttered – and then, for the first time in his life, the Beggar begged. 'Lord, please, I beseech you! Whatever you have planned for me, don't do it!'

'It is not what we have *planned*, my friend. It is what the Flame desires, the Ever-Raging Flame. Let your sacrifice be its fuel, for flesh and spirit are made as diamond in the Crucible of the Flame, and the Flame will one day consume the realms entire. Immolator,' he said. Another figure joined him, tall, his face a twisted, charred ruin, his eyes dazzling with madness. For a moment, as the Beggar looked on him, he seemed wreathed in flames that didn't burn. 'Cleanse this offering,' Rakaros said.

The Immolator, as the Blazing Lord had called him, crouched and laid his hands against the wood. Smoke drifted into the Beggar's senses then, stinging his eyes and choking his lungs. He felt the flames rise from the pit, and the hair on his legs singed to an acrid fume. He looked down. The crystal stones had blazed to a white and implacable heat, and the kindling was beginning to crisp in the fire. The flames licked up and caught at the hem of his frayed rags – and then, in seconds, he was staring at the bare chamber through a whirlwind, his vision a vortex of flashing shapes and searing pain. He screamed into the inferno, and the scream came from the depths of all the pain and fear and horror of his sorrowful life as it fizzled out into fire and ash. And then, for a moment, as the fire scoured the hair from his head and crisped his skin, and before it melted his eyes into twin tracks of sizzling jelly, he saw the figures standing before him as if they were the ones subsumed by flame and he instead were standing at a cool remove – contemplative, at peace, and troubled by no more than the choice of whether to have rat for supper that night or not.

Afterwards, in the calm and purified air of the temple's sacristy on the upper floor, Lord Rakaros leaned against the wall and stared down from the open window at the spread of Carngrad below him. Tin roofs sagged against listing spires, and from the alleyways and souks of the jumbled city came the sounds of street traders and scavengers, of beggars and orphans and those out thirsting for blood. Howls fell across the air, and mocking laughter cackled down the avenues. Footsteps rang out in desperate pursuit. Immediately below him he saw a man in the courtyard dragged down by three faceless women whose limbs were wrapped in barbed wire, their daggers rising and falling in the light of the aether-lamps as they hacked him to death. The victim didn't make a sound. Rakaros wondered if he had perhaps paid for the pleasure. There were those who were so jaded that they desired nothing more than to meet their end at the hands of the Sestrine Sisterhood, and who found an ultimate sensual release in the frenzied attention of their blades.

Scum, Rakaros thought, the rage like a burning coal in his guts. *This whole city is but the kindling for a righteous flame.*

He thought back to the day they had seized this temple from the Splintered Fang, the exultation he had felt. It had been a moment when the Burned Hand, his Scions of the Flame, had been poised on the cusp of greatness, and yet greatness had still not come. Surrounding the temple, searing its corridors with fire and ash, Rakaros had stalked like a conflagration through its chambers, cutting the snake-worshippers down. He had torched their serpent pit, beaten their leader in single combat and laughed as the young fool ran with his surviving followers. Months of squabbling and petty territorial conflict had come to an end in one cataclysmic action, and for a moment the whole city seemed on the brink of capture. What had happened? Why, Rakaros wondered, had they stalled in this lassitude, this stasis, burning beggars from the streets and praying that the fires would light their path? Fire did not stand still. The Ever-Raging Flame ate its way across the realms, unquenchable, from the Viridian Mountains in Aqshy to the seat of the Everchosen, here in the Eightpoints. And yet the Scions stood still, and waited, and scryed the flames for signs that would not come.

Except tonight, for the first time in months, the signs *had* come.

'Lord Rakaros?'

Votremos, the Inferno Priest, entered the sacristy, his staff held before him. He liked to masquerade as an older man, Rakaros had noticed, as if the staff were a necessary aid rather than the trappings of his office. Rakaros had often wondered why. Perhaps the mask of age gave advantages when combat was at hand, deceiving the unwary? The candle seems weak, after all, but in moments it can become a maelstrom.

'Enter, Votremos. The offering went well, I thought. It is often those who have least to lose who make the brightest flame, I have noticed.'

'Thank you, lord. I felt so too. Our Immolator, Xoloxes, seemed particularly pleased with the evening's proceedings. One day, I swear, he will burn away completely.'

'That day will be a blessed moment,' Rakaros said. 'For none among us has a faith so pure.'

The priest came closer, leaning on his staff. 'We have used almost the last of our rage-rock in the ritual, though,' Votremos warned. 'In truth, I'm not sure how to acquire more. A delegation back to Aqshy, to the Temple of Cold Ashes, would be the most perilous journey, but it has perhaps come to that...'

'No!' Rakaros said sharply – and then, more softly, 'No, there will be no need of that.'

'There is a chance it could be found in Carngrad, amongst the souks?'

'I will not trade trinkets with the cheats of this cesspit for something so holy,' the Blazing Lord said. 'Nor will I retreat to the

Temple of Cold Ashes with our mission here undone. We have been sent for a sacred purpose, Votremos – you know this.'

'Indeed, my lord.'

'How are the others? Are the initiates at prayer?'

'Yes, lord – and they've scourged themselves.'

'Good.'

'Katastrian sharpens his blade in the armoury, seeing to the weapons, and the Fireborn have replenished our store of flame-burst pots. Taking this temple from the snake-worshippers was a costly endeavour, but the losses have been made good.'

'Another day is done, then,' Rakaros said. 'Tomorrow beckons…'

The Inferno Priest settled himself on the window seat by Rakaros' side. Together they stared down at the great conglomeration of Carngrad, part metropolis, part labyrinthine shanty town. Both longed to see it scorched to nothing, to raise a pyre so vast that it would catch the attention of the Everchosen himself.

That time will come, Rakaros told himself.

'Is there anything I can help you with, my lord?' the Inferno Priest asked after a moment. 'I come to offer guidance, if it is needed…?'

Rakaros looked at him, and the priest met his gaze. The understanding passed between them of what the flames had revealed, but neither felt able to broach it. Nothing shown by the fire was ever certain; the tongues of the flame spoke a flickering language, and to read them right took not just skill but purity of intention. Rakaros was too self-aware to ignore the flaw in his own heart – the burning coal of ambition, a thirst for power that could quench his true purpose to be a servant of the Ever-Raging Flame. What he had seen in the torchlight of the burning beggar could not be trusted on its own terms, and he needed Votremos to confirm the truth of it for him. To ask would be to admit doubt, though, and to admit doubt was to prise open the first crack in his authority.

The temple had accepted his demand to come here because of the strength of his faith. None other, the elders had understood, would be more likely to gain admittance to Archaon's legions and help fan the flames of his wars. Rage-rock in quantities untold would be their reward, but if his faith was seen in any way as grasping or weak, the whole edifice of their holy mission in the Eightpoints would come crashing down.

He pictured again the warlord of the Splintered Fang, that callow youth, sprinting for freedom as the rooms of the temple crackled around him. They had cleansed this place of that slithering taint, but many times Rakaros had asked himself why he had taken the temple from the Splintered Fang in the first place. Was it to punish blasphemy or to sever the head of a rival? Had his purpose been holy and righteous or the strategy of a selfish mind?

I am tainted by the lust for power, he thought. *And of all things, lust must be burned away...*

'I do need your help, priest,' he admitted. The confession was a burden lifted from his burning heart. 'I need your guidance.'

'The flames showed us something we didn't expect,' Votremos said quickly. 'Tell me, lord – what did you see?'

'I saw...'

He had seen another fire, leaping to the sky like a warning beacon. He had seen desperate pursuit, blood on the wind, the deadly mountains beyond Carngrad. He had heard a child crying, and that cry was a command for sacrifice and death. He had seen the sign of the Everchosen spreading like a stain across the Bloodwind Spoil, a wound stabbed into the heart of reality by the black blade of the Varanspire, and all the holy fires raging across the realms in an unstoppable conflagration. He had seen a ruined temple, and an altar.

'There is something we must do,' he continued. 'We have been given a sign to follow.'

'Indeed,' Votremos said. 'And what is this sign?'

'It is a child. I saw this in the flames. It must be found. Even now, others seek its fate and hope to turn it to their own advantage. They head towards the Fangs, and we must go there also.'

'And what must we do when we find this child?'

The priest nodded, encouraging Rakaros to make that final leap, to piece together the fragments of what he had seen in the fire of the burning beggar.

'We must kill it,' Rakaros whispered, with understanding. 'The Ever-Raging Flame has given us this sign. There is a ruined temple on the outskirts of the Varanspire, and there we must cleanse the child in the holy flame, in the sight of the Everchosen!'

Votremos stood and laid his hand against the Blazing Lord's shoulder.

'This is what we have been waiting for,' he said urgently. 'At last, the Flame shows us the way! It is a test, a quest that we must complete, and then admittance to the legions will follow. We are almost there, my lord.'

Rakaros turned from the view of Carngrad's malignant streets. *Let the cut-throats and the cannibals stew in their own filth*, he thought. *Righteous judgement will come for them in time.*

'Ready the others,' he told Votremos, who bowed at his command. 'We make for the Fangs at once.'

As the priest left to gather the warband, Rakaros unsheathed his blade and tested its edge. There was something else that he had seen in the flames, something that Votremos had not mentioned or confirmed...

Figures on the plains, moving faster than lightning. Warriors in gleaming plate, their eyes blazing with a holy fury every bit as ruthless as the rage of the Burned Hand.

Rakaros sheathed his blade again. He was quite sure that before this quest was done, he would need it.

CHAPTER FOUR

SIGN OF THE GODS

It was colder in the mountains of the Fangs, even here amongst the foothills. A clammy mist seemed to rise from the stone, shrouding the narrow tracks and making every few feet a venture into the unknown. The ground underfoot was loose shale, studded here and there with tough patches of razor grass, and as Ankhad trekked higher into the Fangs he found himself stumbling at every other step. The wind caught between the fissures of rock to sing in mournful tones, and sometimes on the breeze he heard strange, blood-chilling cries that rose to a crescendo and then fell away into a fretful silence. And then the wind would pick up again, whispering through the jagged peaks, drawing its chill fingers against his skin.

He held the baby close to his chest as he walked. Whenever he fell, instinct made him turn and take the blow against his back rather than risk dropping the child. It lay there in his arms, peaceful enough. He stared down at the boy's sleeping face, a lock of his thin black hair untethered from the blanket.

He looks like his mother. Ilthis…

He saw her green eyes flashing in the lamplight, her black hair tumbling down to her bare shoulders, her pale skin. He pushed her from his mind.

I'm sorry, my love. There will be time for mourning, but it is not now.

He had taken little else with him other than the baby and his knife. Three days he had been running, and all he had were the clothes he stood up in and a bag he had snatched as he kicked his way through the hut's rickety walls. He didn't know what had possessed Tarnot to help him, but on the silence of the mountainside he gave the other man's shade his whispered thanks. No doubt he was dead now, dragged to the trough and drowned, but the frenzy of his attack had given Ankhad all the time he needed to escape. He had plunged across the bloody quagmire of the plains as the blood rain fell, sprinting towards the splintered teeth of the Fangs as they loomed in red-streaked shards ahead, the mountains burning in the flash of the lightning storm. He hadn't looked back to see if they were following him, the desperate men and women of Spite, but by the time he reached the foothills he had risked a glance. Spite had glowered in the distance, but the Desolate March between the settlement and the mountains was empty, as far as he could tell. He had taken the paths into the higher lands, rising step by step, heading from the certainty of death to its mere probability instead. The Fangs were no sanctuary, he knew. No part of the Bloodwind Spoil could be called truly safe, but it was better always to move towards danger than meekly stand and wait for it to catch you.

He wasn't sure if they would track him into the mountains, but it was a risk he was willing to take. A child born on the Feast of the Black Spire must be given to the True Gods, or ruination will surely follow. Even now they might be hunting the boy down, waiting to snatch him from Ankhad's fingers and take him back to Spite, where the burning pit awaited.

His hand strayed to the knife tucked into his belt. *Let them try, for it will be the ruin of them all...*

There were more pressing concerns though. He was more used to making orphans than raising babies, but even Ankhad knew that they needed milk. The child would die in this dismal place if it couldn't be fed, and although he was confident he could scrabble his own sustenance from berries and roots, he knew the baby was months off being weaned and would choke if he tried to feed him solid food. As the mists rose, the mountains ringing with the clatter of rockfall, Ankhad allowed himself this thought – that perhaps it would have been better for the child to have died back in Spite. Death would have come quickly enough in the burning pit – Lothin would have seen to it. Better that than this lingering misery, the hollow death of starvation and thirst.

He paused to rest a while, leaning against an outcrop that gave a good view back down the valley he had just climbed. As the mists curled and broke apart, he could see a portion of dun grass, a scattering of boulders, the stunted trunk of a barren tree. He peered into the distance, but he couldn't see anyone following him. He had made no effort to disguise his tracks, doubting that the scavengers of Spite were skilled enough to read them. But there were other dangers in these mountains, and he knew he would do well to take more care.

He laid the baby on the ground at his feet and leaned to drink from a trickle of water that ran down one of the rocks at his back. The water was sharp, gritty with minerals, but it tasted clean enough. He gathered some in his hand and allowed a few drops to drip onto the baby's mouth. The child stirred in his sleep, a frown briefly marring his forehead. His face looked dry and sunken, Ankhad thought, his skin stained with a faint discoloration that spread like a mask across his eyes. He kneeled beside the child and carefully unwrapped the blanket, reeling back from the stench.

With water from the trickling stream he cleaned the baby as best he could, wiping the black meconium from its thighs and drying the child on the sleeve of his tunic. Ankhad had tied the baby's severed umbilical cord with a lock of Ilthis' hair, and he paused a moment to run his fingers over those glossy strands, the last memento he had of his wife. He washed out the blanket and left it to dry on a sun-struck patch of grass. Rummaging in his bag, he found a wineskin and a length of silk from Ilthis' days on the caravanserai. He wrapped the child up again.

The position they were in was a strong one, easy to defend, and Ankhad allowed himself to sleep for a while. He tucked the baby under an overhang of rock at his feet and settled himself on the grass, his knife drawn and held in his hand. Before he fell asleep, drifting on the edges of dream, the image of Ilthis slunk once more across his mind's eye. He saw her walking across a blasted heath, her green eyes igniting in the dusk, the scarf that he had used to swaddle the baby loose around her throat. Then, as he watched, a tangle of jungle plants rose from the ground behind her. The jungles of Ghyran, he thought. He had always been sure that she hailed from that fecund realm, although she had never said. For both of them, their former lives had been subjects of which they wouldn't speak; the pain was too great, and the tales they could have told would have been of nothing but violence, sorrow and bloodshed. As he watched, the jungle through which Ilthis moved began to smoulder and flames began to lick from the undergrowth. Soon, the fire raged in an unstoppable inferno, but still she came on. She was no woman now, but a snake, an emerald serpent coiling in the ashes, its tongue flickering out to taste his fear, his desperation – and then the snake was writhing through a field of bones and skulls, closer and closer, its eyes as green as oceans, as green as life.

Ankhad, it cried, the voice searing into his mind. *Ankhad, protect the Son…*

He snapped awake, the knife in his hand. It was dark. Across the sky came a sound like tearing cloth, a howl that shrieked across the mountainside. The sky flashed above him with eldritch colours, and the wind slithered across his skin like a stream of cold water. He shivered. The baby was crying. He gathered the child close, holding him in his arms until he settled down again.

'Quiet, little one,' he whispered softly. 'Just a storm, that's all. Just a storm passing overhead. Do you hear it? The gods are speaking, and their voice is thunder. They are the power in the earth and the power in the sky. They are for the strong, not the weak, and you are strong, aren't you, little one?'

The baby whimpered and fell still, his breath measured and calm at last.

Protect the Son, he thought.

'I will, Ilthis,' he said to the naked sky. 'I promise. I'll protect him until my dying breath.'

But whose son is he?

He woke early. The mist had burned away and the blanket had dried overnight, so he changed the baby and wrapped him up again. He sprinkled more water on his lips. Strong as he was, Ankhad knew the boy would die today if he couldn't find sustenance.

I will bury you in these mountains if it comes to that, he thought. *Here, high above the Spoil, I will build you a cairn and you will look down on all that might have been, your father beside you. Your father…*

He went on. He passed through chambers of rock that opened

out into long, twisting avenues that snaked across the sharper peaks, sometimes descending into shallow tunnels that passed beneath the jagged overhangs. Rough grass grew at grasping angles in these tunnels, reaching for the light, and from cracks in the walls came pallid lengths of bindweed and haemaflore, their bitter yellow flowers twitching as he passed, dripping their bloody nectar on the ground. He held his breath until he had left them far behind, their rotten stench lingering in the stagnant air.

The paths he followed still led up, a steep gradient towards the peaks. As he walked, the baby tucked under one arm, the other arm spread out for balance against the outcrops of rock, he scanned the barbed landscape around him for threat. It was not just the scavengers of Spite that worried him, although in truth he was sure he had left them far behind. He knew the Fangs were home to any number of creatures, most of them more dangerous than anything he would have found back down on the Desolate March. Beastmen tribes raised their herdstones in these hills, decorating them with talismans ripped from the flesh of those they killed. Cannibal tribes were rumoured to live here too, their caves like rancid charnel houses where they skinned and ate their prey. Raptoryx flocks, prowlers, even the dreaded bat-like forms of furies…

'I'm sure I've brought you into the very maelstrom,' he whispered to the child. The baby looked up at him with its dark green eyes, the irises flecked with shards of emerald. 'Forgive me…'

All seemed quiet, although as he skirted the razor-sharp line of a bisecting ridge and clambered down onto a trail that twisted through a grove of bitter gorse, a strange, keening whine came blowing on the breeze. He stopped at once, crouching down, his knife in his hand. He angled his head to listen, and when the sound came again, he carefully tracked it to the source. Whatever it was, it didn't sound threatening.

The rocktusk prowler lay dead on its side, its flank ripped open and its ribs shattered, its bared teeth glazed with blood. Further down the trail Ankhad found the muscled bulk of a tuskivore, its feathered throat ripped out. The two creatures had killed each other, that much was clear.

He had returned to the prowler, readying his blade to cut some meat, when he heard the keening sound again. He searched amongst the gorse, and then, clambering from underneath the prowler's splayed leg, came two half-blind, squalling kittens. Their horns were little more than soft buds above their eyes, and their teeth were no more than white bumps in their gums, but Ankhad could already see how powerful they would become when they were fully grown. He watched them suckle eagerly at their dead mother's teats, and he was surprised to see that the milk still flowed. The prowler must have died recently, very recently – within the hour at least.

'It is a sign, young one,' he said to the baby. 'The True Gods see your strength and they provide!'

Quickly and carefully he laid the baby on the grass, still swaddled in its blanket. The kittens mewled again, sensing him, the rich milk spilling from their mouths. 'Forgive me,' Ankhad said. 'But the child's need is greater.'

He reached down and took each kitten up by its rear legs, and then he shattered their skulls in turn against the rock.

The baby took to the milk as if born to it, gorging himself on the dead prowler's bounty. Ankhad scooped out the soft, rich brains from the dead kittens and smeared some on the baby's lips, and he lapped it down without choking. He made an incision in the dead prowler's throat and caught the trickling blood into his wineskin. If the baby could drink prowler milk, it could drink prowler blood too – it was a child of the Spoil, after all. Leaving the baby nestled into the prowler's body, he padded down the track and cut the breast meat from the tuskivore. He skinned its great, muscled legs and stashed all the scavenged meat into his bag, and then hurried back to check on the baby. There, as if huddled into his mother's sleeping body, the child drifted into a satisfied sleep.

Ankhad felt confident enough to build a small fire. Night was falling, and they were masked from prying eyes by a shallow depression. As he gathered wood and cut a slab of meat from the prowler's flank, Ankhad felt for the first time since Ilthis had gone into labour that he was no longer so firmly embracing disaster. He was, for the briefest moment, a step out of its grasp.

'A full belly, a warm fire, and no one trying to kill me,' he muttered. 'One at a time is good enough, but all three at once is nothing short of a miracle.'

He mumbled a prayer to the True Gods. By his side the baby snuffled in his sleep.

'Rest, child,' he whispered. 'Rest...' He looked up, and the name fell easily to his lips, as if it had always been there and was just waiting to be spoken. 'Rest, little Allarik,' he said.

The trail was unmistakable, Kurguth thought. Even one of the stone-dwellers couldn't have missed it. The grove of woe trees around him had been reduced to a splintered ruin, their dripping black trunks weeping green sap into the stagnant water of the lake. In the soft mud at the edge of the water a vast sunken footprint was clearly visible – the monstrous cloven hoof of a xaskadon.

'It runs!' Chochola said with excitement. 'But see here, it has stopped to drink!' The young plains-runner capered with excitement. He had been the first to find the tracks, and Kurguth could almost read the thoughts that must have been dancing in his mind. Perhaps the young warrior had seen a glimpse of his future in the Split-Tongue Tribe? Maybe he would become a great tracker, called upon by Burak himself to scout the ground for trails, his keen eyes seeing what others could not? Kurguth had been there himself, as a younger man, always eager to prove his skill, to rise as far and as fast as he could. Fate would see how far Chochola could prosper in the tribe.

'Aye, it has stopped to drink,' Kurguth said, running his fingers gently across the outline of the hoof. It was as big as his chest, from side to side. 'But how long ago? And where is it now…?'

'I will find it, First Fang!' the plains-runner said. He scurried off, bounding along the cusp of the pool, hunting for other signs – but then, as his feet disturbed the water, the pool suddenly erupted in a great spray of pond scum and weeds, and from its depths a foul and gnarled tentacle lashed out to seize him by the legs.

Kurguth threw himself backwards, only dimly aware of the tribe scattering and bearing their weapons behind him. He looked on in horror as another tentacle emerged from the frothing water and wrapped itself around the plains-runner's chest. Chochola screamed in terror, his hands desperately scrabbling for his knife.

'Kurguth! First Fang,' he howled. 'Save me!'

Kurguth unslung his harpoon from his back and hefted the barbed spear in his hand. Others, Burak first among them, were charging into the water, but before any of the Untamed Beasts could attack, the blubbering, wailing creature began to pull.

Chochola burst apart in an arc of blood and entrails. The creature eagerly stuffed each half into its beaked mouth, but before it could settle back down under the water Kurguth flung his harpoon with every ounce of his strength. The rope burned through his hands, and he watched the spear sail arrow-straight, the light catching against the vicious hooks that were embedded in its bone blade. It was with a grunt of satisfaction that Kurguth saw the spear tip pass cleanly into the creature's trembling yellow eye. It bellowed and thrashed its tentacles, but the hooks had sunk deep; Kurguth dug his heels into the mud and pulled on the rope.

Soon, the stagnant water was boiling with the creature's black blood. The Untamed Beasts hacked and stabbed, shearing off chunks of flesh, severing its tentacles, some of them crawling onto its foetid bulk and plunging their knives and swords further into its eye. The creature whipped its tentacles from the water as if scourging itself, baying in agony, the beak snapping open and closed and its thin grey tongue stabbing out and shivering in pain. Kurguth kept pulling, the muscles on his arms as hard as iron, until, with a horrible, wet sucking sound, a great quivering mass came slopping out of the creature's face on the end of Kurguth's spear. At last, no more than a trembling heap of brutalised flesh, the creature fell still. *There is nothing that lives that cannot be killed*, Kurguth thought, wiping Chochola's entrails from his face. *Such is the way of the Bloodwind Spoil.*

'Chochola runs in the belly of the Great Devourer now,' Kurguth told Burak. 'But he has done us great favour by finding these tracks. We can take this beast, I know it.'

Although the xaskadon had paused to drink from the pool, it had clearly not met the same fate as Chochola. Whatever the monster in the water had been, it would have been no match for a beast as thunderously powerful as a xaskadon, a creature so fearsome that in the legends of the Untamed Beasts it was known as the 'moon eater', because its jaws were so vast and strong. To track and kill one would be a feat of profound skill and danger. There were few moon eaters left, Kurguth knew. As long as the Split-Tongue Tribe had prowled the margins of the Spoil, they had never seen one.

'The air whispers its death,' Ekrah agreed. The Preytaker swung the serrated blade of his bone sword. 'Its skull will be a totem for generations to come.'

Burak fingered the brass disc at his neck. 'We have no time to break our path,' he said. His eyes were distant, staring off beyond the mountains towards the edge of the Corpseworm Marches. 'Even now the child moves beyond our reach.'

Ghulassa, one of the other plains-runners, called from beyond the pool, gesturing towards the grasslands ahead. Kurguth nodded and raised his hand.

'The tracks go on,' he said. 'It seems our paths meet as one.'

Burak stared at the ground. He glanced up at Kurguth with a cunning look in his eyes, and for reasons that he couldn't fully explain, Kurguth found himself reaching for the hilt of his axe. Burak bared his teeth, and then seemed to come to a decision.

'On, then,' he said. 'If the xaskadon strays into our path we will deal with it. But do not diverge, do not suffer the lust for hunting to pull us from our true path. We need the child before the moon's turn. We need to find the Mountain's Throat and the temple.'

'It is agreed,' Kurguth said. His fingers drifted from his axe. Burak bounded on, and as Kurguth looked to Mayra he saw that she had taken hold of her weapons too. She met his eyes, her mouth grim. 'On,' Kurguth shouted, and the warband sprinted at his command. The xaskadon ran, and they would run behind it – and if the beast tired before them, they would pounce.

The journey from the Blood Lake Basin had been arduous, even for the Untamed Beasts. Burak had set a punishing pace, but they had covered the ground swiftly, leaning into the hungry miles and not stopping until dusk made of the land a treacherous morass. Then, by their campfires, they rested and told stories, speaking legends of Ghur, myths of the Jagged Savannah and how each had heard the call of the Great Devourer to seek out the Bloodwind Spoil and lay their sword on the altar of the Hunt. Great deeds would they achieve, until the Everchosen took notice and called them to his band. They would ride across the realms at his side, and the grasslands would run red with blood.

They had started the journey with more than twenty fighters, but their numbers had soon been whittled down, the Bloodwind Spoil offering no easy path from one part of its tortured expanse to another. In the remains of an ancient town long since cast down to the dust, they had wandered into a tangle of flenser vines, where Tekraska the Preytaker had been skinned in moments by their ravenous barbs. They had left his steaming corpse for the birds, gathering together whatever totems hadn't been whipped off into the vines' embrace. Further on, two plains-runners had paused to explore a gleaming shard-cluster of strange, mutated rocks, which caught the light and cast it back in a thousand fractured shades. As they laid their hands on the angled planes of the rocks, a blinding flash of light had forced the rest of the warband to cover their eyes. When next they looked, the plains-runners stood as two screaming glass statues, their hearts still twitching in the crystal chambers of their chests. In the flatlands, once they had passed the last foothills of the mountains, the tribe had fought off a shoal of spiny birds that cut down from the clouds and lacerated them with their razor fins. Not a single stretch of the Spoil was free of death, it seemed. Every step was a struggle for survival. Still Burak urged them on, tirelessly exhorting them to greater efforts, until even Kurguth began to feel the impossible – weariness, a bone-deep fatigue that sapped his strength. What kept Burak going? Not glory, not desire for victory, but something deeper. He wanted the child. He wanted the baby's hide on a bloody altar, in the affirming gaze of the Great Devourer. Nothing else would do.

They came across the xaskadon's spoor after another long trek. On the open plains they found a steaming pile of its dung, the stinking mound almost as tall as Kurguth. He covered his mouth as he approached it, using his axe to prise apart the greasy chunks. He could see fragments of indigestible armour, a battered helmet scoured clean of paint, a scattering of bones. Mayra flicked a buckle onto the grass; it was marked with the sigil of the Iron Golems.

The warband laughed when they realised who had been eaten by the beast. Ghulassa and a few of the younger plains-runners pantomimed the Golems' last moments, screeching and running this way and that, and then rolling on the grass with tears streaming down their cheeks. Mayra kicked the buckle away.

'This xaskadon fights on our side!' she said.

'A trade caravan,' Kurguth said. He pointed to the remains of weapons chests, the silvered hallmarks of the Iron Golems' smithy. 'Bringing weapons from Varanthax's Maw to Carngrad, it may be.'

Burak laughed. 'Their fate went sore against them.' He kneeled and plunged his hands into the filth, rooting around until he drew out a long, curved dagger. 'Their feeble iron suits were no protection from the moon eater. Ha!' he shouted. 'If our souls meet on the spirit paths, I will mock their shades!'

Kurguth watched as Burak cleaned the dagger on the grass and tucked it into his belt. *An iron weapon*, he thought. *The steel of our enemies!* But he said nothing, just gritted his teeth and called the warband on.

At last, Kurguth saw, their paths were beginning to split. He paused, chest heaving, and stared towards the horizon. The xaskadon's rampage was taking it further off towards the line of the distant Skullpike Mountains, while the warband's trail curved off towards the Fangs, now more distinct against the roiling, rusty fume of the western sky.

A choice will have to be made, he thought. *Fate hangs heavy on this moment.*

Mayra, leaping onto an out-thrust spear of rock, shielded her eyes with her hand and pointed.

'I see it!' she shouted. 'The xaskadon! We can run it down in a day and it will die beneath our blades!'

Burak stood, impassive. He stroked the hilt of his steel knife and his face was an unreadable mask.

'Leave it,' he said. 'Its fate is not our fate. We have a greater calling to answer.'

Mayra leapt from the stone, snarling. For a moment Kurguth saw the spirit of Neesa move in her, locked to her essence by the helmet she had made of the prowler's skull. 'I can see the dust it raises! You'd hunt a *child* over prey all of us have dreamed of stalking our entire lives?'

'I would,' Burak said. '*This* child.'

'And we suffer only on the strength of your word!'

'You do, young Beastspeaker.' Burak was motionless, seemingly calm, but Kurguth moved imperceptibly to come between them. He knew the Heart-eater would strike her down if he had to. 'Which of us is known as the Bloodseer?' Burak went on. 'My vision is sharper than yours, young one. My eyes see with a greater sight. You think we hunt a child, but we don't. We hunt a god, a rival to the Chief with Three Eyes. Leave the xaskadon, let it be. Its time will come.'

He turned his back on her, unconcerned if Mayra would strike. Kurguth felt something he had never experienced before, a sour feeling deep in his stomach that wouldn't settle. Not fear, but uncertainty. He didn't know what to do.

He stared out across the plains as the trail of the xaskadon faded into the shimmering air. The dust plume settled, and the far thunder of its mighty hooves fell to silence. He picked up his spear and followed Burak. He was the Bloodseer, it was true. He saw further, he always had, and what he saw would come to pass. And so the Split-Tongue Tribe marched on across the plains, and went to hunt a god.

* * *

They came to kill him in the morning.

He woke at once. He could hear them clattering over the loose stone on the other side of the ridge. The fire had burned low, and a vaporous trail of smoke drifted up into an overcast sky. He even felt hungry again, despite how much prowler and tuskivore he had stuffed down his neck the night before.

Nothing lasts, Ankhad thought with a scowl. *I should have learned that by now.*

Lithe as a cat, he scooped up the sleeping baby. *Still alive then, little Allarik. Rocktusk milk has done wonders for you.* He sheathed his knife and ran at a staggered crouch towards the corpse of the tuskivore further down the trail, heading up into the broken ground above the path and then doubling back on himself. He carefully placed the baby down in a small clearing, covering it with loose foliage, and then slipped back along to where the body of the prowler lay next to the remains of his campfire. He lay down, peering around a shoulder of rock into the shallow depression below him.

Bloatflies lazily bumbled away from the body of the prowler, rising to hover for a moment in the chill morning air before settling once more to feast on its coagulated blood. The campfire smouldered on the grass. For the longest while there was nothing but silence. He was beginning to wonder if he had dreamed the noise when he heard the scuff of a boot trying to find purchase on the ridgeline and the muttered curse of whoever was trying to climb over.

'Here,' a wheedling voice said, 'there's a step we can use at this end.'

'Keep your damned voice down,' another voice shot back, harsher and certainly less patient. Ankhad stretched further around and saw a head wearing a tattered cap rise above the ridge, along with two hands scrabbling for purchase. He recognised the figure as it lurched over the rock – one of Spite's mutant slaves, a stunted, vicious little thing with bleary, globular eyes and a rack of rotten fangs in its mouth. It landed by the prowler's body and leaned down to sniff at the corpse, poking the dead kittens and dragging a stick through the embers of the campfire. Warily it peered down the path. Ankhad leaned back, his knife drawn from its sheath. He could see another figure crawling over the ridge, and this one he knew – Grulsham Mof, that backstabbing enforcer, always keen to ingratiate himself with Lothin.

How had they even found him? Every trail he had taken, every track he had avoided, and despite everything they had still hunted him down. Ankhad wondered how many bands Lothin had sent into the mountains. How many had survived? They feared the gods more than they feared him, it was clear.

Ankhad cursed Spite, under his breath. A wretched pit, where figures like Lothin bowed sickly obeisance to the Black Spire but had no idea what that Spire really contained. All they saw was a guarantor of the waste they scavenged, a force that scattered the detritus of war around the Bloodwind Spoil, so they could eke their living from what stronger men and women had cast aside. He had only ever found himself living there because the scavengers of Spite were beneath notice, and in places like that it was possible to be forgotten. For a while, at least.

Curse them all! If the Everchosen turned his unholy gaze for a moment upon such a place, those quivering maggots would slit their own throats in fear...

Grulsham casually cuffed the mutant as he dropped down into the depression. He stood tall where the mutant cowered, and he kicked the embers of the fire into the grass.

'They've been here recently, my master, I would swear it,' the mutant said. 'Feasted on prowler meat, enjoyed themselves a nice fire.'

'They can't have gone far, Treth,' Grulsham said. He stared down the path. He was armed better than Ankhad would have liked, with a spiked mace at his hip and a buckler on his back. 'And we should be more cautious from now on. Ankhad's best days may be long behind him, but he's still not someone to be trifled with.'

'A warrior of renown?' Treth asked. 'He never struck me as dangerous, him or his wife, so pretty, yes...'

'I wouldn't go that far,' Grulsham admitted. 'But I've heard he was once a holy terror of the March, a cut-throat without mercy.'

'Come to make a name for himself, perhaps, to join the legions of the Spire?'

'I couldn't say. It's said he had the makings of a Talon, if he'd struck out to Carngrad with his warband. Who knows,' the scavenger sighed. 'It's all rumour and lies in the end. Could be he started those rumours himself, to keep the likes of us off his back, but be wary all the same. Lothin's reward will be mine, no matter how good Ankhad thinks himself.'

'It's two against one,' Treth sniggered, 'and Ankhad is old. I can't see the baby putting up much of a fight. I'll slit its gizzard if it does...'

'The baby's why we're here, fool,' Grulsham said. He lashed a savage kick into the mutant's side. 'It comes back with us to Spite, and the flames, or the Spire will curse us all.'

Treth yelped and cringed at Grulsham's feet. 'Lead and I will follow,' it whimpered. Its massive bulbous eyes gleamed with tears, and it scrabbled at Grulsham's legs with its stubby hands.

'Better say one and a half against one,' Grulsham muttered.

Ankhad gathered a small handful of pebbles and threw them far off over the broken ground, and as they clinked amongst the stones Grulsham hefted his weapon. 'There!' he hissed. Treth dodged behind the scavenger, and together they scurried off towards the sound. As they passed, Ankhad slipped down from behind the rock and followed them.

He stabbed Treth quickly in the back of the neck, the tip of his blade angled up and spearing out of the mutant's eye. He died with a rising shriek on his lips, and it was to Grulsham's credit that he wasted no time in the counter-attack, chopping down from the backhand and sending the mace whistling past Ankhad's ear. He backed up and peered at Ankhad with frightened eyes over the rim of his buckler, waving the mace in front of him.

'Just the baby, Ankhad, that's all I want! Give me the child and I'll be off.'

'You'll be off soon enough, son. Into the underworld and into the dirt. You'll never see Spite again.'

'Lothin's offered a reward,' Grulsham said. His voice was shaking. He skipped forward and swung the mace, but Ankhad dodged easily aside. Again, he backed off with the buckler up. 'I'll split it with you,' he offered, licking his dry lips. 'There's good Iron Golem weapons in it for whoever brings the baby back. Market scrip as well, and a daemon bottle. A real daemon bottle from Carngrad, none of your fake stuff!'

'What would I want with a daemon bottle?'

'I dunno,' Grulsham said uneasily. 'Keep it on a shelf, like. Use it to threaten your enemies! Imagine opening that one up, seeing the look on their faces...'

'Do you know what happens when you open a daemon bottle, Grulsham?'

Grulsham hesitated. 'What?'

'The daemon gets out.'

He lunged towards the scavenger, his knife raised, and it was the easiest thing in the world to just flick the blade across Grulsham's wrist as he tried to parry with the mace. Grulsham dropped his weapon with a curse, reflexively lifting his shield up to cover his face. Ankhad kicked him solidly between the legs, and then the scavenger was down.

'I thank you for the mace and the buckler,' Ankhad said. He picked up the shield and cracked the rim down onto Grulsham's nose. There was a dull snap, an explosion of blood, and then Grulsham was weeping and clawing at Ankhad's arm.

'Please, you've got to listen to me. I promise, I won't… It-it's the *rules*, Ankhad – I had no choice! The child has to die!'

'Rules?' Ankhad whispered. He knelt on Grulsham's chest, grinning as he pressed the tip of his knife home. Down it went, pricking the bulb of his eye and then sliding deeper into the soft meat of it as the scavenger bucked and screamed under him. 'We're killers, all of us,' he said. 'Hunters of the Spoil. We live in the blackest shadows, enslaved to nothing but our darkest desires. What do we care about *rules*?'

On the blade went, through the punctured eye, and when the hilt met the bone of the socket, Grulsham's body writhed to silence under him.

'Damn your rules,' Ankhad said. 'And damn you, down to the very lowest pits of whatever underworld you believed in.'

When he came back for the baby, he had a moment to thank Grulsham again for the weapons.

Allarik lay there in his swaddling clothes, in the same spot where Ankhad had left him, but on all sides he was surrounded by raptoryx. The cloying stink of them rose to meet him as he clambered over the broken ground. There were three that Ankhad could see, each inching over the beaten grass towards the baby, their razor-beaks low, their leathery frills pressed back against their necks. That was the sign they were ready to strike, he knew. One turned and hissed as Ankhad approached. It spread its wings and its neck frill fanned out in warning, a stench rising from it that made Ankhad's eyes water. He held Grulsham's shield tight against his body, the mace raised against his shoulder.

There was nothing he could do. To fight one of them would be a challenge, but three at once would tear him apart, and there was no way he could get to them before they devoured the child. There was nothing he could do, absolutely nothing, and his fury was tempered only by his grief. That it had come to this…

The baby cried then – not in pain or hunger, but almost as if for the pleasure of hearing his own voice. He had worked an arm loose from his blanket and Ankhad could see it waving in the air.

'I'm so sorry,' he whispered, closing his eyes. 'Ilthis, forgive me…'

But nothing happened. There was only silence, then the contented chuckle of the baby in the grass. When he opened his eyes again, he saw the raptoryx all slowly backing away, their heads lowered, their neck frills hanging slack, their wings tucked into their sides – and then, with a last look back at the child, they all slinked off over the broken rocks and disappeared.

He rushed over to the boy, unwrapping him like a gift. There wasn't a mark on him; the creatures hadn't touched him at all. He looked back to where the raptoryx had retreated, but there was no sign of them, only their sharp, musky stink still lingering in the air.

He lifted the child, laughing, near weeping with relief. He stared down into his face and frowned. Briefly, it was as if a shadow had passed over it, a darkness in the shape of an eight-pointed star.

In Burak's dream he walked the promised paths, and every step burned the skin from the soles of his feet. He took a road writhing in flame, and yet it was wet with blood and poison too. The spirit trail flickered under lightning flashes, and the ground beneath his feet shook to the rumble of distant laughter. The Great Devourer watched, and his hunger was insatiable.

He came under the shadow of the Black Lodge, the dwelling of the Great Devourer, and the weight of it crushed his soul beneath him. He called out. His voice was nothing but the chittering of an ant beneath such unholy power. He drifted off, coming to a cluttered ruin on the outskirts of the Spire, where shadows basked in the eldritch light of the Lodge's campfires. The ruin drowsed beneath a sheet of dust and sand. Down he went, into the tumbled foundations, the broken porticoes and plazas, amongst the shattered columns of ancient days. Deep, deep underground, into forgotten catacombs hidden from the sight of men. On a high altar in the temple chamber, a baby howled in fear. Burak took the crumbling steps and stood before it, the silver knife in his hand. There he stood, on the very cusp of fate.

Bury the child, take its hide...

He raised the knife. The black gaze of the Devourer of Existence swivelled towards him, scouring his spirit away.

I am Burak the Bloodseer, he called. *I have crossed the Bloodwind Spoil and defeated every one of my rivals, and I bring you great sacrifice, lord!*

The baby cried, the green eyes turning to him fierce and strong.

Green light flickered on the edge of the blade, and he stabbed it down as if plunging it into the very bowels of existence.

The warband settled around their campfires. Night, which in the Bloodwind Spoil was always a furtive time of strange screams and black shapes flitting through the darkness, fell quickly on the edge of the Corpseworm Marches. Plains-runners sat in pairs, keeping watch, weapons in hand, but the rest of the tribe turned in an uneasy sleep.

At the edge of the camp, Kurguth and Mayra sat together, the First Fang sharpening the teeth of his axe while the Beastspeaker rested her hands on the sloping skull of her bone helm.

'I felt Neesa's power in me today,' Kurguth said, 'as we ran across the veldt. I was tiring, and then her strength was my strength, and I could run where before I felt I would fall.'

'Last night,' Mayra said with a smile, 'as we camped by the edge of the scrubland, I felt her lie down beside me in the night. She kept me warm, gave me courage.'

For a while, the only sound was the scrape of Kurguth's whetstone against the sharpened teeth. The breeze puckered the flame of their campfire. It smelled of death.

'The Bloodseer will have us press on at first light,' Kurguth said softly. 'The Fangs are near, and he will want us hidden in the foothills before night.'

Mayra fell into silence, but Kurguth knew she was choosing her words before speech. For the Untamed Beasts, words were so much wasted breath; nothing was more eloquent than deeds. She lay down, using the skull helmet as a pillow, and turned to face the First Fang.

'Are you as committed to the quest as Burak?' she asked. 'You think this... *child* is what we must seek, to earn our place on the Great Hunt?'

'I don't know,' he said. Kurguth had an image then of Burak in the days of their youth, his face a mask of warpaint, his arms red with blood from the butchered beasts of the Jagged Savannah. More and more he was drawn to the memory of those times. It troubled him. The life of an Untamed Beast must be lived always heading forward; the past is just the trampled grass that you leave in your wake. Only an unskilled tracker doubles back on the hunt, for he has lost the trail and he must root around in all his failures to find it again.

'I don't see how there can be honour in hunting a child,' he said eventually. He saw by the gleam in Mayra's eyes that she thought the same. 'Burak is possessed by this idea, and I trust his vision, but...'

'It sits uneasily on you. On all of us.'

'Not all,' Kurguth said. He looked reflexively over his shoulder to Ekrah's campfire. The Preytaker would side with Burak, he was sure – and then he shook his head as if trying to loosen the idea. *To side with Burak...* They were all on Burak's side – there was no division, none.

'Burak says the child is not a child, but a god. What we hunt is more powerful than any beast.'

'And you believe that?' She sat up, reaching out to take Kurguth's hand. He felt her palm, dry and warm in his. He raised it up and placed it against his cheek. 'He carries a Golem's knife now,' she said. 'He leads us towards a temple in sight of the Black Lodge, the Varanspire itself. What if he would move us into the Lodge itself?'

'Then we would have stone walls around us, and our voices would echo from stone roofs and stone halls.'

'It would be worse than death,' she whispered. 'Never to feel the wind in our hair, to smell the blood of our prey...'

Kurguth drew her close, and as their lips met a thought strayed across his path – that the Split-Tongue Tribe would not be led by Burak the Bloodseer forever.

CHAPTER FIVE

PATHS OF PAIN

They were no more than a day's march from Carngrad when the Burned Hand passed through the settlement. It was nestled into the borders of the foothills, the mountains of the Fangs looming high above it, casting down a cool shadow that offered some shade from the shelterless plains. Rakaros, at the head of the warband, looked on the filthy scattering of huts and hovels with distaste. Small cook fires gave off a brackish smoke that lingered in what passed for streets and alleyways, cloaking the village in a drifting fume. On the borders of the settlement were patchwork fields where figures were bent double, hoeing the threadbare ground for sustenance. There was a stench in the air of human excrement and rotting food, and here and there the villagers were crouched against the walls of their huts with all the listless apathy of the malnourished and the lost. And yet, Rakaros thought as his Scions moved up behind him, there was something sullen and resentful in the villagers' eyes too. They looked up as the Burned Hand approached, some rising to their feet in evident alarm, others standing from the fields and holding their meagre tools against their chests. He heard doors slamming further inside the village and conversations suddenly cut short, replaced by muttered warnings.

There is no wall here, Rakaros realised, which was unusual for any settlement in these rapacious lands. *And no children either…*

Two guards stood at the head of the cinder path that led into the village. They crossed their spears as Rakaros advanced. He towered over them, but despite their evident fear the guards held their ground. They were wearing leather helmets which bore twisted goats' horns, or the horns of some plains beast. Their weapons were little more than sharpened sticks, with the blades just knapped flint held in place by leather twine. *Pathetic*, Rakaros thought with contempt. He held up his hand to hold his warriors back; there was little danger here.

'State your business!' one of the guards demanded. 'We have nothing for you here!'

'We seek passage into the Fangs,' Rakaros said. 'The road goes through your village and on into the mountains. We would pass through, if you would allow it.'

'The Horned Ones take you,' the other guard spat. He trembled under Rakaros' gaze, and his hands were white-knuckled on the shaft of his spear. 'Go around, if you must. There's another path into the mountains a few miles to the west.'

'Supplies we would have also,' Rakaros said. 'Food, water. We can give good coin for it.'

'We have no need of your coin,' the first guard said. His face was lean with hunger, and his eyes danced with the hint of something that seemed almost like grief. Behind the guards, the villagers were beginning to congregate in the central square, a hard-packed patch of land where a listing well stood and where a solitary twisted tree flung up its spectral branches to the sky as if it were screaming. The villagers bore rusty knives, clubs, flint blades. They were dressed in rags. They were desperate, Rakaros realised. And despite how pathetic they looked, how vulnerable and defenceless, he knew that the desperate were often the most dangerous.

Votremos had appeared at Rakaros' elbow, and the Blazing Lord saw how the priest exaggerated his reliance on his staff. He was holding his cloak close against his throat, as if even in this sultry air he felt the chill wind of infirmity.

'My lord,' Votremos said in an affected, trembling voice. 'Come, let us leave these fine people and seek the other path. Our journey will not suffer for the additional time it will take.'

Rakaros looked over the priest's shoulder. He could see that the warband had slowly split itself into two groups, and that one group had slipped over to the village's flank, on the borders of the fields. The other group hung back on the path, but as Rakaros turned to observe them he saw that they had formed into a column, initiates at the front to swarm any defenders, with Katastrian and the Fireborn behind to deliver the killing blow. The Blazing Lord smiled with pleasure. His eyes met Votremos', and the decision passed between them. As he turned again to the guards, Rakaros felt the low fires in his belly start to burn.

It was a shame, in a way. He would have been content to let them live.

He swept the great two-handed blade from its scabbard and struck upwards in a single move, the sword hacking between the first guard's legs and slicing cleanly up his torso to cut him almost in half. Rakaros took a moment to appreciate the look of devastated confusion on the guard's face before he drew back the sword, and then the blood was sheeting onto the parched ground and splashing at his feet in a bubbling tide. In the same instant, Votremos threw back his cloak and revealed his power, uttering the words of a blasphemous prayer and striking the second guard with the tip of his staff. At once the flames took hold, and like liquid fire they scorched across the guard's body to transform him into a living torch. He shrieked and spun backwards, crashing into a rickety outhouse and setting it aflame. The villagers started screaming, some rushing forward with their weapons bared, others running for their lives. *No matter*, Rakaros thought. *All will pay the penalty of defiance.*

'Holy warriors of the Burned Hand,' he called. 'Kill them.'

The warband roared as one, in the execution of its duty. Xoloxes lunged forward, flames licking from his eyes, and scorched half a dozen of the villagers in a moment. 'Burn!' he laughed. '*Burn!*' The initiates swarmed across the square and hacked the villagers down with flails and hooked axes, with wildly spinning morning stars. Rakaros strode through the press, deigning here and there to dispatch a life with desultory swings of his greatsword. Votremos intoned another prayer, and around him the scum of the village burst into flames, their cries a jarring music. It almost reminded Rakaros of the choir back in the Temple of Cold Ashes, shrieking with the purity of the flame.

Some of the villagers, aware that they had no chance of winning against such a relentless enemy, resolved to sell their lives as dearly as they could. They crowded together by the well, like so much herded cattle, desperately slashing and stabbing with their knives as the Scions approached. Rakaros watched with satisfaction as his initiates lunged in and cut the villagers down, dashing out their brains, disembowelling them with expert swipes of their blades. Men and women caught in a caustic web of fire ran back and forth, deranged, gibbering with agony, until they finally collapsed against the tinder-dry walls of their shacks and set them aflame in turn. Others made a hopeless attempt to escape, running from the village and across the fields, but the other group of Scions had now spread out to catch any stragglers and they watered those fields with blood.

It was no battle, Rakaros knew, no honourable combat against a worthy enemy. But as the flames settled in his stomach, he felt a calmness descend on him that he hadn't felt since chasing the Splintered Fang from their temple – the serenity that only came with the spilling of blood in a righteous cause.

The settlement was little more than blackened ruins and burned corpses when they were finished. There were a few prisoners that Rakaros deigned to let live, it always being good policy to leave alive those who could warn others of your holy fury. The initiates herded them into the centre of the square, casting them down into the blood-spattered dirt. Other fighters tossed corpses down the well or strung up the charred and bleeding bodies from the branches of the tree.

'Lord Rakaros,' the Inferno Priest said. Votremos pointed into the press of bodies. There, cowering and afraid and unable to meet his eye, was a young woman nursing a waxen baby at her breast. 'A wet nurse, my lord? The journey is long, after all, and when we find the child it will need sustenance.'

'Indeed,' Rakaros said, his eyes glittering. 'I had been wondering how to feed the child when it is in our hands. As the problem is raised, though, so the solution is presented. You cannot sacrifice a dead thing, after all.'

'Only the blind would not heed these signs, lord.'

Rakaros stood before the woman. She shrank back.

'How old is your child?' he demanded. A silence that was broken only by the low crackling of the flames from the burning buildings had fallen across the village, and in that silence his voice was like the crashing of thunder. The woman shook her head, mute with terror. 'Speak! Or I have those amongst us who will make you speak.'

'He's not my child, my lord,' she whispered.

'No? And yet you feed it all the same?'

'An orphan, lord... an orphan of the village.'

'I didn't think such a place would practise charity,' he sneered.

'We need them,' the woman said, and then she looked away, as if afraid she had said too much.

'For what purpose?'

'For... for the mountains, lord. For the Horned Ones who live there.'

Votremos took the Blazing Lord's arm, shuffling forward as he leaned on his staff. 'Indeed, I have heard this, my lord,' he said. 'In some of these wretched pits on the cusp of the mountains, they leave out their children for the beastmen who infest the hills. An offering, of sorts. Most primitive.'

The woman nodded eagerly, as if relieved that someone understood.

'He's right, my lord – true it is. The Horned Ones take the children we cannot raise ourselves. It's a great honour.'

'Honour? What nonsense do you talk now?'

'The children, lord. They're raised amongst the Horned Ones, they are. Some are chiefs unto the great herds, it's true! And so grateful are the Horned Ones, they leave us be, and they don't raid or despoil... They look after us...'

Rakaros smiled grimly behind his bronze mask. *Fools!*

'They have been remiss in their duty today, have they not!' he scorned, looming over her. 'I fear you are the victim of a terrible deceit. I will tell you the truth instead, my dear, for the truth is never to be despised. The "Horned Ones" do not raise your offered children as their own. They skin them and they eat them, and they wear those skins or sew them into their banners, whatever the degenerate filth decide. It is not a great honour, unless you consider rotting in the stomach of an ungor an honour. Which, casting my eye over what is left of your disgusting little village, might very well be a preferable fate.'

The woman's eyes widened in horror, and her face was drawn.

Rakaros nodded at the Inferno Priest, who turned and said, 'Katastrian?'

The rest of the Burned Hand encircled the village square, preventing any of the prisoners from escaping. At the sign from Votremos, Katastrian stepped forward, hefting his axe, the blade gleaming redly as if with an inner flame.

'My priest?' he said.

'Seize her.'

The wet nurse begged as the champion grabbed her roughly, wrenching the baby from her arms.

'Leave her be!' one shivering little mutant said. 'Leave all of us be and go on your way! Haven't you done enough?'

'You think to command me, creature?' Rakaros said. 'I am Rakaros, Blazing Lord of the Burned Hand, a Scion of the Flame. From the Temple of Cold Ashes I have come, from the Bright Mountains in far Aspiria, in the Realm of Fire. I pass through here only on a higher purpose that you could not even begin to comprehend. The fire will lead me to the right-hand side of a god. Where, I wonder, shall it lead you?'

Faster than the eye could see, Rakaros lashed out and grasped the mutant by its throat, and as he choked the life from it his fingers seemed to glow. Then, very faintly, pale smoke began to drift from the mutant's neck, and from beneath the smoke came a tongue of flame that spread and multiplied, until the mutant wore a crown of fire and its skin was bubbling in the heat. Its scream seared across the air, rebounding from the slopes of the Fangs, and as it died in the utmost agony Rakaros hoped that every man and beast in a hundred miles could hear the consequence of resistance. The Scions of the Flame were coming.

He threw the corpse into the dirt. Katastrian dragged the woman over by her hair.

'What is your name, child?' he asked her.

'Aceria, lord,' she cried. 'Don't kill me, I beg you!'

'Your life is mine to do with as I will,' he said coldly. 'But take heart, death is not near you yet. Come, you have a task ahead of you that is more important than you can possibly know.'

'What task, lord?'

'You come with us to keep alive that which must die.'

The issue, Ma'sulthis thought, *is not the quality of the substance but the quantity of the dose.*

The Serpent Caller had thought of this often, in his secluded moments. Alone, with only Kathenga for company, he had long meditated on the mysteries of poison. All things, all substances ingested by the mortal creature, could become a poison in turn. The most innocuous foods and drinks would, if taken in excess, prove fatal. Even water, clean water guzzled past the brim, could drown the drinker or dilute his blood unto death. What then of the holy substances brewed by the shamans, by those skilled in the art amongst the Splintered Fang? A drop of Serpent's Sight, as Ashrath had demonstrated, would visit upon the victim the most appalling torments. But half a drop, or a quarter of a drop, or less? Over months and years, the initiates of the Scaled Temple built their immunity through just such an application. Ashrath had done the same, training himself from the youngest age to a full resistance. Was it possible then that each venom was not inherently poisonous but only poisonous by degree? Were they ontologically poisonous, in and of themselves? Or was their effect merely the result of judicious use, and knowledge came less from the understanding of each substance's quality than from the mere ability to weigh and measure?

It was the philosophical heart of the Splintered Fang, Ma'sulthis thought, although such subtleties were beyond most of the clan's adherents. Each poison was both sacrament and weapon, and required both intimate knowledge and humble study. But beyond utility there was another level on which the poison was understood. *It is ironic*, Ma'sulthis chuckled to himself. *The shamans of the Splintered Fang are respected as those who interpret the efficacy of our sacred venoms, but at heart they are simple apothecaries. They calculate the dose with weight and measure, levelling out the ampules like a common market trader. How much of what is holy is mere logistics, in the end?*

He struggled for a moment with the thought, feeling the true understanding drift just outside of his mind's grasp. *How much of what is holy depends on quantity, then, on... excess?*

Few of the warband ever talked to him directly, and he was isolated in a way by this aura of reverence. His bond with the serpents was a source of fear and pride to them, and as the warband crossed the distance from the Hag's Claw Forest towards the Fangs, Ma'sulthis took the opportunity to consider the Horned Krait's position. Kathenga lazily twisted its coils around Ma'sulthis' neck, resting its head on his shoulder.

'Yes,' Ma'sulthis whispered to the snake, 'see with me. Let me look through the crystals of your blind eyes at the ones who follow us.'

His eyes turned the colour of milked venom, and through the snake's refracted gaze he saw Ashrath ahead, striding over the burned ground. Aloof, always glancing over his shoulder, his face betraying his suspicion and his bitterness. His aura was the pallid green of the most powerful venoms, but it was marbled with streaks of purple, red and gold – the colours of ambition and the lust for power, the colours of revenge. He had trained for this moment for years, but now that he had command, he doubted himself. Blindly the snake wove its sight across the field, coming to rest then on Essiltha, the aelf, a Venomblood with needle blades, who walked always at a slight remove from Ashrath, behind and to his left – his weakest side, Ma'sulthis noted, where he had been wounded in the fight with Su'atha. The snake tried to see what the Venomblood would disguise, but her aura was an opaque cloud, buffeting with aelven foresight the attempt to peer through its mysteries. *She walks as if ready to lend her strength to her leader, but a rival must be close to make the fatal strike too. Has Ashrath merely exchanged Su'atha's death for another contender?* He saw the clearbloods walking before her, like an entourage. It was strange, but for one so suspicious Ashrath did not appear to see the danger. *He is looking over the wrong shoulder*, Ma'sulthis thought.

He blinked, and his eyes ran clear again. Kathenga stretched its jaws and settled down to sleep, and the weight of the snake across his body was oddly comforting. He was not a burden but a second soul.

Ma'sulthis had debated whether to warn Ashrath that other challenges would come, but the information would not be new to him. It was better to let events unfold as they would. Everything had led them to this point, from the defeat in Carngrad at the hands of the Scions of the Flame to the failed quest in the forest, the meandering and futile search for Nagendra's Shrine. All had happened as it must, but still Ma'sulthis felt the pang of shame at the Scions' triumph. He remembered the heat in the flaming corridors of the temple, the icons of the Coiling Ones cast down from the votive niche. The Horned Krait had overreached itself, it was true; they had sought open conflict when the serpent would have used cunning, and many blamed Ashrath for his inexperience. Ma'sulthis sighed, feeling the snake-skull mask press tightly against his brow. No matter. He had heard through Kathenga's voice the revelations of the Coiling Ones.

Archaon's heir was abroad, and only Ashrath could save him. Only Ashrath *would* save him.

There was no need for concern.

* * *

88

The path into the mountains was steep and treacherous, and more than one of the initiates stumbled and fell to their deaths before they had left the village far behind. The air became clammy and chill the higher they went, and the rough-beaten earth under their feet became soft shale that was difficult to walk upon. Votremos found himself leaning more heavily on his staff, and it gave him, he felt, a distinct advantage.

After a while, the priest found himself alongside Aceria, who thus far had made no effort to escape. She seemed more sure-footed than her captors, and he doubted that any of them could have caught her up if she had decided to run. Now and again she cast a frightened glance at the Blazing Lord, who strode on at the head of their column, utterly unafraid of whatever the Fangs might throw at them. She was very beautiful, he thought, once you looked past her rags, her sallow skin. It was strange, the places where beauty struck its chord sometimes. *Always,* he thought, *in the most unexpected locations…*

'You fear him,' Votremos said to the young woman. 'You are wise to do so. But know that he is not like the savages you have grown up around. He is dangerous, true, but only to those who defy him.'

'I know that, sir,' she said. 'He is a mighty figure, I think, his eyes like burning coals… Is he a king? I thought him maybe the king come from the Far Spire to punish us.'

'Lord Rakaros? He is no king, no, and he is certainly not the one of whom you speak. We do not recognise such hierarchies in the Scions of the Flame. All burn equally under the Flame's attention, although some burn more brightly than others, it is true. Make no mistake, though – Lord Rakaros is a great figure, entrusted by the first of our order. The Burned Hand could have no better leader.'

'And yourself, sir – the lord seeks your counsel. I think perhaps you are a great figure also.'

Votremos laughed gently to himself. 'I make no such claim,

child. I do as the Flame commands and bring counsel where required. And when necessary, he said, his voice suddenly cold, 'I smite those who require it also.'

'Why do you need me, sir?' Aceria murmured. She looked on the priest. He kept his expression mild, but the sparks of light that danced in his eyes made her turn away again.

'We seek a child of surpassing power in these hills, girl, a baby no less. Babies need milk. You have milk.'

'You would have killed me otherwise? If I had no milk to give?'

Votremos looked down on her. *A simple child*, the priest thought. *For so many in the Spoil, life is the square acre of existence where they graft their living from the mud. Each day is blessed only because it has not yet been visited by the horrors of the day before. Truly, the Flame will cleanse them all, in time...*

'Yes,' he said bluntly. 'Your life would now be as those we left behind. Over. Remember that, child.'

He hefted his staff and moved further up the column.

Ahead, Rakaros felt the sweat steaming from his back. The trail twisted and turned, climbing ever higher, and on either side of the path hung bleak outcrops of rock, wet with the mist that lingered in the dells and hollow spaces. It smelled to him like foul breath, like the breath of the beggar they had burned back in Carngrad. As he walked, his mind drifted back to the Temple of Cold Ashes – the torches on the walls, the fire pits, the clean lines of its tempered stone and the steam rising from the magma flow beneath the precinct. The temple had done him great honour by accepting his demand to lead the mission to the Eightpoints, but Rakaros knew that the weight of expectation was almost a burden too. As he thought back to it, he still remembered the surge of gratification when his name was accepted by the Most Holy. It had been presumptuous to put it forward, but he could not deny the pride he had felt. Pride, and its sullen corollary – shame. Was he truly worthy? Or was he taking the mission only to indulge his baser need for glory and power?

He felt the shame curdle in his gut, and when shame is pushed down it can only ever surface again as rage. *Onwards*, he thought bitterly. *Ever onwards, never stopping until the task is done!*

'Onwards!' he bellowed at those who followed him. He thrashed one initiate with the hilt of his sword, cuffing him further up the track. 'Waste not the time we have, for it presses keenly on us!'

Votremos joined him, struggling to keep up with his leader, such was his pace.

'These mountains are perilous, if what the woman claimed is true,' he said. 'Beastmen haunt these passages and pathways. Perhaps more caution would be advised, my lord?'

'Caution is for the weak, priest,' Rakaros spat. 'I will not lose my prize because we dawdled on the way.'

'"Your" prize, lord? Forgive me for speaking plainly, but we seek the child not for your benefit but for the temple's. In the legions of the Everchosen, we will scour the realms clean and seek out new sources of rage-rock for the rituals of the blessed.'

Rakaros relented. 'You speak the truth,' he muttered. 'Forgive *me*, Votremos. Never let it be said that I didn't value your counsel. But if we do not hurry the matter will be immaterial either way.'

'And how will we know where to find this child? The mountains of the Fangs could hide an army.'

'The Flame guides us,' Rakaros said with certainty. 'Fate puts everything in our path.'

And my fate is not to grasp for something and fail.

Eventually the trail levelled out into a clearing, which was bordered by the flank of the mountain on one side and a jagged, impassable outcrop of rock on the other. A narrow path continued on the other side, heading up higher into the peaks.

The clearing was dominated by a scarred and bloody altar stone. It had been decorated with blasphemous symbols, either crudely carved or painted with blood and filth. On the ground around the altar were littered bones, and the whole clearing stank of death. Looming high above them, as if staring onto the scene, the mountainside itself had been scarred with the suggestion of a leering, bestial face.

'Bring the wet nurse,' Rakaros commanded. The word went down the column, and before long Katastrian appeared, dragging her behind him. She shivered with fear, her eyes wide at the sight that met her.

'Here, fool, is what your Horned Ones do with the children you give to them. It takes not a great leap of the imagination to picture the scene, does it?'

Aceria howled, breaking free of Katastrian's grip and throwing herself to the ground. She covered her face, sobbing.

'Why do you show me this?' she wept. 'Why torment me? The Horned Ones take you! They will be your death, I swear it!'

'Give the word, my lord, and her head is yours,' Katastrian muttered, bringing his axe to his shoulder.

'Leave her,' Rakaros commanded. 'Until the child is dead on an altar of our own, I would trade her life for any of yours. Heed that, all of you.' He stared them down, and not one of them dared to meet his gaze.

There was a clatter of stones from the higher ground, faint and almost indistinct. Rakaros turned, scanning the edges of the clearing. The air buckled in the wind, and the fringes of dry grass that stabbed up from the hard ground shivered in the breeze. The Blazing Lord dropped his hand to the hilt of his blade, aware that he was holding his breath and that the rest of the warband had fallen silent. Even Aceria had stopped sobbing.

'My lord?' Votremos said.

'Quiet. Something draws near...'

And then the drumming began.

Soft at first, it fell as a light patter that echoed from the rock, but then it came louder, more insistent, booming suddenly across the peaks and gathering in the clearing like a hard rain. Rakaros drew his sword and the blade ignited, banishing the shadows from around the bloody altar.

'To arms!' he shouted. 'Cut them down!'

The Blazing Lord pointed to the clearing's further edge, and as he did so the beastmen came boiling over the rise, leaping from the jagged rocks and rampaging down the pathway.

Some wore the mocking remnants of clothes – mouldering loincloths, rags of armour. Others were clad only in their matted fur, their skin stained with old blood and grime. All of them carried weapons, from crude butcher's blades to blunt picks and notched axes, and their war cry as they thundered into the clearing was a cacophony of yelps and screeches, a deafening tide of noise that almost overwhelmed the Scions who stood their ground. Not all of them did. A handful of initiates in the vanguard broke and ran as the first beastmen crashed into them. Some scrambled over the altar and tried to run back to the safety of the path, but they were soon overcome. Rakaros saw one fighter grabbed by the neck, his head slammed down into the rocks at the side of the clearing, a bone-handled knife plunged deep into his stomach. Another had his skull shattered by a blow from a rusty maul, while a third was torn to pieces by the beastmen's gnashing teeth. Some may have broken, but for the rest of the Burned Hand the choice was clear – fight or die.

Rakaros felt all the doubt and shame of his earlier thoughts melt in the cold, clear light that kindled in his chest. He closed his eyes, suddenly calm, and as the wave broke over him, he opened them again to reveal two searing points of light, his sword raised up like a lightning flash, his scorched mouth screaming a wordless exultation. This, he knew, was the freedom that comes from holy purpose, where all the muttered worrying of the self falls clean away.

The beasts were like a herd of wild animals, but their movements did not lack purpose. A dozen of them swarmed around the sides of the clearing to block the path back down the mountainside, while another twenty or so surged forward to engage the Scions, yelping and barking, spittle flying from their yellow teeth, their eyes rolling madly in their heads. Rakaros swung his burning sword and hacked down three of them at once, blood falling like rain and boiling on the edge of his blade. A severed head with cresting horns flew past his line of sight, and he turned to see Katastrian playing freely to left and right with his two-handed axe, cleaving bodies in two, swiping the muzzled face from one beast that was then ignited by Xoloxes in his rampaging frenzy. The clearing was soon littered with bleeding bodies as the Scions launched their counter-attack. Initiates scrambled up the sides of the rock face, turning to fling themselves onto the beastmen below with delirious bloodlust. Flameburst pots arced like fiery comets and erupted amongst the beastmen who had blocked the path, igniting their fur and turning them into screaming torches. Rakaros, a pillar of raw strength, barrelled forward into the beastmen's line on the far side, parrying blows that would have felled a lesser man, hewing to each side until he was stumbling over a pile of severed limbs. The cries of the dying creatures were ear-splitting, a barked hysteria that stoked him into ever more violent rage.

'Protect the woman!' he shouted. 'Votremos, keep her safe!'

He saw the priest nod, jabbing the white-hot tip of his staff into a beastman's eye, ducking down to knife it in the guts. Aceria was cowering under the stone altar, and Rakaros saw the priest pass her the knife before he turned and swung his staff in a head-cracking arc. Votremos leapt onto the altar, intoning his prayers, calling on the Ever-Raging Flame to strike the foul creatures down.

'Purge them!' he called to the sky. 'Wipe them from the face of the unholy earth!'

Rakaros broke through the press to the other side of the clearing, where the path continued up the mountainside. He turned, blade steaming with spilled blood, his attention suddenly drawn by a savage bellow that rang like thunder against the rocks. There, emerging from another crowd of beastmen as they poured over the rocks, came their champion – a hulking brute with twin axes, its face covered in a leather mask that Rakaros was reasonably sure had been made from human skin. It champed its awful teeth and charged forward, hacking a Fireborn's head clean from her shoulders, trampling the corpse under its hooves as it sought out further prey. It neighed and barked, a grotesque purple tongue lolling from its muzzle, its eyes yellow pinpricks of light. Rakaros sent his challenge across the scrum.

'Fight me, degenerate beast! I will burn the eyes from your head!'

'*Foe-ren-der!*' it chanted, champing its blunt yellow teeth and clashing its axes together. '*Foe-ren-der!*'

Rakaros met it head-on, swinging the burning sword in a loop that left a trail of fire across the air. The champion caught the blow on the crossed blades of its axes, lashing out with its hoof to catch Rakaros in the stomach, but as the Blazing Lord fell back, he jabbed his blade forward and stabbed the champion in the shoulder. Rakaros grinned to hear its distress, and at the first sight of uncertainty in the beast's eyes he swung a devastating cross-cut that had the creature desperately retreating.

Katastrian, his axe drenched in blood, moved forward to intercept, but at a sign from Rakaros he backed off. The Blazing Lord struck swiftly, stepping within the sweep of the beastman's weapons and slashing his sword across its face. The blade bit deep, calling a screech from the champion, but as Rakaros moved in for the killing blow, the creature rushed forward and butted him in the chest with its head. The blow was like iron. Rakaros flew backwards as if he had been struck by a mallet, crashing to the ground with the breath knocked from him. Somehow, he had kept hold of his sword, and he brought the blade up to block the beastman's axes as they chopped down towards him. The creature straddled him, gnashing at his face, and the stench from its mouldering hide was grotesque. The eyes behind the leather mask glinted with feral madness, and it was all Rakaros could do to keep its weight from smothering him. He bared his own teeth, drawing on the strength of the Holy Flames, calling up every last reserve of rage and violence in his burning soul. The beastman champion pressed down on him, its axe blades an inch from his face, but Rakaros laughed as the new strength flowed into his limbs. Slowly, he pushed back. The axe blades rose, and the mad glint in the beastman's eye turned first to doubt, and then fear.

'Perhaps when this is over,' Rakaros grunted, 'I will skin you and wear your hide. It gets cold in these mountains, after all.'

He threw the beast off him and sprang to his feet, and as it chopped in again with its axes, howling with rage, Rakaros parried the blow and let fly a vicious riposte. The creature's hand went flying from its arm in a dribbling spurt of black blood.

The tide had turned. What few beasts had survived made a panicked stampede from the clearing, slashing and gnawing at each other in their desperation to escape. A dozen more were cut down as they fled, their skulls battered in by the initiates' morning stars, their legs cut from under them and a flurry of sword strikes hewing them to pieces. The floor of the clearing was a charnel pit, slick with blood and body parts, and over everything came the acrid stench of burning hair.

With ease Rakaros disarmed the champion of its remaining weapon. It cowered against the stone, eyes rolling white in its head, clutching the bleeding stump where its hand used to be.

'Finish it!' Katastrian cried, demented with bloodlust. Rakaros, who, having mastered himself, seemed almost impassive, swung once and sliced the champion's head cleanly from its furred shoulders.

'See,' he said, pointing his blade at Aceria. She peered over the edge of the altar, shuddering in fear. 'Here are your Horned Ones. And they will not be my death!'

He crushed the severed head underfoot; a slop of brains spilled out onto the trampled grass.

'Tend your wounds,' the Blazing Lord commanded his troops. 'But do not tarry. We move within the hour.'

If the Hag's Claw Forest had been a fiendish place, barbed and brooding and full of danger, then the land they moved across on their way to the Fangs was worse. The sky felt no more than an arm's length above them and weighed heavily on their minds. The dark clouds pulsed with unearthly energies, and seemed to follow them across the plains like stalking beasts. As he looked up into them, Ashrath was sure that they buckled in response, reforming into the suggestion of monstrous faces and frowning, vengeful eyes. The Fangs ahead stabbed out of the ground like the jaws of a colossal mouth waiting to devour them, razor sharp, slavering mist down into the valley at their base. The wind was a troubled thing, carrying with it the moans of the dying or the distant sobs of those unhinged by grief.

'Even the stones under our feet are against us!' Ashrath complained, turning his ankle on the uneven ground. Essiltha, who moved with all the grace of her aelven blood, the dagger blades gleaming green on her hip, smiled keenly as if to encourage a child.

'The foot falls where the eye directs,' she said. 'It's just a question of reading the ground.' And then she added, as an afterthought, 'Master.'

Ashrath sent her scouting ahead, out of his sight. His skin itched with sweat, and with the vacant hunger of withdrawing venoms. He looked for Ma'sulthis, who wandered on the edge of the warband with Kathenga, gently stroking the snake's head and whispering softly to it. He thought of beckoning the Serpent Caller to him, but he girded himself instead, unwilling to take another lecture. Let the pain of withdrawal be the spur to further effort; the Fangs were near. Archaon's heir was near.

It was a petulant source of irritation to him that the warband had followed the Serpent Caller's direction, rather than his own, when he told them of the quest. The morning after the duel with Su'atha, Ashrath had called the Horned Krait together and told them of the Coiling Ones' instructions.

'This child,' he had said, 'this babe in arms who even now is in mortal danger, is the scion of the Everchosen himself. The Three-Eyed King calls for aid, and the Coiling Ones will provide it. Blessed are their venoms,' he added, reverently inclining his head. 'When we bring this child to the Spire of the Serpent's Tooth, the spire of his seat, the Everchosen will reward us beyond measure. With his strength at our backs, we will retake our temple in Carngrad, cast down the Burned Hand and bless each of them with a lingering death. This I promise you.'

Agree, damn you, he had thought. *Applause, acclamation, anything!* He looked on their sullen faces; the moment lurched on the precipice. Clearbloods stared shamefacedly at their feet. Essiltha, her hands resting on the hilts of her weapons, stared not at

Ashrath but at Ma'sulthis. *I've lost them*, he thought, and the realisation fluttered in his stomach. *They will cut me down where I stand...* He felt tears prickle behind his eyes. *It isn't fair. It's not my fault, none of it!*

But then Ma'sulthis had stepped forward, and with raised hands intoned the words of a holy prayer. From the undergrowth, sliding cleanly through the grass, a dozen snakes had appeared, and they wrapped themselves around Ashrath's feet. Kathenga had stirred, drawing its lucent gaze across the warband. The moment turned.

'Ashrath Silenthis speaks the truth,' the Serpent Caller had said. 'The Coiling Ones have spoken through Kathenga's maw – they have hissed the holy mission they have bestowed upon us. Only Ashrath can save this child. At the end, he will hold it and he will be victorious.'

The acclaim, so slow in coming, arrived at last. Ashrath had let go of a breath he didn't even know he was holding. The journey could begin.

It continued now, although all the enthusiasm of that moment in the Hag's Claw Forest had long since been drained away. The degrading land had taken it, and the dust of the trail had smothered their zeal. *On*, Ashrath told himself. *Ever on, until I hold the fate of the realms in my hands...*

A few days later they came to a stretch of marshland, but as Ashrath began to cross it he cried in horror and dismay, retching into his hands. The others reeled back, some spewing in the grass, others reflexively drawing their weapons although there was no foe to fight.

'What is it?' Ma'sulthis said, drawing near. Unable to speak, Ashrath pointed at the ground.

It was not marsh, but a field that stretched for miles in each direction, and every inch of that field contained a straining eyeball.

There were thousands – millions – of them embedded in the ground, some smashed and bloody, others wet with tears and madly flicking from side to side. Ashrath tentatively stepped out onto the field, but the clammy feeling of the eyeballs splitting apart under his feet appalled him.

'We must go around,' he said. 'This is impossible...'

'Time is not on our side,' Ma'sulthis urged. 'You know this, master. Distasteful as it is, we must go on.'

'Distasteful? This is beyond grotesque, even for the foul standards of this benighted realm!'

'Nevertheless, it must be done.'

'The Serpent Caller is correct,' Essiltha said. 'If you don't have the stomach for it, perhaps one of the clearbloods could carry you...?'

'Silence!' he snarled. 'You walk a thin line, aelf. Take care that you do not fall off it!'

Ashrath marched on with cringing horror across the field of eyes. The others followed, although he did not look back to check. It was all he could do not to vomit, feeling each eyeball crack like an egg under his feet, leaving a smeared trail of vitreous humour and smashed retina behind him. Ahead, he could see flocks of ragged birds descending to the ground, stabbing their beaks into the helpless eyes and flapping off with their prizes towards the mountains. He risked a glimpse down, and the eyes stared back. They quivered with distress, weeping, staring madly at him, as if trying to bore into his very soul and imprint the full misery of what they were experiencing. What did they see? Day after day, night after night, staring immovably into the black clouds, the blazing sun, watching the sky for the flicker of descending birds and praying in whatever distant mind processed such horrors that this time the birds wouldn't come for them. He tried to imagine a consciousness strapped down, immovable, subject to the most inventive tortures and forced to witness each one without the base human recourse of simply screaming out its distress. It was, it was… He didn't have the words. He shuddered and retched again, and for the first time held closely to the itch in his veins from the withdrawing venom. *Focus on that*, he told himself. *Lose yourself in the unbearable, because at least it is not this.*

He looked to the sky. The dark clouds had reformed themselves into a sneering face that gazed down on Ashrath Silenthis and laughed. He grimaced at it and turned his gaze towards the Fangs.

On, he thought. *On, into the very mouth of death, if need be.*

On went the Horned Krait, until the field of eyes was but a joyless memory behind them.

More days passed, but soon the Fangs, so long a barbed line against the horizon, came more forcefully into focus.

'We reach our goal,' Ma'sulthis said. 'The way will become harder from here.'

'Harder?' Ashrath grimaced. He still felt the liquifying eyes on the soles of his feet. 'If the way thus far has been easy, I dread to think what we face up there.'

'A test, undoubtedly, a challenge such as we have not faced before,' Ma'sulthis said. 'The heir of Archaon will not fall into your hands without a fight, of that I am sure. Nothing accomplished has value if it doesn't demand great struggle or sacrifice.'

And I'd sacrifice every one of the Horned Krait, Ashrath thought bitterly, *if it got me closer to my goal.*

The mountains seemed to rise sheer from the plains, but as they drew closer Ashrath could see the broken ground before them. It rose in gentle slopes into the foothills, sparsely covered with dank foliage and stunted, twisted trees. Reeds and marsh grass grew in spiked clumps on the fringes of the foothills, and Ashrath knew the ground would be boggy, treacherous for a warband unprepared to cross it. He didn't want his last moments to be spent clawing at the weeds while he was sucked down into the morass, Essiltha staring at him with satiric amusement. And what would Ma'sulthis do? He often replayed the fight with Su'atha in his mind and tried to imagine the Serpent Caller's response if it had been he and not the Pureblood who had choked to death on the clearing floor. Divine detachment, no doubt, concerned only with the cryptic instructions of the Coiling Ones…

They paused at the borders of the broken ground, scanning the way ahead. The air felt strangely flat, heavy with a sense of expectancy. Ashrath felt the weight of the warband's expectation on him, all of them waiting to see what he would do.

'Here,' he said under his breath to Ma'sulthis, who lay near him. 'Serpent Caller, I have need of your venoms.' He held out his hand and Ma'sulthis passed him a phial. With twitching fingers, he uncorked the bottle and tipped its spoonful of contents onto his tongue. He closed his eyes and felt the liquid numb his mouth, sliding down his throat like nectar. As it thrummed in his blood, he felt the nausea pass from him, the weight of all that expectation unsettle from his shoulders. He opened his eyes, and the world around him was tinged with emerald.

'Take care, Ashrath,' Ma'sulthis warned. 'The venoms give you strength and clear sight, but they run low. Without them, I worry you will start to fade.'

'If they run out, you will make more,' Ashrath said.

'It is no easy thing. There are the correct rituals to consider, the proper substances. Beware, Trueblood.'

'You worry like an old woman,' Ashrath sneered. His smile was a chill thing, devoid of humour, cold as a serpent's blood.

He gestured to three of the clearbloods, those he knew were aligned with Essiltha. They were crouched in the grass at her side.

'Tsiskatha, Shulishra…' he said. He couldn't remember the third one's name. At their height he must have had over thirty warriors in his warband; so many had been initiated into the Horned Krait as they had made their way towards the Eightpoints from Ghyran. They had been thrown into the snake pits and blessed with holy venoms, and when they came out, they were either dead or Splintered Fang. Now, there were barely more than a dozen, but Ashrath still hadn't deigned to learn their names.

I am a bad commander, he thought. *I'm no leader at all… but the snake inspires through fear, not love.*

The one known as Shulishra glanced at Essiltha for confirmation, and it was all Ashrath could do not to march over there and strike her down. He glared his green eyes at them, and together they rose from their crouch and twisted their way across the marsh ahead, their scaled tabards jingling softly in the dead air.

They moved like true serpents of the Splintered Fang, at least. The clearbloods seemed to flow across the uneven ground, slinking from tree to tree, moving with grace and purpose. Ashrath saw the trace of Essiltha's influence in them, the aelven finesse that made even the most brutal fight into a performance of athleticism and poise. He heard the splashing of their feet as they scouted for firmer ground and could smell the stagnant water as they disturbed it.

The clearbloods reappeared on the edge of the marsh and gestured for the warband to follow. Ma'sulthis, lying in the grass nearby, got up to move forward.

'Wait,' Ashrath said, holding out his hand.

'For what? The way ahead is clear.'

'Just… *wait*.'

'There's a path through the bog,' Shulishra called. 'The ground is–'

She didn't get a chance to finish, let alone draw her weapons. The marshland seemed to boil under their feet, foaming with brackish water, and then in a circle underneath them rose the fanged maw of some awful marshland beast, straining and snapping at the air. Its teeth were as long as spears, crooked and stained, and the blubbery purple lips were pitted with cankers and sores. Ashrath caught sight of a single bulging eye, a slit pupil dancing with pleasure as it mangled the clearbloods and gobbled them down. It bellowed and huffed, and underneath its bestial roar Ashrath thought he could hear the chuckle of some malign intelligence. He grinned, careful to disguise his own pleasure. He looked to Essiltha, and she was staring at him with cold fury, her hand resting on the hilts of her green needle blades.

'Don't think they died in vain,' he said, with feigned sorrow. 'At least we know what to avoid.'

Poor Shulishra, Ashrath thought. *Your favourite by some distance, wasn't she, Essiltha? And never again to share your blanket by the light of the campfire…*

He rose up from the grass, watching the foul swamp creature bubble back down into its mephitic bed.

'Onwards,' he called as he led them through the marsh. 'The Fangs are nearly upon us. And perhaps take care where you put your feet,' he said, looking at Essiltha. 'It's just a question of reading the ground, after all…'

CHAPTER SIX

CALL OF THE PYRE

It was strange how what you owned sometimes ended up owning you. Ankhad had often thought that about Ilthis. At first, she was no more than a woman he had seized on the caravan trail, a prize that he idly assumed he would sell in the Carngrad slave markets for a decent profit. Before long though, she was fighting side by side with the rest of his warband, wielding a blade like any fighter as they struck out across the March. In their chaotic skirmishes with rival bands, or as they plundered the mean villages and hamlets that littered the plains, there came a moment when she passed from mere property to partner. He could never put his finger on that moment, though. How had it happened? When? He remembered how dispassionately she had accepted her enslavement, as if it were a minor inconvenience that she would turn to her advantage when she was ready. The choice to join him as a fellow fighter was one that she had made as well, rather than one he had offered her. Tall, she was, as lithe in combat as a striking snake, with those green eyes glaring from a face as pale as milk...

He had told himself at the time that she was a good fighter, and that joining the warband was just sensible strategy. And all the while, he pretended that he wasn't staring at her whenever she passed the campfire at night, that he didn't dream about her, or wonder if she could ever love a man so steeped in blood as him.

'Damn it, Ilthis,' Ankhad mumbled. 'Why did you have to leave me?'

He tipped the wineskin to the baby's mouth, and the child eagerly drank the heady mixture of prowler milk, blood and water. He had no idea if the brew would kill the boy, but unless another dead cat came across his path with milk still in its teats, he didn't have another option. Somehow, though, he didn't think the drink would harm it. There was strength in the child, but Ankhad could forgive himself for thinking that there was something like purpose too. His dark green eyes, like uncut emeralds, were mostly open now. *He doesn't just look*, thought Ankhad. *He actually* sees.

He sat high up on a perch of rock that gave him a good view across a crumbled valley towards the northern reaches and down the Fangs on either side. Lothin would surely have sent more men, and Ankhad knew he should keep moving. But where? A man couldn't hide in the Fangs forever, especially not with a child that needed care. It was too barren, too dangerous.

'What to do with you?' he said, looking down at the baby as he cradled it in his arms. He had stripped the shirt from Grulsham's body and fashioned it into a kind of sling, the baby tucked into it and nestled against his chest. 'Where shall we go, young Allarik? Carngrad? Maybe...'

Carngrad was the obvious choice. It was large enough to lose themselves in, busy enough that he might be able to find a wet nurse. There were few people there who would recognise him, surely, not after all these years? But his time on the March had been bloody indeed, and the risk that some old rival would see his face... Was it a risk worth taking?

'I don't know,' he said, as much to himself as to the baby. 'I don't know.' He looked down at its open face, the eyes gazing up at him, the mouth an uncomplaining line.

It was not his child. Ankhad knew that. It had never been a point of contention with Ilthis. But then whose – or rather, *what's* – child was he?

From being comrades, they had soon become friends. And from being friends they had soon become something else, something deeper and truer. After that, the needs of the warband fell away, and Ankhad found that the zeal to carve his name on the scarred ground of the Eightpoints was nothing more than an inconsequential dream, something easily forgotten by morning. Before long they had moved on, alone, abandoning the warband to its fate. Leaderless, scattered, no doubt the rest of them were all dead by now. Holy Rhelick, Axkralopos, the Beast, Murmuk'al, Huthor the Flayer – all of them cut down by rival gangs, knifed in backstreet Carngrad taverns or torn apart by the unforgiving landscape. Ankhad barely gave them a moment's thought, those men and women he had fought beside for years. They were killers all. They deserved nothing less.

He and Ilthis had travelled much of the Desolate March, trading weapons here and there, raiding lone caravans, scavenging when the need took them. They fought for hire and fought for others to leave them alone. They were part of the jetsam of the Spoil, two amongst uncounted millions who called the Eightpoints home – the tormented, the fanatic, the lost and the damned, and those who just wanted to live a life free from any constraints.

Years passed and they were content, but then one day Ilthis had seemed unusually withdrawn. She became listless, distracted, prone to directionless rages. She talked in her sleep of strange visions and voices that she couldn't remember by morning. She took to wandering the desert land outside the settlement where they were staying, a place so devoid of consequence it didn't even have a name, staring off towards the burning black spire dimly visible towards the very heart of the Eightpoints. Ankhad kept his distance, not wanting to place her under any pressure. She would stay out for hours, sometimes all night, but then one morning she didn't come back.

A dust storm had risen during the night. The air was a pestilent fog, swirling with ribbons of ochre and tan. Ankhad had covered his mouth with a scarf and set off to find her, calling her name against the whirlwind, labouring through the winnowing sand. There was no sign of her. He was on the verge of giving up and heading back when he heard a feeble cry, and after another hour spent scouting around the plain, he found her lying half buried in the dust. Helping her to her feet, he was shocked to see that she was near full-term pregnant, as if she had moved through a full nine months in an instant overnight.

It happened like this, sometimes; he had heard the stories. The mutating force of the Bloodwind Spoil, a land saturated in the dark energies of Chaos, sometimes induced a weird parthenogenesis in both people and beasts. The results of these malign conceptions were always foul, aborted things, though – slavering ruins that died on first contact with the air, or creatures that were so grotesque a sacrifice to the True Gods was a mercy. They were half things, unsouled, daemonic lives conjured up as no more than a mocking gesture by the dreadful earth. It was no true pregnancy, he told himself.

The others in the settlement had thought it an omen of surpassing doom, though, and quickly Ankhad had gathered their things. They headed across the March, trailing blindly for anywhere they could disappear and be forgotten. Somewhere like Spite, where they could wait for the baby to come and see what awful curse the Bloodwind Spoil had laid against them...

The decision was made. Ankhad headed for Carngrad.

He had traversed the Fangs and now stood at their highest point. The air cut like a razor, and he looked down into the mist-shrouded stretch of the Desolate March on one side and the plains of the Corpseworm Marches on the other. Somewhere to his right, at the far end of the mountain range, he would find Carngrad, and safety of sorts.

'Time is against us, little one,' he said. He huddled into his thin cloak and drew the baby close. The wind rummaged through his hair and stung his eyes. The sky brooded like deep water above him, suggestive of hidden depths and unimaginable predators. 'I have no more food to give you.'

Ankhad looked down into his face and smiled. *You'll be fine, I know it. Somehow*, he thought, *it is not your fate to die on this mountainside.*

The descent was easier than the way up, at least. He kicked against the shale, trotting down a few feet at a time. The trail petered out here and there, and he was forced to scramble over and slip down vast boulders that listed at strange angles, as if placed there by drunken gargants. He came across weird carvings in the stone, glyphs and symbols that he didn't recognise. Etched there during the unnumbered centuries of the Age of Myth, they showed strange beasts and vast monsters – a grotesque serpent seemingly coiling itself around a mountaintop, a massive centaur shattering the earth underneath its hooves. Elsewhere, he found the crumbled foundations of ancient structures – ruined temples choked in purple ivy, palaces long since cast down by the unforgiving ages. He let his mind wander into speculation about those far-gone days, the peoples who might have lived here. Ankhad was no scholar – he could scarcely read – but he had enough lore from his travels to know that the Eightpoints had once been the Allpoints, a place where that smug and sanctimonious false god, Sigmar, had once held court. Long had the ages been since then, though. Long had Chaos carved its mark and bled its poison into the soil.

He rested when he could, never pausing long. At one point, sauntering along a track that curved and twisted against the line of the slope, he had turned a corner only to see a few ragged beastmen skinning a corpse in a clearing ahead. Choking on his heart as it lurched into his mouth, Ankhad had slipped back along the trail with his spiked club in his hands. He could hear the beastmen barking at each other, snarling over the spoiled meat. It was a long detour that took him past them, back up the mountain and then half a mile along before he dared make his way down again.

'That would have been the end of us both,' Ankhad whispered to the baby. 'Or me, for certain. Whatever you're marked for, I'm not sure it's just to be the starter for a beastman's main course.'

That night he rested in a hollow underneath an overhang of rock. He didn't risk a fire, but it was warm enough with the baby huddled up beside him. As he tried to sleep, he pushed the fear from his mind that the child would be dead by morning.

Why am I doing this? Because you're Ilthis' son? Because you're all I have left of her? The Spoil destroys everyone in time – it'll destroy you too in the end. It would be a mercy for you to die now, and not be twisted into something just as awful as this disgusting landscape. Something like me... a killer, a man with no purpose but the spilling of blood. No purpose, until I found her...

He closed his eyes and tried not to think of his wife.

Morning came, and with it a strange, clear dawn that lit the crystal in the ochre stone and for a moment made the mountainside seem beautiful. Ankhad rose and changed the baby and fed it the last of the blood and water. Today was the moment of truth. He looked up into the sky. Either fate was with the child, or it was against him. The only path was the one that led onwards, and on that path would either be survival or death.

'Survival, my son,' Ankhad said. 'I know it.' He kissed the baby on the forehead. 'Maybe I have a purpose after all.'

He stepped down from the overhang onto the trail, but he had only gone a few feet when they attacked. He barely felt the knife go in.

Dawn threw a spear of light against the shrouded mountain. The beam glinted redly on the blade as Ankhad pulled the knife from his gut, his hand coiled around his killer's wrist. He gasped, flinching back as if he could outstep the wound. He stared down into the face of the man who had stabbed him – young, his eyes wide in shock, as if incredulous at what he had done.

Nothing but a boy, Ankhad thought. *Frightened, led astray... a chance meeting on a mountain path.*

No, not frightened, not led astray, and this meeting was certainly not by chance. The boy's face was stained with hard travel and by more than one fight along the way. He had weapons strapped to his back, an old scar against his temple, and he held the blade in an accustomed grip. Ankhad felt the wound pulse and contract in his stomach, the blood spewing out under his fingers as they tried to clutch it closed. The knife had slipped in just under the baby he had bundled to his chest. An inch higher and it would have passed clean through Allarik's body.

Ankhad glared down into the younger man's eyes and turned the full force of his fury on him, twisting his assailant's wrist to the side until the knife clattered out of his grip. He knew a killer when he saw one. He had been one long enough himself.

It was only then that he realised how many of them were on the narrow path ahead. Feverish young warriors with sickle blades and red tunics thrown loosely over their shoulders craned their necks to see what was happening; older fighters with scaled half-cloaks and battered metal shoulder guards were trying to push their way through to the head of the passage.

Ankhad swallowed. *Scions of the Flame! Gods preserve me – there will be no mercy here.*

The trail at this point snaked around two twisted columns of red limestone, falling steeply so that Ankhad still had the advantage of height. It fell away to the left onto a deep escarpment, and as the clouds broke apart and the beam of sunlight withdrew, he could see a long, thin slice of the Bloodwind Spoil's fomenting sky, like red rage made visible.

'Don't kill him!' someone shouted, in a voice that rumbled like an avalanche. Clambering over the rocks and standing on the edge of the escarpment to the left of the trail was the biggest man Ankhad had ever seen. His face was hidden by a mask of beaten bronze, and the air around him rippled with distorted heat. 'I want him alive!' he screamed. 'And do not harm the child!'

As if waiting for the command, the Scions on the path surged forward. Ankhad sneered as he broke the fighter's wrist.

He lashed out with his foot and kicked the younger man to the ground, drawing his spiked club from its leather strap at his waist. He felt the blood bubbling down his front from the knife wound, and he skipped back as the next young fighter in line moved up the path to attack.

'For the Ever-Raging Flame!' the boy cried, twirling his morning star around his head. He was barefoot, lean and eager for the fight. He smelled of ashes, of charcoal braziers and dead campfires.

'Whatever you say, lad,' Ankhad muttered. He swung the club and shattered the boy's jaw, tearing half his face off.

As the downed fighter groped in the dirt, moaning and dribbling blood, the others clambered over him in their zeal and crushed his face into the ground. Ankhad tried to turn and run, but another morning star came swinging towards his head. He desperately parried it, wrapping its chain around the shaft of his club and tearing it from its owner's grip. He skipped another step back up the path, but then hands were tearing at his legs and he had to snap the mace forward to break the nose of the Scion who was trying to bring him down. With a flick of the wrist he stabbed the club's rusty embedded nails into another fighter's throat.

They were swarming him, forcing him back while others scrambled to get behind him. Ankhad struck with the club again and again, stabbing as much as swinging. It was an inelegant weapon, but it was made for just such a brutal press as this – elbow to elbow, face to face, no room to move or manoeuvre, bodies swarming and slashing and stabbing at those in front. Blood splashed into Ankhad's face, and more blood poured from the wound in his stomach, but the more he fought, the more savage and uncompromising he became. He bludgeoned heads and crushed windpipes with the club, he jammed his thumb into eye sockets, and when he had the chance, he bit great chunks of flesh from the faces of those who threw themselves against him. But it wasn't enough. He was being pushed back, further up the path, and every time the surging bodies threatened to overwhelm him he thought only of young Allarik, pressed into his chest, at risk of death from any passing blade no matter how much the Scions were trying to avoid harming him. It was too much. He couldn't fight half as hard as he needed to, and as he raised the club again and again with an arm that felt as heavy as stone, and as he kicked and punched and bit, he felt the darkness descend on his vision. His hands, so steeped in hot blood, were cold. He took a solid punch to the temple, and his vision flared into twirling light. He felt another knife slip into his calf, a third sawing madly at his hamstring.

'Gods!' he tried to shout, but his voice was no more than a puff of breath. The gods wouldn't hear. 'Save the boy! Allarik! Protect him, I beg you!'

He thrashed in a tangle of bodies, a bloody scrum that pinned him to the ground. The baby was torn from him, and it cried its distress across the unforgiving mountainside.

His arms were pinned to the ground, and with a sickening crunch he felt them break. He cried out, felt his teeth smash in his mouth under the weight of the blows.

'Allarik,' he mumbled, spitting blood. Death was near him now. He kicked against it, still struggling against the Scions who held him down. He thought of Tarnot, dragged to the ground back in Spite. He thought of every man, woman and child he had cut down in all the long years of his troubled life, when he had swept like death across the Bloodwind Spoil, and when mercy was just the vice of the weak. Now death was on him. He watched it come close, a tall figure, proud and violent and smoking with flame, bearing a great two-handed blade.

Ilthis, forgive me... Allarik.

The hilt of the sword came down hard, and Ankhad saw only darkness.

They came to burn him at dusk. Rakaros had ordered the last of the rage-rock to be placed amongst the kindling, a symbol of the victim's importance.

'For he is the father of the child,' Rakaros said to the assembled band, 'and he brought it living through the mountains. That is no small thing.'

They placed Ankhad on the pyre, laying him down on the bundled wood, his hands and feet bound. His groans were answered by savage blows, and as the flames took hold his remaining eye sought out Aceria, the wet nurse who held the child on the edge of the camp, wrapped warmly in her cloak. She met his gaze.

Ankhad said nothing, just stared, and his face was the most complete picture of despair she had ever seen.

When he started burning, Aceria closed her eyes. When he started screaming, she looked up into the clouds. They were alive with fire, as if what burned below them wasn't a mortal man but a whole town, a city, a realm entire. The screams leapt up towards those clouds, scratching at Aceria's nerves, clawing their way so deeply into her mind that she knew she would never forget them as long as she lived.

'Hush,' she whispered to the baby. 'Hush, my little one, be still. It's just the wind across the mountains. It's nothing, it's nothing at all.'

She looked down into those green, green eyes as the baby slowly fell asleep.

As the pyre burned, a warrior stirred far down on the loping plains of the Corpseworm Marches. He stood and shielded his eyes against the falling dusk, and where the distant Fangs were cast in all the lurid colours of the sunset, he saw the glint of flame. He saw it rise, and rise again, lancing up to spear the belly of the black clouds that smothered the peak, and on the wind that coursed from those distant mountains he thought he heard a scream – a long, despairing wail of an anguish so deep it had no end. *That anguish will live across these unholy lands until the end of time,* the warrior thought. It would linger on the wind, it would play in all the lonely places of the Spoil, and it would haunt the dreams of anyone who stole an unsettled hour to sleep.

The warrior woke his brothers and sisters, and they girded themselves for war, stowing crossbows, sheathing swords and axes. As the sun set, and as the darkness crept like a murderer across the Bloodwind Spoil, the warriors threw back their rough hide cloaks and sprinted over the dusty plains, and the only light that shone was the eldritch glow of their compass as it led them on into the Fangs.

PART TWO

CHAPTER SEVEN

THE BURNING TRAIL

Night smothered the plains like a shroud when the Untamed Beasts stopped to rest. They set up camp on the edge of a grove of thorn bushes, a jagged gorse that would protect their flanks and offer some protection if they should be attacked. Ekrah directed some of the plains-runners to dig fire holes, to hide the flames of their cook fires from anyone who might be watching, while he sent other plains-runners to scout for game. After an hour, Ghulassa came back with the rancid prey of the Spoil – greasy rodents with eight legs, jackrabbits with iridescent eyes, spiny night-birds caught grazing on bitter seeds. The warband squatted down around their fires and ate, and Ekrah prowled the edge of the camp against intruders. He kept his bone blade unsheathed.

Always, he thought, there were those in the warband who jostled for power or influence, who saw themselves as a Heart-eater but for some obscure misfortune. Such feelings bred anger and resentment, and violence. Challenges were made, challengers cut down. Ekrah was not like that. He was a Preytaker, and the role of a Preytaker is always to move forward as the tribe requires. To move forward is to outrun the demands of pride, and every stop for rest and food chafed against him. He could eat while he ran. He could sleep while he ran. Yet the Heart-eater commanded it, and the Preytaker obeyed. He was not like Kurguth. The First Fang saw himself as Heart-eater – it was visible to the blind. Long had they been brothers, but now Kurguth yearned to be chief, to strike down Burak and take the warband for his own. The Split-Tongue Tribe would be his, to range and hunt as he saw fit. It was coming, Ekrah knew. Kurguth, huddling at night under his animal skins with the Beastspeaker, whispered his plots into her ear. Or perhaps she whispered hers? Maybe Mayra saw herself as Heart-eater, and would use Kurguth to cut down Burak, and then she would cut him down in turn? It was possible. Mayra had in her a savagery beyond Ekrah's comprehension. She was the purest of them, he felt, the closest to the beasts they hunted.

In the morning they ran on, barely stopping to eat. They gathered their weapons and supplies, and Ekrah took the lead as he scouted the land ahead. They passed through a wide stretch of eroded grassland, where the soil was dry and ferrous, like rusting metal. Later, as the light of distant Hysh passed on behind them, they stooped as they ran to lessen the length of their shadows, so they would not give their position away. Ekrah chastised two of the plains-runners for lagging behind. He would have killed them out of hand, for the weak are ever a burden on the strong, but he knew Burak needed every warrior they had for the quest ahead. He threatened them with his sword, and they soon picked up the pace.

The warband stopped after another fifty miles, casting themselves down into the dust as the light began to fail. Night came so quickly here, Ekrah knew. In the Jagged Savannah, back in Ghur, the day's dying was a moment of languid pleasure, stirring and terrifying all at once, as the sky ignited and the sunlight fell against the burning clouds. Here, night was almost shameful and furtive, snapped down like a lid to cover something awful. *The Bloodwind Spoil is a place apart*, Ekrah thought as he patrolled the edge of their camp. *Even the day is no reprieve from the darkness.*

Burak's face was drawn, his chest heaving as he lay down to rest. Yet it had been Kurguth who faltered. Every stage of the march, the First Fang seemed to struggle. He had weakened himself with Mayra, Ekrah thought. Or he was weakening because he did not believe. To hunt a child, a baby, in the mountains... It was not glorious. But it did not matter; it was the tribe's command, and Burak was the tribe. He was the strongest. He saw the furthest.

'Cast around,' Burak ordered. 'Find wood, roots, make a fire. We sleep here tonight.'

'I will take first watch,' Ekrah offered. Burak looked up at him from the ground, eyes glittering with craft.

'Don't you want to rest?' he asked. 'The trail has been long, unforgiving. We have plains-runners to waste on the watch. I need my Preytaker strong.'

'There is none stronger,' Ekrah declared. He looked at Kurguth, who was sprawled in the dusty grass. 'Let me take the first watch, Heart-eater.'

'Very well,' Burak agreed. 'Take your bone blade, Ekrah. Cut down all who challenge us in the watches of the night.'

Ekrah loped off towards the edge of the camp, his sword slung over his shoulder.

What touch of foresight made him look back he didn't know, but when he did Burak was still staring at him, mumbling to himself, his eyes glazed like the eyes of the dead. But it wasn't Burak who drew Ekrah's gaze. He saw beyond the Bloodseer, to where Kurguth and Mayra sat in each other's arms, and both First Fang and Beastspeaker had bound their attention to the Heart-eater's form. They stared at him, talking quietly between themselves, and on their faces Ekrah saw the unmistakable mask of pride, the lust for power.

He stared off into the plains, sitting cross-legged on the ground, his sword resting across his knees. It would come soon, he knew. Kurguth would strike, and Ekrah would defend.

Ekrah, First Fang... he thought, and in the gathering dark he smiled.

'There was Chochola,' Kurguth said. Mayra nodded. He felt her weight shift against his arm. 'The lake beast rose from the waters and tore him in half.'

'Chochola... He runs now on the spirit plains, where the hunting is endless.'

'Talaska, and Daskur,' he said, remembering. 'The lasherbrute trampled them as it ran through the gorge.'

'They were sky-buried – their spirits look down on us and guide us to the right path.'

He remembered others torn and trampled on the way, the numbers they had lost.

'Neesa...'

She turned and embraced him, and when they kissed, he felt a strength in him that seemed to fade when they ran by day. He couldn't explain it. All the years as First Fang, the days when he had grown on the savannah with Burak, and never once had he felt a weakness in him. He cleaved to her for the strength she gave him, and worried that this was a weakness in itself.

'What troubles you?' she asked. She drew his head down to her lap and stroked his hair. 'You have no joy in this hunt. Your strength falters – I see it.'

'And I see the pain in your eyes that we're tasked with such a quest. We run to something beneath us, to something squalid and miserable, the murder of a child on the strength of Burak's visions.'

'There is no glory in this,' she said quietly. 'There are only the visions of the Bloodseer, but rarely have they led us wrong.'

'Rarely, but I have strong doubts. They turn my bones to water.'

'What would you do?' She lowered her voice, glancing over to where the Bloodseer squatted by his fire, staring through the flames, his mouth mumbling secret prayers. He turned the steel blade in his hands, holding it out like an offering to the fire. He still wore his leather helmet, and the branched horns glowed orange in the light. 'Would you challenge him?' she whispered. 'Take the warband for your own?'

Pain spasmed across his brow. Kurguth passed his hand over his face.

'I couldn't do it,' he said. 'Not until the tribe sat on the very edge of ruin and no other road would save us.'

'When you do,' Mayra said, leaning down to kiss him, 'you will have me by your side.'

'Aye, but who else? Ekrah will never turn – he'll heed Burak all the days of his life.'

'Then make his days short.'

Kurguth laughed softly, imagining the fight. Ekrah was fast with the serrated blade, it was true. Face to face, perhaps he would even have the advantage. *But let him try his dancing moves with a harpoon in his belly, and me drawing him closer and closer through the dust, to the edge of my axe...*

'There will be others,' Mayra promised. 'Half the plains-runners would be yours, and in single combat you would cut Burak down with ease.'

'Burak? Maybe, maybe... Did I ever tell you of when we were children?' he said, his eyes glittering at the memory. 'Two more vicious creatures you never saw in your life. Once, I remember, we challenged each other to steal the honey from a butcher-bees' nest, and they nested only at the top of the tallest razor-bark trees in the forest. Up we climbed, up two trees side by side, our hands and feet cut to ribbons on the razor-bark, and when we were only halfway up the butcher-bees started pouring from their nests. They stung us *everywhere*, and the pain was like nothing I care to experience again as long as I live.'

'So, which one of you got the honey?'

'Neither of us. We dropped down and ran as fast as we could, hiding in a stream for half the day until the swarms had disappeared. But then two days later Burak strolled into the middle of our camp licking the honey from his hand. "You did it!" I said, and I couldn't believe it. "How did you get to the top? What did you do about the bees – cover yourself in mud? Smoke them out?" He looked at me and laughed. He'd done no such thing.'

'What had he done?' Mayra asked.

'He had cut down the tree. He took the nest to the stream and drowned the bees. And then he got what little honey was left.'

Later, Kurguth sat with Burak by his fire. In silence, they stared at the flames, listening to the dead, dry wood crackling into dust.

'What does tomorrow bring then?' he asked. 'Do we go on?'

'We do,' Burak said. In the firelight the brass disc at his throat glimmered, and he twirled the knife in the dirt.

'Many have died just crossing the plains. The way ahead will be harder.'

'It will.'

'Many more will die…'

'They will,' Burak said, and he laughed. 'Many and more. Perhaps I will die? Perhaps you will. Or Mayra.'

'Will it be worth it?' Kurguth said, the anger rising in him. 'All these lives from the tribe, exchanged for a child?'

'It will, yes, it will, it will… But I don't think I will die,' Burak said, as if he had long been considering it. He frowned. 'No, because I have seen myself passing through the Mountain's Throat, and I have seen myself standing at the altar in the ruined temple, the child laid out before me...'

'We are to be beaten down to nothing, until only you are left, then. That is what you are asking of us?'

'Not beaten down, no,' Burak said, his voice almost like a chant, 'but whittled, carved, pared back to something stronger. See?'

He reached into the flames and pulled out a stick of kindling, so far unburned, beating the sparks from it against the dirt. He took up the steel knife and briskly carved the tip into a sharp point.

'You take the raw wood,' he said, 'and you whittle it down, casting off the useless parts. And what you are left with is a weapon.'

'Why do you love that knife so?' Kurguth muttered bitterly.

'I don't love it,' Burak said. 'I despise it. Don't you see, my brother? It causes me pain just to hold it in my hand.'

'Then why hold it?'

'Because the Everchosen demands sacrifice to be admitted to his legions. You think sacrifice is doing something difficult, something tough. It is not. It is giving up something that you love, something that is a part of you. I am sacrificing that which makes me who I am.'

'I don't understand,' Kurguth said. 'I feel you are further away from me now than you have ever been. Do you think the King with Three Eyes will welcome us for sacrificing a child? Or will he despise us as weaklings and cowards?'

'It's not your place to understand, my brother. All you must do is be by my side when we reach the Mountain's Throat. I have seen it.'

They lapsed again into silence, and the fire hissed and sputtered before them. Eventually, weary beyond description, Kurguth said, 'I told Mayra of the time we were children, when we climbed for the butcher-bees' honey. Do you remember?'

Burak chuckled, rocking back on his heels. 'Yes, yes, I remember.'

'I told her how we had been stung half to death, how you went back and cut down the tree... I never would have thought of that. You were always different, Burak, always marked by fate.'

'I didn't cut down the tree,' Burak said, laughing to himself.

'Then how did you get the honey?'

The Heart-eater turned to look at him, and for a moment Kurguth felt he was looking into the hollow eyes of a skull.

'I found a merchants' caravan, lost on the trail from Excelsis. I bought the honey with trinkets and beads, like any city tradesman!'

He whooped with laughter and fell back against the dirt, and in the shadows cast by the campfire he looked like some writhing animal, screeching to itself in the very joy of living. Kurguth felt his soul curdle inside him, as if he had been thrust into the presence of something rank and unclean. It was true, what Mayra said – Burak had fallen prey to the lust for iron and steel, for trinkets and trade and the soft pleasures of the city folk. And it had been there inside him for far longer than Kurguth had realised. He felt sick.

The First Fang left the campfire in disgust and walked back to where Mayra waited, and there was something wrenched and broken in his heart. He remembered the Bloodseer's words.

'Sacrifice,' he whispered to himself as he lay down to sleep, 'means giving up something that you love...'

In the morning the Burned Hand moved down the spine of the mountains, and the cries of the child rang out against the dawn. Aceria had fed and changed him, and she rocked him gently as she followed them down the path. The trail was narrow, a beaten track of packed earth that rose and fell against the contours of the Fangs.

'What's the matter, little one?' she said, trying to keep her tone light. 'You've a full belly and this warm sling to sleep in.'

Babies could respond to the emotions of those around them, she knew. They saw the colours of despair, of anger and hatred, and Aceria felt as plunged into the depths of despair as she had ever felt in her life. Her village was a smoking ruin, her belief in the benevolence of the Horned Ones was a bitter lie, and she had watched a man burned to death for nothing more than trying to defend his son. And now she followed the men and women of the Burned Hand to who knew where, to kill a child for what malign purpose she couldn't begin to guess. She looked out over the despondent landscapes that fell away on either side of the Fangs and knew there was no escape. There was only the path that led onwards, and the fate that lay at the end of it.

'Hush, my boy,' she cooed as the baby cried again. She bit back her tears. 'Take heart, young one. Take heart, and all will come good in the end.'

'The child seems disturbed,' the priest said at her side. She huddled the baby closer. Votremos looked keenly at the boy, and then turned his fierce gaze upon her, piercing her with his eyes. She hated him, she realised. Of them all, he was the one who made her soul shrink furthest in her body. The Blazing Lord, Rakaros, was the most terrifying figure she had ever seen, but she feared him as she feared a conflagration, an overpowering event of the natural world. There was something smouldering and sick about Votremos, though – the way his voice dripped richly from his mouth, the way his eyes were flecked with sparks of fire. He was a more dangerous figure than the Blazing Lord, she realised. The Blazing Lord would kill because he must, but the priest would kill just for the pleasure of seeing his victim burn.

'He's unsettled, my lord,' Aceria said. 'Moving all the time like this, and he...'

'Yes?'

'Well, I suspect he misses his father, lord.'

'I'm sure he does. Poor child...'

He reached out a hand to stroke the baby's face, his fingers dusted with ash and soot, but Aceria instinctively pulled away. Votremos grasped her wrist and twisted, his mouth a savage sneer.

'You live on sufferance, girl, for the child's sake. But do not forget you are our slave, and the fires wait for any slave who displeases me.'

He held her wrist a moment longer, staring at her, enjoying the pain in her face, and then he cast the hand down and stalked off towards the head of the column, his staff tapping at the stone.

Rakaros walked near the front of the warband, deep in thought as Votremos approached.

'We make good time, lord,' the priest said. 'The rearguard say nothing is following us, and the ground ahead looks empty. There are the remnants of an ancient city further down the trail, it seems. We could perhaps camp there for the night?'

'See it is done,' Rakaros said. 'How is the child?'

'Fractious, but well. It's remarkable he didn't suffer more on his journey through the mountains. His fool of a father had barely enough supplies for himself, let alone a baby.'

'He is smoke and ashes now. No doubt his shade regrets his actions, but the regrets of the dead are not our concern. What of the wet nurse?'

'She is more insolent than I would like, but she follows as she must.'

'She still has the knife you gave her?'

'She does,' Votremos confirmed.

'I confess, priest, I don't see your reasoning here.'

'It's simple,' Votremos said. 'In utter desperation she would simply run, whether taking the child or casting him to the ground – either way, the child would die before we reach the temple. With a blade hidden, as she sees it, she has a chance. It gives her courage, and keeps total despair at bay. She will continue and she will wait for that chance. But, as she fails to realise, that chance will never arrive. The closer we get to our destination, the smaller her window of opportunity becomes.'

'The mind of the Inferno Priest moves subtly, it seems,' Rakaros said with amusement.

'As it must. My only concern now is our lack of rage-rock.'

Rakaros tried to disguise his impatience. They had used the last of their supplies when burning the child's father.

'Have faith, priest,' he said. 'It was always a resource in short supply, but the Flame will not abandon us. I have seen the temple in my dreams, the burning altar and the bloody knife. All will converge as it must.'

They marched on for much of the day, following the path as it rose higher and higher into the peaks of the Fangs. The shale underfoot became looser, as if the paths had been little used for some time. Sometimes the trail passed through narrow passages of stone, where the rocks bled condensation and where patches of purple moss glimmered in the soft light. At other times, the ground on either side of the trail dropped away into steep escarpments that fell vertiginously down towards the lower slopes of the mountains far below. The trail curved and looped around, and then continued on a straight and unobstructed path that made Rakaros feel obscurely exposed, as if he were being observed by some vast and disinterested power. On they went, and still the false peaks of the mountains leapt into the sky before them, only to diminish and fall away, revealing yet another peak behind them as the warband continued on its way.

The afternoon was well advanced as they came to the ruins. The light was subdued, and the worn stones seemed to emerge from the ground ahead as if choosing that moment to reveal themselves.

Above them as the warband advanced, built into the spires and overhangs of the mountainside, were shattered archways and the tumbled corners of ancient buildings. A listing bell tower was connected to a broken colonnade by a barbed length of wooden walkway, and here and there they saw rough-hewn ladders and half-built shacks. Spiked barriers had been thrown up against the road that led into the ruins, but they were easily cast aside. Despite these signs of settlement, the city seemed deserted.

'The wretched inhabitants have no doubt fled at our coming,' Votremos said. 'I shouldn't think we have much to fear from them.'

'Nevertheless, set a watch tonight,' Rakaros said as he wandered about the ruins. He looked up at the shattered bas-reliefs, the mouldering metal gates and crumbled gargoyles. In its golden years, this place was no doubt a city of some power and influence. A holy place, perhaps, hidden high up in the mountains, its streets resounding to the clash of prayer bells and the sandalled tread of priests. And now, as the great wheel of fate turns ever on, the Age of Myth was cast down and the Age of Chaos came, and what was once holy was profaned. Rakaros felt he had caught a glimpse of time's unsentimental arrow, the straight line that cuts across reality and bends at last, in the unimaginable future, towards a final and permanent rest.

'To the serpent-worshippers, these mountains are Nagendra's teeth,' Votremos told him. 'I wonder what that makes this city?'

'Do you think it was sacred to them?'

'I doubt it, lord. The span of time is too far. Perhaps one of Sigmar's temples was once here? It is impossible to say – it was an age long past, and the lore of that time is long since in the dust.'

'Much of what we move through is dust, in the end,' Rakaros said. '"We ourselves must become as the dust and the ash." Is it not so?'

'A beautiful verse,' Votremos said, with pleasure.

'My lord!' one of the initiates called. He came running up from the other side of the ruins, his tunic torn and blood on his sword. 'Lord Rakaros!'

'Speak,' he commanded.

'Three fighters, Iron Golem it seems. We caught them trying to take the path back down the mountain on the other side of the city.'

Rakaros smiled and felt once more at peace. 'Bring them to me.'

They weren't the greatest specimens of the Iron Golems' might, a faction with which Rakaros and his Burned Hand had clashed on more than one occasion. On the streets of Carngrad, the wary fighter grew to respect the quality of their steel and the durability of their armour, but the three legionaries that were thrown down into the dust at the Blazing Lord's feet were battered and ragged things. Their helmets had been cast aside, and their armour was dented and scratched. All three bore the signs of heavy fighting, though their scars were scabbed and not recent. To Rakaros they looked as if they had spent some time in the mountains, clashing with the flora and fauna of this benighted place.

'What brings you into the Fangs?' he demanded. Sullen, heads lowered, the legionaries said nothing. Rakaros nodded to Katastrian, and the champion's fist smashed down against a jaw. Spitting blood, the struck legionary glanced over to where Aceria stood on the edge of the warband, cradling the baby.

'Our dominar sends us to seek out the child,' he mumbled. He coughed out a tooth. 'Novkorod, of the Black Vambrace.'

'And what does Novkorod know of the baby?'

'He knows the stars converge on its life. He knows the mountains will fall and the storms will rise, and legions will march across the Eightpoints at its command. He would armour this child for all the wars to come.'

Rakaros nodded. 'And for a child this important he sends only you three, does he?'

'There were more,' the legionary admitted. He groaned. 'We have drifted across these accursed mountains for weeks, looking for it! Furies, those damned raptoryx… Not all visions point to the proper path, it seems.'

He collapsed against his bonds, and Katastrian dragged him up again, grasping his chin and holding his head up. The other legionaries, resigned to their fate, kept silent.

'You have done well to get this far,' Rakaros said, 'while guided by false prophecy. Take comfort that your deaths will keep our warriors warm this evening and will feed the Flame to its everlasting glory.'

To their credit, none asked for mercy. Obedient to their laws, they would die – or perhaps they had just recognised in the Blazing Lord a mind where mercy was absent, and death was preferable to the futility of begging.

No matter. The pyres were made, and in the ruins the fires burned. Cooked in their armour, the legionaries wept across the night, and to Rakaros it was the sweetest music. He scryed the fire and saw the flames sweeping through the lands entire, cascading across the realms and burning everything in their path. In the centre of those flames, the fires like a garland of majesty across his shoulders, rode the Three-Eyed King – Archaon, Everchosen. And at his side rode the Burned Hand, Scions of the Flame, with Lord Rakaros triumphant at their head.

CHAPTER EIGHT

PREPARED GROUND

It was like the ghost of an old memory, a haunted thing that slipped across the contours of her mind on the borders of sleep. When she woke, it was a pall on the edge of her vision that she could never quite clasp in her sight. It was always there – a presence that was an absence, a feeling that was a lack of feeling. She moved in the warband's wake like half a person, somehow untethered from herself. She was a Beastspeaker, yet her mind felt hollow without a beast to speak to. She missed not just Neesa – blessed be her shade on the holy hunting grounds – but any creature that hunted and fed on meat. The tribe moved too quickly, ranging too far out of its territories, and there was no time for her to sink into the sacred part of herself that communed with the creatures of the Spoil. And so she ran, Kurguth at her side, her whip coiled at her waist and her knife in its leather sheath, and her mind wandered wide over all the shattered lands they passed through, the deep plains and their scouring dust, the high mountains sharp as any eye tooth. She reached for a sympathetic bond, but always her mind came back empty.

Ahead of her as they scaled the foothills of the Fangs, Ekrah skipped nimbly over the rock. He jumped from one outcrop to the next, his eyes not on his feet but on all the hidden nooks and crannies where an enemy might hide. He had his bone sword in hand, and as he leapt, he held it out for balance. The horns on his helmet were low swept, sharpened, and his furred cloak was thrown back over his shoulders and secured with a length of leather cord. His chest was lathered in sweat, his face streaked with twin tracks of ash and mud. As Mayra followed a few steps behind, she caught him turning to look at her with something dark and covetous in his eyes – and then she realised that he was not looking at her at all, but past her at Kurguth. The First Fang took the track up into the mountains, the rope of his harpoon wrapped around his shoulder, the great jawbone axe held loosely in both hands. He ran, and she could see the labour that went into his breath.

The moment will come. We draw near to it. Kurguth must strike, before he passes beyond his strength. It is not the journey itself that tires him, but the death of his faith in Burak. He is betrayed, and it is killing him.

Ekrah put on a burst of speed, leaping down into the declivity of the path and racing ahead, as if for no more reason than to show Kurguth that he could do it.

'On, Preytaker!' Burak yelled. 'Scout this land, find me my fate!'

To Ekrah, the ground was as an open book to the city dwellers, to those who could scry marks on paper and make sense from their senseless jumble. As he ran, swiftly crossing the ground, it was as if he could see through their eyes when they had toiled up the path earlier that day. A child could read their signs, even the lowliest plains-runner. They had moved as if uncaring who would follow – great courage, or great stupidity.

Ekrah bounded forward, stopping here and there to draw his fingers over the scuff marks in the ground. He smelled the broken stems of weeds and noted the scarred rock where a weapon had scratched it in the passing. He found a buckle from a sandal, a scrap of oil cloth for cleaning a sword. They were careless, whoever he followed. He had the sense of them in his mind whenever he closed his eyes, red shapes that thundered clumsily through the landscape. He smelled smoke and ashes, he felt the warmth of flame. He heard harsh, discordant voices, and–

'Yes...' he muttered to himself. 'It cries, and is fed. The smell of her milk, the trail of the child's spoor, rich and rancid. Here is fate, but...'

He peered up the trail. There was more, a moment of savagery that sat like punctuation on a parchment. Two paths converged, but only one pressed on.

The Untamed Beasts had entered the Fangs from the western side, and they had scouted far along the mountains' backbone to pick up the trail. Burak had known there would be others hunting the child, and here was the proof.

Ekrah turned and shot back down the pathway, sprinting, his bare feet silent on the beaten ground.

They came to Ankhad's pyre near midday. Hysh was at its apex, boiling in the deep, blazing through the anchored clouds. The heat from the circling realm-spheres joined with the light of Hysh to strike the mountains like a hammer blow. Kurguth raised his hand to shade himself and peered down into the ashes as the rest of the warband came up, scuffing the blackened ground with their feet, dragging the tips of bone knives through the cinders. Nubs of charcoal, scraps of mouldering cloth, charred fragments of skull.

Ekrah stooped to pick up the shallow bowl of an occipital bone, its edges scorched, and took it over to Burak.

'Human,' he said. 'Only one was burned in the fire, as I can see it.'

'And if you didn't, no one else would,' Burak said. He took the shard of bone with respect, holding it in both hands and raising it to his nose. He inhaled deeply, his eyes fluttering closed.

'He fought, he fought well,' he said in a drowsy mumble. 'Power was in him, the strength of desperation. He fought for his son. There were many that he struck down, but too many in the end. He was overcome. And then the fires were on him. He burned, he burned away...'

Mayra looked fearfully at the broken ground around them. 'Does his spirit linger?' she asked. 'Those who are killed before they have their vengeance cannot leave a place, and they haunt it until the End.'

Burak touched the tip of his tongue to the shard's frayed edge. 'He does not linger here,' he said at last. 'His spirit is far gone, clear out of my sight.' He placed the fragment of skull back in the ashes. 'No one take this as a trophy or a totem,' he said. 'The bearer of these bones was a brave man, who fought for what he loved. Have peace in the hunting grounds, friend. May your vengeance follow you.'

Kurguth paused by the ashes as the warband moved on. He looked down at the piece of skull.

'Your child,' he whispered. 'The Bloodseer comes to kill it.' He leaned down and placed the tips of his fingers against the shard. 'I will do what I can to make sure that never happens.'

Those who dwelt in the shallow caves that were scratched from the foothills of the Fangs shrank back as the hunters passed, their armour battered but their blades bright. The freaks and deviants who scrabbled in the dust of the Bloodwind Spoil, hating their semblance of life and hating everything that crossed their paths, quailed and fell still as the warriors cut through their miserable freeholds. They closed their eyes and huddled under ragged blankets, waiting for the storm to break above them, but the storm never came. It moved off, across the mountains, and death came with it.

As dawn rose, the light caught glimpses of them amongst the rocks. Tirelessly they climbed. Their armour glinted dully, and if anyone had mustered the courage to look at them, they would have seen that beneath the filth and dust was the hint of something beautiful; a tarnished majesty, a suggestion of elegance and power and craftsmanship.

She was held in the middle of them, as if in a prison; the Blazing Lord, the priest, the older fighters with their scarred faces and burned hands, all surrounded her while she nursed the child and held it safe. Ahead of them, Aceria could see the vanguard of the force as it moved cautiously through the ruins, walking through the ancient sprawl along what must have been the main avenue in the far-gone days when it was still a place of life and civilisation. The high facades of ancient mansions still stood on either side of the street, their stones crumbled and pitted with the elements, and further back in the main body of the ruins Aceria could see the tumbled streets half choked with rubble, and great manses or temples still standing in the gloom. On her right as they entered the city in turn, Aceria could see that the streets went on for miles, curving to hug the contours of the mountain. She felt herself drawn to the wreckage that surrounded them. She imagined she saw the ghosts of old magisters and scholars, of realms-walkers and mages, discussing in earnest tones the latest philosophies. She saw a covered marketplace where men and women in bright clothing traded for goods of surpassing luxury, and saw children playing in the streets, enjoying boisterous games of marbles and catch crystal. There was a sense here of buried majesty that was beyond anything she had ever seen before. Even rumours of this place had not reached them, down in her huddled settlement at the base of the mountains. What had it been like? Would anyone ever come again to build such places in the Bloodwind Spoil? It was inconceivable.

She felt the priest's eyes on her and pretended not to notice. She shuffled slowly and directed her attention towards the baby. It was sleeping now, and the days it had spent drinking her milk had made it strong and healthy. Why keep the boy so hale, though, if the only end for it was death? But then, couldn't that be said for any of them, or for anything that lived? What was the point in struggling for sustenance if the track of your life led only to the grave? She thought of her own child, the long nights she had suckled her, her growing happiness as she had taken in the world around her. Then the ceremony before she was taken up into the mountains, Aceria's mingled tears of sadness and joy… She stifled a sob, clutched the baby tightly to her chest. What did any of this matter? Death was on the wind, blowing from the future and the past, and it cursed everything that ever lived.

Votremos crossed over to where Rakaros strode along the central avenue and took up his familiar place at the Blazing Lord's elbow.

'Everything has unfolded as you saw,' he said.

'There is a "but" there, priest – I can hear it, although the word doesn't pass your lips.'

Votremos laughed softly. 'You know me too well, my lord. It is not so much a "but" as an "and"… Everything goes well, according to our plans, and we near the moment of triumph. How much better would it be if we could inform the Temple of Cold Ashes, back in Aspiria? I'm sure they would welcome the news.'

'I'm sure they would. And yet the mission was given to me, to complete in any way I saw fit – I do not see why I must seek their approval.'

'Not their approval, but no harm could come from keeping the Most Holy appraised. The mission, lord, is to seek admittance to Archaon's legions, and – forgive me – we are not quite there yet.'

'We will be,' Rakaros said, in a voice that brooked no argument. 'On the other side of these mountains, the plains await, and across them lies the temple where the child must die. In the chill shadows of the Varanspire, the Three-Eyed King will see our commitment to his cause.'

'Indeed, lord,' Votremos said. He gave his short, accustomed bow. 'Although the question is immaterial with our stores of rage-rock gone, the blessed aqthracite. We cannot see through the flames to them now. I wonder,' he said disingenuously, 'whether it was wise to use the last of it when burning the child's father...?'

'You try me sometimes, Votremos,' the Blazing Lord said. 'I value your counsel, but do not press me beyond the limits of my patience.'

'I never would,' the priest said – and he thought, *It is a patience that has no limits, because it has no beginnings...* But the Blazing Lord could only understand the holy flames in the moment of their apotheosis. For the Inferno Priest, the knowledge was more complete. Rakaros saw fire and blood, triumph and exultation, but Votremos was cursed to see the way the slow flame took hold, the growing conflagration, and then the sad smothering when there was nothing left to burn. He saw their mission in the round, whereas Rakaros merely saw the target.

Votremos withdrew. And to think that in private he had argued with the Most Holy, the high priest back in the Temple of Cold Ashes. Votremos had tried to convince the high priest that he shouldn't accept Rakaros' claim. It was not right for a crusade of such sacred purpose to be taken because it had been demanded, Votremos had argued. Rakaros' very zeal disqualified him. To be humble and penitent was a more suitable quality, surely? To glow with a subtle, inner fire.

But the Most Holy had overruled him. They would be heading not across the realm of Aqshy to do battle with the feeble forces of Order but to the seat of Archaon's domain, the Eightpoints itself. This was no place for the humble and the penitent, the Most Holy had said, for they would surely die. Rakaros' claim was accepted, and Votremos had accompanied him, trying to temper his pride where he could. Perhaps he was right? The mission was his to complete, and by all intents and purposes he was on the verge of completing it. What mattered pride? What mattered anything but the victory to come?

A cry ahead drew the priest's mind back to the world in front of him. There at the end of the avenue, where the ruined city clutched the edge of a steep drop down into a mist-filled gorge, Katastrian stood and gestured, shouting to get their attention. On the left, a narrow defile led on towards the mountain's flank, which rose in sheer heights above the old city, dwarfing it. The way seemed blocked. From the choked streets, Katastrian turned around to bellow something back down the shattered avenue.

'Perhaps a path has been discovered?' Votremos mused. 'I don't see how else we can manage down that crevasse, especially not with the child.'

'A way will be found,' Rakaros said.

Katastrian raised his axe high in one hand and pointed at the gorge – but then, turning, he stared up into the ruined battlements of the city walls, which stretched steeply above him. Votremos stopped, his arm out-thrust.

'Wait, my lord,' he said.

'What is it, priest?' Rakaros said. He paused, and around him the initiates paused too. There was a moment of silence and antici-pation, both groups of Scions standing there a hundred yards apart, at either end of the avenue, just waiting to see what would happen. Katastrian looked up into the ruins on his right, where the facades of those ancient mansions stared down at him, their empty windows like unseeing eyes. He turned and mouthed some-thing neither Votremos nor Rakaros could hear. He started to run, shouting unintelligibly, and then, in a roaring crescendo of noise, like an avalanche blasting down a hillside, the ruins on either side began to crumble and collapse. Ancient stones, upright for thou-sands of years, trickled from their moorings, and as one stone fell, so it brought down others, and yet more others – and in moments the entire edifice of the city on either side had folded in on itself and crushed the warriors who, belatedly, had tried to sprint to safety along the avenue.

A great plume of dust was thrown up into the air, billowing back down the street towards the remaining Scions. Votremos threw up his arms and turned his head into the folds of his cloak, while Rakaros crouched and turned his back on it, coughing uncontrol-lably. Initiates scattered, shouting in dismay, and the shattering violence of the collapse thundered in their ears until they were nearly deafened.

Slowly the cloud of dust cleared, like a sandstorm blown away on the wind. Rakaros, choking, got to his feet. Where the avenue had been was now a pile of stone and rock, and here and there he could see the spattered remains of those in the vanguard who had tried to escape.

'My… my lord, that's near half our forces!' Votremos stuttered as he dusted himself off. 'Xoloxes, Katastrian… At a stroke, we're–'

'There!' Rakaros pointed. Votremos followed his direction and could see stones dislodge at the head of the pile. An arm emerged, a hand bearing a massive two-handed axe. Slowly Katastrian dragged himself from the ruins, first one arm, then his other arm and his head, his chest. Blood was running down his face, but his eyes burned as bright as ever, caustic with a maddened fury.

'To him,' Rakaros said. 'Give him help!'

A handful of initiates sprinted down the track, but before they could reach the stricken champion the dust began to clear around him. Standing above Katastrian on the piled stones was a lone figure, a sword in hand, a mailed cloak thrown over one shoulder. He was wearing a high-plumed helmet, and the metal glowed with a faint trace of venomous green.

'Well met, Lord Rakaros,' he called down the ruined avenue, and in one stroke he severed Katastrian's head. It tumbled down the stones. 'Well met, once more.'

'*Silenthis*,' the Blazing Lord whispered. Despite himself, a slow smile crept across his lips. He drew his sword, and the blade ignited with a tendril of crimson flame.

Ashrath raised his own sword in a duellist's salute, the blade tapped to the cross guard of his helmet. He stepped down from the pile of stones.

'Let us finish this,' he said, and charged.

CHAPTER NINE

CONVERGENCE

For the briefest moment, Ashrath saw uncertainty in the Blazing Lord's eyes; it was all the encouragement he needed. At last, Ashrath and the Splintered Fang would have their revenge.

Rakaros met him blade to blade, his fiery broadsword casting off a cloak of sparks as Ashrath's swing struck down. The Blazing Lord counter-attacked immediately, turning the defensive strike into a sudden jab and then hacking the blade with brute force to push the young Trueblood back.

'Fate seems to have granted you a second chance, snake-worshipper,' he rumbled. 'Try not to waste it this time.'

'Have no fear, Rakaros – I won't. I look forward to mounting your head on a spike at our temple gates, when we take it back from you.'

The Blazing Lord laughed and redoubled his attack.

It was all Ashrath could do to ward off his blows. The Way of the Splintered Fang was sinuous, indirect, trading brute force for speed and skill. Their poison blades meant the merest scratch was often enough to bring an opponent down, no matter their size, but as Ashrath tumbled and ducked, skipping nimbly over the loose stones of the broken avenue, he couldn't find the gap he needed in Rakaros' defence. For his size and the unwieldy nature of his great two-handed sword, he fought with all the dexterity of an expert fencer. Parry and riposte were followed up with huge, crunching swings, the Blazing Lord using the edge of his blade like an axeman chopping wood. A few minutes into a fight that Ashrath had hoped would be over by now, he felt himself beginning to flag. He remembered their first fight, the bitter duel in the corridors of their stolen temple, and the cold realisation crept up on him again – Rakaros was going to win.

It was a near-fatal mistake, to feel doubt in the middle of a fight. Ashrath steeled himself and started to back up, drawing closer to the ruins in the hope that the bigger man would lose his footing on the uneven flagstones, or even that he could escape up into the complex of arches and walkways and gain the advantage of higher ground. For the first time, he began to sweat.

Around them the two warbands clashed in a mad clangour of steel. Scions were spitted on pale blades; Splintered Fang were beaten into the dust with flails and short swords. It was a mess of sprawling violence, the molten fury of one meeting the serpentine agility of the other. Here and there, members of the Burned Hand who had been too slow to dodge a cut felt their blood curdling in their veins from Splintered Fang venom. Some bent double to spew out their liquifying organs in gouts of black slime, while others shuddered in bone-breaking seizures, their teeth shattering as their jaws clamped shut. Elsewhere, clearbloods howled in agony as they burst into flame, their skin crackling, their lungs scorched by the superheated air. Some took the fight upwards, into the ruins, duelling amongst the upper stories and charging across wooden walkways to knock their opponents onto the spiked barricades far below. The ruins rang with groans and bellowed war cries, with the frenzied clatter of weapons.

As Ashrath warded off each strike from the Blazing Lord's burning sword, he risked a glimpse at the mayhem around him. Despite the desperate defence of the Burned Hand, it was clear that the Horned Krait were winning. Ashrath's bare dozen fighters had evened the odds in moments, and the Scions of the Flame had been caught entirely off guard. It was a maelstrom, a chaotic carnival of bloodshed and death.

But where in Nagendra's name is the damned child?

The memory of that previous defeat burned in Ashrath's mind as he fought. He knew the Blazing Lord was stronger, more brutal, seemingly tireless. As he parried and duelled, still backing away, he tried to read the pattern of blows that Rakaros was unleashing on him. It was pure offence, a blistering assault that was almost impossible to defend against.

In desperation as much as anything, Ashrath lashed out and saw the Blazing Lord strike his blow aside. And yet, he thought, Rakaros' movement had seemed clumsy. It had felt more like a reflex than anything that had been learned in proper training. Ashrath feinted left and swung low, and as Rakaros blocked the strike he swept his sword up as if he intended to slash the Blazing Lord's face. Rakaros made the expected defence, stepping with his weight on his right foot and pivoting as he drew the great sword up to meet Ashrath's blade. The Trueblood tried again, feinting right this time, and again Rakaros fell into the accustomed defence. For the first time in the fight, Ashrath felt something like hope. Rakaros was nigh unstoppable in attack, but his skills as a warrior were perhaps his undoing when forced onto the back foot, where he had only a limited repertoire on which to draw. For Ashrath, schooled in the flowing, serpentine methods of the Splintered Fang, defence was as much a part of swordplay as assault. For

Rakaros, though, it was mere afterthought; rarely did he expect to be on the losing side in any duel.

'Something amuses you, serpent-lover?' Rakaros muttered.

'Indeed.' Ashrath grinned. 'I was picturing the image of your corpse once I have killed you.'

He slashed at Rakaros with sudden fury, his sword a streak of silver light, but the blow was yet another feint. As Rakaros swept his greatsword up to meet it, Ashrath stepped inside his guard and slammed his shoulder into the Blazing Lord's chest. Rakaros stumbled backwards, and although he was quick to recover, the opening was enough for Ashrath to draw a line of blood from his unprotected arm. His grunt of pain was the purest satisfaction.

It was only a moment of relief though. Fire shone in his eyes as Rakaros came on, the blood dripping down his arm, the greatsword held in a low grip almost as an afterthought. His other hand was balled into a fist, as if he were going to beat the life from Ashrath with his bare hands.

Again, the Trueblood was forced back. Almost in despair he parried the relentless strikes, and in moments his arm was numb with the force of each blow.

'What does the image of my corpse look like now?' Rakaros laughed. 'Does it still amuse you? Or perhaps you mistake it for your own.'

It was only the crumbling span of an archway that prevented the next blow from taking off Ashrath's head. Rakaros' sword bit deep into the masonry, spitting a spray of dust into Ashrath's eyes. He hissed and swung blind, but then the Blazing Lord's great fist came crashing into the side of his helmet, knocking him to the ground. He spat blood and raised his sword to block the killing blow.

Curse you, Rakaros! Curse you down to the very lowest pit of Shyish!

He cringed as he stared up into his death – Rakaros, standing triumphant above him, sword raised.

But the blow never came. There was a blaze of golden light, a crackling explosion as something like a lightning bolt struck the ground between them. Rakaros flew backwards, crashing into the rubble. Scrambling to his feet, ready to sell his life as dearly as he could, Ashrath looked wildly around. He could see bodies tumble from the ruins on the other side of the avenue, could hear screams and bellowed war cries. There was a flash of steel, a glint of dull armour, and another lightning bolt crackled into the wall above his head, scorching the stone.

'*No!*' Rakaros shouted as he gained his feet. His face was seared with burns, and Ashrath was shocked to see something like fear in his eyes. 'Scions!' he screamed. 'Fall back! Defend yourselves!'

Ashrath took cover as Rakaros retreated into the ruins, crouching behind a notched pillar and peering through the rusted metal gate in its side. He stared, and all the doubts he had felt in the fight with Rakaros seemed like hard certainty compared to what he felt now. He looked, and he couldn't believe what he saw.

They came like something out of myth or legend, charging into the flank of the clashing warbands. They appeared from nowhere; suddenly, the ruins on the other side of the avenue were their hunting ground, and they killed at pace. Each warrior was easily seven feet tall, armoured in a massive suit of pale cream warplate that was tarnished with the dust and misery of the Spoil. They held short swords with viciously sharp blades or short-hafted axes, and most of them bore brutal, compact crossbows that shot dazzling shards of light. Each lightning bolt punched through human flesh with ease. They had animal-skin cloaks thrown back over their shoulders, roughened-leather kit bags, grappling hooks, rope, and despite their size they moved with a speed and fluidity that rivalled the Splintered Fang. It was their faces that disturbed Ashrath the most, though. Entirely enclosed in war helms, each was a vacant, emotionless mask. He looked, but he couldn't see a trace of pity or even anger behind those black, hollow eyes. Something in him rebelled from the sight.

Stormcast Eternals… He had heard the rumours, had even spoken with those who claimed to have seen them. Back in Ghyran all knew the legends of an age gone by, of how the Everqueen was rescued by Sigmar's mighty Stormhosts. But since passing from Invidia's forbidding jungles to the heart of Chaos in the Mortal Realms, Ashrath had never thought to see one for himself. For the champions of Order to have made the journey to a place where the very stones on the ground were saturated with the dark energies of Chaos… That made them bolder and more dangerous than he could possibly have imagined.

They sprinted through the ruins, leaping gaps, spinning and hacking and slashing, pausing only to take snapshots with their crossbows. Ashrath leapt from cover and ran deeper into the ruins. He saw Essiltha frantically pirouetting away from one of the Stormcast warriors, her needle blades a blur as she blocked stroke after stroke. He had time to smile at her obvious distress, but not enough time to watch the outcome of the fight. On Ashrath ran, ducking the sharp hiss-crack of lightning bolts, somersaulting over downed Scions and Splintered Fang alike. He slid to the ground and stabbed up as one Scion tried to cut him down, earning himself a face full of the Scion's blood. The skirmish had become an open battle, a furious tangle of swords and axes, of whips and throwing knives and panicked screams.

He scurried around a corner, some blind instinct making him throw himself to the ground just in time to avoid the lashing swing of a Scion's flail. Ashrath leapt up and struck back, but then another Scion appeared on his right side. Warily he circled round. He pulled his dagger from his belt with his left hand, and the knife gleamed with dark poisons.

'On this blade is the Kiss of the Krait – do you know what that will do to you?' he said. 'Imagine what happens to a corpse when it's left out in the sun for a few days. And now imagine that happening to your bodies in the next ten seconds...'

The two Burned Hand fighters exchanged glances, and the instant their eyes were off him Ashrath spun and slashed left. The dagger caught one Scion high on the shoulder, notching the skin through his ripped tunic. He gibbered and howled in a peeling crescendo, thrashing about in the dust as the necrotising venoms rippled through his flesh. Blackened and as soft as wax, it bubbled and split and soughed off his bones in an acrid spume. The other Scion retched, although he had presence of mind enough to keep up his sword. Ashrath would have enjoyed making this last, but he didn't have the time – he needed to rally the warband before they were all killed.

He was about to feint right and flick his blade up into the Scion's throat when the fighter's head was suddenly enveloped in a thrashing hood of scaled green – Kathenga, snapping forward from behind and plunging the curled talons of its teeth deep into the Scion's eyes, injecting its coruscating venoms directly into his brain. So complete was the fighter's agony that his scream was soundless; his mouth stretched open like it would split, and after a moment his dissolving brains were trickling down his face.

'The battle goes against us,' Ma'sulthis said as the dead Scion collapsed to the ground. 'We need to regroup.'

'It goes against all of us,' Ashrath said. He stared at the chaos on the avenue. He couldn't see Essiltha, but there were still scattered groups of Splintered Fang trading blows with the fire-worshippers and desperately defending themselves against the Stormcasts. 'Is there any sign of the child?'

'None that I have seen.'

'We need to find it, and find it fast. Gather up who you can, send them round the flanks – don't stand and fight, we can't win that way. Find the child, do you understand? Find it!'

'It will be done. Come, Kathenga. Leave your feast for when this is over.'

Ma'sulthis scooped up the great snake and wrapped it around his shoulders. He disappeared into the shadows, working his way around to the end of the avenue. Ashrath gathered his breath, crouching down amidst shattered stone and rusted metal.

When this is over, he thought, *even if we win, there won't be much of a warband left to command...*

He struck down another of the venomous clearbloods, chopping his blade in one smooth motion to cut straight through her neck and shoulder, splitting her to the navel. The two disjointed halves of the Splintered Fang fighter wavered in a geyser of blood and then tipped queasily to each side.

There were too many of them. They emerged from the cracks in the ruins, slithered from the upper storeys and dropped down behind and in front of him. Rakaros swallowed his rage. Individually these foes were beneath contempt, but in concert they could easily swarm him. So far none of them had managed to strike him with their poisoned weapons, but no matter how many he bludgeoned and eviscerated, more seemed to take their place. At the same time, he was painfully aware of the Stormcast Eternals on the fringes of the fight, the tireless hunters who had shattered each warband like a thunderstorm. Each glimpse he had of them as they cut and run and leapt made him feel as if his eyes were going to burn out of his head. That they should be here, that they should be *here* in the Bloodwind Spoil, in the Eightpoints, in the realm of the Three-Eyed King and in defiance of the Ever-Raging

Flame, was a blasphemy he couldn't countenance. He yearned to strike at them, to pierce that pale, encrusted armour with his holy blade and send them streaking back to their cowardly god – cringing Sigmar, cowering in far Azyr...

But everywhere he turned, these damned snake-worshippers hounded his steps, jabbing with their daggers, slashing with their knives, snapping barbed whips at his face. He felt himself slowly pushed back into the ruins, his sandalled feet crunching over fragments of stone. Constricted by the crumbling walls, each swing of his sword met the ancient brick as many times as it met flesh and bone.

Rakaros threw back his head and roared with anger. He could see Votremos on the other side of the avenue, incandescent, his staff like a pillar of living flame as it boiled a Stormcast hunter in its armour, until the armour cracked apart and a lance of lightning went streaking up into the aether. Rakaros bulled forward and cleaved one of his opponents in two, turning on the backswing to direct even more force into a high, swinging arc that tumbled two heads to his feet. He felt his lips charred with fire, his hands dusty with soot, and his tongue was a tongue of flame. More died under his sword, and yet more, but still they came, and still they cut and stabbed, and sheer weight of numbers meant that sooner or later a blade was going to make it through. Breathing hard, the Blazing Lord held his sword low in a fool's guard, inviting attack, conserving his energy and waiting to make a counter-cut. He was knee-deep in bodies, and there was little space for manoeuvre.

That it should come to this, backed into a corner by these scum...

The pain lanced up from his ankle, like a sliver of ice, so cold it made him gasp. He looked down in time to see a streak of red coiling its way between a crack in the stones, the snake retreating after spearing him with its venom. And now the cold was creeping up his leg like a vine, twisting and reaching higher, sending spears of agony into his chest, his heart. Rakaros staggered back, and then a knife went in, and another. He lashed out with the hilt of his sword, felt another blade slide smoothly across his neck, parting the skin. He shouted incoherently, stumbling to the ground, desperately trying to hold his sword up, seeing the flame flicker out and die on the blackened blade. Another knife, another...

He was down on his back, leaning against the bodies of those he had killed as if calmly lying down to sleep. The fighters of the Splintered Fang surrounded him, their weapons sharp and bright. He held out a hand. Where were his Scions, where was Votremos? Poor Katastrian, beheaded in the ruins... Xoloxes, crushed, his flame gone out at last. And where was the child?

'You dare... to challenge *me!*' he tried to say, but the words died on his lips. The blades were raised, and–

Lightning, falling in bursts, like ruined stars. A spray of red crystals fell like rain, blood cauterised in the lightning storm, and then the bodies were on him, smothering him, blackened holes in their chests, their heads evaporated by the scouring bolts. Rakaros whispered as the dead bodies fell – praying or begging, he couldn't say. He held out his hand. He felt his heart stutter and fall still in his chest as the poisons wrapped their coils around it.

Where is the child... Where is he... Where...

And then he felt nothing at all.

Since the Scions of the Flame had burned her village, Aceria had found herself plunged into moments of fear and horror so foul she didn't think they could be surpassed. From the attack of the beastmen by their stained altar, to the sick and cloying attention of the Inferno Priest as he monitored the baby, every day had revealed a new facet of her nightmare. But this swirling, chaotic skirmish amongst the ruins scared her more than anything since Rakaros and his Burned Hand had first marched into her settlement.

When the ruined walls had fallen, smothering half of the Scions in an instant, Aceria had gasped with what she was surprised to find was joy. There he went, the champion with his monstrous axe, crushed by an avalanche of stone and rock. And when Katastrian struggled out of the wreckage, Aceria looked on, incredulous, as the young warrior with the great plumed helmet and the gleaming silver mail took his head clean off with a mere flick of his wrist. In the blink of an eye, the bars of her cage seemed to widen. A key had turned in the lock, and although Aceria wasn't naïve enough to think that these new figures would offer her freedom or escape, she grasped eagerly at what they did offer – opportunity.

Dimly she was aware of Rakaros and the young warrior coming together in a clash of swords, but she soon left their duel behind. As the Scions surged forward, and as their rivals leapt up to meet them, Aceria bolted for the safety of the overhanging archways to her right. She sprawled behind a pillar, arms tight around the baby as he shifted and wriggled against her chest. She felt the knife under her cloak, reassured by its weighty presence.

'Hush, child, quiet now – let me think.'

Peering from around the pillar, she saw members of the Burned Hand die under the blades of the Splintered Fang. Blood sprayed freely, and the air took on a pungent, coppery taste as it spattered in the dust. Keeping her head down, she tried to hurry through the broken stones and head further down the avenue, back to the narrow trail that had led them up to the ruins in the first place.

A body slammed to the ground in front of her, kicking up a plume of dust – one of the rival band, helmetless, his hands scrabbling for a dagger in his belt. He snarled with terrified rage, and then one of the Burned Hand threw herself on top of him and stabbed him in the throat. Aceria ran left, deeper into the ruins, hardly heeding her direction. Bloody shadows flitted along the walkways above her. Further on, a dead eye gazed down unseeing at her through a gap in the slatted wood, where a ruined face leaked blood onto the flagstones of what had once been an elegant forecourt. For one dislocated moment, as she cowered in her hiding place, Aceria wondered what those far-off days must have been like. Had the people who lived back then ever imagined, even in their most fevered nightmares, that the colonnades and cloisters of their beautiful city would one day ring with the bestial war cries of the cut-throats and bandits who fought here now?

Black shapes darted past the open space ahead of her. She shrank back. Off to her right she could see a rough-hewn ladder leading up to a teetering platform, and then a narrow walkway that led to a short drop on the other side of a pile of stones. Far above, bright Hysh was drowsing over to the north, and the light was slowly changing. She could hide, keep her head down, wait for both warbands to hack each other to pieces and then escape when it was dark. It would work, she knew it would. Although she thought no further than that pile of stones, Aceria knew that her only chance of survival was to run with the baby and hide herself in the deepest and most obscure parts of the Bloodwind Spoil, so none of them would find her – or him – ever again.

'I will not give you up,' she whispered to the child. 'They won't have you, I promise.'

In faint shards and brief flashes, while she waited for the way ahead to clear, she had time to picture herself and the baby in something like peace. In some hidden hollow or insignificant slum, she would raise him and take care of him, and he would become strong, able to defend himself. She would look after him until he could look after her. They would be inseparable, and in his growing strength and purpose she would somehow atone for all the misery and mistakes of her life so far – the child she had given up to the Horned Ones and their rancid altar, high in the mountains... their banners of cured skin...

'Give him to me, girl,' a voice hissed behind her.

He seemed to glide over the rubble, a black hood shadowing most of his face, the rest of it covered by a dull bronze mask in the shape of a snake's skull. Around his shoulders, sliding with deadly patience, an enormous serpent with glittering yellow eyes swung its head. The hooded man reached out for her, for the baby at her chest. Aceria pressed herself against the stone, fear flooding her system like a poison, paralysing her. The swaying head of the monstrous snake followed her every move, hypnotically. She stared into its crystalline eyes, saw herself refracted in a hundred dancing shards deep in the core of each bulging orb, and although every fibre of her being wanted to run, she couldn't move. Sweat streaked down her forehead. At her breast the baby started crying. She was trapped, held prisoner by the serpent's petrifying gaze.

'This will be over for you soon,' the man said. 'A small, sharp pain, and then you shall know peace, I promise. It is what you want, isn't it, more than anything? Peace... the chance to rest... to rest at last...'

Her hands moved of their own volition. Her fingers plucked like dead things at the knots of the sling, and even the baby's cries seemed to come from some unimaginable distance.

'Peace... yes,' she said, and the snake swayed closer. Its eyes were a thousand mirrors casting back her reflected soul, and each splinter of her life danced madly in the glass. The pain of hunger, the pain of beatings and raids, the pain of childbirth, the pain of giving that child to the beasts of the high mountains, the indescribable pain of seeing what those beasts had done... It had all been pain, every second of it. She stumbled through a land built on pain, where it leached into the very soil and made of the air a caustic fume. All she wanted in that moment, as the battle faded to a dim recollection of distant cries, was for it to be over at last. She would give anything, anything at all.

With a blinding flash of light, the snake's blunt head erupted into a plume of red mist. The cauterised neck reared back, its stump a weeping scab, and it thrashed like a vine in a hurricane. Aceria, freed from the transfixing gaze of its yellow eyes, wiped its blood from her face.

'Kathenga!' the hooded man screamed, and the agony in his voice was more profound than Aceria would have believed possible. Weeping, wrenching the snake mask from his face, he cradled the stump in his arms and wept bitter tears. 'Kathenga, my son...'

He didn't even flinch as the axe came down. Aceria reared back as an armoured demi-god followed up his blinding shot with a brutal swing of his weapon, burying it in the hooded man's face. He crumpled into a bloody ruin.

Aceria stood there, transfixed, as if the snake had still been staring at her. The light was blocked by the figure's massive shoulders, and its pauldrons were draped in the reeking skins of some plains beast. In one hand it held a bulky crossbow, and in the other it wielded its blood-stained axe. Aceria looked up into a pale, blank mask devoid of mercy. Silently, the dead-eyed thing looked back at her, and under the unbearable weight of its gaze Aceria thought the last thin sinews of her sanity were going to snap. Slowly, it hooked its crossbow to its belt and reached for her, fingers stretched wide, the armoured gauntlet spattered with blood–

No, she realised. Not for her at all, but for the child which trembled in her arms.

'Please,' she whispered to its pitiless, silent face. 'He is all I have.'

Its attention snapped away from her, and its axe whipped up to block a rapier thrust that came streaking out of the shadows. Two of the snake-worshippers leapt and jabbed their knives down, the blades screeching off the heavy armour. The warrior hacked back at them, and then Aceria was running, her head clear. The open ground ahead was empty, and like a rabbit bolting from cover she whipped across the flagstones and reached the ladder.

She tightened the straps of the sling, made sure the baby was secure and put her hands to the rungs. She could hear the frenzied sounds of men and women dying behind her, could hear the blistering hiss-crack of the armoured warriors' crossbows, could even hear the bellowed war cry of Rakaros, the Blazing Lord, as he killed or was killed in turn. She ignored it all. Up she climbed, taking care not to knock the baby's head against the rungs, onwards to something like safety.

Halfway up she felt a circlet of fire around her ankle. She shrieked in pain and looked down to see Votremos, the Inferno Priest, grinning maniacally through the slats at her, his hand grasping her foot.

'Don't think you can escape me so easily, you filthy peasant!' he cackled.

She fell, crashing to the ground on her back, all the wind knocked out of her. Votremos limped round to her, his staff gone, a ragged slash across his face. Still his cruel eyes glowed with their flecks of fire, and his spittle burned against her skin as he clambered over her.

'Give me the child!' he roared. 'The Ever-Raging Flame is not done with either of you yet! Give him to me!'

'You want him?' Aceria wept, beyond herself. 'Then take him! Take him, and damn all of you for the murdering scum you are!'

She wrenched the sling from her shoulders, tumbling the baby into Votremos' lap. The child cried out. The priest looked dumbly at her, confusion moving like pain across his face. He held the baby in his hands, looking down at him as if unable to believe that Aceria had given him up so easily or that he would now have to care for him until his evil schemes were complete.

'Such a small thing,' Votremos said. 'Innocent – and yet doomed to die.'

He looked up at her, just as she thrust his borrowed dagger into his eye.

'Let me give you back your knife,' she hissed.

The priest reeled back with a wordless howl. She snatched the baby from his lap and laid him carefully on the ground, and as Votremos thrashed in agony she drew out the blade from his smoking skull and stabbed it down, again and again, straight into his foul and brooding heart.

The blade still quivered in his body as she hurried on with the child. She had done it. Despite everything that had happened, she couldn't help but smile.

She was free.

They heard the fighting long before they reached the top, climbing the last few feet of rock to take up positions on the outskirts of the ruins. Burak chuckled and muttered to himself, his eyes scanning the scene that lay before them with a hunter's expert appraisal.

'Now, look there!' he whispered. He pointed to a demolished manse on the left-hand side of the avenue, its gate a rusted tangle of scrap and its cloistered walkway no more than a few bare pillars jutting from the rugged earth. Suddenly, out of the darkness came a dozen armoured giants swinging axes and slicing swords, unleashing a pitiless barrage of lightning bolts from their crossbows. Hidden by the craggy ridge, the Untamed Beasts watched these ironclad warriors in their animal skins and uncannily impassive face masks cut through the warring bands with brutal precision.

'You were right,' Kurguth admitted. He felt Mayra tense beside him, ignored Ekrah's barked laugh. 'We were being followed.'

They had turned from the path early the day before, on Burak's insistence. Collapsing to the ground, his mouth frothing with spit and his eyes rolling in his head, the Heart-eater had ridden the spirit trail with the scent of danger in his nose.

'They come!' he had gibbered. 'With holy blades and bloody vengeance, they come!'

'Who?' Kurguth had demanded. 'What do you see?'

He had cradled the Bloodseer's head in his lap, wiping his face clear of the sweat that poured freely down it. So many times he had done this when they were children, standing over Burak while the sight was on him, fighting off those bitter rivals from other tribes who mocked him or would seek to do him harm.

Burak, my old friend, the visions are getting worse. They are hollowing you to the core.

In time, his spirit had resettled into his body. His breathing had grown less heavy, and his eyes had flickered into life again. Kurguth had helped him up.

'Kurguth, First Fang – oldest of my companions,' Burak had whispered, as if seeing him for the first time. 'Mayra, Beastspeaker... mate of Kurguth, your children will be like wolves to men.' He had laughed, throaty and hoarse, and fixed them with that keen, cunning glare that always made Kurguth reach for his axe. 'I see it all,' he had said.

'Who comes, Burak?' Kurguth asked. 'Who did you see?'

Burak had looked back down the trail, its twists and turns like the coils of a snake unravelling down the mountainside. 'Those who would do us harm, who would take the child for their own ends... ones not of the Spoil, but of high and blinding Azyr...'

He looked up into the blistering sky and was silent.

'Now,' he said. 'Let not the hunters become the hunted. Leave the trail, let us take the unexpected path around the side of the mountain. Come, my Split-Tongue Tribe, follow your Heart-eater in the glory of the hunt!'

They had scaled the side of the mountain at the point where the path veered off to the right, finding in the rough stone and clumps of bitter weeds enough purchase to make their way around and out of sight. Up they had gone in the staggering heat, hand over hand, weapons slung to their backs and fingers trembling on the rock. Mayra, as agile as a two-headed mange-goat, leapt from point to point, clawing her way to the top. Kurguth, the muscles in his arms screaming with the effort, had to drag his bulk up every inch of the cliff, and he didn't dare look down. The wind had coursed over him, plucking at his animal skins, threatening to tear the helmet from his head. And then, a bare few feet from the cusp, they had heard the unmistakable sound of battle.

'Burak the Bloodseer sees all!' the Heart-eater said now. 'Long have I felt the weight of these armoured ones on my spirit-sense. Even we can't outrun them for long, my brothers and sisters, for they never tire and they will never give up. A great purpose lies heavy on their hearts. But if we can't outrun them, we can at least lead them where we want them to go.'

'They have hearts?' Mayra questioned. 'They look more like... like...' She lacked the words and snorted with frustration.

'They have hearts, and blood, and flesh,' Burak said. 'Sigmar the Craven's finest warriors, it is said. They are men and women, of a kind...'

Mayra uncoiled her whip. 'Then let us kill them, and cut the hearts out of their metal suits,' she snarled. 'They have dared to hunt us, and the sight of them offends me!'

'Hold fast, my Beastspeaker,' Burak hushed. 'To be hunted is no fine thing for an Untamed Beast. But it is not us they truly hunt, but what we hunt in turn. See,' he said, pointing again. 'Tell me what your eyes understand.'

As Burak fixed the two-clawed dagger-fist to his hand and unsheathed his great jawbone axe, Kurguth followed his directions. He saw a young woman reel back from a hooded figure, one of the Splintered Fang, far off amongst the ruins on their right.

'I see her,' Mayra said.

Kurguth swallowed. 'She has… she has the child.'

They watched as the hooded figure was cut down by one of the armoured giants, whose vacant face plate was as expressionless as a skull.

'Now it is time for us to play our part,' Burak said. 'Ekrah, with me. We will go hunting for the child through the ruins. Kurguth, Mayra, lead half the warband around the left-hand flank, head towards the ravine and guard our escape. Stick to the shadows and the fallen stones, avoid fighting where you can. Prey must be postponed, my brothers and sisters – the Mountain's Throat is near.' He pointed again to a cleft in the rock far over to the left of the skirmish ground, where the line of the gorge met the fold of the cliff. 'That is where we will find our path – I have seen it. Keep the way clear and we will be with you soon, bearing the greatest prize in the Bloodwind Spoil.'

Burak, Ekrah and half a dozen plains-runners scrambled over the edge of the rock and ran, hunched over, from cover to cover. They disappeared into the ruined city.

'Come,' Kurguth said. Mayra held his arm and glared at him. 'Now is not the time,' he said roughly. 'Let us wait and see where this Mountain's Throat leads, and then the decision will be made.'

He glanced at the mayhem before him – the spinning blades, the furious clash of weapons, the split and mutilated bodies littering the ground. Far off, a spear of lightning stabbed up into the bleak, prismatic sky.

'Spirits watch over me,' he muttered. 'Be my guide.'

He was sprinting along a ladder that had been slung flat between the broken corbels of some decaying edifice, and beneath him, running in the shadow that it cast, was the hulking form of one of those armoured monstrosities. It stared up at him, and Ashrath stopped suddenly, flipping down onto a lower platform and doubling back on himself.

'Nagendra curse you!' he shouted.

It was still following him. It had his scent, and it wouldn't give up.

He leapt to grab the jutting prow of a gargoyle high overhead, swinging his weight forward and managing to reach the cornice above it. Groaning, his arms like water, he hauled himself up and over. A lightning bolt seared up from below, singeing his shoulder.

'Ah! Nagendra curse *all* of you, you vicious–'

Another bolt slammed into the stone at his feet, scorching it black. On he ran, and when he looked back over his shoulder his heart sank like a lead weight in his chest. It had climbed up after him. It was still coming.

He had his sword in his hand. He sheathed it awkwardly at his hip, then tucked and rolled from the edge of the cornice to fall two storeys down onto the ladder he had just left, crashing through it, spinning wildly and finally coming to rest in a heap at the bottom. He coughed and rolled onto his back. Dust fell around him like soft rain, and the air was bruised with lines and spirals of black. Everything seemed very far away. He looked up into a slice of sky framed by the building's edge, high above him, and for a moment he was content just to lie there gathering his breath, letting the muscles in his legs spasm and contract.

He closed his eyes.

When he opened them, the Stormcast warrior was standing there in silhouette, poised on the edge of the ruin above.

'Scales of Nagendra!' Ashrath cursed. 'Don't you ever tire?'

Scrabbling through the wreckage, he ran across the avenue on wobbling legs, his chest heaving. He followed the line of the gorge on his right-hand side, which stretched bottomless like some vast and ravenous maw down to the Fangs' lowest foothills, thousands of feet below. Scions of the Flame slew Splintered Fang around him, and Splintered Fang slew Scions of the Flame. The ground was sticky with spilled blood. He drew his sword, slashed a clumsy parry against a blow that came out of nowhere, tripped to the ground, rolled, retched up a string of saliva, felt the burn of venom retreating from his veins, tripped again. He looked around; it was still coming.

'Come *on* then!' he roared, with the last of his breath. He stood his ground with his sword in a tail guard, resting on its tip as much as holding it ready. 'Fight me! Fight me and take my name back with you to your feeble god, with all the blessings of Nagendra! I am Ashrath Silenthis, Trueblood of the Horned Krait, and I will cut you down or die in the attempt!'

It came on with all the power of the storm, crashing over the ground towards him. So massive was the warrior that it blocked out the light, and it seemed to glow with an inner fire, dazzling and opaque. Ashrath flinched in horror from it, only just managing to raise his sword in defence. The Stormcast knocked him flat with one blow of its axe. Ashrath rolled to the very edge of the gorge, his arm aching from blocking the strike. He looked down into the abyss, and the wind whistled up from the depths, cold and furious.

His sword was on the ground by the Stormcast's feet. It said not a word as it kicked the blade back to him.

'You will come to regret that,' Ashrath said, his voice shaking as he got to his feet. He picked up the sword. He could barely lift it. 'Few who give Ashrath Silenthis a second chance live to give him a third, let me tell you.'

Where was his warband? Where was Ma'sulthis, and Essiltha, curse her a thousand times? He stood on the very edge of the precipice. The Stormcast warrior could push him off with its little finger.

Some last vestige of his arrogance came surging back into his blood. As the venoms faded from his system, leaving only weakness and doubt, the deeper lust for glory, which had wrapped its tendrils around his heart for as long as he could remember, lent strength to his sword arm. He raised the green blade, alive with venom, although he supposed the Stormcast's armour made his poisons useless. No matter. The Coiling Ones would guide him. He would cut this giant down and take his helmet for a trophy, and he would find Archaon's heir and take him to the Varanspire, the Spire of the Serpent's Tooth. There, he would accept his place at the Everchosen's side. It was meant to be. It had been seen.

He was Ashrath Silenthis, and there was no one alive who could master him.

He came on with new heart, still with the ravine at his back, whipping the blade high and fast to slash at the Stormcast's immobile face. Its axe came up, and under its guard Ashrath thrust, his sword tip screeching against its breastplate. He feinted left, cut right, jabbed and swung. Each time the Stormcast parried, far faster than he would have imagined. It backed away a foot or two, and Ashrath realised that he was being deliberately overextended, made to exhaust himself on futile gestures until his strength was utterly gone. That moment was surely near, and he had barely made a mark on the Stormcast's armour.

He tried to jab the tip of his sword into the ridged leather at the warrior's elbows and upper thighs, beyond the encircling plate, but each time the axe came down and battered his strike aside. His arm was buzzing with pain now, and the sword in his hand felt triple the weight, like a length of riven steel. He could hardly hold it any higher than his chest. Then, at the first sign of hesitation, the Stormcast advanced.

The axe whistled past his head, only missing his shoulder because he dropped to the ground and rolled away. As he tried to stand, the Stormcast sent him sprawling with a vicious kick. Ashrath slithered to the edge of the gorge, rolled again, tried to raise his sword to block the axe strike that fell like a meteor towards his face. When the axe struck home, the sword shattered like glass.

Su'atha, you should be with me now... he thought. *Forgive me, old friend. The Serpent's Sight was not well done, and it has blinded me to all that was true.*

He closed his eyes for the mortal blow.

It didn't say a word as it died. Ashrath flicked his eyes open to see Essiltha high up on the warrior's shoulders, her legs wrapped around its neck, and the twin needle blades shimmering as dusk crept closer over the ruined city. The white pupils glittered in her evil black eyes, and her grin was like a bright and savage scar across the smooth aelven planes of her face. She plunged the daggers down into the Stormcast's neck, down through the soft leather where the breastplate met the pauldrons, and as the warrior called out in an agony so sorrowful it almost brought tears to his eyes, Ashrath stabbed up with his broken blade into the unprotected space beneath its arm.

Light poured from the empty sockets of its faceplate. The armour began to shimmer, and as Essiltha executed a perfect backflip from its shoulders, the Stormcast Eternal erupted in a blaze of lightning so pure and blinding that it threw Ashrath back off his feet. His foot touched earth, touched air–

And then he was falling backwards, clawing at nothing, tumbling from the lip of the cliff in a flash of light, with all the breath whipped clean from his lungs and the gorge opening its depthless mouth to swallow him down...

Kathenga...

He thought, and the thought took form. Through waves of pain that crashed against a distant shore, he peered through the darkness and saw the serpent disentangle itself from the void. Kathenga lived, greater than he had ever been before.

The blind crystal eyes glowed like stars, like cut amber embroidering the dark. Each shard of light that caught and glittered in those eyes erupted across the endless span of the cosmos.

Ma'sulthisss…

His consciousness pulsed with pain. All was black, and then slowly the serpent's swaying head drew near. He was but a mote of dust in its orbit. Behind it, hanging in the firmament like clustered nebulae, were even greater shapes – vast scales that defied human comprehension, forked tongues that ran like rivers of light throughout the Mortal Realms entire.

The Coiling Ones, his consciousness thought, and the thought was like a spiral of dust unravelling across an abyss.

The Coiling Ones as they will be, Ma'sulthis, with all the power of the Mortal Realms accrued to them, if you have the strength to carry on. Archaon's heir is in mortal danger now.

I have the strength, he thought. *I do! I am broken and cast down, oh Holy Ones, but what strength I have left is yours to use. Send me back! Kathenga! Grant me in death what you always granted in life. Help me now!*

The hiss of the serpent was the sound of a billion storm clouds unleashing their rain on a billion parched deserts.

You will go back, Ma'sulthis, but not as you were… Seek Nagendra's Son in his moment of need, for his hour grows near. Seek him, Ma'sulthis… Seek him!

I will, he thought, and all the properties of that vast cosmic silence began to spin, faster and faster, a vortex that drew him down towards Kathenga's cataclysmic jaws…

'This one lives,' Ekrah whispered. They crouched in the rubble, and the Serpent Caller at their feet moaned and twitched. There was a wet, sucking sound coming from his ruptured throat. By his side, as thick as a ship's cable, lay the headless corpse of his snake.

Burak drew his steel knife and stabbed down once.

'He lives no more.'

The Bloodseer scanned the ruins on the other side of the street and saw Kurguth's band move stealthily through the wreckage to the fold in the cliff at the other side. The armoured ones, Sigmar's Storm, had moved on and were mopping up the last resistance at the line of the gorge. They would have to move quickly.

'Come, Ekrah!' Burak grinned. He touched the tracks on the ground. 'The prize is almost in our hands!'

They caught up with her on the outskirts of the city.

Ekrah was glad she had run. He hadn't hunted properly for weeks, and for a Preytaker to bend himself to any other task was to distort himself into something false and dishonest. He felt it like a lie sitting heavily on his mind, but when the hunt was up the lie evaporated into truth.

Burak had flushed her from cover. The young woman burst from the twisted vines of some thorn bushes that smothered the western edge of a once-great plaza. She ran across the broken flagstones towards the opposite edge, her bare feet slapping against the ground. Ekrah looked to the Heart-eater. Burak nodded indulgently and gave Ekrah his head, and then the Preytaker was bounding over the littered ground, keeping to her heels, letting her exhaust herself. The plains-runners fanned out to the left and right, herding her towards a cluster of low-lying walls, all that was left of the city's once-formidable defences. Ekrah watched her gaze in terror over the ruined walls, here at the very edge of the ancient city, where the great cyclopaean stones had slumped into each other and subsided, a shattered breach more substantial than anything the most determined enemy could have made. She stared down at the jagged tiers of the mountainside below her as it fell away towards the great plains of the Desolate March.

Ekrah could almost read her frantic thoughts as she scurried back and forth along the edge of the breach. Would she jump? She seemed to be weighing up her chances. Would she be able to find handholds, footholds? Would it be possible to climb down to the next level and somehow gain the lower track that twisted across the mountain's flank, a hundred feet below? Or would the uneven ground betray her, and would it send her and the baby tumbling down to be broken apart on the rocks like ripe fruit? Ekrah slowed as he approached her. He drew his serrated blade, a length of bone studded with the razor-sharp teeth of a mastazyr. The woman turned around, and her eyes were a mass of panic that seemed to draw the very light towards them. She held the baby, trembling, stuttering, but when she looked at Ekrah – his warpaint, the horns sweeping back from his battered leather helmet, the stink of him like a feral beast – it was like all hope had died in her. He could see it in her face – slack, resigned. She stared at him with the eyes of an animal run to ground, with no more sense in it to fight.

'I was going to raise him,' she said in a tired, wounded voice. 'He would be mine, and I would be his. He would... He will protect me. Don't you need me to go with you? I can feed him, look after him, I...'

'We have no need of you, my daughter,' Burak said, not unkindly, as he came near. 'The child has only a short distance yet to go, but we must travel quickly. You could not keep up.'

She nodded. He reached out his hands.

'Horned One,' she moaned. The whisper choked into a sob. She held out the baby. He writhed in her arms, but he didn't cry. Burak gathered up the child, smiling, whispering prayers to it in a low, sing-song voice. The woman closed her eyes. Tears cleaved a track down her face – and then Ekrah swung his sword.

CHAPTER TEN

HUNTERS OF THE
BLOODWIND SPOIL

The remnants had broken and run – Splintered Fang, Scions of the Flame, all the ragged survivors stricken by their defeat. They staggered for whatever paths off the mountain they could find, throwing their weapons aside, some disappearing deeper into the ruins and hiding themselves in forgotten cellars or the mouldering shacks of the scavengers who had fled at the Scions' first approach.

Bodies, crumpled and broken, were cast around the old avenue like so much despised refuse. The light was dropping low, the course of Hysh having drawn it far out across the Eightpoints to circle more distant segments of its brutal landscape. A noisome wind picked up, faint with the scent of death, and it curled like a sorrowful song across the peaks of the Fangs. After the clash of weapons and the cries of the dying, the ruins thrummed with silence, and in this silence the warriors of the Stormcast Eternals began to regroup.

'Antigonos!' Damaris called, striding quickly through the wrecked streets. Her cloak was torn, and her armour was scratched and spattered with blood. It had been a pale cream once, gleaming with power, but the long weeks in the Bloodwind Spoil had encrusted it with dust and filth. She took off her helmet. Her skin was like burnished bronze, and her eyes, although ringed with strain, were clear and fierce. Whatever else the Bloodwind Spoil had done, Antigonos thought, it had not lessened her zeal.

Antigonos, Hunter-Prime of the Tempered Blades, stood there cleaning his axe in the centre of the avenue, issuing orders, staring up at the listing span of the archways that surrounded him. Something in their configuration, in the style of the gargoyles that mournfully gazed down on the wreckage of their once-proud civilisation, clawed at his heart. His thoughts drifted through all the discarnate horrors of his many reforgings, the gulfs of time that divided him from the man he once was and the being he was now. Those memories were little more than flares and streaks of light, vague images distorted and made strange by his distance from them. But somewhere in that former life, in the days before the God-King had chosen him for the ranks of the Tempered Blades, there had been a city much like this. He was sure of it. There had been cool gardens and shuttered walkways, balconies and cloisters and sun-struck market squares. There had been peace, and life, and love...

He couldn't remember. But of all the places he had been in this repulsive land, this was the only one to make him feel something more than outright disgust. In the flame of his soul, even here, these ruins spoke of better days.

'Speak, Damaris,' Antigonos said. 'There's no sign of the child – I'm assuming some of them have managed to escape with him?'

'Yes, Hunter-Prime. The barbarians we tracked across the Corpseworm Marches and into the mountains. In the confusion they managed to seize it.'

Antigonos gritted his teeth. It was no small thing to evade a

Stormcast ranger in the wilderness, but these savages had managed to do it. Through the paths and defiles of the mountains they had run, hard on their heels, but then the trail had died. Antigonos had thought it no real matter because the peak and its hidden ruins had soon revealed themselves. There they had found what they had long sought – the child, around whom swirled such deadly rumours, as well as those who would smuggle it on towards its final destination.

'Where are they now?' he demanded.

'The cliffs on the other side hide a labyrinth of passages and tunnels,' Damaris said. 'They lead down off the mountain, as far as we can tell. The savages have disappeared through one of them, but which I cannot say.'

Behind his helmet, Antigonos closed his eyes. Just being in the Bloodwind Spoil subdued his mind. He felt the malign presence of the landscape as a constant pain high in his temple.

'We lost two noble hearts in this fight,' he said, 'those who ran far across the worst this sickened land could throw at us.'

'They return to the God-King,' Damaris said. She whispered a prayer. 'We will see their likes again.'

'Will we?' Antigonos sheathed his weapon and gathered his things. 'We don't fight in the Mortal Realms here, Damaris. This is the Eightpoints, the domain of the Everchosen. Chaos leaches all that is good from the very air, and a soul may have a troubled journey if it needs to find its way back to High Azyr.'

'I saw the lightning strike into the sky,' she insisted. She laid an armoured hand on his arm. 'They will find their way home.'

'Let us pray for them when we have the time,' he said. 'Gather the others. We have another long journey ahead if these beasts run us the same race as they did before.'

He called up into the air, and after a moment a distant speck resolved itself into the wheeling form of a bird. Trailing light, iridescent, its wing feathers bold shades of cerulean blue, the aetherwing plummeted towards the ground and angled up at the last minute to hook itself to the Hunter-Prime's gauntlet. It furled its wings in a nimbus of grace and power, consenting to the hand that Antigonos gently stroked along its dorsal feathers.

'Take wing once more, Starglider, seek them out,' he said softly. 'They cannot hide from your eyes. Go!'

He threw his arm out and the aetherwing streaked up into the firmament, soaring off towards the high cliffs that masked the fissures leading out of the mountains. There the Untamed Beasts had fled, bearing their prize, and there the Vanguard-Hunters of the Tempered Blades would cut them down.

'Lead on, Damaris,' he said. 'We have one chance at this. They must not reach the altar with the child. If they do, everything we have fought for here will be utterly lost.'

Everything hurt. He would have said his pride hurt most of all, but that would have been a lie.

Above him stretched the flank of the gorge, the rock pitted with scrub grass and pale moss. He could see a segment of the riven sky, where dusk was falling. When he rolled onto his side all he could see was the abyss and the faint traces of the foothills far below. But he lived, and for Ashrath Silenthis that was enough. Where there was life there was hope – and where there was hope there was the chance of revenge.

He had fallen onto a narrow platform, a slice of the ancient city that had once stretched out far across the gorge. A bridge, perhaps, a sheltered walkway – who knew what arcane science the elders of that place had once used to span such a distance. Now, it was just the jutting remnants of its foundations, and it had saved Ashrath's life.

His face prickled with heat from the blinding flash of the dying Stormcast warrior, and every muscle in his body screamed with the effort of standing. He pressed himself against the wall. The wind moaned like a spectre around him, ruffling his hair, tugging at his mailed snakeskin cloak. He had no weapons and his helmet was gone. He looked up at the short section of the cliff-face wall, more than twice his height to the top. What, he wondered, would be waiting for him if he made it up?

There was only one way to find out. Slowly, Ashrath set himself to the task.

The first few feet were encouraging. The rock was scarred and easy to scale, the roots of the scrub grass tough enough to take his weight. He levered himself up off the platform, and although his arms trembled with the effort, he found himself narrowing the distance. But then the angle of the clifftop changed subtly, edging out no more than a foot or two, enough to make a difference. His feet pulled away from the surface, and he was hanging there in mid-air by the strength of his arms alone. Again, he wriggled his toes into the gaps, pressed down, hauled up. The muscles in his arms and shoulders felt like they were slowly being torn away from his bones, and his feet were bleeding. He gritted his teeth, snarled and swore and felt the sweat lashing down his face. Closer came the lip of the cliff, jutting out above his face. If he could just reach out and touch it, hook his fingers over the edge… And then the roots of the scrub grass gave way.

He had time to make a muffled cry, to suck air into his lungs and feel his eyes widen, even to picture in a moment of blind panic what his body would look like as it tumbled all the way down to the bottom of the gorge, spinning end over end, trailing a scream like the ribbons of a kite. With a desiccated little puff of dust, the grass unplugged from the mountainside and Ashrath fell back…

Strong hands encircled his wrist. He looked up to see Essiltha's narrow face, her eyes squeezed shut with effort, the muscles bulging in her arms like thin cords.

'Don't let go!' he shrieked, and instantly wished he had been silent. Essiltha had time to laugh, that low cackle, harsh and sibilant. She pulled, and then there were other hands around his shoulders, grabbing his arms, dragging him up over the edge of the cliff. He could have wept.

They lay there in a tumble, Ashrath and what remained of the Horned Krait. Essiltha, a handful of clearbloods; that was it. They had been annihilated.

'Thank you,' he forced himself to say. Essiltha nodded, got to her feet and limped back to her weapons. Her hair was stiff with dried blood, her face grimy with dust and sweat. The clearbloods helped him up, but Ashrath batted their hands away. 'Is this all that's left? How did you survive?'

'We hid,' Essiltha said bitterly. 'Or we ran. I'm sure a few of our comrades are still running, as fast as their feet can carry them down the mountain.'

'Cowards,' Ashrath spat. Essiltha whipped around, her black eyes blazing.

'Cowards?' she sneered. 'They fought for you, Silenthis! Most of them *died* for you. Burned Hand, Stormcast Eternals, for Nagendra's sake! When all was lost, can you blame them for breaking?'

'And what am I supposed to do with four clearbloods and you?' he countered. 'Where is the child, do you even know that?'

'The Untamed Beasts,' one of the clearbloods said. 'I saw them take it through the canyon. The Stormcasts give chase even now.'

'Damn the child!' Essiltha snapped. 'You dragged us from Invidia through the raw hell of that Realmgate. You took us across the nightmare of the Bloodwind Spoil to Carngrad. You lost our temple to Lord Rakaros, let us trawl around the Hag's Claw Forest for months in search of that shrine – and why? For glory? So you could play at being a great leader? So you could become the mighty warlord you have always dreamed of being, no matter how many are cast aside in your wake!'

'I am a great leader,' he said, and even he realised how petulant it sounded.

'If you were, you wouldn't need to say it,' Essiltha told him.

'The Coiling Ones chose me,' he pleaded. 'You know that. I'm blessed by them to achieve great things – you cannot doubt it! Don't you remember the ceremony in Invidia? I drank the venoms and I didn't die. I am a Son of Nagendra!'

'Ma'sulthis chose you,' she said, turning her back on him. 'But for what ends I do not know.'

'Because he spoke with the Coiling Ones, communed with them, saw what they showed him! This child is our chance, Essiltha, our one and only chance to come out of this with real power. Please.' He took her arm, gently, turning her around to face him. 'This child *is* Archaon's heir – there can be no doubt. Why else would so many be fighting for it? Why else would Sigmar, curse his name, send his best warriors to track it down?'

She looked into his eyes. Deep in those black hollows, hidden in the warp and weft of that aelven mind, Ashrath thought he saw the calculations taking place.

'One more chance,' she said quietly. 'But I promise a blade for you if you lead us astray.'

'I won't.' He forced himself to smile. 'And I won't forget this, Essiltha.'

She narrowed her eyes. 'No,' she said. 'I'm sure you won't.'

They gathered weapons and supplies from the dead. The Scions of the Flame had not got off lightly either, and Ashrath took small satisfaction as he wandered around the battlefield that they had seemingly been cut down to a man and woman. He found a knife, a replacement sword, and slashed the throats of the few survivors. No doubt others, like the renegade warriors of his Splintered Fang, were still hastily running from the field. *Damn them all*, he thought. *The horrors of the Spoil will do for them in the end.*

He found Ma'sulthis in the rubble, sprawled by the corpse of Kathenga. He stood over the body, searching his feelings, waiting for grief to surface from the depths of his anger. Long had the Serpent Caller championed his cause. In a wily and ambitious young fighter, Ma'sulthis had seen something like greatness, and he had moulded and crafted Ashrath to the leadership of the Horned Krait. Guided by his dreams of the Coiling Ones, by the silkily insinuating voice of Kathenga when he communed with his serpent familiar, Ma'sulthis had watched him rise to glory. He could not give up now. Ashrath looked down on the Serpent Caller's body, lifeless in the dust, and a tear came to his eye.

'You *idiot!*' he snarled. He kicked the corpse with fury, crouching to ransack the body, searching with trembling fingers all the folds of his cloak for the phials and philtres of venom, the elixirs that had given him such strength and confidence for so long. 'Where are they, you old fool? What have you done with them?'

They had been too long from the temple, and Ma'sulthis had not had the chance to brew more. What little of the venom remained now soaked into the dirt at his side, and the bottles lay in shards around him. Eagerly Ashrath snatched up these shards, licking the glass until he cut his tongue, pawing the ground and spooning handfuls of dirt into his mouth so he could suck the venom from it. He felt a vague trickle in his blood, the thrum of old strength returning, but it wasn't enough – not nearly.

Sprawled in the dirt, frantic and desperate, he turned to see Essiltha watching him with disgust.

'Let us go then, *Trueblood*,' she said. 'The storm-warriors give chase to the Beasts, and the Beasts are running. We don't want to be left behind, do we?'

CHAPTER ELEVEN

LOST AND DAMNED

They had been wandering for hours when they found the rusty stream. Ashrath threw himself to the muddy bank and lapped the water like a dog, gulping it down no matter how disgusting it tasted.

'There's probably blood in there,' Essiltha said. She stood aloof, her hand on her hip. 'Or worse.'

'I don't care,' Ashrath said, water dripping down his chin. 'I can't remember the last time I had something to drink, let alone the last time I ate. I don't suppose that would bother you though, would it, aelf?'

Essiltha laughed, a musical phrase that broke against the surrounding walls. 'It's true, we can go longer than mere humans without sustenance. You're surprisingly limited as a species, in so many ways.'

'Limited, maybe,' he said. 'But I'll wager there's one area in which we excel.'

'Oh? And what would that be?'

'Our ambition.'

'Well…' she said, looking around the narrow confines of the gorge. 'Your ambition has certainly taken us this far. Whether that's a good or a bad thing, though, remains to be seen.'

Night had passed briefly, as if frightened to outstay the dawn. The light now swelled against the mountains, but deep in these twisting ravines it was still dark, cool and damp. They had followed unnumbered paths, coming up against dead ends, fissures too narrow to pass through or sheer drops that led only to a plummeting death. They had retraced their steps a dozen times already, and now they found themselves in this shallow declivity, where water trickled in a stream from the rock and where the walls leaned up on either side to enclose them like a bowl. They were lost, and Ashrath knew it. The knowledge was a twisting pain in the back of his neck that he couldn't ignore, a dull sense of panic that rose higher and higher from the pit of his stomach.

He flopped down on the grass at the side of the stream, where it frothed and bubbled from the stone. He was exhausted – beyond exhausted. *Oh, for a taste of the Serpent Caller's venom…* His veins throbbed with its need. The backs of his eyes itched. All of this would be a damn sight easier if he could just clear his head, take some time to properly *think*.

The clearbloods took off their helmets and scooped water from the stream, some of them falling to the grass with their arms slung across their eyes. Only Essiltha stayed on her feet. She looked down at Ashrath, and the expression on her face was one of almost aristocratic hauteur. The aelves of Ghyran were rare enough, and rarer still was it to see one amongst the tribes of the Splintered Fang, but Ashrath had often thought how similar they seemed to snakes – how much closer they felt to the cold menace of the serpent. Her black eyes ranged freely over his face, and he found himself looking away.

'What next, *Trueblood*?' she said. He felt the sting every time she used his title. Ashrath dried his hands on the grass and forced himself to stand up. His knees were shaking.

'We'll rest here a moment and then head back, try the next turning. Or we can split up, take a different canyon each until we find the right one.' Black spots were dancing in front of his eyes. He passed his hand across them, trying to make it seem as if he were thinking. 'Look for tracks, maybe. Those Stormcast scum must leave a deep footprint, and I'm sure they know where they're going.'

'Unlike us,' she said. 'It must be so much easier to be on their side, don't you think?'

Ashrath snapped. 'Damn your insolence!' he hissed, jabbing his finger in her face. 'What other choice do we have but to go on!'

'Go back?'

'…What do you mean?'

'Exactly what I said. This is futile, Silenthis – we've failed. *You've* failed. We're going to die in these mountains, and we may as well die heading back to what we know rather than stumble on into what we don't.'

He was aware of the clearbloods stirring behind him. Some sat up; others stood and milled uncertainly near the two warriors.

'Go back *where*?' Ashrath demanded. He laughed, but all humour was dead in him. 'Carngrad?'

'Why not? The Burned Hand are dead, and they could only have left a skeleton crew back at the temple. Why not take it back? Start again, build up our influence, build up our power.'

'There's only six of us, you stupid aelven fool! What chance do you think we'd have in Carngrad, of all places? We'd be prey, pure and simple! Iron Golems, Corvus Cabal, those skinless Unmade freaks. Gods, the damned Talons themselves… They'd cut us to ribbons! We'd be dead the moment we set foot through the gates!'

He felt the blood was going to burst from his veins. Sweat trickled down his brow, and the panic that had been slowly stewing in his gut was ready to erupt. Trudging after Essiltha, all the way back to Carngrad, to sneak through its treacherous streets like beaten dogs and slip inside their temple once more, the temple that had been taken from them and profaned by those fire-worshipping bastards – it would be beyond degrading. It was impossible.

'Master,' one of the clearbloods said tentatively. He stood at Ashrath's elbow, one eye fused shut from the beating they'd taken up in the ruins. 'Essiltha speaks the truth, I think. The Venomblood is right – we can't go on. We're at the end of our strength here – we've nothing left.'

'What's your name?' Ashrath asked him mildly.

'My name? I'm… My name is Thus'ana, master.'

'When I want your opinion, Thus'ana, I will be sure to ask for it.'

In one clean and practised motion, Ashrath pivoted to the side, drew his sword from its scabbard and swept it up to slash the clearblood's stomach open. He stepped aside to avoid the spray of blood, the loose jumble of intestines that spilled out onto the grass, hissing like a nest of vipers. The clearblood dropped to the ground and tumbled into the stream without a word.

'There, Essiltha, do you see? Now the water *definitely* has blood in it.'

He didn't feel it at first, the cut was so smooth. The first thing he noticed was Essiltha skipping back, her knife up, the blade coloured a rich and oily yellow. He looked down at his left forearm and saw a thin line slowly widen, a little trickle of blood leaking out to drip down to his wrist guard. He looked up. The tip of Essiltha's knife carved a figure of eight in the air, and her other hand was on the hilt of her needle blade. She was smiling at him, a cruel and half-amused smile, like someone watching a mortal enemy stroll unwittingly into a trap.

'What have you done, Essiltha?' Ashrath said. He gave her a

smile of his own and raised his sword. 'You think to poison me? I'm a Son of Nagendra, a Trueblood – there's no poison from any serpent in the Mortal Realms that can kill me.'

'Who said it was poison from a serpent?' she said.

Ashrath looked down at his arm again. The skin was turning, very faintly, a sickly shade of yellow. His forearm felt deadened somehow, detached – as if it didn't belong to him and would at any moment start drifting off.

'What…?'

'Do you think I picked all those flowers in the Hag's Claw Forest because I liked the smell? They were harrowmask flowers, you arrogant fool. One of the deadliest poisons in the Eightpoints.'

She sheathed her knife and calmly strolled over to pick up her gear. The clearbloods settled their helmets on their heads again and prepared to leave. Ashrath stood there, gripped by a mounting sense of wild, unanchored dread. He turned his head, and it felt as if he were being buffeted by a gale, and that each inch he moved was taking him a thousand years of the most impossible effort.

'It's slow-moving,' Essiltha said, 'so I imagine you won't be dead for hours. But you'll feel every moment of it as your muscles seize up, your heart slows, your eyes gradually shrivel and die in your head. And when you're blind, and suffocating, and going into the first spasms, you'll still be able to hear them when they come near.'

After an eternity, Ashrath said, '*Who?*'

'Raptoryx, furies maybe – I'm sure I saw one earlier, coasting over the peaks. Beastmen, skinwalkers, cannibals… The list goes on. Perhaps the Stormcast hunters will come back and find you, and in their contemptible mercy put a lightning bolt in your head? That would be a shame, but it'll be out of our hands by then.'

Another eternity, an aeon on the mortal earth. '*Where?*' he said. He dropped very slowly and deliberately to the ground, until he was kneeling in the grass.

'Not Carngrad,' she said. 'It pains me to admit it, but you're right there. Back to Ghyran, I think, to the jungles of Invidia.' She looked around at the darkened hollow, the sparse and greasy grass, the trickling stream the colour of mouldering blood, the body bobbing in its sway. 'Here is where your story ends, Ashrath Silenthis. This is where glory gets you... glory, and ambition.'

Gently, almost without malice, she put her foot to Ashrath's chest and tipped him over onto the ground.

'Come,' she said to the clearbloods. 'Let's go home.'

It wasn't pain, as such. Pain is an event, a journey; it has a beginning and it has an end, one way or the other. This was more like an eclipse, a new state of being overlaying the old. Everywhere he looked inside himself, Ashrath saw someone new staring back at him – an impostor wearing his face, subtly altered, mortifying the old flesh and the old spirit and blending it into something grotesque and unrecognisable. It was well named, the harrowmask flower, because that's what its poison felt like it was doing – it excruciated, and it disguised, and before long 'Ashrath Silenthis' was just the persona being torn away and casually thrown on top of his body's slender architecture, discarded by the totality of the poison.

And yet, usurped as he was, there was still a shard of Ashrath in there. He felt the poison slowly creeping up his arm, saw as if from outside himself the harrowed skin begin to turn like curdled milk. Clotted and thick, the poison had not yet crept all the way up into his heart. He blanched at the thought of what would happen when it did, if only this merest tendril in his system could dislocate him so completely. His face was pressed into the grass, and after a thousand years of concerted effort he managed to twist his neck around. He stared down the length of his wounded arm. He turned his neck again, and what felt like aeons later he saw his other arm, the fingers of his hand curled into a fist. His body felt like a thin veneer painted over a canvas. He fired thoughts down into his limbs and was encouraged to see his fingers twitch. He looked at the wound on his left arm. He looked at his right hand. He looked at the hilt of his sword, lying just out of reach. It was like looking at the forms of an equation, frowning over the solution and then suddenly seeing the right calculation. And the result sent waves of nausea and grief crashing through his system.

Time moved slowly in the hollow that afternoon. As the light lengthened and contracted, as the air grew first warm then chill, Ashrath engaged in the greatest struggle of his life. It was a struggle that felt as long as the grinding of the cosmos, from its first spark to its final dissolution. He reached for and touched the blade. He curled his fingers against the handle. He ploughed every last inch of his strength into raising himself from the grass, lying his wounded left arm against the ground and lifting the sword above his head.

The entire lifespan of material reality rose and fell in the time it took him to raise the weapon. He held it high in a hand that wouldn't move, and he stared down at his left arm as if it belonged in another dimension entirely. The horror of the moment looped and spun through his mind, and even as he tried to bring the sword down, he seemed to see his left arm shearing off from his body in a gout of blood. He looked again, saw it still twitching in the grass as he tried to move it, saw the wound leaking its pale poison. He strained every sinew to make the sword come down faster, but it was like he was trying to cut through the very earth, through the crust and mantle of the Eightpoints itself. Coiling Ones, what if it didn't work though? What if he was maiming himself for nothing, and when the foul deed was done, he would be lying here with the poison still trickling through his system, his blood pumping out into the grass! *Gods save me! Children of*

Nagendra, heed my prayer! He wanted to cry out, but even opening his jaw to speak was an act beyond him now. Still the sword came down, and as its motion reached its terminal point Ashrath realised with absolute distress that he couldn't stop it even if he wanted to. The act had been put in motion; all that was left was to watch it play out. And so in one screaming, maniacal chop, straight onto the joint of his elbow, the blade came down, the severed limb then springing away in a hot jet of blood as if eager to escape from a prison where it had been incarcerated for far too long.

It was as if all of creation itself had passed in the time it took Ashrath to unstring his belt and make a tourniquet, to quieten his blood as it beat out of his stump onto the grass. He screamed then, long and loud, boiling off his grief in one heart-wracked roar, the walls of the canyon projecting and amplifying the scream so that it seemed to those who might have been passing in their shadows as if the very peaks of the Fangs were howling for help, or for death, or just in the sheer misery of existence in this awful place, in this awful time.

He dreamed then, falling into unconsciousness. They weren't dreams as he understood them, but something he seemed to dwell inside for a while – strange, unravelling shapes, and strange bursts of colour that quickened in the murk. Slowly, with infinitesimal patience, those shapes and colours reformed themselves into coherence. What had been a vast, humped shape of iridescent green suspended in the darkness gradually revealed itself as the coiled ring of a mighty serpent, something so vast and powerful that it was almost beyond his comprehension.

Coiling Ones, Ashrath's consciousness thought, and his consciousness was afraid. He tried to turn away, but the shape of the Coiling One was so cataclysmic that whatever direction he turned only showed him another aspect of the same.

Ashrath Silenthisssss...

It was a voice that rose from his bones and his blood, from all the sinews of the universe around him. Quaking, forcing his consciousness to look in full awareness of what he was seeing, Ashrath turned and allowed the voice to pass through him. It was Kathenga, he thought. It was a shape and a voice familiar to him in some way, a mask adopted by a higher power, designed to make the translation easier.

Ashrath, your time is not yet come... Glory still awaits you, power at the side of the Everchosen's heir...

How? he cried. *All is lost! All is in ruins!*

Not all is lost, not yet, but the hour draws near. Look to the earth, see your salvation. Pick up your sword and fight, Ashrath Silenthis... Fight, and do not give up now... The greatest prize is still yours to take. You will have Archaon's heir in your hand before this is finished...

He screamed into the void – and then his eyes were struggling open and he was gazing out onto the hollow by the stream. He saw his severed arm leaking blood into the grass, saw the dead clearblood face down in the water. And then, glinting in the soft and muted light, he saw a pale shape begin to move on the other side of the clearing.

The shape, tentative at first and then more confident, drew closer. It emerged from a gap in the rock and writhed slowly across the grass. It was a snake the colour of milk, and as he stared at it, unable to move his eyes, Ashrath saw that it was translucent, or that it was phasing slowly in and out of reality. One moment he could see the grass through the shimmering mist that formed its skin, and the next it appeared as solid as his severed arm lying just ahead of him on the ground. Fixed in space or adrift in time, the snake's impassive rectilinear motion brought it closer and closer to his face. The forked tongue flickered and withdrew. The eyes like glowing antimony stared unblinking at him. It came closer and closer, until it paused and swayed in front of his face, the tongue flicking out to brush against his skin.

'Ma'sulthis...?' he said, and as he looked into the spirit-snake's cryptic, opaque eyes, he knew he was looking in some way at the eyes of the Serpent Caller, whose body even now was lying in the wreckage of the ancient city far behind him. 'Ma'sulthis, how is this possible?'

The snake, inscrutable and as cold as the deep void of the unreality that had birthed it, inched forward. The eyes bored deep into Ashrath's soul as it opened its jaws and lunged forward to strike, and when its fangs plunged deep into the flesh of his throat like knives of ice, he felt the harrowmask poison boiling out of his veins, replaced by venoms more powerful than any he had ever experienced before.

Ashrath swam through the darkness at the edge of death and headed for the light. He opened his eyes. He felt the grass under him, heard the stream still trickling from the stone. He looked to the stump of his elbow and saw that the blood had congealed into a hard crust. There was no sign of the spirit-snake, and when he reached his other hand up to feel his throat, he could find no mark from where it had bitten him. He felt...

He stood and picked up his sword, swaying and light-headed. He could feel the venom in his blood, pulsing, pulling like a magnet towards his target in the distance – Archaon's heir, the Blood of the Everchosen.

He felt like Ashrath Silenthis once more. After sheathing his sword and tightening the tourniquet, with a snarl of pain and rage and violent frustration on his lips, he turned from the clearing and started to run.

CHAPTER TWELVE

VALLEY OF THE DEAD

Say one thing for the savages, Antigonos thought. *They hide their tracks well.*

He crouched to brush his fingers against a shallow indentation that was picked out by the shadows against the declining light. He saw a crushed patch of grass, the wet underside of a disturbed pebble. They were the faintest traces, barely visible to anyone who did not know where and how to look. Behind his face plate, Antigonos smiled at the cunning of it. He imagined himself a lesser scout, eagerly seizing on this evidence and hurrying along the track in search of further signs.

'They think to fool us along this path,' Damaris said. 'They're not stupid, I'll give them that.'

Antigonos stood up. He looked towards the only other trail they could have taken, which curved around a spur of the cliffs and disappeared further into the maze.

'No prey should be underestimated,' he said. 'Even the lowest animal has a natural craft that would put any of us to shame. But still, their intention is clear.'

Damaris readied the others to take the second path, but Antigonos stopped her.

'They know what we are,' he said. 'They know that we hunt them. Tell me, what would you do?'

'Send us the wrong way,' Damaris said. 'They can't outrun us or outfight us, so they must outfox us.'

'Which is exactly what they almost did.' He pointed at the marks on the ground and the trail they indicated. 'This is the way they have gone. They want us to think these marks are deliberate, a ruse, and so take the second path instead. But that in itself is the ruse.'

Damaris laughed lightly, and the sound boomed inside her helmet. 'Like you say, Hunter-Prime, a natural craft.'

He looked up into the sky. As the black clouds began to gather, he saw the trailing light of Starglider moving slowly across the sphere.

'She sees,' he said. 'The way narrows, the prey is near. Philemon, Leander – take the lead, scout the way ahead.'

The two warriors nodded and drew their weapons. They ran off down the track as if unencumbered by the weight of their armour.

Antigonos picked up his axe from the ground. 'Run, my hunters!' he said, and swift as the wind, the hunters took flight.

She had felt their presence grow the deeper they went underground. Burak led them through the tunnel, cackling madly to the child he guarded in his arms, and as they turned the last bend of the channel in the rock, their feet kicking through the low curls of mist and the walls converging above them, Mayra felt something dark and feral snarling on the borders of her psyche. It was like a fierce shape unfolding on the outskirts of a campfire, held at bay but waiting for the embers to burn low. She gasped as the fingers of her beast-sight brushed against them, these strange beings. Beyond or beneath their animal nature, brute and wild as it was, there was something alien and unfamiliar to her, a sulphurous mental reek that almost stopped her in her tracks. *Daemons*, she realised as she touched against those soulless, Chaos-saturated minds.

The other Untamed Beasts, attuned to the wild as they were, felt it too. They paused in their headlong flight towards the Mountain's Throat, apprehensive, impressed by the cold ice of superstitious dread. For Mayra, though, it was much worse. She felt their ravening attention at once, and as the tunnel opened out into a chamber that was marked by a forest of sandstone pillars, she cried out in pain. The furies, suddenly disturbed, ruffled their leathery wings and screeched.

Burak turned to her at once, gripping her arm. His voice was low, urgent, skating the very edge of panic. His eyes gleamed greenly in the luminescence, and Mayra was shocked to see the fear that was lurking there.

'If we fight here, we die,' he said. Mayra squeezed her eyes shut, pressing them against the furies' morbid chatter as it trickled through her mind. 'The Mountain's Throat is close. Mayra, my Beastspeaker, you must calm their evil blood or all of us are dead!'

A plains-runner scurried down the path from the ravine behind them.

'Speak, Tuk-kho,' Burak said. 'Do the armoured ones follow?'

'They are near, Bloodseer, very near,' the plains-runner said. Her eyes were wild. 'They have our scent!'

'Can you do this, Beastspeaker?' Burak hissed. 'Can you save us all?'

Mayra opened her eyes.

'I can.'

With the beasts of the wild, it was a connection of purest sympathy. It was a question of opening one mind to the insight of another, joining them for a moment and walking the same hunting paths in the shadow world – to *become* each other in some way, so that Mayra was the beast and for the briefest moment the beast was Mayra. The hierarchy between them, Beastspeaker to beast, could only grow once the architecture of that connection was in place.

With these *things*, though… Mayra stared up at them as they scrabbled around their perches by the tunnel's ceiling, fixing them with a glare as forceful as a lash. She scanned each in turn, probing them, reading the contours of their minds in the same way Kurguth or Ekrah would read the contours of the living earth.

There…

The alpha, dominant and more monstrous than the rest combined. She felt it growling at her, its lithe, predatory intellect slipping off her mental grip like oil on water.

'Come to me, beast of the Bloodwind Spoil,' she muttered. Her eyes rolled in her head, and blood leaked from her nostril. She reached out her hand, and like a fist her beast-sight struck out and knocked the creature from its perch. It shrieked, leaping up, the stinking bat wings flapping frantically. It howled and struggled. It was like she had caught the creature in the coils of her whip, and as the rest of the warband nervously watched, they could almost see the lineaments of Mayra's beast-speech stretching away from her, a gossamer thread of unbreakable power. Then, like the turn of the seasons on the plains of the Jagged Savannah, the furies were suddenly in Mayra's grip. The alpha landed at her feet and made foul obeisance to her. Burak roared with delight, as if he were a child and had seen a trick of surpassing skill pulled off right in front of his nose.

'You have the Speech indeed, Mayra, and you speak it more

fluently than any I have ever seen! Our lives have passed safely through your hands, my sister!'

Mayra, exhausted by the effort, dismissed the fury from her sight. With that same jerking motion, it flapped raggedly back to its perch.

'They won't harm us now,' she said. 'The way is clear.'

Burak, half crouched, roughly stroking the baby's head as it rested in his arms, stared at her with his dancing eyes. He grinned craftily, showing his pointed teeth, the blackened gums. The brass disc glinted at his throat.

'Stay and hold them up, Mayra,' he said. 'The armoured ones. Use the furies, fight for us, keep the storm-born from us until we pass the Mountain's Throat.'

Kurguth stepped forward. 'You would leave her here to die?'

'Not die, my First Fang, but fight. You want to fight, don't you, Mayra? Punish these armoured fools for making us their prey...?'

'Leave Ekrah instead,' Kurguth argued, pointing at him. 'He can–'

Ekrah, scowling, pushed forward and thrust down Kurguth's arm. 'You would have me die to save your woman, is that it?'

'And what of me?' Mayra demanded of him. 'You think me too weak to fight?' She spat on the ground. 'Here is all I give for the armoured ones.'

'Mayra–'

'Ha! Fools that you are,' Burak laughed. 'You could all stay and die for however much I care! Only the child matters now, don't you see? Make your decisions quickly, brothers and sisters, for the armoured giants thunder down the path, and their will is bent on murder.'

Kurguth drew Mayra aside, beseeching her in a low voice only she could hear. 'Don't do this, my heart. To stay is to die.'

Softening, Mayra reached up and touched his face. She kissed him, and when she looked at him again her eyes were hard and clear, undaunted.

'No fate is ever written,' she said. 'Even to speak it aloud isn't to make it true. And if I die, then we will meet on the hunting paths, Kurguth, my heart, and we will live forever on the trail of mighty beasts.'

'You would give your life for this madness?'

'I would give my life for our chance at glory, and so would you. We are of the Split-Tongue Tribe,' she said, and her face was hard and dark as obsidian. 'Death means nothing to us.'

'Your death means everything to me,' Kurguth said, and his voice was tight with passion. 'There will be nothing left for me here if you are gone.'

'You will have Burak, and the tribe.'

'Burak...' She saw the agony sweep across his face as he spoke the Heart-eater's name.

'The choice comes closer now,' she whispered. 'It lies waiting on the path, and you only have to pick it up. Does he live? Or does he die?'

'He has led us this far,' Kurguth said. 'But he has led us only towards death.' He looked into her eyes, and she could see that all his doubts had been burned away. 'I will kill Burak for you,' he said. 'I promise.'

'When the time is right,' she said. 'Get out of these mountains, follow him wherever he leads. You will know the moment.'

'I hope I do.' He leaned down to kiss her again. 'Hunt well. Hunt true.'

'With me, First Fang,' Burak called from further up the tunnel. 'Despite my words, you are the one I need most of all when we reach the Mountain's Throat.'

They moved on as the storm began to break – Kurguth, Ekrah, Burak and all the plains-runners who remained with the warband.

Tuk-kho whooped for them to follow, and then they were sprinting through the mists.

When they reached the other end of the valley, Kurguth looked back and saw Mayra standing with her bone whip uncoiled, proud and fierce.

She was staring not at him but in the direction their enemies would come.

They came to a gloomy path that twisted its way through the body of the mountain, the walls of rock rising sheer and high above them. Water glistened on the stone, and the rock face was streaked with a gleaming efflorescence. The path was narrow at first, and the ground was covered in a low-lying mist that scuttled with strange, foul-smelling insects. Lank foliage grew from lower down the walls, and their leaves dripped like slobbering tongues. Soon, further down the trail as it plunged deeper into the mountain, the high walls of the channel merged at the top to form a ceiling that blocked out most of the light, leaving only a green eldritch glow to show them the way. There were bones hidden in the mist, and the Stormcast warriors crunched over them as they ran – disarticulated skeletons, shattered skulls, femurs that had clearly been gnawed by sharp, devouring teeth.

'Beastmen?' Leander said. He held up one of the bones, the bowl of a human pelvis.

'Possibly,' Antigonos said. 'Or Chaotic beasts of another kind...' He glanced warily up towards the distant ceiling, where the twin sides of the ravine walls had come together. The passage they moved through had led them deeper underground, into the belly of the mountain itself. Antigonos could feel the pressure of those millions of tons of rock above him; the vast, soaring peaks of the Fangs balanced precariously on this hollow space in their heart. 'We are in the tunnels now,' he said quietly. 'And who knows what creatures call this place home. Keep your eyes sharp, but we must move swiftly.'

Further on, the tunnel opened up into a wider stretch that was marked by great stone columns that marched irregularly down its length, like the pillars of some vast, chthonic cathedral. Light still fell from the walls and ceiling high above them, the glow cast down by the luminescent mosses that infested the stone. The Stormcast rangers paused, fanning out instinctively, their pistols raised to cover each other. Above them, the high ceiling was a leaden sheet, and they could hear the dull sound of distant thunder. Further up the tunnel, the way they had come, flickers of lightning cast the ravine in a weird, flaring light. Condensation pooled dankly on their armour.

Pillar by pillar, the rangers moved cautiously through the chamber, and it was when they were halfway across that Antigonos heard Starglider screech. He looked up to see the aetherwing hurtling like a fire arrow mere inches from the ceiling. A spindly, ragged shape, dark and indistinct, followed close behind her. A creature of the heavens, she had risked her natural dread of enclosed spaces to warn them, and the thing that trailed her was so instinctively disgusting that Antigonos had raised his pistol to shoot before he even knew what he was doing.

'Antigonos!'

He spun around. Damaris was firing blindly up into the pillars. Leander and Philemon had crouched back into a fighting stance, weapons ready. Other rangers were sprinting back towards the main group. He heard a shriek on the air, a repellent, jabbering laughter.

'Furies!' Antigonos cried. 'Hunters, bring them down!'

They fell from the pillars where they had been roosting, dropping slowly to the ground and then jerking up on their tattered wings with a cackle. Their eyes were spots of crimson in a sea of black, their bodies blotched and leathery. Lengths of matted hair hung down from their chins, encrusted with blood. The stench that came off them was stupefying, a noxious wave of gangrenous flesh and sulphur. Antigonos gagged and shook his head to clear it.

As one, the boltstorm pistols unleashed their scouring shot into the air. As the lightning further up the ravine crackled and fell still, flaring up to cast the vale in its quivering glow, the furies descended to their prey. Some collapsed to the ground, pierced by the Stormcasts' bolts, their wings torn apart. Others swooped down to carve tranches in the warriors' armour, spinning off only to turn and launch themselves down in another withering stoop. Antigonos chopped wildly with his axe even as he tracked his targets and brought them down with his pistol. As one fury crouched before him and sprang into a leap, Antigonos smashed the butt of his axe into its face and threw it back to the muddy ground. Off to his left, past Damaris, he saw one ranger dragged into the air by three of the beasts, his armour torn open and his life cast away in a blur of claws and teeth. There was a shattering discharge of light, a thunderous explosion that rocked the walls around them as his soul surged off towards the balm of High Azyr – bold Heraclius, who had once run the length of Aqshy's Great Parch to warn blessed Hallowheart of an impending Khornate attack. *Fly, my friend*, Antigonos thought. *May your soul seek the solace of Azyrheim. One day I will join you on the Anvil of Apotheosis.* He grimaced with rage and redoubled his blows. *But not this day!*

Slowly, the rangers began to gain the initiative. Much of the furies' assault had relied on surprise and the natural advantages of flight, but as the Stormcasts shot them from the sky, they began to retreat to their blood-smeared roosts. Up they flapped to the tunnel's natural rafters, crouching there like monstrous bats and shrieking at the armour-clad warriors who moved through their territory below.

Philemon picked up Heraclius' axe and hefted his own storm sabre to his shoulder. His boltstorm pistol was a broken ruin and he cast it to the ground. There was a deep gouge across the face of his helmet and his greaves were smeared with blood from where he had stamped one fury to death.

'There seems no end to the horrors this place can throw at us,' he growled. 'Do you still think the savages came this way?'

'I don't know,' Antigonos admitted. He gazed up into the black air, but he couldn't see Starglider. 'The trail is impossible to read now.'

'The furies would have gone for them too, surely?' Damaris said. She rotated her arm, stretching the pain from her shoulder where one beast had dug its claws past her armour. 'Maybe they're little more than the piles of bones we passed, or they're being torn to bits on top of these pillars as we speak?'

Leander crunched another magazine into his boltstorm pistol. 'Either way,' he said, nodding laconically towards the other end of the open space, 'they're coming on again. And this time they're not alone...'

Shrieking like a daemon, a warrior of the Untamed Beasts came rushing across the mist-drenched ground, the furies flapping wildly behind and above her. Charms and a necklace of teeth rattled at her wrists and throat, and she wore a helmet carved from a beast's skull, the fangs of the dead creature framing a face dark with bestial fury. She lashed out with her whip, and as Leander ducked the blow his shot went wide, streaking off into the darkness at the other end of the clearing. The woman howled wildly, and in moments the furies were swooping to strike the Stormcast warriors once more.

'Shoot them down!' Antigonos cried.

Boltstorm pistols flared in the gloom, and two of the furies fell from the air vomiting blood. His armour streaked with gore,

Antigonos moved through the furies like a hurricane, the bones that littered the ground crunching under his feet. He parried blows against his gauntlets, struck out with his axe and severed a fury's head. He looked for Starglider, but the tunnel's mouldering ceiling was unlit by her presence. He saw Damaris thrust her sabre through another fury's chest, and as the foul creature howled its agony, she drew her armoured fist back and smashed the teeth from its jaw. He saw Leander, with preternatural calm, choosing his targets and unleashing a hail of fire from his pistol. And he saw Philemon roaring with a joy as savage as that which animated the Chaos creatures, hacking left and right with his twin weapons, making of the tunnel walls a bloody canvas.

The barbarian warrior fought like a fury herself, darting, snarling, stabbing. She was relentless, but on her own she could not make a real difference; as soon as the furies were dead, Antigonos knew, she would quickly follow them. Another creature went down, its head split in half from Philemon's handaxe, then another, disembowelled as Damaris swept past with her storm sabre.

In the end, only the woman was left. She growled from the depths of her skull helmet, her whip snaking sinuously through the mist, her teeth bared and bloody. In her other hand, blade down, she held a knife made from what looked like sharpened bone. Antigonos held up his hand to warn the others back, and as they butchered the last of the furies, he slowly approached her.

There would be no surrender, he knew that. The air shimmered in the mist around them, dank and cold, beading on the woman's skin. Her panted breath came in a plume from her open mouth. Antigonos was about to say something, to throw her off guard before he attacked, when the whip was suddenly coiled around his throat and the woman was jerking him forward. He stumbled over the piled bones, one hand reflexively raised to loosen the cord of the whip. The savage leapt forward like a pouncing cat, her knife flicking out to strike his face mask. Before Antigonos could reach her, she screamed her war cry and kicked against his stomach, flipping backwards even as the whip snaked from his throat and flicked out again, the embedded teeth at the end smashing into his wrist and sending his axe spinning to the ground. Again the whip danced past him, the weighted lash striking between the plates of his armour, and every time he moved to block it the lash whipped back and struck again.

Warily he circled her, weaponless, his arms half raised. She feinted with the knife, skipping back and cracking the whip against the ground. He could see Leander draw a bead with his pistol, but Antigonos shook his head.

'You have no means of escape,' he said to the savage. 'Is this what you saw when you thought of your end? Buried deep underground, in the cold tunnels beneath the Fangs?'

'Death stalks the hunter as well as the prey,' she said, a wolfish grin on her face. Her accent was thick with the sound of Ghur – the rushing plains, the brutal mountains, the rivers and trees. 'Death comes for all, and none can outrun him. The Great Devourer will have his fill.'

'Of you, perhaps. But not of me.'

She sneered and snapped her wrist forward, dragging back the stock to send the lash screaming at his face. Antigonos sidestepped and caught the cord around his wrist, pulling back with all his god-forged strength to drag the woman to him in one irresistible movement. Her eyes widened in shock, but before she could let go of the whip and jump back, Antigonos had crashed his fist into the side of her head. He felt the bone shatter under the impact, and as her eyes glazed over, he drew his hunting knife from his belt and, with something like sorrow, plunged it into her chest.

Her body dropped to the ground. The cavern was silent; the fight was over.

One more had died, and now they were only four – Antigonos, Damaris, Leander and Philemon. The death was too near to weigh on the Hunter-Prime, but he knew the force of it would catch up with him somewhere on the journey ahead. A moment of snatched rest, perhaps, a reflective turn as they covered the ground, and then he would see Heraclius' face and hear his voice and remember him as the noble warrior he had been when he fought by his side.

He cast aside his battered helmet and wiped the blood from his face. Damaris, her chest heaving, spat blood on the ground. Leander, of few words at the best of times, said nothing as he cleaned his weapons. His face was a mask as unreadable as the face of his war helm, but Antigonos had known him too long to mistake the fury locked behind those dark eyes. They had all lost something this day, and the day was not over yet.

Philemon scouted ahead, picking through the wreckage of the fight and trying to find the trail. Antigonos knelt by the body of the woman. Her skull helm, the cranium of some vicious-looking beast, had cracked when she fell. He wondered if she had hunted that beast down herself, taken its mighty skull as a trophy. Hammer and throne, but she had fought well...

Woman... he thought. *She's little more than a girl.*

In death, bruised and battered though she was, there was still something lithe and graceful about her. She was like a hunting cat, he thought. The cast of her features, the shade of her skin, reminded him of Ghur – but Ghur as it had been, perhaps, in a dim and distant past that he could barely recall. He frowned. She looked like someone he had known once, he was sure, back in all the dead centuries before his first forging. He couldn't remember; it was too faint, too distant from where he now stood. After reforging, it wasn't so much that your memories were locked out of sight, but that they felt like tales vividly told by an old companion – unforgettable in the moment, but somehow fading out of sight as the years advanced. All you could remember was the tone they had been told in.

At the other end of the tunnel he found Starglider. In death she had killed the one who had killed her, her claws having disembowelled the fury that held her in its slavering jaws. Antigonos prised her body from the creature's mouth. He held her in his arms, and the grief in him was deeper than any he had felt before. He looked up at the high black ceiling of the tunnel, glad in a way that the sky was hidden. It would be forever dead to him now, because it did not have her in it.

Philemon returned from the other end of the catacomb, sprinting through the mist between the pillars as if the fight had taken nothing from him. Already Antigonos felt his own strength returning. *Our armour may be tarnished, but our hearts remain pure.*

'There's no sign of them,' Philemon said. 'The trail ends.'

'What do you mean? These are cunning folk, Philemon – are you sure they haven't turned you from the right path?'

'No, Hunter-Prime – there is no path. The tunnel ends against a wall of rock.'

He was at a loss. They couldn't have doubled back on themselves, not without running into the rangers in the vale. The way ahead was blocked, and yet somehow the survivors had gone on.

But there are other ways to travel, for us if not for them.

He placed Starglider's body reverently on the ground. 'Damaris,' he said. He saw the strength returning in her too, the will to complete their mission no matter the cost.

'Yes, Hunter-Prime?'

'Ready your astral compass. It will show us the way.'

Damaris took from her belt a dull orb caged in silver, and as she held it up the orb started to glow like a glimpse of starlight in a cobalt sky. Its surface swirled and contracted, and then gradually it began to flow like a stream of crystal water, casting out a beaming luminescence that bathed them all in blue. In an azure flash, the Stormcast rangers seemed to vanish, running along the celestial cusp as they sought out new paths to bring them off the mountains.

Night reached across the ruins, dipping its fingers into all the hidden spaces, caressing the bodies of the dead. On the margins of the skirmish ground, raptoryx and other fell scavengers stirred, drawn by fresh bounty. The wind rustled sadly over the broken stone.

In a sheltered space beneath a demolished cloister, a pile of bodies began to stir. One rolled away in a tangle of limbs; another seemed to sit up, its head lolling grotesquely, before it pitched forward and fell. A raptoryx, skittish and nervous, scuttled off. A feeble groan drifted across the silence, and in the darkness beneath the bodies came the glow of two burning eyes. A voice, harsh and weakened, called out desperately from amongst the dead.

'Flame protect me, give me strength!'

The light descended along the hidden pathways of the mountain's flank. It flickered like an ember burning low, like a spark smouldering in the dirt. But still it went on – falling sometimes, tumbling down the slope, but never stopping. Nothing could smother it, and the further it went, the deeper it burned.

Lord Rakaros was coming.

CHAPTER THIRTEEN

THE MOUNTAIN'S THROAT

Fear gripped him, and he was ashamed of it. Even as he ran it crept at his side, a deformed and sallow facsimile of his soul, an evil reflection that he didn't recognise. He longed to cut it down. The First Fang should not be afraid. Death is nothing to him – but it was not his own death that he feared.

Kurguth heard from far behind the shrieking of the furies, an outraged cackle high on the winds. The air shuddered around the Untamed Beasts as they ran, buckling with the breath of the storm that blew down the tunnel from the ravine at its head. Between the lightning bursts and the first pattering of the rain, Kurguth heard the song of battle rise. He thought of Mayra cracking her bone whip above her head, facing down the armoured hunters, and his legs nearly gave way beneath him.

Die well, my heart, he thought, gritting his teeth, and he sent the thought winging its way back to her. *Die like an Untamed Beast.*

The channel of the tunnel was high and narrow, and it twisted so much that from his position at the back of the warband Kurguth could not see Burak and the child at the front. He could hear him though, the baby wailing along the trail, disturbed by their frantic pace. Ekrah was running at his side, and as Kurguth glanced at him he caught a glimpse of the Preytaker's undisguised contempt. Kurguth opened his mouth to spit some insult for the Preytaker's insolence, but his mouth was dry and there was no space between his ragged breaths in which to speak. He turned away, focused instead on the path ahead.

The hunt for the child had nearly destroyed him, he knew. His leg throbbed with the old injury from his fight with Khask of the Iron Golem, and his heart was racketing about his chest like a trapped bird. This was going to be the end of him. Strangely, the thought was one of resignation, not rage. All beasts must meet their end in time, and the Great Devourer will have his feast. He sees all, and he consumes all. Kurguth looked to the clammy ground and ran on, biting back the taste of blood.

I will not be First Fang much longer. He tightened his grip on his axe, and as Ekrah sprinted on ahead of him he seemed to see Mayra's fierce face rise in his mind's eye. *I will not be long behind you, my love.*

The Mountain's Throat...

It had always been more of a phrase than an image, a form of words that hung like stars in the firmament, heavy and dazzling, and just out of reach. Burak felt compelled towards it though, always, and the further they went, the more convinced he became that his intuitions were right. They were on the true path; the Mountain's Throat would reveal itself when it needed to, and not a moment before – the tunnel that led from the mouth of the mountain through its guts, the passage they would have to brave to escape the gnawing violence of the Fangs.

Burak laughed quietly to himself, directing the laugh down

at the baby that squirmed in his arms and cried, the dark green eyes opening and blinking in the wind-lashed air, staring up at the Bloodseer as he led this merry dance through all these bloody acres of horror and destruction.

'Peace, peace, my child,' Burak sang. He clutched it tightly under one arm, and it rested in the cradle of his dagger-fist. His axe was slung across his back, and with his other hand he held the steel knife. The brass disc at his throat jumped and jangled as he ran. The baby, as if hypnotised, reached up to touch it.

'Oh, perhaps you're a Golem then, eh? You're drawn to it, little creature, aren't you? I wonder, I wonder... Well, if I had a snake at my throat I wouldn't be surprised if you reached for that too! It doesn't matter which tribe or band you favour, my boy, the altar will sing with your blood all the same.'

He bent to kiss the child on the top of its head, the downy hair tickling his lips. Burak laughed again, a wild and careening sound. He could see the altar as if carved from the mist before him, hidden deep within the catacombs of the ruined temple. There, struck by falling light, in the shadow of the Varanspire, the altar lay. The Hungering King's eye was trained upon it. He saw himself, Burak the Bloodseer, lay down his animal-skin cloak and place the baby upon it. He saw the steel knife rise and fall, heard the whip-crack of thunder, the pealing afterburn of Archaon's gaze turning full upon him. He saw it all, and his vision was true.

Kurguth had once asked him about his visions, when they were young warriors first pledged to the tribe.

'What do they feel like?' he had asked. 'How do you *know* they're true?'

'True?' Burak had said. 'I know they are true because they come true.'

'Not all of them.'

'Just the ones that matter.'

Kurguth, reaching almost beyond his capacity to frame the thought, had said, 'But how do you know which ones matter?'

'Because they are the ones that come true...'

'But who sends them?' Kurguth had said, exasperated. 'Don't you ever wonder? Where do they come from? Do they come from the Great Devourer?'

'Maybe... I don't know,' Burak had said, but in truth he had always known. What happens inside your mind is all you can really trust. The voice that ran in parallel to his thoughts, commenting on them and interrogating them, framing them in ways he didn't consciously understand, had always been there. Ever since he was a boy, he had felt he had two minds inside him, two voices, two ways of seeing the world.

Oh, Kurguth – if you could crack my head open and spill those secrets on the stone, how light my life would be...

He couldn't imagine that any of the others in the warband thought the same way he thought. He looked to Ekrah, leaping ahead on the trail. He glanced to the plains-runners who flanked him, to Tuk-kho and Ghulassa and the others, to poor Kurguth fading further by the moment, defeated by Mayra's necessary death. It was possible that inside each of them there were just vague impulses, a sense of hunger, the track of instinct, and nothing at all like the teeming cornucopia of Burak's thoughts. They didn't understand what the Great Devourer was; only he, Burak, was truly aware. The Devourer was created inside each of them, in some way, in how their thoughts and lusts and desires took shape inside their minds and found expression through their bodies and their actions. It was so simple, but none of them could really see it. They saw themselves as living in the shadow of a mighty force, but they didn't realise that they were *all* that mighty force. *They* were the Great Devourer, all of them a shard of his ravenous hunger, a tooth in his cataclysmic maw. Even the Everchosen, the Hungering King himself, was but part of this grand design. It was all so simple.

'That is the truth of the visions,' Burak whispered to the baby. 'I dream them, or I invent them, but the end is the same. They are true because I *believe* them to be true. *I* am the Great Devourer, as much as the Great Devourer is part of me.'

The baby looked at him, and for no longer than the span of a heartbeat his face seemed marked by a terrible, laughing shadow.

They came to a wall at the end of the tunnel, where fronds of lank weed hung heavy from the stone and the rock was stained with lime and calcium. The mist lapped up against the wall like a tide, and in the narrow dell the air was chill and dead, smelling faintly of sour breath. Kurguth wiped the beads of moisture from his forehead and watched Burak as he approached the wall. The Heart-eater was cautious, as if he were approaching a sleeping beast. Kurguth saw him reach out to touch its flank, patting his palm to the cold, wet stone and close his eyes.

'The Mountain's Throat,' he whispered. 'The passage from the mouth to the gut… It should be here.'

Kurguth slammed the heel of his fist against the stone. 'There's no passage here, nothing! The armoured ones cannot be far behind, Burak!'

'No,' Burak mumbled, 'not far. Not even Mayra could hold them off for long.'

Ekrah craned his neck to look up the sides of the tunnel wall, as if there would be an opening there for them to reach. The walls dripped with slime, greasy to the touch. Even Ekrah looked apprehensive, and with a questioning glance he met Kurguth's eyes. The First Fang grimaced, and gripped his axe.

Burak carefully sat on the ground, his legs crossed. He rocked the baby back and forth, cooing softly to it.

Kurguth checked on the path, but there was no sign yet of the pursuing Stormcasts. Suddenly, far behind them, a flash of golden light strobed the darkness, bursting with a sound like a meteor scorching through the sky. The walls of the tunnel flickered and were still.

'See, Kurguth!' Tuk-kho said. 'Another is dead then, yes? I saw one die like that amongst the ruins, killed by the snake-worshippers.' She gnashed her teeth in a grin and kissed the hilt of her blade. 'Mayra has made them pay!'

There was silence now, where before there had been the dim sounds of combat. One more dead, one more armoured giant sent back to its golden God-King, but there had been more than one of them to start with… The mist rippled and fell still.

Kurguth turned back to the stone wall and saw Burak still in the same position, sitting on the ground amongst the tides of drifting mist, mumbling to himself, or praying, or talking to the baby. Mayra, the plains-runners… All those miles since the Blood Lake Basin, all this ground devoured by their feet as they ran and ran and ran. So many dead, until there were now no more than a dozen of them left. Kurguth looked back to the line of the ravine, and he felt a chill move through him, gripping his bowels, turning his knees to water. It was not fear, he knew, although it almost felt the same. It was rage.

He stared at Burak and remembered every fight, every blow, every insult he had taken in all the years of their youth. He remembered every time he had defended the Bloodseer from those who would have cast him out – cursing him as a madman, gods-touched, weak in the head. He felt, as if living it again, every skirmish they had fought together on the savage plains of the Jagged Savannah, as Burak gathered his own followers and made the Split-Tongue Tribe a force to be reckoned with. He shuddered to recall the hellish journey through the Mawgate in Ghur, called to the Eightpoints by Burak's visions, the desperate paths they had taken to sneak past the nightmare legions of the Everchosen as they poured along the fortified route to the arcway. And then the skirmishes across the Corpseworm Marches, around the ringed mountains by the Blood Lake Basin – the raids and reprisals, the feints and sorties, all the violence they had meted out and received in turn, deaths unnumbered and unmourned, deaths that all took them one step closer towards a goal that always seemed just out of reach...

'For what,' Kurguth said in a low tone. He took a pace towards the Heart-eater. 'For what?' His voice was louder now, strident, questioning. 'For *what?*' Burak did not turn. His head was bowed low over the baby. The wall in front of him dripped with water. Kurguth unslung his axe. '*For what?* You killed all of them!' he shouted. 'You killed her as surely as if you'd plunged the blade in yourself, that steel blade you dare to hold in your hand!'

He swung high and fast with the axe, bearing it straight down towards Burak's head, straining to cleave the Heart-eater in two. His vision was blurred with tears and spit flew from his mouth as he snarled with the effort, and as the axe came down, he closed his eyes – but Burak did not move.

Shards of bone splintered and flew away, and when Kurguth opened his eyes, his arm numb, he saw Ekrah with his serrated blade extended, having blocked the blow. Mightily they strained against each other, Kurguth trying to force the Preytaker's sword aside, Ekrah trying to throw up the First Fang's axe. From the ground, Burak said, 'So, is it to be like this, then, my brother?'

Kurguth gritted his teeth. He looked at the plains-runners. Some had drawn their knives, backing away; none had edged closer to the First Fang. He glared at Ekrah, whose eyes flashed with anger behind the narrow slits of his helmet.

'It is,' Kurguth said.

He jumped back, breaking the hold, and slammed the butt of his axe into Ekrah's face. The Preytaker reeled, whipping his sword around to parry a blow that didn't come, skipping back to hold the weapon high as he got the measure of his foe. Kurguth, axe held loose at his side, felt the rage upon him. His breath was tattered, sucking oxygen into his lungs, pumping blood into his muscles. He cast his harpoon to one side and it disappeared into the mist at his feet. His vision was drowning in red. He bared his teeth as if preparing to rip the Preytaker apart and devour him. Still Burak hadn't moved, and more than anything that made the anger boil up and subsume him utterly.

He lashed out with his axe. Ekrah, reading the moment perfectly, danced forward and slashed left to right, dragging his sword vertically to block Kurguth's blow. But as the heavy axe blade entangled itself with Ekrah's sword, Kurguth simply dropped it, dragging Ekrah's guard down, opening him up to a headbutt into which Kurguth put every ounce of his anger and hatred, his boiling rage at the death of Mayra and at this squalid end Burak had dragged them all into. Kurguth felt something shatter in his own face as he hit the crosspiece of Ekrah's helmet, a bone cracking above his eye, but there was still enough power in the blow to send the Preytaker flying backwards, his sword careening off into the mist. He crashed against the wall of the tunnel, blood pouring from his nose, his eyes dazed and wild. Kurguth leapt towards him, pummelling him in the stomach and chest, ripping the helmet from his head and snapping an elbow into his eye. Ekrah screamed. He pushed Kurguth back and fell to the ground, rolling away, clutching his ruined eye, his other hand desperately searching the shrouded ground for his sword. Kurguth stood over him, heart lurching in his chest. He felt he could wrench the Preytaker apart, limb from limb, with his bare hands.

'You will never be First Fang now, Ekrah,' Kurguth laughed.

Blood sheeted down his face from where the broken bone above his eye had split the skin. His head rang with strange, distorted sounds, and he felt as if only his anger was keeping him upright. The moment it drained away, he would collapse – and he would never get up again. Around him, the plains-runners wailed with uncertainty, some with knives drawn as if to attack him once the Preytaker fell.

Let the cubs play, Kurguth thought, *while the prowlers are fighting.*

Ekrah sank back and leaned against the wall. His eye was a mess of blood and pulped flesh, and half of it was running down his cheek. Kurguth stood over him, and he was about to reach down, to throttle the life from him or even tear his head from his body, when he heard Burak's voice whispering low in his ear.

'Kurguth, my brother, don't you remember my words?' There was a crack in his voice. His breath was a light breeze against Kurguth's skin.

He felt fire in his chest, a searing pain that lanced straight through him. He couldn't breathe. And then, somehow, he was kneeling on the ground, and the wall of the tunnel was in front of him, stained and weed-choked and stinking of death. He tried to speak but the words died in his mouth. The pain crackled and blazed, blinding as the sunrise, and the cold mist was wrapping itself around him like a grave shroud.

Kurguth opened his eyes, and through bleary vision looked down and saw the two tines of Burak's dagger-fist protruding from his chest. Blood dripped from them, deep and red, and it took Kurguth a moment to realise that it was his.

'Burak…?'

He felt the steel blade resting lightly against his throat. Its touch was as cold as the night.

'Sacrifice,' Burak whispered, 'means giving up something that you love. Something that is a part of you. I give you up, my brother.'

The last thing Kurguth saw was the spray of his blood arc wildly against the stone, and where the blood reached, the stone began to split and draw apart, slobbering open with a stench of decay. Inside the stone there was darkness, and the darkness deepened and drew nearer, until all there was in the world was darkness, and light was but a hazy pinprick an eternity away. Kurguth tried to reach for that light, but the distance was too far.

Mayra, he wanted to say. *I failed you... I failed all of you. Great Devourer, hear my prayer! If nothing survives of me, I call for vengeance on this man... Kill him. Kill him before it's too late...*

But there would be no more speech now, no light, no feel of the wind in his hair as he ran the frantic courses of the hunt. There was nothing at all.

'See, my brother,' Burak said, weeping as he laid Kurguth's body down. 'I needed you after all. I always needed you. And the Mountain's Throat has opened for us at last.'

They dragged his body into the tunnel, and as they passed its threshold the opening began to close, meshing perfectly once more, until all that could be seen in that clammy dell was the trailing mist. Burak laid the baby on the ground and paused to cut the heart from Kurguth's chest. He bit deeply, gorging himself on the meat, and felt Kurguth's spirit surge inside him – raging, burning, incandescent. When he had eaten his fill, he passed the heart around. Ekrah, his broken eye covered by a length of cloth, ate next. Tuk-kho, Ghulassa and the surviving plains-runners ate what was left, and as the last morsel was swallowed, Burak took up the baby and dipped his bloody fingers against the child's lips. He grinned wildly as he did so, his pointed teeth gleaming in his blackened gums. He could feel the mountains around him pulsing with life – with each mangy beastman hacking its prey to death; with each raptoryx shucking a mouthful of carrion down its throat; with each grasping vine and poisonous root sucking the life from the earth.

'Ekrah,' he said, 'you are now First Fang, my right hand. Tuk-kho, you are now Preytaker, my eyes and ears, the knife I wield.' He looked at the ridged and fleshy sides of the tunnel walls – the Mountain's Throat, which led clear through the Fangs to the other side, to the plains of the Tormented Lands and the buried altar where the baby would die. 'Now, my tribe, the last stage lies open before us. Through the Mountain's Throat, and all that remains is the temple and the altar – and the glory beyond.'

PART THREE

PART THREE

CHAPTER FOURTEEN

REMNANTS

When night fell on the Bloodwind Spoil, only the unwary stayed abroad. Those who wanted to live took shelter.

In the Tormented Lands, though, shelter was hard to come by. A wilderness wracked by sandstorms, it stretched in a monotonous spread between the Fangs and the Varanspire in the distance. Strangler-roots prowled the hollows and the banks of brackish streams, looking for prey, and the very earth was a poisoned residue of ancient magics. Here and there across its vast expanse were the ruins of observatories and temples from the Age of Myth – tabernacles to forgotten gods, orreries where philosophers of old would scry the heavens, wizards' towers and the palaces of merchant princes. All were now little more than the jumbled stones of their foundations, and they were few and far between. As night descended, cast like a black sheet across the scrubland, a traveller would have little recourse but to pitch his tent and hope he lived to see the dawn.

But now, deep in the dismal steppes, a light was faintly glowing.

It shivered on the horizon, shrinking and then flaring higher, but never more than the suggestion of a flame. It was light, and it was life – that was all he knew. That was enough. He drew his robes around him and staggered on.

Rassa watched the meat crackle on the spit as Grex fed more wood to the flame. Taglen turned the handle, and she felt her stomach lurch with hunger; she could almost taste the grease on her lips. Around them, the shadows cast by the fire crept and lengthened, reaching up into the crannies of the enormous skull, into the cleft of the brainpan and the sockets of the eyes. It was as big as a house, this skull, big enough for three of them and more. As the two men cooked the meat, Rassa pulled her blanket tight and looked around at this strange place where Grex had brought her. They sat on a floor of fine silt, and behind her were the half-buried teeth of the creature's upper jaw, each tooth taller than she was. A rough panel of wood had been thrown across the nasal passage and secured with a length of leather cord. The rest of the skull's pale interior had been decorated with soiled curtains and frayed rugs, and from rusting nails hung bags of rank-smelling herbs and the dried carcasses of rodents and bats.

While one of the eye sockets stared down only into the dirt of the Tormented Lands, the other gazed up at the gravitation of the turning sky. Rassa could see the wheeling progress of the arcane orbs – Illuminated Hysh, maybe, or even High Azyr. She shuddered as they passed and as the cold music of the cosmos seemed to dance a moment around the skull's interior. The window of the eye was like the picture of a dream, she thought – framed, bordered, hinting at a greater meaning that was always just out of reach.

They had fallen in with Taglen three days ago, and he had brought them across the parched lands to where the Beldam lived.

'She is a great witch,' Taglen had said, 'powerful and respected. If we stick with her, none will steal our scavenge.'

'What's in it for her?' Grex had asked, reasonably. 'If she's so powerful, what use are we?' He had wiped his snout with his stump and shrugged, and Rassa had nodded agreement. Taglen was rangy, thin as dried driftwood, and there was a lump against his neck that in certain lights looked almost like a vestigial head.

'Errands,' Taglen had said with enthusiasm. 'Cooking and cleaning, fetching all the wart-bugs and dead-man's-fancy she needs for her spells!'

Grex had agreed, and so the three of them had approached the Beldam's hovel, this half-buried skull lying stark against the maundering steppe, to offer their services. At night, lit only by the meagre stars and the quaking flame of her cookfire, the skull had seemed no more than a cave or a hut, but by the sepia light of day all of them had seen it for what it really was. The Beldam had let them inside, had fed them from her stocks and had then vanished with a promise that she would be back by morning.

'What is this place?' Rassa asked now. She could smell the meat too and silently begged the men to finish with their cooking. 'I've never heard of anything with a head so big it would leave a skull this size behind it.'

'It's a godbeast, got to be,' Grex said. He sounded certain, but Rassa had long since learned that Grex's certainty was as good as an admission of his ignorance. 'Fell from the Darkness Without, crashed down here, died – there you go,' he concluded.

'What happened to it?' she said.

Grex sniffed. 'I don't know. Some god or another killed it, probably. Smited it with their hammer or blasted it with some lightning bolt or another. You know what gods are like, in the old tales. They're always doing things like that.'

'Why?'

'Beats me. They're gods – they do what they want.'

Taglen scoffed at Grex's theory. 'It's no godbeast! You'd know all about it if it was. You'd have half the Spoil fighting over its remains if that was the case. Powerful magics still in those bones, I've heard.'

'So, if it's no godbeast,' Rassa said, 'what was it?'

'Haven't a clue,' Taglen said cheerfully. 'Don't care neither. It's shelter, that's all that matters. You don't want to be out there at night, the lord protect us.'

'The lord protect us,' both Grex and Rassa whispered. Rassa touched the eight-pointed star that hung around her neck, a twist of metal Grex had made for her many months ago.

'Have you heard?' Taglen went on. 'Rumours are flying like furies out there – I can't make head nor tail of them. Uproar in Carngrad, it seems, the Scions of the Flame at the Splintered Fang's throat. An Iron Golem convoy's clean vanished coming from the Skullpikes.' He lowered his voice. 'Something about a child, I heard, a great sacrifice to the lord, or...' He lowered his voice even further. 'Maybe it'll grow to a great warrior who'll cast the lord down.'

Rassa gasped. 'Don't say that!'

'It's just what I've heard,' Taglen said quickly. 'I'm not saying it's true or nothing, just the word that's going around in the scavenger camps.'

Grex sat back. Despite the fire, he shivered. 'That's not all,' he said in an ominous tone. 'I've heard that–'

'What have you heard, boy?' a great voice interrupted. The Beldam stood there in the doorway, hunched and glowering at them with her pale eye. She held a wicker cage in one hand, and from inside it came frantic squeaks and growls that she silenced with a strike of her staff. With a wordless look she made Grex scurry over to close the door behind her, and then laboriously she set about storing the supplies she'd gathered – the screaming mandrake roots, the bitter herbs, the bug-eyed land shrikes. Outside, the mutant steed she used to trawl across the nearby fields huffed and lowed. Rassa hated that thing; it was like an awful cross between a pig and a lizard, and it stank. 'Been listening to gossip and hearsay, have you?' she said. 'Been frightening yourselves with idle tales?'

'None such, I swear it!' Grex stammered. He bowed reverently, and the Beldam snorted with contempt. She thrust four clay cups at him and bid him pour the sour beer. Grex filled each cup and passed it round, daring an extra swig when the Beldam wasn't looking.

She was old, older than anything Rassa had seen in the Spoil in all her young life. Not much made it that far. Her pale eye roved like a glow-bug, never settling for long, and the other eye was hidden behind a lank tangle of hair that dripped down her forehead. She had a hump that near unbalanced her, and she made her way with an iron-tipped staff she claimed she had found in the ruins of a great wizard's laboratory, left over from the time of Myth. Slowly, the Beldam sat herself down by the fire and sniffed curiously at the meat.

'Is that not ready yet?' she scorned. 'You'll damn near burn it to a crisp if you're not careful.'

'Nearly, mistress,' Taglen grovelled. He turned the spit faster, and a gobbet of fat spat into the flames and hissed.

'What were you talking about then?' she demanded. 'You know I don't like rumours and tittle-tattle. Rumours make people afraid, and there's enough to fear in the Bloodwind Spoil without having to make anything up. Lord protect us...'

'Lord protect us,' the others said.

'Your home,' Rassa said quickly. 'We were talking about the skull, about... Grex thinks it's a godbeast.'

Grex stared, affronted. 'I never,' he snapped. 'Meaning, I was just thinking that maybe–'

'You're more of a fool than you look, then,' the Beldam said. 'It was no godbeast. In truth I don't know what it was – I didn't kill it.'

'What did?' Rassa asked.

For the first time the old woman smiled, and it was a dreadful thing to see. 'Now there's the right question to be asking,' she said.

'Stormcasts, maybe,' Grex said. He was feeling bold. The food was almost ready, they had fire and shelter, and nothing was trying to kill them. That was luxury itself, in the Spoil. 'That's what I'd heard, the rumours. The storm-born are abroad...'

Taglen and Rassa both immediately made the sign of the star against their chests. Taglen sucked in a shocked breath, and Rassa felt like she was going to be sick. She closed her eyes and rocked back on her heels, mumbling prayers.

Of them all, only the Beldam seemed unaffected. She became quiet, seemed almost to deflate as she sat there by the fire. A look of vast sorrow came into her face, and with a stray twig she poked at the flames.

'Is that what they're saying out there?' she said. 'Stormcast Eternals...'

'Everyone knows they're not real!' Rassa wailed. 'Just stories, just legends to frighten decent folk.'

'Decent folk, eh?' Grex snuffled. 'And where are you going to find any of them in the Spoil?'

'You know what I mean,' she said. 'Gods-fearing folk, those that worship the lord.'

'Is it true, mistress?' Taglen asked the witch. 'Are they real, or just stories? I've never seen one.'

'Nor would you have lived long if you had,' the Beldam said quietly.

'Have... have you seen them?'

'Once,' she said. 'A long, long time ago.'

She told them, then, in a halting tone as she reached back into the deep chambers of her memory, about a young girl and her father and the hovel where they had lived deep in the Desolate March. Low stone walls, it had, bolstered by scavenged wood and flaps of canvas. They scratched a living from the bare earth, grew bile-berries and kept a pair of skeletal kyne. It was life – such as life was in the Bloodwind Spoil. They feared the gods and worshipped the Great Lord in his distant tower, and so bare were the surrounding lands that few bothered them.

'My father used to tell me tales of the olden times,' the Beldam said. 'Stories to frighten me before I went to sleep. Of the hated God-King and his pantheon of the weak, and of the cringing wretches who bowed before him across this land before the True Gods came. Great cities they built, temples to flatter his arrogance. Wizards threw up their towers and delved into the sacred mysteries. The realmgates stretched their arcane roads throughout the realms, and the arcways kept them safe.' She laughed bitterly. 'Though not for long.'

Chaos came, she told them, and threw down the feeble foundations of Sigmar's empire to the dirt. All was slaughter and ruin, and the Great Lord, the Everchosen, set up his spire in the centre of the land. The great cities fell to ruin, the wizards' towers were thrown down and the temples despoiled. All was covered by the dust of ages – but the God-King never forgot. Relics and treasures untold were hidden in the earth from the time of Myth, and Sigmar brooded mightily on them, forever out of reach. Until…

'Until when, mistress?' Taglen said. The meat was ready, and he pulled each piece off the spit as Grex held out the plates. The Beldam was silent for a moment, and when she continued, her voice was cracked by the pressure of her memories.

'Until he forged the Stormcast Eternals, his warriors of gold and silver, his weapon in the wars,' she said. 'Nowhere is safe from them. Even here, as deep in the Eightpoints as you can get, they come. Not in flashes of lightning, not in hosts for open war, but as hunters slipping through the gaps, swift-running across the deserts, scouting through jungle and forest. They have arcane ways to read the land and find the hidden paths that carry them.'

'And you actually saw one?' Grex said. He held a plate out to her. She started eating, picking at the meat.

'I did, and more than one. Our home, where I lived with my father, was no hovel, it seemed. Once it had been something else. The entrance to a chamber, a vault, a temple? Whatever it was and whatever secrets it stored, the memory of it had hung heavy on the God-King's mind, and he sent his hunters to find it.

'I remember waking up,' she said, 'late in the night. The screams of old spirits out there never bothered me. They were a lullaby to me in those days. But then one night, the screams suddenly stopped, and the silence was like nothing I had ever experienced before. It was the silence before a storm, the silence after an atrocity. My father took up his pitchfork and stood at our door, and I remember staring from the window when they appeared. Like gods, they seemed – three giants who dwarfed my father, and he was a tall man. Their armour was a dull gold, and they held swords and axes in their hands. They had tattered furs across their shoulders, and their helmets were like the masks of the dead. And when they spoke, my father quailed.

'"Step aside," their leader said. "You squat on holy ground, scum, and I would not see it profaned a moment longer." My father, brave as he was, did not step back. Their leader took off his helmet, and his face was a terrible thing – scarred, marked with savage warpaint, twisted with rage and hatred. I have never forgotten it. It haunts my dreams still.'

She was quiet again, for a moment, as she ate. Rassa, shivering under the blanket although the night was not cold, looked at the Beldam's strained face.

'What happened?' she asked. 'Did your father let them in?'

'He did not. And so they cut him down, without mercy. They ransacked our home, tore up the flagstones, descended into a chamber I had no idea was there. And when they were finished, they disappeared as swiftly as they had come, and they gave not a thought to the child lying there at their feet, sobbing, cradling her dead father. Sometimes,' the Beldam said, 'I wish they had cut me down too.'

The ate together and said nothing, and in Grex's face there was something like shame. He should never have mentioned it. Rassa glanced to the eye socket high above them, the framed circle of the night, and she thought of swift hunters haunting the Spoil. 'Lord protect us,' she whispered under her breath. Outside they could hear the Beldam's steed munching at its fodder, shifting its ponderous bulk against the dirt.

Taglen, hoping to break the tension, said, 'You've given me the hand again,' he complained. 'You know I don't like the hand.' He held up his meat – a human fist charred by the fire. Grex protectively drew his plate away; he had a nice slice of cheek.

'You takes what you're given,' he said. 'Isn't that right, mistress?'

'Eat your meat,' she said. 'It's not often we get a wanderer out here, and we eat what we can find.'

Rassa nodded in agreement; she was happy with her foot.

Sullenly, Taglen addressed himself to his plate again, chewing the dry meat from the fingers. He sighed. Wanderers were rare, it was true – you had to take what you could get.

The knock at the door boomed through the empty skull, and each of them froze, meat half raised to their mouths. Taglen looked at Grex; Grex looked to the Beldam. Rassa touched the star at her throat, and the Beldam held up her staff. They sat there in absolute silence, not even daring to swallow what was in their mouths.

The knock came again, heavier and more insistent.

'Begone!' the Beldam shouted. The tip of her staff began to glow as she got to her feet. 'There's nothing for you here!'

The door shivered under the blow and flew open, and standing there in the light of the fire was a trembling figure, huge, dressed in tattered robes, its eyes as bright as embers. Grex howled and hid himself behind Taglen, and Rassa pulled the blanket over her head as if that would save her. Only the Beldam stood her ground, her staff held out and her rotten teeth bared. The figure looked at each of them in turn, its arm reaching out and its mouth slowly opening to croak a single word before it collapsed to the ground:

'*Help...*'

He had no idea how he found his way off the mountain. The pain in his stump had been too great, eclipsing everything. All he could think of was the call of the venom in his veins, the pulsing agony of his missing arm. Ashrath had put one foot in front of the other, and the venom had guided him. Gift of the Coiling Ones, of the spirit-snake, it had sung like a twisting melody inside him. All he had to do was follow the line of its song.

During the day, he crawled into the dry hollows of the scrub and rested for a while, or he found loose cairns of rock and sheltered in their lee while the sandstorms blew over. He may have slept; he may have dreamed – he couldn't say. When darkness fell again, he continued, pacing a trail that existed only as a high, discordant whine in his head, calling him ever onwards.

He walked now over rough ground, dwelling inside the pain. His remaining hand was clamped like a circlet above his elbow, pressing deep into the muscle. Sometimes he whimpered at the agony; other times he laughed. Still the venom shot and fluttered through him, greening his sight, colouring everything with a faint tinge of emerald. When the light failed and the night swept over the land, he could see traces of heat in the dirt around him – rodents, scuttling insects that existed as a patch of flaring red in the murk. Quick as a snake, he dropped to the ground and snatched one of them up, a squirming beetle as big as his fist with a greasy, furred abdomen and two glittering compound eyes on wavering stalks. He crunched it to a bitter paste and gagged against the flavour, but it was sustenance at least. It would keep him going, and to keep going was now the sole and guiding purpose of his being. He wiped the paste from his mouth and checked again that his sword was still shackled to his hip. He would need the sword before this was done. It was one of the few things he knew with any certainty.

The light bronzed, and distances withdrew. Everything seemed flattened around him, two-dimensional. Puffs of dust quickened in the wind, and a warm breeze harried the steppe. He could see faint shapes on the horizon, like shacks or huts huddled into each other. He turned away from them, hunching down, scurrying now to keep his profile low. When they had receded far over to his left, he turned again and headed on. He had as if floating in his mind's eye the image of a temple thrown down by the immeasurable ages, reduced to a scattering of stone and the bare suggestion in the earth of its long-forgotten foundations. Buried in drifts of sand, choked by scrub grass, it hid its secrets deep. But there would be more to it than met the eye, he was sure. There were stairs, and chambers, and long corridors made of cyclopean stone – and there would be an altar, where a baby would lie crying.

Ashrath hurried his pace, as if he could hear the crying of the baby on the breeze.

'I am almost there,' he shouted through dry, cracked lips. 'I will walk at the right-hand side of a god!'

Days passed, many nights – he couldn't say how many. Ashrath stumbled on, and the plains around him seemed neither to recede nor grow wider. It was as if he had been walking always in one spot, pacing a narrow patch of ground and never moving any further. The featureless spread of grassland and thorns, of desert drifts and rocky outcrops and narrow, meandering streams stained the colour of gangrene, began to weigh against his mind. He looked for caves or hollows, for anything that seemed to lead underground – for underground was where he needed to go, where the child would be taken. The venom in his blood had told him.

When night was on him again, he crouched by the edge of a stinking stream and splashed water against his face. He rested for a while against a tooth of rock, staring out at the limitless land as it vanished in the gloom. A lone campfire wobbled against the horizon some distance away, but apart from that the land was lost in a sullen murk. He looked up into the branching night, the trail of arcane orbs planing smoothly across the velvet sky. The realms spun and twisted around him, and the Eightpoints brooded viciously at the centre of all creation. He closed his eyes, dizzy suddenly, thrown off balance by that maddening cosmic scale. Behind his eyes he saw the stars coalesce into the coils of Nagendra's children, the Coiling Ones, vast as eternity. His blood cooled, and he began to shake. Was this how Ma'sulthis had felt when he communed with them, when Kathenga's eyes, like shot amber, turned their blind gaze upon him and the Coiling Ones began to speak through his mind?

Ashrath squeezed the bridge of his nose and tried to clear his head. Why him? Why Ashrath Silenthis? What did they see in him that he couldn't see in himself? Every day since the ceremony in Invidia he had demanded obedience and respect as no more than his due, convinced that his destiny was merely sitting there waiting for him to pick it up. As Ma'sulthis had dripped the poisons into his mouth, Ashrath had shrugged off their effects to demonstrate his power. As the Serpent Caller chanted his prayers, Ashrath had felt the Coiling Ones' attention slide gracefully towards him, and it all felt like no more than he deserved.

But everything had gone wrong since then. His destiny had run along a crooked path, full of pitfalls and disasters. He had brought his warband through the Realmgate to the Eightpoints, certain he would draw Archaon's favour the moment his feet touched the soil, but every step he had taken since then had led him only further into ruin. That foolish feud with Rakaros and his Scions, jostling for territory in that foul quarter of Carngrad, had invited only fire and destruction. And then the quest into the Hag's Claw Forest, searching for the rumoured Shrine of Nagendra, an ancient relic of the Eightpoints' earlier days, led on by legends that in the end proved to be nothing but lies. The duel with Su'atha, his greatest warrior. The journey into the Fangs, the fight with Rakaros and the Stormcasts that almost destroyed them – and then Essiltha's betrayal, curse her name unto the very ends of time itself! Essiltha – he would never stop praying for her death, as long as he lived!

He clutched his wounded arm and grimaced. The pain was unbearable, but the self-pity was worse. Ashrath ground his teeth and lay down in the dust. What were mortal men to the gods, that they should torment them so? Why, when a god spoke, was your first instinct to believe its words? This could all be no more than a cosmic joke to them, a petty amusement that had cost Ashrath everything he had.

Light caught his eye, far off in the distance. A strange blue glow seemed to unfold there, thin and wavering, growing stronger as it shot across the steppe. Instinctively he crept for cover, pressing himself against the rock. The blue light flickered and then was still, and in the air Ashrath thought he could smell a hint of ozone, like a field after a lightning strike.

'Stormcasts,' he whispered to himself. He watched the darkness for an hour, but the blue light didn't come back. He lay down to sleep for a while, and in his dreams the light dazzled and jumped like a will-o'-the-wisp, like the caged flame of some spirit saturated with an ancient malice.

He found Essiltha's body not long after dawn.

He had been following the line of the stream, which curled and twisted across the steppe towards the bleak shard of the Varanspire still many miles distant. The tower sat there on the horizon, plunged into the heart of the Eightpoints, the nail on which the angle of the Bloodwind Spoil hung. Just to look at it hurt Ashrath's eyes, but the stream seemed to stretch in that direction and the bank was easier ground to walk on than the rugged surface of the plains. He headed on, lulled by the babble of the oily water, occasionally stopping to watch the progress of some lumpen mass as it turned and rolled on the tide – bodies, mostly, their wounds bled out, or severed limbs and headless torsos. Ashrath watched them sink beneath the water, only to surface again a few feet further on. The refuse of the shanty town around the complex of the Varanspire, perhaps. He wondered where the stream ended, what inland sea it vomited these bodies into. He turned away, the pain in his stump reduced this morning to a dull, insistent ache.

Ahead, there was a tumbledown shack made of tin, a dead tree twisted like a tortured soul beside it. Essiltha had been nailed to that tree, her throat cut, her body decorated with bloody wounds. Her arms were outstretched, and her head lolled on her shoulder. Her eyes were gone, eaten by the birds. She looked like she had died in pain.

The tree groaned beneath her, and from a jagged rend in the bark something that looked like a tongue emerged to lap at the dripping blood. Ashrath kicked it, and the tongue slapped back into the gap.

He stared up at the aelf for what felt like hours. He looked into her eyeless face, the smooth and beautiful angles now drawn with pain. He tried to feel the joy he had promised himself when he saw her corpse, but there was nothing in his heart but a flutter of... He couldn't even say. Sorrow? Regret? It was neither of those things. Perhaps all he felt was the weight of his solitude. He was now alone, utterly. He had taken them all from the jungles of Invidia, leading his warband with all the confidence of a conquering prince. He had been so sure of himself, convinced that glory was his for the taking. And now he was the last of them, sole survivor of the Horned Krait, adrift in the wastelands of the Bloodwind Spoil, and everyone who had followed his banner was dead. He clenched his teeth.

Ashrath looked around the listing hut and found the bodies of the clearbloods Essiltha had taken with her, scattered in the dust. All of them had scorch marks from lightning strikes against their chests, and one had been beheaded. He wondered how long Essiltha had fought, whether she had sent any more of those lightning scum up into the heavens. *Damn them, damn them all...* He thought about cutting her down, but with one arm he didn't think he could manage. The tongue, a gross purple thing dripping with slime, tentatively emerged once more to lick the blood that dripped down the trunk. Ashrath took his sword and split the tongue down the middle, bifurcating it like a snake's. Something squealed and shivered inside the tree. He laughed, and it was a cold, vicious sound.

Let her rot, he thought. *It's no more than she deserves.*

His arm ached in sympathy, but as he left the shack behind, he felt something bend and quiver inside him, greening his sight even deeper. It stoked a fire in his belly. He was seething, he realised, hot with a growing fury. There was just him, him alone – very well then, alone! And even if this was all just a jest on the

Coiling Ones' part, then the joke would be on them in the end. He would not give up. He was Ashrath Silenthis, and his ambition eclipsed the world.

'Let them all beware!' he snarled. 'All of them, every last living thing in this poisonous land!' He drew his sword and held it high above his head.

'Ashrath Silenthis is coming!'

CHAPTER FIFTEEN

HUNTER'S PREY

In the dream it lies before him, shimmering in the crystal mist. From a distance it looks no more than a jumbled heap of stones furred with moss, but the closer he comes to it the more its old form reveals itself. Sand and the silt of ages past have buried most of the temple. There are two great stone slabs on either side of a crooked doorway, the door having long since rotted into the dust. On a lintel above the doorway is a carved symbol blurred by time, a twin-tailed comet. The darkness beckons him in, tenebrous and cool. His feet meet the first flagstones, a flight of stairs that lead down into the murk. He pauses a moment on the threshold, and then forces himself on. His heart thumps harder in his chest, hard enough, it feels, to break his ribs. His breath frosts in a plume of smoke before him. The clammy air grips his skin and makes him shiver.

He comes to a corridor that trickles with the drip of water, and as he walks old torches flare to life on either side of him. The corridor stretches on, arrow-straight, deeper and deeper into the ground. All he can hear is the drip of water, the muted scuff of his bare feet on the stone. Here and there along the corridor the stone has fallen away, leaving gaping holes in the floor that he must steel himself to cross. He paces back, pauses, runs and leaps – and a patter of rock falls into the abyss beneath him. On he goes, and the dream unfolds before him.

Eventually, the corridor opens out into a wide chamber, so wide that he cannot see either side of it in the gloom. Across a floor of cracked flagstones, creatures scuttle and gibber. There is a stale smell in the air, of long-dead things desiccating in the silence. He crosses the chamber, his steel knife held low and ready, but nothing emerges to attack him.

In the centre of the chamber he stops to listen. He can hear his heart beating, and he can hear his breath whistling through his nose. The dripping of water somewhere behind him, the low hum of the wind coursing through a gap in the stone. And after a moment he can hear something else too, very faintly at first, and then more insistent. A cry that softly pierces the silence. The cry of a child.

He moves more quickly across the chamber, and as he gets closer to the middle the torches flare in their brackets around the walls. Cold green light emerges from the flames and is cast down onto a vast stone altar. The edges of the altar are chipped and worn, the stone stained by unsentimental time, but he has the sense that this huge platform of rock has stood here since the beginning of the ages, and it will still be here once all the ages have been burned away. The altar came first, and the temple was built around it. When the temple is ruined utterly, the altar will still stand.

Cautiously he approaches it, his knife held up. Creeping closer, taking the first step onto the dais where the altar stands, then the second, he peers over the edge. Lying there in the middle of the bare rock is a boy child, naked and alone, kicking out his legs and paddling with his arms. His eyes are open and they are green, and as they turn to look at him, he feels something shrink away inside.

'There,' he says in his softest voice, baring his sharp teeth in the semblance of a smile. 'Quiet now, I'm here. I'm here for you...'

He holds the knife in his right hand. The blade is a line of purest silver. The baby looks at it, his eyes wide. He rolls onto his front and begins to crawl across the altar, and then he stands up on wobbling legs, although he is no more than a few days old and still far too young to be walking. The baby comes nearer, staggering like a drunk across the stone. Burak the Bloodseer trembles, and the knife drops from his hand. It clatters to the ground with a sound like a ringing bell. He looks again at the baby, but it no longer has a human face. There is a shadow across it in the shape of an eight-pointed star, and as Burak stares at the child he sees the centre of the star begin to spasm and unfold. In the middle of the baby's forehead another eye blinks open, black as the void, and when it stares at him, Burak feels it peeling away every last atom of his soul. He wants to scream, but his voice is dead in his throat, and the baby is getting closer. Its mouth distends, unshackling a rack of fangs, and it reaches up to claw the skin from Burak's face, drawing him down towards those gnashing teeth, sharp as needles, the black third eye blazing into his mind and paring it away to nothing, while its green eyes shimmer and glow like infernal orbs staining the night sky. And as he feels himself being devoured by this thing, he can hear the fire laughing, and the ground beneath the altar slithers with a thousand snakes – but none of this matters, because he is being devoured by the Three-Eyed King, torn apart, every morsel consumed, until nothing is left in the dead chamber of the forgotten temple but the ghost of his memory, shifting and fading in the sombre silence – in the end no more than a chill breath of air that flickers the torch light and is at last completely still...

Burak snapped awake and fought for breath. His heart heaved and faltered, and for a moment of disjointed panic he was completely paralysed.

A dream, just a dream! he told himself.

The cold tendrils of prophecy hadn't wrapped themselves around his neck, freezing his brain, stealing the strength from his muscles – it had been no vision. It was just a clammy extrusion of his racing mind.

Slowly, taming his breath and focusing on the earth in front of his face, Burak forced himself back into the present. He was lying on the ground, and the warband – what was left of it – was lying near him. They had camped overnight in a clearing amongst the tall grasses that bordered a sparse forest, not far from the foothills of the Fangs. Long had the tunnel stretched, the gullet of the Mountain's Throat, leading them through its ribbed and rubbery expanse deep into the bowels of the rock. They had hurried through the musty dark, feeling their way as much as seeing, barely stopping to rest. Eventually, the tunnel had tapered to a cloying gap, a rank extrusion of crusted filth high on the flanks of the Fangs' northern expanse. Ahead of them had stretched the barren scrubland of the Tormented Lands, and the end of their journey.

The baby gurgled under his arm, wrapped in his furs. It was awake and seemed content, and it would not devour him as the thing in his dream had devoured him.

'You wouldn't do that, would you?' he said, his voice shaking. He stroked its head and cupped the baby's cheek in his palm. 'Not to old Burak, not to me.'

He got up and fed it blood and oats from an old skin, a gruel the Untamed Beasts often relied upon in the wilderness. The baby lapped it up and seemed happy. Burak frowned as he cradled it in his arms. The child should have been dead long ago, and if nothing else marked it out as special, then it was this. Some force kept it going, and it was seemingly untroubled by all the horrors it had experienced in its short life. It had barely been fed on the mother's milk it needed – gruels of blood and fibre were no substitute at all. A child of the Bloodwind Spoil… Burak wondered if it was drawing its sustenance from the air that surrounded it. From the mutating earth and the gangrenous winds, from the harsh rains that hammered the land – perhaps it had everything it needed?

He smiled down at it. 'You are no ordinary child, are you? The Great Devourer will gorge on your spirit, my son, gorge until he's fit to burst!'

He woke the rest of the warband, and they readied themselves to go on. The trees around them were studded with weeping cankers that smelled of rot, and as they woke up, some of the plains-runners began to vomit into the dirt. Ekrah grimaced as he fitted his helmet across his ruined eye. Burak had found it amusing to make a half-blind man take the first watch, but Ekrah had sat to the duty without complaining. *That's Ekrah for you*, Burak thought. *No task is too much for him. My First Fang…*

There had been no sign of the Stormcast warriors during the night, but Burak knew they were near. They shadowed and watched and waited, but they did not strike. He was under no illusions as to how long the warband would last if they did, especially in open ground. What puzzled him was why they didn't. He looked again at the baby, holding him up to the light, inspecting him as if he were a choice cut of meat.

'What do they want with you, I wonder?' he muttered. 'When they could take you away from me in an instant, why don't they reach out those armoured hands, eh? I wonder, my child, I wonder… yes, I do…'

They skirted the line of the forest, moving swiftly. The grass came up to their chests, and with every step Burak was sure some lurching horror was going to spring up and rend him to pieces, but they were no creature's prey that day. The grassland stretched in a wide crescent around the borders of the forest and they kept to its shelter, pausing now and then, ducking down and hiding amongst the stalks while they scouted the ground ahead.

The land reminded him in many ways of the Jagged Savannah back in Ghur, where he had grown to manhood with Kurguth by his side. As they ran on, he recalled a time when they were simple plains-runners, the lowest of the low, sent out by the elders to flush game from the forests around their territory. Kurguth, thinking it a great honour, had leapt to the task at once. Burak had followed, dawdling, leaning his spear against his shoulder, enjoying the opportunity to get away from the baking meadowland and into the forest, where the light fell in placid beams and the ground was refreshingly cool underfoot. Kurguth had stalked the forest paths, thrashing the bushes with his spear, sending predator birds in a frantic scramble for the treeline.

'Why hurry?' Burak had said. 'Let the others wait for their game. I'm happy stalking these old paths and keeping the sun off my head.'

Kurguth had snorted with derision. 'And what do you think will happen to us if they find out we've being taking our time for no more reward than cool shadows and a pleasant walk, eh? I dread to think of the thrashings we'll be due.'

'Are we children, to fear chastisement?' Burak said. 'Life is short – let us take our ease where we can.'

Kurguth jogged ahead, sweeping his spear through a stunted barrel of gorse. Two fat quail erupted from the bush and scurried off into the grass.

'There are worse than game birds in these trees,' he said. 'You should keep your eyes open. If we're torn apart by a xaskadon because you were too busy dreaming, I'll kill you myself.'

'There are no xaskadon here,' Burak said. 'You'd know all about it if there were.' He sat down on the grass and leaned against a tree, closing his eyes, the spear planted in the ground beside him. 'Besides, this is not where I die.'

'Oh? Seen that in one of your visions, I suppose?'

'I have.'

'Where do you die then?' Kurguth asked. Despite himself he was smiling. 'King of Ghur, I suppose, sitting at the top of a throne made of all your enemies' bones, and the Everchosen himself bowing down before you...'

Burak had laughed. Kurguth stood before him, leaning on his spear, mouth twisted in a grin. The light painted stripes against his dark skin, and with squinted sight he would almost have blended into the forest around him.

'Not King, no, but I will be Heart-eater one day. I have seen it, and it will come to pass. The Split-Tongue Tribe will be mine.'

'You, Heart-eater!' Kurguth scoffed. He roared with laughter, and the noise sent more prey flapping from the branches. 'If I live to see the day, it'll be too much! What about me, then, what do I become? See that in any of your visions?'

Burak smiled softly, looking away. 'You? You will be my First Fang, Kurguth, and fight at my side.'

'I will?' He was quiet for a minute, contemplative. Burak knew that Kurguth lived only in the moment, that his ambition stretched no further than the next woman, the next fight, the next hunt. Give him a task and he did it, straining every sinew, but the long days ahead were not his to worry about. 'First Fang... Well, that's something to think about,' he said. He hefted his spear, held it high above his head. 'Kurguth the First Fang!'

Burak laughed again, but his eyes were sad. The vision had come on him late the night before, as he tried to sleep. His grass mat had swum in front of his eyes, and the stars above had bent off true, hazing into a milky swirl. He had collapsed, face down, and as the ice gripped the back of his neck, he saw the future unfold in a spread of disjointed images and flashing lights. Burak, sprinting across a strange landscape, a child in his arms. Kurguth, comforting a woman Burak didn't recognise, a young Beastspeaker. And then Burak cutting the heart from Kurguth's chest, tears pouring down his face, bending to lift the organ to his mouth as his teeth sank in – and all the rage and sorrow of the First Fang thrashing through his blood. That was what he had seen. It would happen in time, there was no doubt. Tomorrow, a week from now, a decade. It would happen.

He looked at Kurguth, who stood there with his back to him, staring towards the treeline, dreams of the future swimming through his head. Kurguth, as if feeling his eyes on him, turned and barked a laugh.

'You're such a dreamer, Burak! None of that will ever happen. Heart-eater, First Fang… Come on, we've a task to do now, in this moment, not in all the moments to come.'

Burak joined him. He laid a hand against his shoulder. 'I'm sorry, brother,' he said.

'There's no need for sorry,' Kurguth said. 'Who would you be without your visions, anyway?'

He slapped him on the back, and together the two plains-runners disappeared into the undergrowth, whooping and striking the bushes with their spears.

Such a long time ago, Burak thought now. There was no thread that linked this moment to that; it may as well have been another life. As he ran, he whispered a prayer to Kurguth's shade. He had died because he had to; there was no other way. It had all been foreseen.

Ekrah drew near, running swiftly through the grass. Burak halted and held up his hand, and the others all crouched low in the concealing stalks.

'Tuk-kho returns,' Ekrah said. 'The armoured ones are near, Sigmar's chosen. They hold back.'

'Are we seen?'

'Tuk-kho says no. They scout for our trail, but in these grasses…'

Burak nodded. It was true – even the most cautious and vigilant beast would have left a track any fool could read in vegetation like this. They must have seen it. They kept their distance. But why?

Wrapped in furs in Burak's arms, the baby jabbered contentedly to itself. The Heart-eater contemplated those green eyes, the strange discoloration across his face that seemed to darken and fade depending on the light.

'They want the child,' Ekrah said. 'They would steal our glory from us, deny us our place beside the Everchosen.'

'Maybe, maybe,' Burak muttered. 'Or they want not what we have, but where we are taking it…?'

He signalled to Tuk-kho, who crawled through the grass towards him.

'Ekrah, First Fang of mine. We must hold them off, let the hunters become the hunted. Draw them into the trees, then we will see how well Sigmar's chosen can really fight.'

The flame burns before his eyes, leading him ever on. Rocks melt in its holy light, and the path turns into a river of liquid stone. He falls and the flame picks him up. He is blind and the flame allows him to see. The poisons roil in his blood, but the flame burns them all away. He staggers down the mountain with only the flame to guide him, walking secret paths known only to the fire.

Ahead, warped by distance, a dark smear against the northern sky ignites into a coruscating pillar that limns the land with streaks of amber and crimson. Varanspire, he thinks. It is the end of all things and the beginning, the fire and the ash, the seat of the Ever-Raging Flame.

A temple rises amongst the flames, the image of a child…

The fire dances in front of his eyes, flaring like a comet-fall, like a meteor, like everlasting life. He leaves the mountain behind and travels level ground at last. One foot takes the place of another. He follows the secret fire, and it burns, it burns...

He surfaced queasily, aware of voices mumbling nearby. Opening his eyes, he saw only smears of light and dark. A pinwheeling pain began to spread throughout his body. He tried to speak, but his words were ashes in his mouth.

'Eat,' someone said nearby. 'You must eat.'

A rancid gruel was smeared against his lips, the edge of a wooden spoon. He opened his mouth and choked it down.

'He will live,' a voice said. 'Though the lord knows how.'

'Lord protect him,' said another voice.

'Lord protect him.'

'So... shall we eat him now?' another voice said.

'We'll see,' the first voice said. 'This one has power, though. We must wait a while yet.'

'But there would be such good eating on him. And I'm so hungry...'

He tried to move his head, but the flame receded and grew dim. He fell away into unconsciousness, his fingers reaching for a sword that was no longer there.

When Rakaros surfaced for the second time, his head was clear. He was lying on a dank mattress, covered by a flea-ridden blanket. He was in a room of some kind, a chamber the colour of old bone. He looked up, into a circular window open to the night sky. The void was a star-strewn orb that turned and wheeled above him. A humid breeze buffeted the curtains that were drawn across the chamber. He struggled to raise himself and saw four figures hunched over a low fire, sorting scrap – shards of armour, an old knife, rusted plates and spoons.

'Where am I?' he said. He was shocked to hear his own voice, how weak it sounded in his ears.

One of them, an old woman hunched and stinking of sweat, hobbled near. She held her hand to his forehead. He tried to move but the pain was too intense. The old woman lifted the blanket and examined the bandages that had been wrapped around his torso.

'You have healed far faster than I thought you would,' she said. She turned to the others, who cowered by the fire. 'Didn't I say he had power?'

'Who are you?' Rakaros demanded. Again, he tried to rise, but the pain of his injuries forced him back onto the dirty mattress.

'Mere wanderers in the wasteland, sifters of the scrapheap and the grave,' she said. She trundled back over to the fire and stirred the cook pot. 'The Tormented Lands hold little for those who cannot take it, but we get by as best we can.'

'The Tormented Lands?' Rakaros said. He knew that wilderness. To walk across it would take days, weeks, if he didn't die of thirst and hunger first. But beyond it, on the other side, led the road to the Varanspire.

'Here,' the old woman said. She brought over a bowl of broth. Despite himself, Rakaros felt his stomach respond. She sat by his side and spooned the chunks of meat into his mouth. He glanced to the fire and saw the body parts, the severed hands and feet. Still he ate. A man who didn't eat what he could find soon starved in the Bloodwind Spoil.

When he had regained his strength a little, watching them with a wary, penetrating eye, he said, 'Why didn't you kill me? I imagine food is scarce in these parts, and I flatter myself that I would keep you going for some time.'

The old woman laughed, croaking like a marsh rat.

'What good is poisoned meat to us?' she cackled. 'You've burned most of it out, as far as I can see, but I'd rather not take the chance.'

'You mean to heal me, then?' Rakaros said. 'But not too much…'

'There's more to it than that,' she said. 'I don't know who you are, but I can see you're not like this scum.'

She indicated the others around the fire: a sallow young woman with no teeth and a great, seeping boil on her face; a man as tall as a reed and thin as a skeleton; and a third figure, grotesquely snouted, with close-set eyes and a stump where his hand should have been. They all bobbed their heads at his attention, approximations of a bow.

'Where are you from, my lord?' the snouted one said. 'Not from the Tormented Lands, that's for sure!'

'I am Lord Rakaros, Blazing Lord of the Burned Hand,' he sneered. 'A Scion of the Flame. I come from far Aqshy, the Realm of Fire.'

As he spoke, he felt something of his old strength return. This was who he was, damn them all. Damn the snake-worshippers and their ambush, and damn that fool Silenthis! He clenched his fist. It ached for his sword.

The old woman's eyes glittered. 'I thought the Scions' fire burned in you, lord. I have seen it before, lighting the streets of Carngrad itself.'

'Then you know what I am capable of, woman,' he said, throwing off the blanket. 'If indeed you are a woman… If you have weapons, I will take them, and food for the journey – even if it must be the offcuts of whatever unlucky wretch crossed your path before.'

The old witch scuttled off into a corner and came back bearing a lacquered box, jewelled and polished and smelling of charcoal. She held it before him and opened the lid. Rakaros glanced down and his words died in his mouth.

'*Aqthracite…*' he breathed. 'Rage-rock…'

The stones, and there were only two, shone dully on a bed of red velvet. Each was no bigger than a seed, if that, but there was no mistaking them. Rakaros could smell the power in them; he could taste it as it stained the air around him.

The witch snapped the lid shut and hid the box away in her tattered robes.

'Weapons you shall have, lord, and this. But not yet, not yet...'

Rakaros seethed. 'You want payment, is that it?' he said. 'And what do you think I have to pay you with? A pound of my flesh? A hand, would this do?' He held out his fist, but it trembled before her.

'Nothing so drastic, lord, just... answers that I might be looking for, questions I might have. Promises you might make.'

'What questions? What promises?'

The old woman settled herself by the fire again. 'Are you from the Citadel, perhaps? Or are you going there?'

'Are you taking the trials for the lord's guard, sir?' the young woman interrupted. 'Oh, say you are, please! Lord protect you if it's true!'

'Lord protect you,' the others intoned.

Rakaros frowned. His head was swimming, and the broth was on the turn in his stomach. 'What lord? What citadel?'

'The Varanspire,' the old woman said. 'Archaon Everchosen's seat.' The cannibals clasped their hands to their chests and closed their eyes. 'Are you making the trials for the Varanguard?'

'Me?' Rakaros scoffed. 'At this stage I think I'd have trouble killing any of you, let alone duelling with any of those fell champions. I am no black pilgrim, fools.'

'Then what do you seek out here in the wastes?' the old woman cut in. She looked at him sharply. There was more there than her doddery front might suggest.

He thought carefully. Caution was all, but he knew his time was running short.

'A child,' he said. 'A babe in arms. There are those who would use it for their own ends. I would use it for mine instead.'

The snouted one looked at the reedy mutant, and the woman hid her face from him. Rakaros, his eyes keen, fixed the little pig-man with his baleful gaze.

'What do you know of it? I see by your face, scum, don't try to hide it from me.'

'N-nothing, lord, I swear it! Just rumours winging their way across the scavenger camps, that's all it be.'

'And what do those rumours say?'

'A child, lord, like you said. It'll grow to a mighty warrior, some claim, who'll... who'll challenge the Everchosen for his throne...'

Rakaros laughed, bitter and cruel. 'I doubt it'll get even the ghost of a chance. Whether it's Archaon's heir or his deadliest rival, it matters not to me.'

'Then why do you seek it?' the young woman asked.

'Because it is a trial, set by the very highest. A test. The child is marked, that cannot be denied. Whoever finds him and presents him as sacrifice will win a prize beyond your feeble comprehension.'

'Yes,' the old woman muttered. 'Rumours abound, and they make more sense now... It is said that warriors of the Untamed Beasts have him now, the babe.'

'Those degenerates? Then give me the aqthracite and let me be quit of this loathsome place – I will hunt the hunters and add their hides to the pile.'

'That's not all, my lord,' the witch slyly said. 'The hunters are already hunted, and you must take your place behind them. Stormcast Eternals, I have heard... warriors of Sigmar's chosen, fell of temperament and deadly – they give chase as well.'

His vision was streaked with black and he had to grip the wall to stop himself from falling. 'Then I will kill them too, and the God-King's frustrated wailing will be part of my reward!'

The woman gave him a guileful smile. After a pause, she

produced the lacquered box. Rakaros took it from her, a tremor in his hands.

'Take this with my blessing, Blazing Lord. Regain your strength, seize the child. But you must promise me one thing.'

'What? Come, make your demands, woman. Time is pressing!'

'Kill the lightning-borne! If they fall under your blade, make them die for all they have done to me. Kill them, if it is the last thing you do!'

It was like rising after a long fever, the illness broken at last. He swallowed the shards of rage-rock and felt them burn inside him, searing into his lungs, his heart, his stomach. His blood ignited, and the coals of his eyes smouldered with renewed vigour. He looked on the squalid shelter and its mean inhabitants with the burning light of judgement in his eyes. Their words came back to him, the phrase they had used as he lingered near to death.

'"Lord protect us," you said. Is that right? You call on the Everchosen to defend you, to keep you safe?'

'He is the Three-Eyed King,' the young woman said. 'He sees all.'

'And you think he cares a damn for your miserable lives?'

'We're true followers, my lord,' the pig-snouted mutant said. 'We have faith in him.'

Rakaros looked on them with contempt. 'You think he is some snivelling god of mercy,' he rumbled, 'to raise a shield above you and save you all from your petty troubles?'

The rage was in him now, stoked and furious. He leaned down to the fire, plunging his hand into the flames. He drew out the metal spit on which they had roasted their cannibal meat. He held it like a sword as he advanced on them, and they shook before him.

'You speak blasphemies,' Rakaros whispered. 'He is the Ever-Raging Flame, and he consumes utterly.'

'Please, lord!' the old woman cried. 'Mercy, haven't we helped you, fed you, given you that which is most holy to you!'

Her face contracted, as fast as a snake, and from the glowing tip of her staff came a dazzle of blue light and flame. Rakaros was wreathed in smoke, but when the mist cleared, he was untouched.

'Mercy?' he said. 'Ask yourself – does the fire offer mercy to the wood?'

He raised the spit above his head and struck, and his eyes blazed like the very pits of hell.

The yellow grass ruffled against their greaves as they approached the trees. Spread out in a line, the Stormcast warriors seemed isolated from each other, lone knights daring to broach a russet darkness, their weapons drawn. Leander was far over on the left flank, his boltstorm pistol levelled from the hip. Antigonos and Philemon took the centre, while Damaris covered the right. The treeline, a patchy scrub of red thorn and tussled undergrowth, was silent and empty, and the branches were bare of birds. The sparse trees beyond the grass dripped with illness and were plagued with boils and lesions. It was a dank, gloomy place, devoid of life – another patch of sordor and decay in the heart of the Bloodwind Spoil.

The grass bristled its dry stalks as they waded through it. Damaris, her sabre drawn, looked over to Antigonos for reassurance, but the Hunter-Prime seemed withdrawn, detached. As they passed through the threshold of the trees, she heard Philemon ask if they should perhaps skirt the forest instead, but Antigonos said nothing in reply. He just bowed his head, his shoulders slack.

'Antigonos?' Philemon said. He looked at Damaris, but she could only shrug. It weighed on all of them, this awful place. There was not much that could break the god-forged spirit of Sigmar's chosen, but if anywhere could, it was the Eightpoints. They had been here for months now, scouting the margins, subsisting off meagre rations, following trails and rumours about the child. Now, at last, their target was in sight. But so many of them had been lost, and of the four who remained Damaris knew it was doubtful any of them would live to see Azyr again – at least, not in their present form. All they could hope for was the agonies of the Anvil, the bludgeoning skills of the forge-smiths working their souls once more into new flesh and blessed Sigmarite. Damaris tried to ignore the twinge in her belly at the thought. Unlike Antigonos, it was a process she had gone through only once, when first called to the ranks of the Eternals, and although she could barely remember it, she had no great wish to experience it a second time.

What has it been like for him? she wondered, looking at the Hunter-Prime. Five times he had passed through the soul-mills, folded and beaten and rehoused in a new form. How much of him was really left? Damaris thought of the cut-throats they had found by the banks of the stream, lost members of the snake cult who had clearly fled the battle in the mountains. To kill them was one thing – they deserved nothing less – but to have tortured her like that, to have nailed her to the tree, still sat uneasily with her. She saw again Antigonos' face as he had hammered in the nails with the butt of his axe, the aelf wailing in agony before he slashed her throat. He had shown not pleasure, or rage, or even the catharsis of revenge, but just a blank indifference that was somehow worse. This was what you did in the Bloodwind Spoil, his face seemed to say. You didn't just kill, you mutilated and you maimed, for no other reason than your ability to do it.

Antigonos seemed to come around to himself again. He straightened, shook his head clear. He had discarded his helmet some distance back, and his face was strained and scarred. He lacked nobility, Damaris suddenly realised. That was what was wrong with him. The thought shocked her. That was what this place had done, and it was more grievous a wound than anything merely physical.

It is bruising our very souls.

'Here,' Leander said in a low voice. He beckoned the others over and showed them the patches of matted grass on the edge of the trees. 'Someone camped here last night. The grass is still flat – they could only have left a couple of hours ago, at most.'

Antigonos nodded, staring down into the flattened grass as if expecting it to give him answers. Damaris looked to the trees – and then she drew her boltstorm pistol. A flash of green cloth, perhaps, a hint of red. She stared from the wavering grass towards the treeline ahead of her, and the shadows fluttered as the breeze took hold of the branches. Their rank leaves slavered together, and a stench of disease and rot came wafting from the forest.

'Hunter-Prime,' she whispered. 'Movement, about twenty feet in.'

'Our quarry?'

'Possibly.'

'Spread out,' Antigonos said. He waved Damaris off to cover their right flank, where the forest dipped down towards the banks of a moribund lake, its surface rippling greasily. Leander ran through the grass in a crouch, skirting the edge of the forest, his boltstorm pistol in hand. Damaris saw him staring into the gloom, his pistol held up at the ready. He turned to say something to Antigonos, but before she could even shout a warning Damaris saw a horned figure smeared in warpaint rise swiftly from the long grass and swing a savage bone blade at Leander's neck.

The hunter had no time to bring his pistol to bear, and instead relied on the protection of his armour. He threw his shoulder up to catch the blade on his pauldron, but the razor-sharp bone skidded against the metal and caught him high on the temple instead. The helmet saved his life, but still Leander sprawled down into the grass – in the perfect position for another of the savages to skip out from behind the trees and ram her knife deep into the hunter's throat, again and again.

Damaris screamed, a frantic mixture of rage and grief, and let loose with her pistol. The shot was wild, unfocused, and it sent Philemon crashing to the ground to avoid it. The two savages had vanished as suddenly as they'd appeared, slipping like ghosts back into the trees.

'Hold, Damaris!' Antigonos shouted. He ran to Leander, Damaris behind him. The hunter – veteran of a hundred campaigns, one of the greatest marksmen in the chamber, the warrior who had tracked Khiz'krxy'x the Neverborn for a thousand miles across the Crystal Henge – lay choking in his own blood. His eyes were wild behind the pale armour of his faceplate. Antigonos carefully removed his helmet.

'Lie still, my friend,' he whispered.

Leander nodded, spitting blood, grasping at the Hunter-Prime's hand. 'It won't be long now...' he retched. 'We will meet again... in the halls... of Azyrheim. I swear it.'

He tried to speak again, but all that came from his lips was a bloody froth. His face spasmed in pain. Antigonos bent down to kiss him on the forehead, and then ushered the other warriors back. Leander's armour began to dissolve in a coruscant haze, the discarded anchor of his blazing soul as it thundered off into the heavens.

Damaris saw the truth of it in the Hunter-Prime's face; Leander might well undergo the agony of reforging, but for Antigonos such a trial would be the end of him. He may see Azyrheim again, but what emerged on the other side of the Anvil would not be Antigonos as any of them remembered him – or as he remembered himself.

'Now we are three,' Philemon muttered.

Antigonos grimaced and pressed his fingers against his eyes. 'Now we are three,' he said. 'And we must go on. We can't let the savages escape.'

'But how do we know?' Damaris said. She had tears in her eyes, but she wouldn't wipe them away. 'They run us a merry dance, but we have no way of knowing if it leads in the right direction. If we lose them, we could never find it!'

'We won't lose them,' the Hunter-Prime reassured her. He looked into her eyes. She saw no doubt there, no uncertainty, only a hard and brutal faith. Damaris' gaze faltered. 'Trust me. Follow me now,' he said, 'for a little while longer.'

'Until the end,' Damaris said. She held out her hand and Antigonos took it in a warrior's grip, wrist to wrist.

'Until the end,' Philemon said. 'Until every last one of these savages is food for the crows.'

'Until we have what we came for,' Antigonos said. 'Nothing more. Nothing less.'

The hunters, more cautiously now, stowed their weapons and slipped into the woods.

Ekrah and Tuk-kho caught up with the others at the edge of a poison swamp, where the green water bubbled with the faces of the drowned. Burak laughed to hear of the Stormcast's death.

'Well done, my fighters!' he said. 'One more cast up to the God-King's domain!'

'Only three remain, Bloodseer,' Ekrah said. His chest heaved with the run, and Burak could see the exultation gleaming in his eyes from the kill. 'They must draw off now, their numbers are so low.'

'If only one remained, they would still fight on,' Burak warned. 'Don't underestimate Sigmar's chosen, my First Fang. We will deal with them in turn, but the moment draws near and the temple awaits. I have seen it,' he said eagerly. 'It haunts my dreams, and its foundations are close.'

The faces in the swamp surfaced briefly and screamed, but the

Untamed Beasts were deaf to their cries. They headed beyond the forest and the grasslands, running for a day and a night, running on towards the blasted plains that lay in the shadow of the Varanspire. Burak clutched the child as he ran, and the moment nearly overwhelmed him. He could see with his keen eyes the ruin in the distance, the foundations of its buttresses and battlements like shattered teeth. Every sinew of his body responded to it with new speed and deeper hunger.

'Run, my brothers and sisters!' he bellowed. The wind carved tranches in his hair, and his feet were a blur beneath him. He shouted with incoherent joy.

They were almost there. The Devourer of Existence was near, waiting, poised to witness the victory of the Bloodseer.

He set a fire inside the skull and laughed as it burned. The stench of the bodies reached him as they caught the flames – the rancid stink of charred flesh and rendered fat, the waft of stale sweat from their burning clothes. He breathed in the smoke, felt the rage-rock respond in his blood and sinews. The fire was a sculpted mass against the sheet of night, bowing and stretching, the flames leaping from the pyre as if trying to ignite the very heavens. Rakaros luxuriated in it. At his side he held the metal spit the cannibals had used to turn their meat. A blunt knife, a flask of sour beer – there had been nothing else worth salvaging from their mess. He was armed as poorly as any scavenger, but he would prevail all the same.

The flames rose higher, bursting from the socket of the skull's empty eye. The rage-rock that boiled in his system called up images and portents of his fate from the flames. He stared at them with unblinking eyes, and the images were like a swatch of shadows moving on a cave wall. He saw the Untamed Beasts move fleetly through the grasslands, the baby in their grip. He saw the Stormcast Eternals, battered but unbowed, stalking their every move. He saw the temple, and the black smear of the Varanspire on the far horizon.

He was about to turn away when another image boiled in the flames and caught his eye. Rakaros paused, watching it unfold in streaks of orange and vermillion. Hypnotised, compelled, he watched the ruins of the temple as they rose before him, carved from flame. He saw the pylon falling into disarray, the inner court smothered under the weight of its collapsing roof. He saw the wide-spaced columns of the hypostyle fall like toppled trees. He saw time's unforgiving gaze turn everything to dust, and underneath that dust, deep underground, he saw an altar; and as he watched the altar crack, the lid splitting into two pieces and falling away to the ground, he saw what lay inside – and he laughed, long and cruel.

The fools! All of them. They have no idea...

The massive skull cracked and split with the force of the fire inside it. Rakaros found the tethered steed the cannibals had used to carry their spoil from their scavenges across the Tormented Lands. The beast, some vile reptilian amalgam, shied at the flames, but the Blazing Lord would brook no wilfulness. He struck it across the muzzle and clambered into the saddle, kicking his heels to the creature's sides and turning it towards the centre of the Eightpoints, where the black shard of the Varanspire sucked all hope from the land. There, in the shadow of its baleful influence, he would find what he sought – the mark of the Everchosen's favour, the sacrificial child.

And he would find something else, too. Something long buried that would gain him more than mere admittance to Archaon's court...

CHAPTER SIXTEEN

BURIED SECRETS

The body and the soul cling to the balm of happy memories, and pleasure is rarely forgotten. The company of good friends, lovers, families, the taste of the finest zephyrwine, the feeling of a full belly after a feast – all are a comfort in times of need, lights to banish darkness, hope to guide the hopeless on.

But one of pain's chief properties, Antigonos knew, was how quickly it could be forgotten. The fear of it lived on in some feral quadrant of the soul, but it was nearly impossible to recall with the conscious mind. Physical pain, anyway. He thought of the Anvil of Apotheosis in Sigmaron, the mighty forge where the warriors of the Stormcast Eternals were hammered into being from the base clay of their mortal souls. Forged, and then reforged when death cast them back up to the celestial halls – and then reforged again, and then again, until in time what remained was an animating soul that had lost any memory of what had once made it human.

The pain of reforging was something Antigonos could certainly remember, and with a searing clarity.

The making of these immortal warriors was an agony both physical and spiritual at the same time. Every atom of a warrior's being was pared away and purified, cleansed and rebuilt under the unsentimental attentions of the Six Smiths. It was scoured and restored, reincarnated once more, and clad again in fresh-forged Sigmarite armour. The natural wastage of this process always led to imperfections, though, lacks and losses that were amplified down the ages as each Stormcast Eternal fell in battle and was rebuilt. Antigonos knew it well. His last reforging had been as violently eclipsing as all the others put together, and at the end of it he knew with perfect clarity that some essential shard of him had been left behind on the Anvil's face. Whatever had linked him to his former life had finally been chipped away, forever.

It affected them all differently, he thought, as his last two warriors ran with him to their fate. Some became mere shadows; others were struck as if by a heavy grief and were unable to carry on with the duties that had been tasked to them. For Antigonos, losing those memories of the man he used to be was like losing an old friend – only he couldn't remember the friend's face, or why they had even been friends in the first place. It was just gone, and what he missed was the sense of something rather than the thing itself.

It had been made worse, somehow, by setting foot in the Eight-points. He remembered that moment, as they had drawn on their hunters' skills to evade the marching legions on the roads from the arcways. They had slipped into a degraded zone of filth and mayhem, and his soul had abjured every element of it. But then he saw the stern determination of fresher-forged heroes like Damaris, and it shamed him. Antigonos admired her almost naïve sense of duty, her need to avenge whatever awful moment had called her up into the ranks of the Stormcast Eternals in the first place.

She is equally strained by this awful place, he thought, *but she girds herself against it and carries on.*

He wondered what it had been, the moment that had marked her out for Sigmar's attention. For even the closest comrades it was often a private grief, rarely shared. For Antigonos, it was so far back in the mists of time that he could barely remember it. The impression of a city, a place of cloistered peace… That was all he could bring back to mind.

He felt ashamed at his own weakness, angry at his self-pity. As they crossed from the grasslands, bypassing the diseased forest, he tried not to think of what the Eightpoints was doing to him. He flinched at the memory of the aelf by the riverbank. They had disarmed her and her paltry retinue in a perfect ambush, shooting down her foot soldiers and wounding her without any loss to themselves. The snake-worshippers' lives were always going to be forfeit, but as Antigonos pressed his boltstorm pistol to the aelf's bleeding forehead, Damaris had interrupted.

'This is the one who killed Erastus,' she said. She pointed at the aelf, who grinned up at them through her broken teeth. 'I recognise her now. She was in the fight on the mountaintop. I saw it, by the cliff edge.'

'Is that true?' Antigonos demanded, but all he got for a reply was a gob of spit and a reeling cackle. *She is brave*, he thought. *Brave, when all she faces is death…*

He would ask it of none of them, so he did it himself. He beat her to the ground and dragged her over to a salivating tree, being careful not to let its corpulent tongue touch him. Shards of metal from the tin shack were all the nails he needed, and before long she was hanging there from her ravaged hands, screaming, begging for death.

'The pain you bear is only what you have earned from your evil,' he said. His voice was dark and pitiless. 'And I will see you paid in full.'

As they had turned to go, the other hunters exchanging troubled glances that were all too visible to the Hunter-Prime, Antigonos had felt some small part of himself recoil from what he had just done. What was the point of it, what purpose did it serve? *It is a response*, he had told himself. *An appropriate response to this awful place in which we're going to die.*

At last the grasslands fell away, and a blasted heath unrolled before them in unbroken downs towards the distant Varanspire. The sight made his eyes ache. They could wander for a hundred years in this bleak landscape and never once stumble across what they had been sent to find. He looked for traces of their quarry in the broken scrub grass, and Damaris hissed a warning as she spotted them far ahead.

'Move out,' Antigonos told his hunters as he steeled himself. 'We'll circle them, approach them from the other side and see at last where they're going. Damaris?'

'Yes, Hunter-Prime?'

'Ready your compass.'

'Is that wise?' Philemon said. He had his axe and sword in hand already, now combat was near. 'This close to the enemy's spire?'

'It doesn't matter,' Antigonos said. 'Stealth is no more use to us.' He tried to smile, to reassure them, but all he had left was a twisted grimace. 'They have led us this far, but we have to get to the chamber before them, or on their heels at the very least. If they find out what's hidden in that altar...'

They all nodded. Damaris unhooked her compass from her belt, and the caged blue light began to gleam, its holy glow revealing the hidden paths that would take them on towards their goal.

Antigonos closed his eyes as the light enveloped him. This would be his last mission, he knew. Win or lose, there would be no coming back from this.

* * *

It was a jumble of faded stone, half buried in tussocks of grey grass. Here and there old pillars erupted from the earth like the bones of some buried creature, and there were the suggestions of ancient walls and grand battlements, now fallen into long decay. Old masonry lay scattered in the grass, and at the heart of the ruin they could see the entrance to a half-buried chamber and the suggestion of a flight of stairs that led down into the darkness. Damaris, who had the keenest eyes, pointed this out as they hid themselves amongst a covert of thorn bushes half a mile distant.

'This is it,' Antigonos said grimly. Damaris nodded at his side. She could feel it, somehow. There was buried power here, buried threat.

They scouted wide and looped around, running swiftly along the dusty channel of a dried riverbed that bordered the temple complex on its western flank. They kept their heads down and their weapons drawn. As they left the riverbed, climbing up its crumbling banks, they kept the horror of the Varanspire at their backs and approached the ruined temple from the other side. The Varanspire, foul locus of the enemy's power, brooded in the far distance, repelling light.

Damaris had fought against the followers of Chaos for decades, as both mortal and immortal, and she had long heard the stories of the Everchosen's citadel. Champions of the plague god had died under her sabre, drooling tales of Archaon's seat. Scions of Khorne had declared themselves black pilgrims to the court of the Three-Eyed King as she cut them down, and even amongst the Stormhosts of the Tempered Blades there were those who told campfire stories about the hated Varanspire, wondering how the Allpoints could ever be taken back while Archaon commanded his hosts from this black fortress at its very centre. But all the stories and legends she had heard about it could not prepare her for its bitter resonance once she fell into its orbit. Even though it was still miles away from them, it felt claustrophobically near without any intervening feature to hide them from its dread gaze. Damaris almost felt that it was leering over her shoulder, and it conjured up a feeling in her of squirming, abject horror.

In the land towards the rear of the temple, a hundred feet away, the ground was humped like a series of funeral barrows, and the Stormcast warriors hid themselves amongst its folds. Damaris crept forward, hidden by the fringe of grass that covered the slope, and scanned the ruins ahead. There was no entrance on this side, as far as she could see; there was just a scattering of toppled pillars, time-worn walls and austere stone scoured by the bitter winds. The ruins lay there in the silence of the ages, grey and desolate, a grim reminder of everything that had been lost when Chaos came.

She found herself wondering what this land around her would have looked like in those distant days of myth. What was now bare moorland, arid and ploughed by a thin, wheedling wind that cut through the gaps in her armour, could once have been a great complex of temples and holy places. Under the dry grass there could be the remains of ancient roads, wide avenues stretching from every corner of the Allpoints to the grand cities where humans, duardin and aelves had all lived their lives in peace and prosperity. She felt something wild and bitter well up inside her at the thought of what had happened here, as if the memory were still fresh and personal to her and not something that had occurred centuries ago, in another age of the Mortal Realms.

The gods themselves have walked this earth, she thought. She tore up a handful of the grass and it melted to a black slime in her hand. Disgusted, she wiped the smear away. *Sigmar, Grungni, Alarielle...* She had seen the frescoes on the white marble of the Sigmarabulum, had seen naïve renderings on the panelled walls of humble taverns in the backstreets of Azyrheim. How long would the great war go on before this place could be taken back?

Damaris had grown up on tales of the Realmgate Wars. The heroic example of the Stormcast Eternals had always guided her spear in the days when her people fought against the fell tribes of Chaos. And now here she was, a young woman from Brazier, on the edge of Aqshy's Great Parch, raised to immortality. Here she lay, on the grass of the Eightpoints, in a place that was almost an echo of the Realm of Chaos itself. She wondered what her parents, Sigmar rest their souls, would have thought if they had lived to see her now. And then, as Damaris tried to picture their faces, she realised that the image she had of them was old and faded; little of them truly came back to her mind. They were the dream of an old memory now, nothing more.

Antigonos stirred beside her as they watched for the savages, waiting to see which way they would go. She glanced at him, keen and feverish, his cropped hair making his lean, gaunt face look almost like a skull. His attention seemed bent only on what lay ahead, with not a thought for what might come after. There was a ravenous look in his eyes that was almost repellent. Damaris quelled her unease. How degraded would her parents become in her mind's eye once she had been on the great wheel of reforging as many times as he had? How little of them would be left? And if they were no more than the memory of an absence, how little would she care? This was the sacrifice that was demanded of them, she knew, those heroes who were swept up from their last calamity to the ranks of the Stormcast Eternals. With Antigonos lurking in the grass beside her, though, Damaris began to feel something like despondence for the first time. It lowered itself on her like heavy weather, diminishing her horizons, covering her sight in an insubstantial murk.

'I see them now,' Philemon growled. He had crept up the slope beside Damaris, and he parted the fringe of grass with his fingers. Together they looked over the scrubland towards the ruins, the grey stone flecked with spots of rain. 'They're running single file, crouched low.' He pointed, and Damaris saw them in turn, the warriors of the Untamed Beasts moving through the harsh landscape, keeping to the contours of the ground. Philemon rolled onto his back and checked his weapons. 'They could be coming this way, taking the path of the riverbed.'

'No, look!' Damaris whispered. Her sight had always been the sharpest amongst them. 'They're turning off. They're heading straight for the temple.'

She strained her eyes, and she could see them flit between the broken stones, sprinting from pillar to pillar. One by one they passed between a henge of disordered rock and entered the central chamber of the temple, dipping down and vanishing into the darkened passage as if diving into the earth itself. There were six or seven of them, she thought, perhaps more – it was hard to tell. And then, as if answering them on the breeze, came the wailing of a child.

Antigonos was already standing as the last of the Untamed Beasts entered the chamber. His boltstorm pistol was in one hand, his axe in the other. As the lank breeze caught at his cloak, whipping it back from his shoulders, and with the light seeming to strike the worst of the tarnish from his armour, Damaris thought he looked how she would always remember him – as a hero, bold, undaunted by the worst disasters or the greatest dangers. He was a knight of the Tempered Blades.

The line of the river had taken him far towards the west, where the route of the highway burned in the night with torches and braziers, with all the song of endless war. There, Archaon's legions marched to lay siege to the arcways and bring ruin to the Mortal Realms.

Ashrath turned back to the east when he thought he had put

enough distance between himself and the Stormcast Eternals. He had followed their light as closely as he dared, keeping enough distance between them as possible. He scouted forward now, keeping low, trying to lose himself in the parched tussocks of the tundra. He dropped onto his front, daring to raise his head and peer through the stalks of grass. There was no sign of the Stormcasts now, and carefully Ashrath pushed himself to his feet with the tip of his sword. The stump of his severed arm thundered at his side. He could smell the death in it, the flesh beginning to turn beneath the rough bandage he had wrapped around it.

Not yet, he told himself. *The Coiling Ones would not lead me this far only for me to fall now.*

He hurried on, veering off the path and ducking behind an isolated outcrop of stone. Ahead of him, half a mile away on the other side of a bare apron of grass, the ground rose to a dusky knoll, where listing sandstone pillars abutted the ruins of some ancient structure. Moss-covered stones were cast about the slope of the knoll. He could see, shaded in the grass, the suggestion of a plaza or precinct. He peered out across the dead land, and, straining his sight, he could just see in the centre of the ruins a crumbling chamber.

Movement caught his eye. Figures seemed to emerge from the grass on the sloped ground, and they sprinted quickly between the ruins, darting from pillar to pillar. Ashrath watched them one at a time cautiously enter the central chamber, disappearing like dreams into a darkened doorway. The last of them paused for a moment, turning as if to scan the land around him. Ashrath huddled behind the rock, peering out through the smallest possible gap to see this last figure plunge into the darkness as well. As he did so, Ashrath could hear a plaintive child's cry ring out across the heathland.

The heir…

When he was sure they had disappeared, he eased himself out from his hiding place and quickly sprinted across the grassland towards the knoll. He clambered up the shallow slope, slithering through the grass as he skirted the edge of the ruins. He slipped into the remnants, jogging quickly past the last foundation of an old internal wall. Perhaps it had been a battlement, he thought, designed to protect the complex from any attack? If so, it had proved unable to defend against the implacable advance of time, that most dangerous enemy. Nothing could halt that foe in its tracks.

On, Son of Nagendra... the venom seemed to say. Ashrath paused, unsure if he had imagined it, but then the voice came again, weaving through his blood, and it was old and familiar.

The hour draws near, the time is upon you, Ashrath Silenthis. Strike like the Horned Krait. Take what is yours.

'Ma'sulthis,' he said. 'Old friend, I didn't think to hear your voice again. You have saved me once already, saved me from Essiltha's venom.'

The Coiling Ones saved you – they took my soul and sent it back, the voice whispered. *They are not done with you yet, Ashrath.*

'I never understood why I was chosen,' Ashrath said. He clutched the stump, stifling the pain. 'The Trials of Nagendra, the poisons I ingested, and none of them ever harmed me. But why? I acted as if leadership of the Horned Krait was mine by right, but in truth I have always been terrified... I have failed at everything, Ma'sulthis, everything.'

Self-pity unbecomes you, Son of Nagendra. The Gods are wilful and act only to their own accords, but you cannot deny that you were the one they chose. The Coiling Ones are the true children of the Great Snake, and we follow in their path, to their glory and to our own! Go now, seize what is yours, and the Varanspire will open its doors to you!

'But what chance do I have!' he pleaded with the voice, with himself. He crouched, furtive and afraid, amongst the stones. 'Starving, mutilated, half-dead already – I'll be cut to pieces!'

Trust in the favour that has brought you this far, young True-blood. When all is done, you will be the last one standing, and the child will be in your hand. This I swear.

Ashrath gathered up what scraps of courage were left to him. His green sight was on him now, the venom sour in his blood. He saw the ruins not as a man would see them, as a jumble of cast-down rock, but as a snake would see them – a predator's lair, a complex of hiding places where the hunter stalks the unwary, waiting to strike. The pain in his arm was a clean pain now, a reminder of what he had lost and what he could still gain.

He hissed under his breath and slithered between the stones.

Rakaros had flogged the creature to the very edge of endurance as he urged it across the heath, stabbing its flanks with the metal spit, screaming at it with all the guttural fury he could muster. The beast's rank hide, like cracked leather, wept under the blows. More used to the Beldam's leisurely progress as she harvested her materials or picked clean the occasional corpse, it was utterly unsuited to this mad pursuit. Still, Lord Rakaros did not relent; he thrashed it again and again, bringing his fists down against its neck, until eventually it could take no more and plunged to the ground, throwing the Blazing Lord head over heels onto the tundra. The breath was knocked from him, and the force of the fall ignited all the agonies of his previous wounds, but his rage eclipsed everything – he launched himself at the creature and rained down a frenzied series of blows that spattered its blood up into his face. Deaf to its sorrowful cries, Rakaros lost himself in vengeance until the beast was little more than a mass of steaming flesh.

When he had recovered, he threw away the bent spit and wiped his hands against his ragged robes. A lesser man would have been lost, but as Rakaros looked around him he felt the pull of the temple nearby. He had passed many ruined foundations, a dozen ancient structures that were little more than hollow shells held up by the habit of the ages as much as anything else, but each one he had dismissed. He would know it when he found it; all he had to do was continue in the direction his blood commanded.

His eyes swept over the bleak moorland, but they were caught at once by a haze of shadow far off towards the north, where the centre of the Eightpoints and the very tip of the Bloodwind Spoil met – the locus of all power in this disordered realm, where the black blade of the Varanspire stabbed into the earth. He felt a shard of ice enter his soul as his gaze fell upon it, and he was shocked to find himself almost afraid. Gathering himself, Rakaros did not pause a moment longer and hurried on.

As he ran, his mind was drawn back to the moment in the Temple of Cold Ashes when he had put himself forward for the mission to the Bloodwind Spoil. The muttered outrage from his fellow aspirants still rang in his ears – that he would be so bold as to demand the task, rather than wait to be chosen by the high priests. But what was the flame if not bold? Does fire cringe and snivel, waiting patiently for permission? Or does it seize and destroy instead? In its unquenchable fury, does it not devour the very substance that gives it life?

It was what he was doing now, he knew. All was lost, every member of the warband that had accompanied him from Aqshy on his holy mission was now dead – and yet he still stood forward and demanded the task. He would never shrink from it. The Ever-Raging Flame had seen fit to tear all his comrades away, to leave him here stranded and alone, but so be it. He would endure, and through enduring he would triumph.

Thundering over the turf, Rakaros roared his outrage without a thought for stealth or self-preservation. Unarmed, wounded, he would fight to the bitter end, and he would take what was rightfully his. The child would die in holy fire, and the blaze would be so appalling that the Everchosen himself would be forced to take note.

He glanced to the shade of the Varanspire once more, and the ice in his soul melted.

Heed me, Everchosen. The task is nearly done.

CHAPTER SEVENTEEN

STORMVAULT

The corridor stretched on before them, disappearing into a darkness that seemed to reach out from the catacombs ahead, ink-black and smelling to Burak of ancient dust and forgotten decay. He stood warily at the bottom of the stairs, the long flight of worn stone steps abraded by centuries of passing feet, that had taken them from the chamber's listing entrance down into the very depths beneath the earth. The sweat cooled on his skin, and the air was chill around him. Long had they walked already into the temple; long had they still to go.

Ekrah stood at his side, holding aloft a burning branch that he had lit on the cusp of the chamber's entrance. He had torn a wind-dried vine from the chamber's outer wall, wrapped an old rag around it and set it alight with his flint. Without the torch, Burak knew, it would have been impossible to force his surviving warriors down here. He could have asked them all to charge a xaskadon head-on and they would have done it without question, but what he was asking of them now went against their every instinct. The Untamed Beasts were creatures of the wild, of veldt and plain and jungle; they were not creatures of the deep, like grots or duardin, to seek these dark and hidden places.

Burak cradled the baby in his arms and stared into the darkness ahead. The corridor was low and wide, and here and there the roots of subterranean plants fell trailing from the ceiling like the cobwebs of monstrous spiders. There was an inch of unbroken dust on the great stone slabs of the corridor's floor, and a few feet ahead, on the edge of the radius cast by Ekrah's torch, Burak could see what looked like a mouldering skull. There was no sound save the dripping of water far in the distance, and when he spoke Burak's voice fell flat in the dead air.

'Ekrah,' he said. 'Take the lead. Tuk-kho?'

'Yes, Heart-eater?' Tuk-kho said. She stood at Burak's elbow, clutching her daggers, her teeth bared.

'Stay at the back, see we are not followed. The rest of you?' He turned to Ghulassa and his remaining fighters. There were no more than six of them left now. 'Protect me at all costs. Protect the child – see it comes to no harm.'

Burak turned to Ekrah, who still stood there staring into the shadows. 'You have the honour of leading the way, First Fang,' he said. 'Are you afraid?'

Ekrah started, as if he had been stung. 'No, Heart-eater! I fear nothing. No man or beast that walks or crawls holds any terror for me.'

'Well, if our luck holds,' Burak told him, 'it will only be man or beast that we have to worry about.'

Ekrah nodded and stepped forward, his torch flaring in the murk as he held it aloft. On they went, creeping like grave robbers into an ancient reliquary.

They prowled on in silence, senses alert, weapons ready. The dust muffled their footsteps, and in the closeness of the air the clink of weapons and the scuff of leather sounded muted and hollow. After a while Burak noticed that Ghulassa was at his side, the young plains-runner tensed for combat, his knife held in a loose fighting grip. Burak remembered when the plains-runner had first pledged that knife to his service, and he reminded the boy of it now.

'Do you remember, Ghulassa? Few have been as bold as you who came to seek admission to the Split-Tongue Tribe.'

'I remember, Heart-eater,' he said. He grinned despite himself. 'Death was near me that day, I think.'

'Nearer than you imagine – how you crept past my guards, I'll never know! We woke up to find you sitting there in the middle of the camp, head shaved, naked, that knife across your knee...'

'Actions are more eloquent than speech,' Ghulassa said, an old edict amongst the Untamed Beasts. 'I had to show you my boldness, for you would not have taken my word for it alone.'

'True, true,' Burak said. He remembered the Preytakers dragging Ghulassa to the dais where he sat, throwing him down into the dirt for judgement. 'I'll never forget your words, though, the words that made me take you into the tribe. Do you remember what they were?'

'Of course,' Ghulassa said. He closed his eyes for a moment, reverently, as if recalling holy speech. 'You asked if I thought your seat was a throne, that you were a king to whom I must pledge my service. "No," I said. "But you will have a throne to come. You will join the Hungering King on his rampage through the realms, and a throne you shall have in the end. I have seen it." That is what I said, Burak, and I will never forget it.'

Burak's eyes shone in the dark, snatching the light from Ekrah's torch. 'Yes...' he hissed. 'The throne to come... I will never forget either. And I will never forget your dedication, young Ghulassa, your boldness and your loyalty.'

The passage stretched on for a hundred yards or more before they reached the first turning. Warily, Ekrah paused and looked around the corner, casting the flame from his torch into the new stretch of corridor. On the ground at his feet there were more bones and some rags of cloth, and the desiccated remains of what might once have been a walking staff.

'I do not like it, Burak,' Ekrah said. 'The air ahead smells of death, and–'

'The smell of death should not worry a First Fang of the Untamed Beasts,' Burak scorned. 'A First Fang deals in nothing but death.' He kicked the rags on the ground. 'But we are not the first to come this way, I see.' He peered down the new passageway. There was an itch at the edge of his mind. A presence, almost, a force that felt as if something were lightly pressing against the stuff of his soul.

Ghulassa bent to the powdered bones, turning them over in his hands. He held up the rags and sniffed them, and then cast them onto the ground.

'Too many years have passed,' the plains-runner said. 'These bones are of one who walked this place long before any of us were born.'

Ekrah's torch flickered and flared, and the crackling flames threw jagged shadows against the crumbling stone walls around them. Burak could feel a passage of warmer air trickling past him, coming from deeper into the catacombs. The baby cried softly in his arms, and then settled down to sleep.

'Do we go on?' Ekrah asked. Burak looked into his face – the ruined eye gummed with scabs, the harsh planes of his cheekbones and jaw, the other eye dauntless and unafraid. Truly, Burak knew, Ekrah would throw himself on his sword rather than be thought a coward.

He looked down the new passageway ahead of them, trying to

stare past the ring of light thrown out by Ekrah's torch. The rough, uneven walls on either side were worn and pitted. The flagstones were patched with lichen, and here and there they had broken away to leave gaps and hollows in the floor. Burak inhaled deeply, feeling again that warm channel of air as it was exhaled down the corridor towards them. He looked at the bones on the ground, the filthy rags. 'Wait,' he said to Ekrah. 'Ghulassa?'

'Heart-eater?'

'Take the lead for the next stretch.' He looked at the plains-runner, who eagerly stepped up. Burak smiled and patted the boy's face. 'Prove your devotion to me once more.'

The young warrior needed no more encouragement than that. Gingerly he stepped out into the corridor, his knife held at his left side. He trailed the fingers of his right hand against the wall, and at every step he judged the ground as if reading the spoor of a hunted beast. Some of the flagstones were discoloured, and on others it seemed as if the dust had once been disturbed, many years ago. He stepped over the gaps in the flagstones, Ekrah following close behind with the torch held high to light his way. Burak came next, and then the rest of the plains-runners, some of them muttering prayers, others nervously clutching the charms and fetishes that were tied to their wrists.

Keenly Burak watched Ghulassa, and when they had all walked a few more yards down the passageway he raised his hand to Ekrah's shoulder, halting him. Ghulassa turned, his mouth open to speak – and then there was a hiss of air, a juddering snap, and Ghulassa stood there with a metal spike through the back of his head, the point jutting out of his eye and quivering to the last few beats of his heart. The young warrior's other eye was vacant with shock; he hadn't even had time to scream.

Carefully Burak approached, seeing where the spike had stabbed out of the wall, where Ghulassa's foot had brushed the pressure pad on the flagstone floor. Ekrah raised his torch, and in the dancing light Ghulassa's face seemed almost alive again. Burak patted his cheek, careful not to get blood on his fingers.

Your journey is over, he thought. *And you did as you promised, through all the trials and dangers we have faced. Run in the great hunting grounds – you have earned the Great Devourer's favour. But I wonder if this is really how you saw your end? Prophecies and omens are uncertain guides at the best of times...*

He shivered and pushed the nagging doubts away. 'Take care,' Burak whispered to the warriors behind him. 'It seems we would be wise to watch our feet...'

The catacombs stretched on ahead of them, smothered in shadow.

But I do not die here, Burak told himself. *Not impaled upon an ancient trap or crushed beneath a deadfall – I do* not *die here.*

He went on, scanning the ground ahead, a murky path only partly lit by Ekrah's torch. Each step was as much a leap of faith as the result of cold calculation. Once more the dust on the ground was undisturbed, and there were no more rags or bones to mark the end of another unfortunate. However far they had come into the catacombs beneath the Tormented Lands, they had pressed on further than anyone had ever done before. Burak glanced up at the corroded ceiling, where fronds of vine roots stretched pale and dead across the stone. He tried to imagine the millions of tons of earth and soil and rock above him, the buried bones of immeasurable creatures long since passed out of legend, the weight of the Bloodwind Spoil itself pressing down on his head. The breeze, like a rank and gelid breath, drifted across his bare skin. It smelled of decay, and of the long-drained wells of ancient power now rotted down to nothing.

'Step where I step,' he said. 'Walk where I walk, and do not stray from the path. Or poor Ghulassa's fate will be yours.'

From deeper in the chamber, which was slowly revealed by the pulse of Ekrah's burning branch, came a soft cry of distress – faint, like a name being called in desperation. Burak grinned to himself. He held the child in one arm and drew his steel knife in the other, and the brass disc at his neck shivered in the torchlight. They were not alone, it seemed. Others dared these secret chambers and fell victim to their ancient snares.

Burak laughed. As if in answer, the baby began to cry, and its voice wavered down the corridor ahead of them to disappear into the darkness.

From their position at the back of the temple complex, the Stormcast warriors watched the Untamed Beasts slip noiselessly into the central chamber and disappear into the earth. Now, rising from the broken ground where they had been hidden, Damaris led them swiftly across the short stretch of scrub grass to the base of the knoll, the slight rise in the centre of the plain where the temple precinct had once dominated the surrounding landscape. They climbed up between the ruins of old foundation stones, through the demolished walls of external chapels and blessed sanatoria, where ancient steles carved with myriad holy symbols lay smothered in the grass. Damaris touched her fingers to the wind-smeared outline of a twin-tailed comet that had been carved at the pinnacle of an obelisk that now lay broken in three pieces on the ground, just a relic left forgotten on this unholy earth.

'There is something of immeasurable power here,' Damaris said. 'I can feel it.'

It pressed at the edge of her mind as they clambered on through the fallen stones and ruined outbuildings, a feeling of great apprehension that blurred when she tried to consider it more carefully. She felt a strange and almost sentient presence slowly reform to admit them. There was something here that wanted to be forgotten, Damaris felt, and it was trying to scour the understanding from her mind even before she had properly absorbed it.

'What you feel is the residue of an ancient system of defence,' Antigonos said. 'Thousands of years have passed, and still some fragment of it stretches out to ward itself from prying fingers – or from prying minds. It will not harm us, though, if we're careful.'

The Vanguard-Hunters crept closer to the central chamber and crouched behind a fallen architrave.

'Do we follow?' Philemon asked. 'We could rush them as they fumble through the dark, make short work of them in the tunnels?'

'No,' Antigonos said. 'The passageways beneath this place are cramped and dangerous – they would have the advantage. And they would hear us coming no matter how quiet we tried to be.'

He pointed beyond the chamber, to a cluster of pillars and stones far over on the other side of the hill. Damaris followed his direction, looking over to what had once been a hypostyle atrium, where all that was left were the leaning columns that had once supported its roof.

'There are other ways inside this vault,' Antigonos said. 'We can outflank them. We can reach the altar before them, and we'd have the advantage of surprise. Come, my hunters. Let us seize at last what we have come here for.' He raced off across the grass, Philemon and Damaris following close behind.

On the edge of the slope that led down to the plains, where the breeze stuttered fitfully through the short grass and carried with it a carrion stink from the direction of the Varanspire, Antigonos stooped to inspect the ground. The columns of this sub-temple rose aslant above them, leaning into each other, some balanced precariously and threatening to fall at the merest breath of the wind. Damaris looked up into those leaning trunks, where dust trailed in ribbons from the worn stone. That they had survived this long was a miracle, she thought. She prayed that all they saw here would one day be rebuilt, to the glory of the God-King and to the benefit of all who served him.

Antigonos crouched and examined a split in the stone of the temple floor. With one firm stamp of his armoured boot he cracked the stone in half, and the sundered piece crashed down into the shadows below.

'There is an undercroft beneath us,' he said, peering down. 'A chamber of some sort. The drop looks steep, uncertain...'

'A leap in the dark,' Philemon said. Damaris could almost see the smile behind his helmet – bluff, undaunted, ready to follow his Hunter-Prime anywhere. She steeled herself, felt that ancient presence skim once more over the contours of her consciousness.

'I'll go first,' she said, but Antigonos was already feeling his way into the gap. As he climbed down, the shadows almost rising up to meet him, Damaris unhooked her compass and let its celestial light guide their way.

They dropped onto the top of a long slope of rubble and earth, which stretched down onto a disordered tier far beneath them. The light from Damaris' compass cast a pale and eerie glow, and as they climbed down the scree, she saw that they were in a small antechamber or portico to a vast room that loomed in the darkness beyond it.

Shadows leapt up the walls around them, slinking over the faded carvings of scenes from ancient myth. Godbeasts unknown to Damaris thundered in onyx and marble through the celestial void, and the gods stood resplendent in all their emblazoned glory. Where the stone was cracked and broken, though, the tendrils of vines had crept through, and on the ground at their feet was a drift of dead leaves and dust. The air was stale and close, threaded by a musty smell of incense and rotting parchment. The clatter of pebbles echoed around the chamber, and when Antigonos spoke his voice boomed massively back at them.

'This way,' he said. 'And watch your step – these ancient places are more dangerous than you would think.'

They clambered down the slope and reached the chamber floor at last, pacing quickly across it, stepping lightly over the broken stone and leaping over a latticework of tangled roots. The antechamber receded behind them, swallowed up once more into the subterranean gloom. Ahead, only the glow from Damaris' compass kept the darkness at bay.

Eventually, looming up in front of them, came the edge of the portico. A long flight of stone steps stretched down into the darkness beneath them, so wide that the light from Damaris' lamp did not reach either side. The steps had been saddled and worn by use. She thought it must have been a processional route once, where pilgrims and worshippers in ages long past walked in holy purpose, dozens abreast. Now, this whole complex was not even a rumour in the lands around them, despised where it was thought of at all, or forgotten by those who eked a miserable existence in the Tormented Lands. They headed down the massive flight of stairs, walking abreast – down, ever down into the dark of the catacombs beneath.

They came to the edge of another chamber, vast and cavernous, and so oppressively dark that Damaris felt almost apprehensive as they approached it. She held up her compass light. The Stormcast warriors moved forward, cautiously, Damaris in the lead. Suddenly she skidded to a halt, throwing her arms out for balance – before her there was nothing but a yawning chasm in the ground, a gorge that had split the chamber apart and plunged down into the inky dark with no hint of how deep it went. She lifted her compass. The other side of the gap was but a faint line etched across the shadows.

Philemon crouched at the edge and dropped a stone into the chasm. A solid minute passed... two... then three. Nothing. He looked at Antigonos, who stood there on the lip of the cliff, staring off at the other side.

'Grappling hooks?' Philemon said. 'We could throw a line across and crawl over the rope?'

'The distance is too far,' Damaris said. 'The rope wouldn't stretch, if we could even make the throw.'

'What is this anyway?' Philemon said. He stood up and angrily kicked another stone into the darkness. 'A moat? What's the point of it?'

'This is unstable ground,' Antigonos said. 'I would have said it was a split from an earthquake, but the lines are too regular.'

In the darkness Damaris scouted along the line of the gorge, until she came to the denuded nub of what must have once been a bridge. Two parapets bracketed the shattered line of an avenue, where a roadway would have stretched out across the gorge. She could imagine it in ages past, the ceremonial procession made more glorious by the vacancy beneath it, the span of the deck as it curved out in an elegant sweep across the deep. Age had withered the stone and sent it crashing down into the void; there would be no crossing here.

The Stormcast warriors ran further along the edge of the chasm to the point where it met the chamber wall. The wall stretched across the gap, and Damaris could see that it was roughly surfaced with ivy roots and coarse stone. She pointed. 'There,' she said. 'We could climb across. There are handholds, footholds – I'm sure we could do it.'

'Better that than go back,' Philemon agreed.

'Always on,' Antigonos muttered. 'On, ever on...'

Damaris went first, confidently prising her fingers into the fissures of the rock, lifting her weight first onto one foot and then the other, swinging out and already stretching for the next handhold. An updraught from the chasm below snapped her cloak out from her shoulders; without pause, she unhooked it from the clasp and sent it fluttering down into the abyss.

'Be careful,' Antigonos called as he stowed his weapons. He took his own cloak off and drew his gauntlets from his hands, letting them fall to the ground at his feet. Philemon did the same, and then swung himself out onto the rock surface to follow Damaris' lead. Antigonos powdered his hands with dirt and took the rear.

The distance could have been no more than fifty feet, but to the three Stormcast hunters it felt like miles. Despite their god-forged strength, their fortitude and will to continue, by the time they were halfway across their muscles were beginning to shake. Sweat lashed down Damaris' forehead, and she felt her fingers tremble at every grip. Her feet in their armoured boots scrabbled at the stone, and more often than not she had to kick at the wall to force a foothold. It was as if the very shadows beneath her were trying to pull her down. She kept her sight fixed to the wall in front of her, only turning to search for the next handhold.

'Don't look down,' Antigonos called, as if reading her mind. 'And whatever you do, don't fall... I dread to think how far it goes, or what gnawing madness lies at the roots of this land.'

Eventually she could see the edge of the other chamber, a stepped line that gradually emerged as a grey smear from the darkness. She grinned, and suddenly her efforts seemed easier. She looked back to shout encouragement, but when she saw Philemon her heart lurched in her chest.

He had found the crossing more difficult; it was obvious. He had thrown off his helmet halfway across, and his face was red with strain. All Stormcast Eternals were near-giants, infused with the energies and power of the heavens, but Philemon had always been an imposing figure. Often, Damaris had joked that he had been rejected from the ranks of the Paladins and had taken up the mantle of a Vanguard-Hunter as a second choice; he was that substantial a fighter. In battle his bulk was an asset; here, it was a hindrance. As she turned, she saw him reach out for the next handhold, overstretching and grasping instead at the cord of some subterranean vine, the plant then yielding to his weight and unravelling from the rock in a cloud of dust. Philemon's eyes widened, and his mouth opened to a gasp – and then, as Damaris looked on in horror, he was falling, tumbling backwards, his other hand slipping its grip from the shallow stone, his breath sucked in with shock.

'Philemon!' Damaris screamed. She made a reckless leap, dropping down to snatch at his hand, grabbing at the rock wall at the same time, but she was too late; her fingers passed through his, and as she looked into his eyes for the half second before he was engulfed in shadow, she saw not fear or dismay, not even anger at the end of his journey, but something like regret. It was not regret for himself, she knew – he went to his fate with all the stoic endurance she would have expected – but in some way it was for her. Regret that she should have been brought this far, that her fate would no doubt be to die here too. Regret that all these deaths would lie most heavily on the shoulders of their Hunter-Prime, Antigonos, who even now gritted his teeth to the loss and forced himself onwards.

'Philemon…' Damaris cried again, but the chasm was empty, and her voice was swallowed by the void.

The lightning never came. Wherever he was, however far down he had gone, Philemon was still falling.

At last they emerged into open space, after what had felt like hours creeping through the dark. Down and further down the passageways had led, deeper into the earth, the gradient sometimes subtle and sometimes steep. The Untamed Beasts had come to other stairways that flowed down into the darkness, and the air became oppressively close. Ekrah had fed more rags to his torch, but Burak had begun to worry that it would soon burn out. He tried not to think of what it would be like once they were plunged into permanent night down here, lost and groping in the pitch. He shuddered.

Eventually, a faint glow broke the darkness ahead and they came out of the passageways into a vast chamber, where thin columns of light fell down from some hidden break in a ceiling unimaginably distant above them. The walls were as wreathed in vines as any jungle bower, and the air was feverishly charged with the latency of old magics. Ekrah tore a dried vine from the wall at the side of the stairs and quickly made another torch, which he passed to Burak. The Heart-eater felt his hair prickle on his scalp, and in his arms the baby wriggled with distress. Ekrah stood at Burak's left side, his sword in hand. It was the side where his smashed eye wouldn't hinder him, Burak knew.

He is not my right hand, like Kurguth, the Heart-eater thought, *but he is my left. Kurguth, forgive me for your murder, my old friend... All is about to be accomplished, though, I swear it. Your death was never in vain.*

Ancient flagstones crumbled under their feet as they stepped cautiously into the chamber. Beneath the covering vines, the walls were decorated with massive, faded frescoes of times unknown to the Untamed Beasts – times when gods walked amongst men, and when war was a distant and glorious thing. A time before the Great Devourer filled his belly with the lies of the weak.

Ahead of them, lit by a slanted spear of light that called up all the silicate colours in its stone, was a vast altar that seemed to radiate power. It stood there in the middle of a wide dais, on a tier six feet higher than the tier beneath it. On the lower tier, a twisted mass of sculpted metal lay like some arcane model of the solar winds. Burak found his mind turning from this weird sculpture even as he looked at it, as if it were somehow too great for him to comprehend. Even the altar felt too large to be contained by this space, too big for the eyes to see. It dominated even a room this huge, a hall for the gods, and as he stared at it Burak felt that it was somehow repelling his sight. It was too pure, too powerful – and it disgusted him.

He bared his teeth in a snarl, drew his steel dagger and sent his warband on across the marbled floor.

'Guard me now as you have never guarded me before!' he shouted. He rushed forward with the child mewling in his arms. 'The Everchosen's eye is on us now!'

They had taken but a bare few feet into the chamber when a bolt of lightning streaked across the hall, impossibly bright, and scorched Ekrah's shoulder. He cried out, but the wound was a glancing one; in moments he had his sword up, sweeping out before him. He threw his torch to the ground, and it cast up its eerie flicker on the scene. The survivors of the Split-Tongue Tribe circled around Burak, and from the shadows on the other side of the chamber came the vengeance of heaven – the Stormcast Eternals, weapons drawn, charging into battle for their craven god.

'Untamed Beasts!' Burak called. He bounded on towards the altar. 'Kill them! Kill them before it's too late!'

She parried the first blow and swept the head from the savage's shoulders with her storm sabre, whipping her elbow back to smash the one who was trying to flank her in the face. The barbarian dropped to the ground, moaning and clutching his jaw. Damaris stamped on his neck as she circled around, the vertebrae crunching under her foot. Three more of them dashed to the side to head off Antigonos, who had split to Damaris' left and headed for the altar. They leapt on past the dais and came at him in a blur of bone knives and axes, but then Damaris lost track of the fight as she was enveloped in her own. Two more of the barbarians confronted her. One of them scuttled across the chamber floor like a grot, hunched and wary, her teeth bared by the leather bit in her mouth. Two yellowed orruk fangs rattled from the strap that kept the bit in place. Her eyes glared with madness, bloodshot, crazed. The other savage, a big man with a vicious-looking serrated blade, the polished leather of his horned helmet gleaming in the torchlight, held his sword at guard. He trod warily across the dusty flagstones, bare feet scuffing lightly on the stone. His right eye was a crusted scab, and his face, half hidden by the flared helmet, was twisted with rage, but Damaris still recognised him from the ambush at the edge of the diseased forest.

'You!' she said. She lowered her sword and pointed at him with the blade. 'You're the one who killed Leander.'

'Aye, storm-born,' he growled. 'And I'll be the one to kill you too!'

He cut the blade down and knocked her sabre aside, then swung low with a swift backhand.

Damaris blocked the blow easily, but then the smaller fighter, gnashing her filed teeth, rolled under her guard and jabbed at the gaps in her armour. Damaris felt the bite of a blade behind her knee, and it brought a gasp from her mouth. She kicked out, but the small fighter skipped away and snapped a throwing knife towards her, and as Damaris knocked it from the air the bigger man came whaling in once more with his sword. They were experts at this, Damaris belatedly realised. They looked like animals, like feral beasts, but they had more skill with their weapons than most. This wasn't random savagery, but precise swordplay.

She caught the first blow against her breastplate, the second against her left vambrace. The big man dodged her lunge and shoulder-barged her backwards, scraping the bone sword with a piercing shriek across her pauldron. Damaris caught the return swing of his sword on the crossbar of her own, twisting her grip and throwing his blade upwards, and then as the barbarian cut down again, she swept her sabre up to shatter the bone sword in two. To his credit, the savage didn't even flinch; instead, without losing any of his momentum, he stabbed forward with the broken hilt and caught Damaris across the forehead, opening a gash in her skin that poured blood down into her eyes. The Stormcast hunter swung wide, stepping backwards, tripping over the young woman who had thrown herself behind her. Damaris crashed to the ground, and before she even had the chance to draw breath, she felt the knife slip wetly into her throat.

Blood gushed from the wound, spewing from her mouth to spatter her armour. She tried to scream, but her lungs were choked with it. Through matted eyes she saw the woman draw the knife back for a second blow, her face a mad mask of hatred. Damaris had dropped her sabre, but as the knife came down, she blocked it with the bare palm of her hand, the bone blade stabbing through the meat to pause an inch from her face. The pain was extraordinary, but she twisted her arm to the side all the same. Two of her fingers were sheared off as the blade slipped out of her hand, but she had opened the savage's guard. Damaris spat a mouthful of blood up into her face, watched her reel back, and then jammed her thumb deep into her eye.

The savage howled, and Damaris tried to howl with her, the blood gurgling in her torn throat. She lifted the fighter off the ground and slammed her head down onto the flagstones, again and again, the skull shattering, brains jetting out to cover the feet of the big man, who looked on in horror. Damaris crushed what was left of the barbarian's head in her fist.

'Tuk-kho!' the savage cried. He threw himself at Damaris. Both were now weaponless, but they hammered at each other with fists and feet, with teeth and nails. The Untamed Beast fought like his namesake, like something feral and without inhibition – wild, more dangerous than any trained foe. He crashed his fists into Damaris' face, splitting her nose, and those blows she couldn't block beat the breath from her. In any other circumstances she would have had the best of it in moments, but the blood was pouring freely from her throat and her vision was dark. Chill fingers were creeping into her soul. She kept her hands up to block her face, but she was being pushed back, forced down onto her knees. She caught a ringing punch to the side of her head and hit the ground, but as the savage followed up, she kicked his legs from under him and chopped her forearm down onto his throat as he fell. He gagged and spluttered, but before he could roll away, she was up on top of him, her hands wrapped around his throat, fingers crushing his windpipe. Blood jetted from the wound in her throat to cover his contorted face, and in moments he was masked in it. Damaris kept pressing down with a manic strength, until she felt beneath her thumbs the notches of his broken spine. His tongue rolled fatly from his mouth, his lips covered in pink foam, and his one remaining eye strained fit to burst through the crossbar of his helmet. Damaris was trying to scream, her vision awash with blood. No force on earth would ever make her stop squeezing this man's neck.

She looked up. Far over on the other side of the altar, Antigonos clutched a wounded arm to his chest and dispatched the last of his foes, splitting one of the savages' heads in half with a swing of his axe. The bodies of the others were in pieces on the ground. He turned, saw her, opened his mouth, shouted silently–

Why couldn't she hear him? He looked so pale, so worn. There was almost nothing left of him. This would be it. If he died here, then all that he was would be lost. And then Damaris felt warmth spreading through her, and she raised her fingers to feel the tip of the knife jutting from her chest. She heard as if from miles away the laughter of the man who had killed her, the crying of the baby that he would now take to the altar stone.

'Antigonos,' she tried to say, but the word wouldn't come. She tried to reach for him as he ran towards her, but then he was brought down in turn. She saw a blurred figure crash into him, both of them rolling and falling the short drop from the dais where the altar glowed in its column of light. She turned and saw the chief of the Untamed Beasts sprinting towards it with glee, a knife slick with her blood in his hand.

Antigonos, she thought. *We have lost... The vault is unguarded – we have failed you.*

Forgive me, Sigmar, my liege. I will do better next time, I promise. Antigonos, I promise...

But Antigonos was very far away now, and she was falling – falling not into darkness but into the light.

CHAPTER EIGHTEEN

BLOOD OF THE EVERCHOSEN

He hit the ground and pain lanced through him. His left arm was numb and lifeless at his side. Blood dripped freely from the wounds the Beasts had put into him. He had killed them all in a frenzy, witnessing the severed limbs and the gaping injuries he inflicted as if they were coming from a distant dream and not happening right in front of him – a nightmare of sharpened teeth, glaring eyes and stinking, meat-rank breath. Fighting them had been more like fighting the scuttling menace of skaven or grots – insignificant warriors when taken in turn, but deceptively dangerous when faced in concert. Still, it should not have come to this. He should not feel this weak.

The Penumbral Engine, clouding my mind – the arcane energy of a distant age, dormant, but still reaching out to mask its presence from me. The deaths I have caused, the weight of my failure...

The savages were more like animals, Antigonos thought, practically immune from observing what they did not understand. The presence of the ruined Penumbral Engine barely seemed to affect them at all.

They had fought with desperation, but even in his debilitated condition Antigonos had been more than a match for them. They had stabbed at the exposed gaps in his armour, bleeding him, draining his strength, knocking his boltstorm pistol from his hand. He had been pushed back while he tried to shake the fog from his mind, but instinct and training had kept them at bay, and then a rising fury saw him cleave left and right to hew his tormenters to pieces. Arms tumbled to the ground; blood splashed against his armour. He did his butcher's work with dour efficiency, until the Untamed Beasts were little more than ruined carcasses on the temple floor.

As the last one fell, Antigonos looked wildly for Damaris. He saw her on the flagstones on the other side of the dais, choking the life from the last savage, screaming wordlessly, her face and armour splattered with blood – and then the Beasts' unholy chief, with sly amusement, was running forward to plunge his dagger into her back. Antigonos screamed a warning, but it was too late. He saw the blood heave from her body as the knife was drawn out, saw Damaris fall and roll over, reaching out, her eyes frosting with death – and then the motes of gold began to agitate around the tarnished cream of her armour, and her form slowly softened into mist. From the earth rose a piercing beam of light that arced through the chamber, shatteringly bright, disappearing into the further reaches of the ceiling above.

'Damaris,' he had whispered. 'Farewell, daughter of the storm, hunter of the Tempered Blades. Avenge this moment. And… remember me, if you can.'

Before he could go to her, something slammed into his side and sent him tumbling from the dais. He hit the ground, the breath knocked from him.

'I doubt she will,' a hissing, slithering voice said behind him. 'It doesn't seem to me that you've done much worth remembering at all, chosen of Sigmar.'

Antigonos reeled around, scrabbling for his axe. There was a flash of steel, red pain, and then he was clutching the bleeding stump where his right hand used to be. He cried out, and through blurred vision looked onto the foul thing that stood before him, its face pale and streaked with green veins, its hair lank and greasy, the yellow, weeping eyes that glowered at him bisected by a snake's slit pupil. The man, if that was what it was, had only one arm; the other ended in a scaled stump that twitched and leaked a corrosive green venom onto the flagstones.

He recognised the creature, somehow – or rather, he recognised the type. It reminded him of the aelf woman he had killed out on the Tormented Lands, one of the snake cult who had fought in the mountains, who he had left nailed to a tree. This was one of them, he was sure, transformed, come seeking revenge or in search of the child that even now Antigonos could hear crying as he was brought to the altar. He risked a glance over his shoulder, and he could see the barbarian chief struggling against the force of the Penumbral Engine, his head bowed, an expression of naked pain on his face and the baby clutched to his chest.

Antigonos pushed himself backwards, slowly, until he reached the edge of the dais. He cradled his wounded right arm in his shattered left, and he felt the strength draining from him. The snake-worshipper advanced slowly, sinuously, his sword tip weaving and flowing in the air like crystal water. Antigonos looked for his axe and saw it off to the side, no more than an arm's length from him.

An arm's length… while I'm cursed with wounds in both.

He felt the power of the Penumbral Engine, still so potent despite its long disrepair. And beneath it, whispering on the edge of his mind, a susurrus of arcane energy from the altar itself – and from what had been hidden inside it.

'Go on,' the snake-worshipper said, following his line of sight.

'Take it. Pick up your weapon and strike me down – you know how much you want to.'

'What I want, scum, has nothing to do with it. I do my duty, not my desire.'

'Do you? I wonder... I haven't seen many of your kind, storm-born, but there is a look in your eyes that I recognise well. Hunger, lust, the thirst for murder... The lightning hasn't burned that from you, I see. Or maybe the Spoil has planted it in you, instead.'

'Get it done,' Antigonos spat. 'Kill me, boy, as I killed your aelf friend out on the plains.'

'Essiltha...?'

'Was that her name? I didn't think to ask. And I doubt she could have answered at the end, she was in so much pain.'

The snake-worshipper paused. He lowered the tip of his sword. He seemed to drift away, and for a moment his face cleared into some semblance of its normal state. Young, and strangely innocent, Antigonos thought. A boy led astray, a young man who had let ambition and wild promises poison him as surely as the venom in his veins.

Then the child cried out from the altar behind them and the snake-worshipper's eyes flickered back with a pale, envenomed gaze. He grinned, and his teeth were like fangs.

Antigonos breathed out and closed his eyes. He didn't know why, but the image that came forcefully to his mind was of his first night in the Bloodwind Spoil – himself and Damaris, Leander, Philemon. The others of the hunting party too – Heraclius and Erastus, and Starglider weaving the heavens, coursing untouched through the manic reek. They had risked a fire, circling around the low flame and girding themselves for the task ahead. The place they had found themselves in was appalling, and the night around them was laced with awful screams that faded on the breeze. Despite that, he was not afraid. He had looked over his warriors, his comrades, his friends, and he was not afraid. Even if he died here, died for the last time, it would be worth it to have served as their Hunter-Prime – for they had obeyed the summons, and they had armed themselves for the fight ahead without a murmur of dissent. The quest had failed, but they had each gone to their fate like heroes. It had been an honour to lead them, the greatest honour of his life.

Antigonos opened his eyes. He smiled – and then he lunged for his axe.

It was hard to tell what was real and what not in this subterranean place. A creature of the veldt, a hunter of the wide and unobstructed plains, Burak the Bloodseer felt the weight of the catacombs pressing down on his mind, crushing his thoughts, blinding him with its tenebrous light. The closer he forced himself to the altar, the worse it got, as if he were trying to push himself through some invisible force. Everything around him took immense concentration to realise – the knife in his hand, the crying child he cradled in his arm, the altar stone's sacrificial table.

The mute power of reality, pressing up against the force of my visions. It is the will of the Devourer, testing me. Am I strong enough to break through this fog, to make the sacrifice?

He bared his feral teeth and howled into the pressure that ranged itself against him. In his arms, the baby howled too.

'Our paths diverge, child! I go to hunt at the right-hand side of a god.'

He wiped the knife on his cloak, cleansing it of the storm-born's blood. Iron Golem, Splintered Fang, Scions of the Flame and Stormcast Eternals – the Bloodseer had defeated them all. Every vision, every head-splitting prophecy that had crawled its way across his brain, had come true. The long, ostracised years, the decades of mockery and threat, were coming to an end. As Burak laid the baby down, unwrapping the swaddling cloth, he seemed to feel again every dismissive cuff and beating he had ever taken as a child, from those who feared or hated him as he slowly came into his power. More than that, he felt every life he had taken as he honed his skills and grew his warband, every rival he had knifed in the dark or bested in single combat as he took over the Split-Tongue Tribe. He lived again all the murders he had committed, the friends he had killed on the bloody path to glory, enslaved by the truth of his visions – Kurguth most of all, his brother... He saw the splash of blood against the rock, the Mountain's Throat swinging open to lead them deep under the stone. Did Kurguth's shade still linger there on the mountain paths, he wondered, haunting the mist-wreathed trails, condemned to wail its dismay across all the nights to follow? It had been a dishonourable death. Of all the ways Burak had betrayed his friend, that one was the worst.

The child cried again and brought him back to the present moment, the hinge of fate, where the long years of the past prepared to meet the pivot of the future. Burak scanned the shadows quickly on either side, flinching as a jagged burst of light streaked up from somewhere on the other side of the altar, a golden breach in the darkness of the catacombs that cast them with an eerie, flickering glow.

So, the plains-runners have dealt with the last of the lightning-borne, he thought, cackling to himself. *Back to face the displeasure of his vengeful god... So be it.*

All then had failed in the challenge except Burak – the stick had been whittled down to the sharpest point, and now it was ready to strike.

'I am the one who will anoint the altar, who will wash it in blood, my child,' he said. 'None other.'

He placed the child on the altar. The baby seemed to calm itself, lying on its stone bed. Thin, malnourished, but still strong; it stared at him with its deep green eyes, and for a moment Burak faltered. He remembered his dream and shuddered, seeing again the child crawl across the altar to devour him – but then the moment passed. It had been a dream, not a premonition. After all these years, he knew the difference. There was no truth in it.

But as the child stared at him, a point of light seemed to ignite in each eye, a reflected flame that flickered and grew. Burak looked up quickly, knife ready. There, on the other side of the altar, smouldering and dark like a column of black fire, stood Lord Rakaros. His armour was gone, his body was a mass of scars and he had no weapon, but his eyes were pits of flame more terrible than the mightiest conflagration.

'You have done well to make it this far, Beast,' he said, his voice rumbling through the cavernous chamber. 'But your time on the hunt is over. The sacrifice is mine.'

Wary of the last time he had been in the presence of a Stormcast Eternal when it died, Ashrath threw himself aside as he struck the killing blow. Even with his eyes closed, the burst of light was near-blinding, the power and energy that radiated from it scorching his skin and the noise a deafening blast that made his ears ring. When the moment was over, there was nothing where the Stormcast had lain but scorched stone.

Ashrath quickly clambered up the lower tier, cursing at the pain in his arm. He sneaked to the side of the altar, and as he crouched and peered around the corner, he could see the leader of the Beasts standing triumphantly at the sacrificial table, wiping his blade on his cloak. The child was crying. As the Untamed Beast laid it down and stood before it, he became strangely still, as if frightened of the decision he had to make, overawed perhaps by the momentousness of what was occurring.

It is the Everchosen's son, Ashrath thought, steeling himself to act. *No wonder your blade falters at the final cut, Beast!*

He gripped his sword, tensed his muscles for action. His teeth gnawed hungrily at his bottom lip, and the stump of his left arm burned and twitched with the venoms that were coursing through his veins. His green sight flared in the gloom, and in its emerald glow the altar seemed to pulse with arcane energies, as if already absorbing the molten essence of the sacrificed child. He felt its force grinding into his mind, turning him away, trying to scour all thought of it from his memory. He would not let it happen. He was a moment away from apotheosis, from the final vindication of his every move since leaving Invidia. The Horned Krait were no more, cast to the winds of the Spoil, but Ashrath Silenthis lived on, and he would be victorious.

'Ma'sulthis,' he whispered under his breath. 'Hear me now. Lend me the strength of the Coiling Ones, let your venoms gird my arm and guide my blade.'

He was poised, ready to leap, when he heard the voice. Low, it was, booming resonantly around the buried chamber, rebounding from the walls with all its force redoubled. Despite himself, Ashrath trembled to hear it.

Lord Rakaros! Blood of Nagendra, he lives!

The Blazing Lord leapt the altar in a savage bound, ignoring the flash of Burak's blade as he staggered backwards in shock. Rakaros kicked Burak's arm and the knife clattered to the stone floor. With a roar of defiance, he lashed out with his fists and pummelled the Heart-eater to the ground.

Burak rolled away, his disbelief soon replaced by rage. That this fire-worshipping madman thought he could seize the child and steal his glory! Burak snatched up the knife from the flagstones and struck back, darting first left and then right – feinting, stabbing, sweeping the blade out on the backhand to slash a ribbon of blood from the Blazing Lord's chest. Rakaros grunted with pain, but again he came on, wildly swinging his fists. Burak was the faster fighter, without a doubt, and as powerfully built as any of his warband had been, but Rakaros was a brute of a man; every stab and slash Burak managed to inflict on him was like a pinprick, soon shrugged off. No matter how quick he was, he knew, eventually one of the Blazing Lord's blows was going to connect.

Suddenly there was a dull pain in his head. As if from a hazy distance Burak saw a handful of his own teeth rattle across the ground, and then the ground was sweeping up to meet him. He smashed into it face first, his nose bursting, blood drooling from his mouth. He turned, dazed, just as Rakaros launched a crippling kick into his ribs. Burak felt them crumple in his chest, and he gasped as he scrabbled at the ground, as if he could claw back the breath that had been beaten from him. Above it all, he could hear the baby crying, its soft wail higher even than the ringing in his ears.

'Wait, my child,' he groaned. 'Burak will be with you soon.'

Rakaros scooped up the knife from where it had gone flying out of Burak's hand. He tested the edge of the blade on his thumb.

'Iron Golem work,' he said. His voice sounded to the Heart-eater as if it were coming from underwater. 'To a barbarian like you, I would have thought good steel would be anathema.'

'It is,' Burak laughed. He was choking on the blood that was pouring from his nose, and he rolled onto his front so he could hack it up. 'Good steel,' he coughed. 'And cities, and temples – all make me sick to my stomach.'

'You're little better than an animal,' Rakaros said, standing over him. He winced as he raised his arm, the knife held high. 'Some snuffling beast with a cunning sense of survival, but no vision, no awareness of the part you've played in grander schemes. You deluded yourself to think you could succeed on this quest. Victory was always mine for the taking. The Ever-Raging Flame will have its due, and only I am worthy enough to give it.'

Burak struggled to his knees and held up his head for the coup de grace. 'I am an animal, yes,' he said. 'A beast, untamed. I'm sure you know that the beaten dog, when bested, presents its throat to the victor and hopes for mercy?'

'You shall have none from my hand.'

'Do what you must then, Blazing Lord,' Burak said. Rakaros raised his arm to strike. 'But remember – I am no dog.'

The knife came down and Burak lunged left, taking the blade deep into his shoulder. He screamed in agony, but before Rakaros could draw out the knife, Burak had writhed up and grabbed his forearm with his right hand. He twisted around, pulling back and bracing Rakaros' arm, and then he punched up with the flat of his left hand against the hinge of Rakaros' elbow. Burak grinned to hear it snap, to see the jut of the broken bone come splitting out of the Blazing Lord's arm in a spray of blood. Rakaros bellowed in pain and fell backwards towards the stone dais, and as Burak wobbled to his feet he tried to haul the knife out of his shoulder.

His vision went dark. He felt the steel slither wetly from his flesh, but before he could bring the knife to bear Rakaros swung wide with his left hand and crashed his fist into Burak's eye. The Heart-eater dropped, half blind, his head swimming. He clawed around for the knife, felt it at his fingertips, brought it up to sink it into Rakaros' stomach. He felt the blade go in, felt the blood pour freely over his knuckles until the hilt was slick with it. But then Rakaros had grabbed a fistful of his hair and was hauling Burak towards the altar, huffing and wheezing with pain. He knocked the knife away; it skittered across the stone. Burak, his scalp ablaze, punched the wound in the Blazing Lord's stomach – once, twice, spraying blood across his own face. He felt his jaw crack as Rakaros lunged up with his knee. He spat, gibbered instead of speaking. The knee came up again and something snapped in his eye socket, and then again it hammered up into his cheekbone and broke that too. Burak felt himself hauled up, dragged by his hair, raised off his feet – and then the edge of the altar was screaming towards his face. He kissed it once, twice, three times, each time leaving a wider smear of red spattered across the stone, scraps of flesh, teeth, a chunk of his tongue. All was blazing fire, a deluge of pain.

'Anoint the altar!' Rakaros was screaming. 'Anoint the altar, wash it with your blood!'

Everything was bright, blinding, warm and cold, both near and far away – and then Burak was not falling towards the altar but floating above it instead. He felt lighter than air suddenly, unburdened, as if all the visions in his head had found a final release at last. They were cast out onto the stained altar stone, scattered to mix with the blood and the brains that lapped towards the baby, who cried out and kicked his legs.

Everchosen! Lord of the Black Lodge, wait, don't turn your gaze from me, I beg you! The child will die by my hand, I have promised!

He tried to reach for it, straining to grasp the baby with hands that were no more than mist and thought.

Kurguth, forgive me! I have failed! Stay your vengeance in the hunting grounds, brother, please! Forgive me!

But as his spirit melted away into nothing, Burak poured out all the wounded horror of his soul into a scream that was mere silence in the chamber where he had died.

The sound of a crying child, the smell of death, the stale air of the buried chamber. Rakaros held on to these things. Everything seemed to be spinning away, hiving off into the aether. He gripped his soul as he had once gripped his sword, refusing to relinquish it. He felt his wounds gape and contract, vomiting blood. His right arm was ruined. He had lost everything but his will to power – and he still wielded that like a deadly weapon.

The last of the rage-rock burned away inside him, and as its holy force dissipated, he knew that it was all that had been holding him together. With redoubled force the agonies of his wounds assaulted him. He blacked out briefly, and when he came to again, he squinted into the gloom. The columns of sunlight that fell from the ceiling now slanted to a deeper angle and moved away from the altar. The body of the Untamed Beast, its head no more than a gory stump after Rakaros had beaten it to pieces, lay at his side. The baby had stopped crying. Rakaros crawled to the edge of the tier where the altar stone was waiting for him, but it was too much, far too much. To climb such a mountain was utterly beyond him.

'Flame,' he muttered, and his voice was wet with blood. 'Give me strength… At the end of it all, give me the strength to continue.'

Ashrath took a moment to enjoy the dazed expression on the Blazing Lord's face as he stepped from the shadows with the baby in his arm. His sword was sheathed at his hip; he wouldn't need it now.

'Fate seems to have granted you a second chance,' he said, with as much malice as he could muster. Rakaros opened his blood-gummed eyes and stared at the Trueblood with bitter resignation. He sighed, such a deep and fatalistic breath that for a moment Ashrath wasn't sure if he had died or not.

'So, it ends,' he whispered hoarsely. 'The Everchosen's test is over, and I have failed. We have all failed.'

'All?' Ashrath said with glee. 'I think not, Lord Rakaros. After all, here I stand, at the end of all things. *I* have not failed.'

Rakaros laughed softly, a terrible, hacking noise that quickly degenerated into a violent fit of coughing.

'Haven't you? Look at yourself, Silenthis. Whatever you are now, it is not what you once were. You have won something, it's true, but I'm not sure if it is the prize you really sought.'

'What I have won,' Ashrath said, pressing his heel to Rakaros' throat, 'is the endless gratitude of the Three-Eyed King.' He clutched the baby, feeling it snuffle up against him. 'I have Archaon's heir, the Prince of Ruin, and the Varanspire will open its gates wide for me. For me, flame-worshipper, and no other!'

He eased the pressure on Rakaros' throat as the Blazing Lord began to laugh again.

'Archaon's heir, is that what you think?'

'What else?' Ashrath spat. 'For this much bloodshed, this much suffering?'

'It was a sacrifice for us, and for the Untamed Beasts. And Sigmar alone knows what the child was to the storm-born. And for you it is the Son of the Everchosen. I wonder, Silenthis, I wonder... Who's to say what forces moved us here, and for what dark purpose in the end? The True Gods? The Ever-Raging Flame, or your Coiling Ones? We are playthings to them, I sometimes think, nothing more. Take care, Silenthis. If I know nothing else, I know this – that child is not what you assume. Nothing could survive this that was not meant to survive.'

He laughed again, and a spasm of pain flashed across his face. He coughed up blood, opened his eyes wide in torment.

'The Horned One!' he groaned. 'She was wrong, in the end...'

'Who?' Ashrath demanded. He leaned in to hear the Blazing Lord's dying breath.

'The wet nurse... Aceria. She said... the *Horned Ones* would be my death, but...' He grinned, an evil smile of shattered, blood-flecked teeth. 'I see no horns on you, snake-worshipper!'

Ashrath stood, and the smile he gave the dying man was ecstatic. He pressed his foot again to his throat, and before he stepped down, he said, 'You forget, Lord Rakaros of the Burned Hand.

I am Ashrath Silenthis, Trueblood of the Splintered Fang. Trueblood of *the Horned Krait*.'

He felt the bone crack under his heel as he broke his neck. It was the sweetest moment of his life.

'Long has your road been, my child,' he said to the boy as he turned from the altar. 'Through dangers uncounted. But it is nearly over. Come, your father awaits you.'

He stepped from the dais. The path out of the catacombs would be long and arduous, and the journey to the Varanspire more dangerous still, but Ashrath was not afraid. He would never be afraid of anything ever again.

Behind him, the altar settled into the shadows as the slanting beams of light moved on. It was getting late. The day was almost done.

EPILOGUE

THE BLOODWIND SPOIL

They killed the snake-thing as it stumbled from the ruins, blinking in the light – just another mutant of the Bloodwind Spoil. The first arrow took it under the chin and sent it staggering backwards, and then the next two thudded into its chest. It was down in moments, dead soon after that.

'You could have hit the child, you fool!' one of them shouted.

'I hit what I aim at,' the other said nonchalantly. 'I don't miss.'

They took the child and handed it to the old man, who fed it from a leather flask. It drank hungrily, its eyes flashing green. They pulled their cloaks about them, drew scarves across their mouths as the dust storm picked up. The light was fading, and on the horizon the black spear of the Varanspire was wreathed in corposant, stark against the coming night. Smoke rose from the shanty town around its base – cook fires, the pyres of sacrifices. They turned away and headed back to the caravan.

'We're not going on to the Spire?' the old man said.

'No,' came the reply. 'What's the point? The Three-Eyed King is abroad, somewhere in the realms. Anyway, he'd have no interest in what we have here.' He looked at the baby, stared deep into those green eyes. 'To Carngrad,' he said.

'Very well,' the old man replied. He covered the child in a fold of his cloak. 'To Carngrad.'

As the caravan set off across the Tormented Lands, the storm blew in from the direction of the Desolate March. Ribbons of sand snaked across the scrub, lashing the stunted grass. A breaker of dust rolled and billowed from the horizon, smothering the lands like a tide. Soon, the slanted pillars of the temple were swallowed in the storm and the foundations of the ancient battlements were just faint suggestions under tons of sand.

By the time the storm had passed over, there was little sign that anything had stood there at all. The temple had gone; the Bloodwind Spoil was a hungry land, and it had devoured it completely.

ABOUT THE AUTHOR

Richard Strachan is a writer and editor who lives with his partner and two children in Edinburgh, UK. Despite his best efforts, both children stubbornly refuse to be interested in tabletop wargaming. His first story for Black Library, 'The Widow Tide', appeared in the Warhammer Horror anthology *Maledictions*, and he has since written 'Blood of the Flayer' and the novels *The End of Enlightenment* and *Warcry Catacombs: Blood of the Everchosen*.

YOUR
NEXT READ

COVENS OF BLOOD
by Anna Stephens, Liane Merciel and Jamie Crisalli

The Daughters of Khaine bleed the realms dry in the name
of their god across three linked stories that show both the aelves' skill
at war and dedication to their bloody-handed master.

An extract from
'Trisenthni the Unseen'
by Anna Stephens,
taken from the portmanteau novel *Covens of Blood*

She was a witch-aelf of Khailebron, a Daughter of Khaine, and she slid through the night like steel through velvet – silent, lethal and true. The great fortress city of Greywater Fastness was intermittently dark and subdued, though never entirely, for even this late there was business to be done and perimeters to be walked. The great forge complexes run by the wealthiest duardin families operated day and night, and now they lit up the heavy smoke hanging over the city, casting a sulphurous yellow glow over rooftops and along streets.

The air was acrid, heavy with soot and hot metal, rent by the deep-throated scream-hisses of quenching steel. Yet despite the Greycaps' vigilance and the hellish glow from the forges, no one saw the aelf pass, for she was Trisethni the Unseen, and the title was no mere posturing.

Lord Rygo's mansion sat high upon the central hill of the city, where the breezes did much to carry the worst of the smoke away. Here were situated the most expensive properties in the Fastness, exclusively occupied by merchant lords, nobles, and members of the Council of the Forge or the Grand Conclave.

Trisethni's disdain did not show on her cold, beautiful features, though it burned hot within her. These people worshipped glory and wealth, comfort and reputation, when they should worship the gods who kept them safe from the Forces of Chaos; the gods who blessed them with the resources and knowledge needed to manufacture their weapons and black powder. Instead, they were enamoured of their own skill, blinded by greed and arrogance and the bright flash of gold coins.

Footsteps sounded up ahead and the aelf stilled in a shadow as black as spilt ink. Her silver-blonde hair was muted with charcoal, her boots, trousers and tunic in shades of grey and deep blue. She splayed a gloved hand across her face to break up its outline lest forge-light or moonlight should glint upon her. The sentries marched past, silent and alert – but neither silent enough nor alert enough to spot her. Trisethni watched them go, and then slipped back onto the road and increased her pace. She didn't have long.

The aelf didn't like Greywater Fastness, hating its stink and endless hammering, the black skies and black walls and black rain that fell. But her soul and devotion were to Khaine, to Morathi his First Daughter and the High Oracle, and to her coven. She would endure the contempt of Greywater Fastness' other, lesser, races with the outward inscrutability common to both her species and her religion.

The Khailebron sect of the Daughters of Khaine did not have a home temple, preferring to wander the Mortal Realms in response to the tides of war and fortune or the dictates received from Morathi herself. For the duration of this dictate, the Draichi Ganeth sect was hosting them in their temple here in this smoking, desolate, dead place of rock and metal.

She headed towards Rygo's confection of a mansion for the

second time that night. The first had been with her sisters, clad in armour beneath their cloaks to perform their ritual blade-dances at the coming-of-age celebration of Rygo's son. Trisethni did not know why the boy was to be so honoured with their presence, but it was not her place to question the commands of Hag Queen Belleth. The war-coven had attended and they had performed, their every movement composed of death and grace and worship, moving in step, matchless in their abilities – and they had been insulted. Rather, Trisethni's sister Itara had been insulted when some stinking-drunk human had told her she lacked the grace to blade-dance with the others. Itara had, rightly and instantly, slaughtered the scum for his sacrilege.

Just the memory of it set Trisethni's rage to burning anew, hotter and brighter than the largest duardin forge, for an insult to one member of the coven was an insult to all, and by the time they had departed the panic-stricken mansion and reached the temple, they were clamouring for permission to return and wreak holy vengeance.

The insult would not have been borne by any of the aelven races, let alone those who had pledged their lives to Khaine, god of battle and Lord of Murder. Belleth had listened to their complaints and shared their outrage. While she did not at this time want outright war with the humans of Greywater Fastness, she had sent Trisethni to be the silent blade of justice, streaking through the night to carve retribution from the bodies of the perpetrators.

Trisethni ground her teeth together at the blind arrogance the surviving human guests had displayed in the aftermath of Itara's righteous slaying. Once the initial screaming and running had faded, after the Greycaps arrived at a run and looked at their opponents and wisely did nothing but form a non-threatening line between the Daughters and the humans, some of the guests had spoken eagerly from that supposed safety. Their mouths uttered false solicitations, their hands and eyes told the lie that they did not share the dead man's opinions of Itara – or indeed all the witch-aelves who had done them the honour of performing – and all the while they stank of unearned superiority and pitying derision.

You are beneath us. You are savage. You are animals, their smiles and hearts proclaimed, and not an aelf there did not see past the lies to that inescapable truth.

As she sped through the night, it pleased Trisethni that she would prove them right in one of their beliefs. The Daughters of Khaine were savage, because life was savage in the endless struggle against Chaos. And before the dawn fought the forge-light for possession of the sky, Rygo and his whelp would know just how savage existence could be. The humans would need to invent a new word for what she would do to them.

Trisethni's saliva was coppery with the need for blood. *I am the blade of my sisters' just vengeance. My retaliation on their behalf shall not be swift, though it shall be brutal. It shall last for hours. And all humans will be reminded that the Daughters of Khaine are true servants of justice, and of blood.*

The aelf ran the last mile over the rooftops of the houses ascending the soft curves of the hill, springing from gable to eave to ornamental tree until she reached the crest and the largest, grandest buildings, each set back behind its own protective wall. Trisethni had memorised the layout of Rygo's gardens – a wonder in the stone, smoke and metal of Greywater Fastness and its bleak, uninhabitable surrounds – and the approaches to the main house, as well as the three large rooms she and the rest of the blade-dancers had been permitted to enter. Permitted. As if they were a troupe of common mummers. But she was deep into the concentration required for her mission now, and the thought – the outrage – skated over its surface without leaving a mark.

There were house guards patrolling the base of the wall and none of the trees were within jumping distance – she'd have to cross open ground to reach the little orchard. Trisethni waited until the pair of guards had vanished into the gloom and then leapt from the top of the wall, covering ten feet and rolling once to take the impact out of her landing, and sprinted into the shadows. Her keen ears told her she remained unnoticed.

From there it was two hundred paces to the house, eighty of them within the trees. Once she was on the lawns and among the flower beds, there would be little cover, but it didn't matter. Though the humans found it more comforting to think of them only as blade-dancers or pit-fighters – little more than brutal savages who fought for the Forces of Order – the truth was that the Khailebron were the spies, saboteurs and assassins of the Daughters of Khaine. Concealment and subterfuge, the blackened blade in the night or the slip of poison into a cup, were their tools in trade. A hundred feet of open garden was no obstacle to Trisethni the Unseen.

Grinning at the ease of outwitting the dull-sighted human guards, the aelf sped light-footed across the grass, using the low shrubs as cover, and flung a grappling hook from thirty feet out. The hook, muffled in black cloth, flew long and high and true, wrapping around a second-floor balcony balustrade with a muted clatter. Trisethni didn't wait to see if anyone was alerted by the noise; she swarmed up the rope and over the balcony, drawing it up after her, and lay pressed against the smooth, cool stone until she was sure she was undetected. Two more guards patrolled by below her and she caught a glimpse of their grey hats – Rygo was spooked and had supplemented his private guard with others. Just how she liked it.

Trisethni packed the hook back into the small bag she carried across her back and pulled out a stiff loop of wire and a blackened, narrow blade. She worked the blade in between the window frame and the lock, pushing to create a small gap, then fed the wire through and felt around until it hooked the latch. A twist and a quick upward jerk with the loop, and it slipped free. She stepped into the house as soft as liquid shadow.

Humans were so trusting. Give them high walls and enough weapons and night-blind guards and they considered themselves impervious to retribution. Trisethni's lesson would be for more than just Rygo and his mewling pup; it would be for them all. The whole of the Fastness. The whole of Ghyran. The Daughters of Khaine fought for Order and for Light, and there wasn't a human whose opinion meant anything to them. This house's fate would ensure no one ever forgot that again.

The mansion was sprawling and opulent, as befitted a member of the Grand Conclave. Wealth oozed from the walls, displays so ostentatious they became tasteless. So rich they looked cheap. The heavy carpeting silenced Trisethni's footfalls, but would also deaden those of any guards; she proceeded cautiously but fast, gliding along the corridor. It was lined with rooms, many with the door closed and the distinctive sounds of breathing emanating from within.

Rygo's party guests inhabited these rooms, guests who had stood by and let Itara be abused. If there'd been more time, she would have chased them down one at a time or in groups, spilling blood for Khaine, but tonight it was Rygo as host and his son as guest of honour who deserved the full measure of her fury. The rest would benefit from mercy they had no right to expect.

Trisethni pulled a mask from her bag and tied it tightly over her nose and mouth, then took a paper packet from a pouch. One by one, she opened the doors and ghosted into the rooms, using a long feather to waft the powder coating the paper over the slumbering occupants before stealing back out and shutting the doors. No one in this house would wake at Rygo's screams. No one in this house would ever wake again.

*In the name of almighty Khaine, in honour of his prowess and his
subtle arm, I dedicate these deaths. May he look on me with favour,
though these endings draw no blood in his name.*

That is still to come, she added to herself with a toothy smile
as she removed the mask. Anticipation stroked its fingers across
her scalp and began to whisper in her veins as she padded up
the stairs to the third floor, where the private suites were located.

She left the tainted mask, the feather and the empty paper on
a small table in an alcove, arranged beside a large, gold-painted
vase. The mask's silk was painted with the Khailebron sigil, but
Trisethni placed it face down so it couldn't be seen without being
handled. She smiled again, wondering who would turn it over
when the house's fate was discovered – and if they would live
long enough to identify the Cult of Khaine as the bringers of justice to this house.

There would be sentries stationed throughout the lower levels
of the house to guard against intrusion. Trisethni didn't know
how many, but she knew they'd come at the first sounds of fighting or the first screams. Another slow smile stole across her face.

Crouching at the top of the stairs, the corridor sweeping away
to her left and right, she scanned the darkness. Rygo and his
son, Rygel – *how original* – would have the entire third floor to
themselves; Rygo's wife had died two years before. Each man had
a guard stationed outside their door and the soft tramp of feet
indicated at least one more walking another, unseen corridor or
room. Guards downstairs she'd expected – it was why she'd entered
the mansion through the second floor. For Rygo to have or need
guards on the private floor spoke of paranoia in excess of what
she'd expect even for a lord.

*He knows the insult given to my sister. He is expecting me,
perhaps.*

Reaching into her bag, the aelf retrieved a different packet. She didn't need a mask this time. The tiny black spheres shifted against the paper and Trisethni tipped them into her hands. Rising fluidly, she called out: 'What? Who are you?'

The guards' attention snapped towards her. 'What?' one responded in dumb incomprehension. 'Who are *you*?'

'How dare you enter the lord's house uninvited,' Trisethni growled. Confused but obeying their training, the guards trotted towards her from either end of the corridor, pulling short swords as they came. As soon as they were in reach, she threw the spheres. Warmed by her body heat through the gloves, the sudden cooling as they sped through the air caused them to pop, releasing the gas inside.

Trisethni back-flipped down the stairs to the landing, well below the reach of the coiling fumes. Coughing, spluttering and then the snarling of rage drifted down to her, and after a count of ten she sauntered back up. The guards lunged at her and the aelf held up her hands. 'You will do as I command,' she said softly, and they halted. She gestured at their uniforms. 'Kill all those dressed as you are dressed, and those wearing grey hats who patrol the grounds, but quietly, that you might take them all. Let none come up to the third floor. Go.'

They passed her in a silent rush, teeth bared and eyes black with compulsion. *Dressed as you are dressed.* When the last of the non-compelled guards were dead, they'd turn on each other, unable to stop the need to kill. Waving her arms to dissipate any last traces of the gas, Trisethni took the left-hand corridor first. Time to see who slept where – and who got to watch the other die.

It was the boy's room. Rygel. Newly come of age. An adult now, but one who would never get any older. He didn't look like an adult as he sprawled drooling among the silks and quilts of his bed, though; he looked young. He looked innocent. Almighty Khaine would be pleased to receive his life in offering.

The assassin backed softly out of the room and left the door ajar, then hurried along the corridor to Rygo's suite. She could just make out the sounds of combat from the ground level, too quiet for human ears. Would the Greycaps in the gardens be aware and, if so, would they come to the guards' aid or summon help first? It was an idle query; Trisethni would slaughter any who tried to stop her. She slid in through the door and leapt, lithe as a cat, onto Rygo's immense bed. The thump of her landing was enough to stir him; the press of the sciansá at his throat enough to bring him to full, icy-cold wakefulness. Trisethni crouched over him like the avenging spirit of murder she was.

'Let's visit Rygel,' she breathed.

'Who – who are you?' Rygo stuttered. 'Guard!'

They waited for twenty heartbeats, Trisethni's smile growing in time with Rygo's blanching. 'Oh dear,' she lamented. 'No help.' She slid off the bed, keeping the blade against his throat, and wrapped her hand around his arm, dragging him to his feet. Rygo winced at the force of her grip and then gasped as moonlight crossed her face.

'Aelf,' he hissed. 'What is the meaning of this?'

'I think you know, but I'll tell you both in Rygel's room. I dislike having to repeat myself,' she said, hauling him towards the door. The man dug in his heels and resisted, so Trisethni spun behind him with a blade-dancer's grace and her sciansá nicked at his flesh, drawing a crimson bead of blood. 'Walk. Walk or I take your fingers one by one.'

He balked again, just for a second, and then all the fight went out of him in a rush. 'Whoever's paying you to do this, whatever their price, I'll double it,' he babbled as she marched him along the corridor towards Rygel's room. She said nothing. 'Triple. I'll triple it, I swear. In Sigmar's name, I swear it.'

He seemed suddenly to realise where they were going, because he slowed and then fought them to a halt. Trisethni let him, let the fear build. 'Ten times,' he said, his voice hoarse. 'Ten times whatever you're being paid if you let me and my boy go.'

She shoved him in the back, got him moving again, her lips peeled back at his proximity to her. His body heat passed through her clothes; his fear-sweat clogged her nostrils.

'Everything I have,' he moaned.

'Open the door.'

'Please.'

Trisethni sighed, spun him so his back was to the door, pressed his hand against the stone of the wall and severed his little finger with the wicked, razor edge of her blade. Rygo sucked in a breath to scream and she slapped her hand over his mouth, turned the door handle and shoved him backwards into the room. Only then did she let go and the shriek she'd muffled found its way out.

Trisethni locked the door and pocketed the key. When she turned back, Rygel was sitting up in bed, yelling in shock at the sudden commotion. *Humans. Always so loud, so emotional.*

Rygel fumbled with the lamp on his table and turned up the flame. Rygo had his maimed hand clamped in the other and held in front of his face. He was grey and still screaming as he stared at the space where his finger should be; maybe he'd never stop. Trisethni relished the screams of her foes, but this one was simply embarrassing himself. She brandished the sciansá; Rygo sucked in one last deep breath and then closed his mouth. Sweat poured into his eyes and his chin wobbled as he fought to master the pain.

'I am Trisethni of the Khailebron war-coven. We did you and your whelp the greatest honour of your miserable lives earlier this night by performing our blade-dance for you. The response of one of your guests was to insult my sister.' Trisethni's voice lowered into a growl and her fingers flexed on the hilt of her sciansá. Outrage and fury built anew in her breast. 'You have no honour, and you sought to strip the same from us to, what, make your own inadequacies seem less? Believe me, in that you failed. You will pay for the insult, and all in this stinking prison of a city will know the Daughters' honour is intact and untainted.'

'I didn't... the insult has been paid for,' Rygo squeaked, trembling all over. 'The man is already dead!'

'The man is, yes. But who encouraged him in his folly? Who was the corpse's friend?' She didn't bother making it easy for him, knowing the moment of realisation would be sweet. For her, at least.

Rygo frowned amid his sweating and bleating and bleeding, but then horrified recognition dawned and, slowly, he twisted towards the bed. Rygel was standing by its side now.

'You fool,' his father breathed. 'Tell me you didn't. Tell me you're not so stupid.' He was almost begging.

Rygel's warm brown skin drained to grey. 'I... it...' he stuttered, but no more.

Trisethni felt a blush of satisfaction and another rush of justified anger. There was no battle-joy to sink into with this assignment, but that was simply another sacrifice the witch-aelves of Khailebron made for their god. Alone of the Daughters of Khaine, when it was necessary they forewent the wild blessings of bloodlust that united them with their lord. To be the subtle arm and poisoned cup instead of the frenzied, joyous killer was their pride and their curse both.

Rygo turned back and seized both her forearms in a grip strong with desperation. Trisethni raised an eyebrow.

'He's a boy, just a boy, a stupid, snivelling wretch. He didn't know what he was doing. A foolish prank, honoured Daughter. We will pay reparations to you, your sisters. Many reparations. A donation to the cause of the Daughters of Khaine, however much you ask. My son will make a public apology–'

Trisethni twisted her arm free and whipped up her sciansá; the point scored through his cheek and eyebrow, a thin red line that an instant later began to gush with blood. Rygo screamed and fell back, both hands clutching the new wound. Rygel screamed too, and seized up the lamp and threw it at the aelf.

Trisethni leapt towards the bed. The lamp smashed against the door and spilt burning oil in a pool across the wood and the rugs. Hissing in fury, she batted the boy aside and ripped the silk hanging down from the wall. She threw the material over the flames and stamped them out, her rage hotter than the burning oil. The last thing she needed was the house to burn down – no one would find her message if the occupants were nothing but charred corpses. By the time she turned back, Rygel had fled, leaving his father coughing and bleeding on the floor. Human loyalty left much to be desired.

Trisethni slammed the hilt of her blade into the side of Rygo's knee – he wouldn't be running anywhere now – and set out in pursuit of the boy. The suite was a warren of rooms, at least a dozen, but no human had ever outrun an aelf and this one wasn't to be the first. She caught him by a window and slammed his face into the wall next to it. He crumpled, and Trisethni bound his hands with cord from her pack, and dragged him back into the main bedroom.

Rygo was hammering on the scorched door and calling for his guards, his injured leg stretched out before him.

'Stop that,' the aelf said. 'They're dead or dying – no one's coming for you. You've done this to yourselves. Arrogance has blinded you to any consequences that don't involve increasing your wealth. Weapons and gold are your god and guiding light. Neither will save you.'